Viva Voluptuous

Viva Voluptuous

Sarah A. Clark

Winchester, UK
Washington, USA

First published by Sassy Books, 2014
Sassy Books is an imprint of John Hunt Publishing Ltd., Laurel House, Station Approach, Alresford, Hants, SO24 9JH, UK
office1@jhpbooks.net
www.johnhuntpublishing.com
www.sassy-books.com

For distributor details and how to order please visit the 'Ordering' section on our website.

ISBN: 978 1 78099 798 8

A CIP catalogue record for this book is available from the British Library.

Design: Stuart Davies

Printed in the USA by Edwards Brothers Malloy

I dedicate this book to all the sassy, feisty,
curvy girls – you rock!

Acknowledgements

Massive love and huge amounts of thank you kisses have to go to some of the amazing people who've been cheer leading me through the ups and downs of writing this story.

My lovely Dad gets top billing as the first person who told me I should write. Of course, I ignored his advice for years. My late granddad gave me his old typewriter when I was little and let me rattle away on it for hours, pretending to be a reporter, and Dad encouraged me to keep it up, until eventually I listened. I love you, Dad.

My amazing Mum, who told me every time I thought I might have another idea for a book, *"well sit down and write it then"* – I love you too. I sat down and I wrote it!

A great big sloppy kiss to my best mate Murray Burgess who always, always believes in me.

A shout out goes to gorgeous lady Lindsey Williamson who read my rubbish first draft and actually liked it…

One for lovely Claire Robinson, who's been telling everybody for the past year that she has a friend who's writing a book. Hey, I couldn't let you down, could I?

And another one for my fabulous g-friend Vanessa Harding who's been there cheering me on all the way, as ever.

Special thanks to fabulous Lisa Lister – I couldn't have done it without you, beautiful!

And last but not least, I have to say a massive thank you to my wonderful fiancé Andrew Banham. You restored my faith in man-kind, you've made me laugh, you've been an absolute rock and I know you can't wait to read the book so that you can see if your catchphrase is in there somewhere. I love you to bits, and can't wait to be your Mrs. Mwah!

I hope you all enjoy it…

Chapter 1

"Ell, I have to be honest, I really don't want to come to Dublin with you. You're a lovely girl and I would love to have met you when I was younger as I think we could of had a lot of fun. After what happened with Rachel, I just don't think I'm ready for a proper relationship with you. I hope we can still be friends. Sorry. Mark xx"

My breath caught in my throat as I digested what I was reading.

I, Ellie Johnstone, had been dumped.

The perpetrator of the brutal dumping had done it out of the blue by email, while he was at work, knowing full well I couldn't call him to make a scene. And I *would* make a scene.

Feeling slightly dizzy, I re-read the message that had just, quite frankly, ruined my afternoon.

How could he? I know we didn't have the most conventional of relationships, but I was so in love with him I didn't care that we'd been seeing each other six months and never actually slept together. We'd got close to it once, and when he said he wanted to take it slowly, I thought it was cute - when I'd got over the humiliation of being rejected, obviously - but after a while it just got...tedious. Our relationship seemed to consist of me feeling let down and a bit frustrated because of the numerous ways I'd try to engineer getting him alone in my flat, and the numerous excuses he came up with for not being able to come in. I blamed myself.

He blamed Rachel, his ex.

She was beautiful. I'd seen the pictures he still kept in his wallet. She had fallen out of love with him after being married for five years, except she'd neglected to tell him. He only found out when he'd discovered the text messages she'd been sending to her lover. Who also happened to be his brother. I made every excuse for his lack of interest in me physically, but deep down, I started to believe it was because I was a big girl and Rachel was younger, more glamorous and *much* slimmer than me.

I hated that he made me feel like that.

When we met, he'd said that he loved the fact I was confident about my body even though I was a size 20, but after months of going out with a man who quite obviously didn't fancy me, my confidence was in shreds and I was having to stretch my own body-positive credibility to believe I was the sexy, voluptuous beauty I kept trying to tell myself I was.

I'd needed three very large glasses of Pinot Grigio to get me back to the bedroom with Mark that disastrous night. I'd been so nervous – he was the first person I'd got close to since I'd split from my ex-husband and I hadn't exactly been around the block. In fact, you could count all the men I'd slept with on the fingers of one hand and still have fingers left over. Eventually, we ended up in my bedroom and just as things were about to get *interesting*, he sprung back like he'd just burned himself, shaking his head and muttering, "I can't do this."

He'd drunk too much to drive home, so he stayed the night, yet he couldn't have slept further away from me if he'd been in the house next door. The next morning, he was out of the door at the first chirp of the dawn chorus. I pretended I was okay, but that kind of rejection? It stung. Convinced I was about to be dumped right there and then, I was straight on the phone to Zoë, as soon as it was sociable, bawling my eyes out. Only Zoë and Lauren, my two closest friends, knew that Mark and I had a celibate relationship. Everyone else thought we were a lovely couple, they even commented on it. 'You two are so lovely' and do you know what? That was fine by me. I gave them the smug smile and let them think we were love's not-so-young dream. I thought he might be coming round to the idea of a 'normal' relationship, and by normal, I mean a relationship involving sex, really good sex, when he suggested we get tickets for Glastonbury in the summer – but now here I was, dumped, miserable and stuck with two tickets to the festival I wasn't even that fussed about going to. I had bought them as a surprise birthday present for him, because that's what 'cool' girlfriends do.

There's nothing like being dumped to kill your ability to write.

My work for a beauty website may sound terribly glamorous, but being 'Spa Editor' for *Glammazon* sounds far more fabulous than it actually was. I did get sent on the occasional visit to a new spa or salon opening, or to try out a brand-new treatment, which definitely counted as a major perk, but most of the time I sat at home in my little flat, typing out pages and pages of dull copy for a website that was desperate to get to the top of the Google rankings, even if it made the content itself virtually unreadable.

I still hadn't replied to Mark's email.

Usually I'd be the first person to come up with something clever to say, but I was literally lost for words, which for a writer, is not a good sign. I kicked myself for suggesting a weekend in Dublin, because that's what normal couples do, and we weren't normal, were we? We were technically just a couple of mates who hung out, and I was his freaking agony aunt, listening to him whine on and on about his cheating bitch of an ex, her personality disorders and how much he hated his brother for sleeping with his wife.

I did start to write a reply, but when the words wouldn't come, I simply typed, "Whatever. Have a nice life." and hit send.

Muttering the word 'arsehole' under my breath, I logged onto my Facebook account, changed my status to 'single' and added, "Don't ask. Just send chocolate."

So I was single. Again.

That meant I'd have to actually go out. I'd have to sign up to dating sites and put myself back out on the market. I also didn't know where I'd left my mojo, I couldn't remember stumbling across it recently. It's funny how going a long time without any action whatsoever makes you forget what it's like and you actually stop wanting it. Far from being desperate for sex, I was feeling really quite ambivalent about the whole thing. After the poor, and rather embarrassing, fumble with Mark where I was brutally rebuffed, I wondered if I'd ever get naked with a man again. The very fact he'd taken one look at me with nothing on and practically run screaming for the hills had done nothing to boost my body confidence. I had my own blog dedicated to plus size positivity, yet after that night, I felt like a bit of a fraud, giving it large about being large, when, in reality, I was letting a man make me feel about as sexy as a plate of cold sprouts.

I'd started my crusade against the diet industry after calling time on the waste of my energy that had been diets and weight loss. I'd taken dieting as far as I could - to the point where I gave in, ended up becoming really depressed and eating myself silly for about a year. I'd been having a hard time at work, and it *somehow* resulted in me going from a size 14 to a size 20. Despite walking everywhere and going to the gym, I stubbornly stayed just outside of the 'acceptable' size range for women. It had taken years, but I had made my peace with being fat, it was a fragile peace, but I refused to let myself be bullied into the cult of skinny by anyone, especially men. I'd bought into it for far too many years; reading celebrity magazines that pointed out cellulite and weight gain, letting people make me feel bad about myself. It made me angry that so many gorgeous, intelligent and frankly rather lovely women I knew had bought into the idea that in order to be acceptable, they needed to starve their bodies into submission and make themselves miserable on Slim Fast for weeks on end. I'd even seen a dear friend completely consumed by body hatred and eating disorders, but even that hadn't stopped me trying to get slim, and as a result I'd ruined many a lead up to a special event by trying to lose weight ahead of it, which was pointless, because as soon as I'd get to the wedding/holiday/party/event I'd pig out, stuff myself silly and end up fatter than I had been before I started.

I had to work pretty hard to get rid of the self-hatred that years of dieting and gaining weight had left me with but enough was enough, I'd given up diets for good and decided that if the world didn't love Ellie as Ellie was, they could sod right off. I even started blogging about being a curvy girl and loving it. Darren, my ex-husband, disapproved of this greatly, telling me I was silly for 'signing myself up to that cause' but I ignored him and decided that no man was going to make me feel bad about my size ever again.

Except, I hadn't bargained on Mark.

He made me feel as if I was faking my inner vixen, pretending to be sexy and confident when inside all I really wanted was for him to rip my clothes off and make me feel wanted. Fat chance of that now.

I consoled myself with the thought that he was way more psychologically damaged than I was, and wandered into the kitchen to pick out a cookbook.

Ever since I was a little girl, when I was stressed or upset, I'd bake. I loved to experiment in the kitchen – although my experiments were legendary among my friends and family for not going quite right *a lot* of the time. I'd never really been clever enough to make up my own recipes, but loved tweaking the recipes I found in books to see what would happen. My flat was usually filled with the smell of cake, which was probably why I was never short of visitors, and if there was one thing I could *definitely* cook, it was cupcakes. My blog had started off as mainly a foodie thing, but since my plus-size epiphany it had morphed into a blog where I talked about life, love, fashion and cake.

Today my kitchen experiment was going to have to be Banoffee cupcakes. Mark hated bananas, so it was like an act of defiance. I mixed up the eggs, flour and butter with a little bit more aggression than I'd usually use for something as delicate and girly as a cupcake, added the mashed banana and fudgey bits and splatted the mixture into the pretty pink cases with a thwack. My stroppy mood and rubbish aim resulted in a lot of cupcake mixture missing its target, but eventually, I had 12 reasonably well-adjusted cupcakes ready to bake. Just as I was putting them in the oven, my Blackberry pinged. It was Zoë. Bad news certainly travels fast, especially when you can't resist adding it to Facebook as soon as it happens.

"Did you dump the freak?" Zoë had texted.

I wiped my sticky hands on my leggings and texted back, "No, he dumped me. Seems Dublin was too scary for him. I hate him. I love him. I dunno. Am upset."

"I'll be over in half an hour," was Zoë's response.

Chapter 2

Zoë was probably my best friend in the whole world. I was close to Lauren too, but Lauren was always busy and had moved to London from Cambridge a couple of years back so we didn't see each other as much as we'd like to. Zoë was a writer, like me, and lived over the other side of the city and she was easy to get to. We used our impoverished writer-girl status as an excuse to meet up for coffee on a very regular basis, so much so, that I could tell you exactly when the summer drinks or Christmas red tops would start appearing on the Starbucks menu, and had a very detailed memory of the Costa and Café Nero menus too.

Zoë went through phases of being vegan, raw food, caffeine free or just plain awkward, but her endearing personality meant that the baristas didn't seem to mind serving her whatever she wanted. It might also have been her big brown eyes, killer size 16 curves, tumbling auburn pre-Raphaelite curls, or the way she wiggled in and out of coffee shops, or *anywhere* In fact, wearing the most inappropriate, but beautiful footwear known to woman.

I loved Zoë insanely; in fact I probably had a bit of a girl-crush on her. We met at a bar in Cambridge when we were out with mutual friends. I used to work for a hideously anally retentive media agency that was full of image-obsessed career bitches, and Zoë had tagged along with one of the nicer people at the agency on one of their social outings. We'd hit it off straight away, while being slightly judgemental about a super-bitchy woman from the office. She'd been trying to get freelance writing gigs with local agencies, and as an in-house dogsbody/writer I talked her out of it. I told her to stick to her passion, which was writing about body image and general kick-ass feminism. Zoë was passionate about body confidence, and worked with some of the teen magazines to try and encourage a no-diet approach. She wasn't getting very far with that – they were all whip-licked by their advertisers like everyone else - but she'd had a few articles published recently and was starting to make a name for herself on the positive body image blog scene too.

Zoë turned up with the perfect 'get over that loser' kit. A bottle of pink fizzy wine, a bar of butterscotch flavour Green and Black's chocolate, and my two favourite pick me up films; 'Eat, Pray, Love' and 'Letters to Juliet'. Pictures of Italy could always make me smile.

She let herself in, dropped the goodies on the sofa, kicked off her floral wedges and ran towards me. "Oh darlin'," she said, as she hugged me tight.

That was it. I started to cry. I'm not a delicate crier when I get going either. I gulp and snort, my nose runs and I screw my face up like a newborn baby gasping for its first breath. Zoë just squeezed me hard, not even needing to say anything as I made horrible snotty noises, leaked mascara all over her top, wailed and sobbed. A good ten minutes of unladylike snorting later, the worst of it had subsided and I was down to the occasional snuffle.

"So, what did he actually say?" Zoë asked.

"He emailed me." I replied, sulkily.

"Emailed you? What a total weasel!!"

I laughed. The word weasel always had that effect on me.

Somehow, between us, Zoë and I ate all 12 cupcakes, warm from the oven. I hadn't even had time to frost them and make them look pretty. They complimented the two bottles of sparkling wine that we managed to polish off while watching our girly films and fantasising about being back in Italy. We both adored Italy, especially Verona. Two years ago, we took to the Venetian islands and Verona together – we were so proud of the fact we did it on our own without a tour guide telling us we had to be back on the coach every two hours. We harboured romantic daydreams about going back and spending a decadent week or two being kissed by beautiful Italian boys, eating fresh pasta and drinking Prosecco.

Unfortunately, our budgets right now only stretched to watching movies about Italy, and in my case, the virtual reality walk through the Piazza san Marco in Venice on the treadmill at the gym. I was getting by on what *Glammazon* paid me to write reviews of body lotions and face packs for them, but I wasn't well off, and the money I'd made from selling the house I'd shared with my ex was dwindling fast. I promised myself every month that I wouldn't touch it but every month something just 'came up.' Like shoes. Or food shopping, on a particularly bad month. I was so lucky that I'd managed to find the flat I was living in now. I was living on one floor of a gorgeous three storey house overlooking the tree-lined park, with two bedrooms, one which was exceptionally small but I could just about fit a desk in it, a living room, bathroom and an unusually large kitchen to call my own. As long as I kept up the £875 a month rent, that is. The rent, bills and boring stuff took up practically everything I made from the writing job, and I'd been taking money out of the 'one day I'll buy a house' pot for months now.

"So, dollface," said Zoë after *Letters to Juliet* had once again reduced us both to sniffles with its soppy ending, "what are you doing tomorrow night, now that you are minus Mr boring, born-again-virgin Weasel?"

I giggled, despite myself.

"God knows." I said, "I should see Lauren, it's been weeks. I haven't told her I'm a single lady again yet. Do you fancy a Saturday night bar crawl? The three of us on the prowl?"

"That would be fab," Zoë said. "I could do with a night out too, I found these adorable shoes on eBay and they look so damn gorgeous with my spotty halter neck dress that it would be criminal not to give them an outing. And we definitely need to get you some man-action!"

I rolled my eyes. "I'm off men."

"Don't be silly. You just need to find yourself a hot younger man and get him to buy you drinks all night. Work those curves lady, stick out the cleavage, and you'll have them eating out of your beautifully-manicured hands."

I looked down at my nails. Zoë might have hot pink nail polish adorning her perfectly filed nails, but my poor excuse for talons refused to grow. They were all different lengths and hadn't seen a bottle of OPI since my last spa trip six weeks ago. Feeling unsexy and unwanted had taken its toll on my beauty routine. I couldn't even remember the last time I'd shaved my legs. I'd been working on the theory of the no-shave Law – that is, if I didn't shave my legs and I grew my bikini line out, Mark would want to get me naked. Clearly, my cunning plan didn't work. Now I just had a lot of depilating to do and grotty looking nails.

Zoë had to get to a yoga class and so I was all alone again by 7pm. I'd sent Lauren a text but not heard anything back – this wasn't exactly unusual as she was probably the busiest person I knew. She'd had her own events business for years, but hit hard times and had to ditch it to go back to working in marketing two years ago. She was good at her job, and had managed to get herself promoted to account director within a few months, but she was a workaholic and she was often taken advantage of. It wasn't unheard of for Lauren to still be in the office at eleven at night. She'd moved to East London once the commuting had got too much, and was living in the smallest bedsit known to woman. She usually came back at the weekend, either to stay with her on-off boyfriend Colin, Zoë or me.

Bored, I decided to fire up the laptop and do some blogging. Now I'd calmed down a bit. I checked my email.

Nothing from Mark. The weasel. Once again, I'd given him an easy way out. I should have been a diva, and demanded a face-to-face explanation, but I'd just let it go. I was never one for a confrontation. I'd probably think up an incredibly cutting email response at three in the morning and be too lazy to get out of bed and send it. I'd forget it by the time I got up too, of course.

I looked at the figures for the blog. I hadn't updated it for a week or so and I was down to 21 views the day before. I really wished I could spend more time on it, I loved blogging. It had always been the one place I got to just be me. I just had so much to do for *Glammazon*, and they'd negotiated my fees so low that I had to work really hard to make any kind of decent living. I sneaked in writing the odd blog post on *Glammazon* time, but to be honest, after six hours straight writing product reviews stuffed with keywords designed to keep Google happy, all I really wanted to do was switch off and watch repeats of *Mad Men*. The blog was my creative outlet but I'd been seriously neglecting it.

I typed in my title, and something just kicked in.

WEASEL!

"I haven't told you about The Weasel. I used to refer to him as The Boyfriend and I've been telling you how great he is for the past six months, how we're going to Glastonbury together in June, and how in love we were. Well, I was *in love with him. But he didn't love me. He's a weasel, and he's just dumped me.*

By email.

What's more, we spent six months, a week and three days as girlfriend and boyfriend and never got much further than kissing. I tried everything in my curvy-girl arsenal to tempt him into my boudoir, but he ignored my womanly ways. I wore the sexiest undies when we went out…just in case. Then I didn't shave my legs for over a fortnight because I was trying reverse psychology, tempting fate. That didn't work either. He's either gay, or he just didn't fancy me. What's more, all this time I've been desperately trying to stay my confident plus-size self and it's been a lie. I feel like crap.

The fact he didn't want me, made me feel like a slut for wanting him. He rejected me, and at the same time, if I made any comments about it, he made me feel like I was a nymphomaniac! In the end I just forgot about it. My sex drive drove off. My libido disappeared. He didn't show me any affection, and I felt like I was his sister, not his girlfriend.

He'd say things that made me think he wanted me, he'd tell me I was bloody amazing, that he thought the world of me and that I was special to him. What a load of crap. My two closest girl-buddies have been telling me to dump him for weeks but I'd fallen for him in a big way and wouldn't listen.

Girls know best!

I've never had a relationship like this before. It's always been me making the man wait a 'respectable' length of time. I'm used to being the one in control, I'm used to turning them down, but now it's the other way round, I feel bad. It sucks. Anyway, we're not together anymore, I'm a single lady, and I'm going out this weekend, with my girls, to get my 'tude back.

I'll be donning my best strappy heels, getting my hair done, painting my nails foxy purple and hitting the town to forget that The Weasel ever existed. Wish me luck!"

Chapter 3

I woke up full of the joys of spring, until I quickly remembered my newly single status. I pottered into the kitchen, switched on my coffee machine and made myself a big mug of wake-up juice in an attempt to bring myself kicking and screaming into Friday morning. It was only 7.15am, but I had a whole lot of copywriting to do for *Glammazon* about body scrubs and I had to artificially cajole my brain into thinking about keywords and contextual links.

My Blackberry was flashing at me and I picked it up, glancing down the list of email messages. Delete, delete, delete. Nope, nothing from he-who-shall-forever-be-named-Weasel. Irritated at the lack of communication, I gulped my coffee, wandered over to the laptop and fired it up.

Half an hour later, despite the coffee and a slightly stale pain au chocolat I'd managed to liberate from the kitchen cupboard, I was still half asleep and staring at the blank page in front of me. I had a target of 3000 words to write today and so far, I hadn't managed one solitary word. I'd been absent-mindedly staring at the screen, surfing Facebook and trying to conjure up enthusiasm for waxing lyrical about mango and coconut body polishing treatments that cost almost as much as a weekend in Ibiza.

I knew I shouldn't have done it, but I wasn't thinking straight. I clicked on the link to the *Daily News* website hoping for something fluffy to read about celebrity romances or soap spoilers - deliberately ignoring weight loss and cellulite stories - but then I found myself drawn to a story about a recent report proving that diets don't work, and also saying that fat people who exercised were healthier than thin people who didn't. The article was slightly condescending in the usual *Daily News* style, but at the end there were already over 500 comments from readers. Knowing that if I read any further I was likely to put myself in a raging bad mood, I should probably have just closed down Internet Explorer and got on with some work. Unfortunately, my masochistic tendency won out.

"It's nothing to do with being fit; fat people are disgusting and offensive to look at"

"Put them all in a concentration camp and see if they come out fat...eat less and move more is all you have to do."

"Lazy slobs just need to get some self-control, if I ever put any weight on I just watch what I eat for a few weeks and I'm back in my size eight jeans, these repulsive fatties disgust me. If I can do it, so can they, they are all just greedy weak-willed pigs who have no pride, gluttonous nobodies who need to put down the fork and pick up a gym membership."

"Revolting fat people, it's not diets that don't work, it's the fat pigs' legs...if they took them out for a run instead of to the fridge occasionally they wouldn't be so disgusting!"

I could feel the tears prickling at my eyes, but I wasn't feeling sorry for myself, I was feeling angry as hell. I was a size 20, but I probably went to the gym more in a week than some of these nasty, judgemental idiots had done in their entire life. I was far from stupid, I ran my own business, I was creative, intelligent, well-spoken, and what's more, I was a far nicer person than any of these self-congratulatory, ignorant arseholes could possibly be. Why did they assume that because someone was fat, they were a stupid, pie-shovelling glutton who wouldn't know a lettuce leaf if it smacked them in the face? Did their assumptions describe my two best friends, Zoë, a size 16 who was quite possibly the most glamorous and gorgeous woman I knew, who had men chasing her all over town or Lauren, a size 18 stunner with a mane of gorgeous, sleek chestnut brown hair, big brown eyes and a smile that could charm grumpy old ladies out of their place in the bus queue. Lauren, who dressed in designer gear and managed a team of ten people, was considered one of the best in her business and actually ran half marathons when she wasn't working. I had always said I'd join her one day – I usually said this when I'd had a few glasses of wine, but whenever the opportunity arose I was mysteriously busy.

I'd made it halfway down the first page of comments before I could take no more. Angrily, I clicked back onto Facebook and tried to pretend I hadn't just churned up all the grotty feelings from the day before. Images of Mark's size ten, glamorous blonde ex-wife kept popping into my head, and I tried desperately to replace them with images of going out tonight with the girls and getting plastered.

I was too upset to think about work. There was only one thing for it – a session at the gym. The treadmill was going to take the brunt of my increasing frustration, and maybe, while I was pounding it hard, I'd get some inspiration for the copy I was supposed to have written for *Glammazon*'s web director by the end of next week. I put my faith in the endorphin high, changed into my gym gear and headed out into the freezing rain to the bus stop.

There was only one treadmill free when I got to the gym, so I decided to skip the warm up and head straight for it. Setting it to a higher level than normal, I hoped that the extra effort would bring on a much-needed hormone rush to flood my body and take away the sheer rage I was feeling right now. I stuck Tinie Tempah *'From Miami to Ibiza'* on the ipod and stared at the images of the Italian Alps as they went by on my screen. As the beats kicked in, I started to walk, but no matter how hard I tried to focus on pretty Alpine views, I just couldn't stop thinking about what I'd been reading. It played on all my fears about not being good enough for Mark, and I was angry with myself for letting strangers, and a weasel, make me feel so bad about myself.

As I broke into a run, I felt the defiance begin to kick in.

Not good enough? Too damn good more like. As for those

idiots online, I'd like to see them running, doing a Zumba class or working out. I bet they couldn't run their own business and a house at the same time, work a pair of Louboutins like Lauren after a day of putting designers in their place, or make a whole room full of people fall in love with them like my girl Zoë. But we were all fat girls, and therefore repulsive and lazy. Fat people were always shown as being a bit stupid on TV. We were loveable but dim. Always unlucky in love. The fat kid was always the one who was bullied. Well no more, fat people needed better press, and I was the girl to get it for them. My blog would be an ideal place to start, but right now, I only had 20 readers. It wasn't the ideal way to start a fat girl revolution but I was so sick of people assuming I was greedy and lazy. I'd had it all my adult life.

"Aren't you supposed to be on a diet?" Sandra, the cow I used to work for would simper, as she took her time nibbling her salad sandwich. She was a size six at most and delighted in bringing sweet treats in to the office and offering them around, while complaining that she was "watching her thighs."

"Watching them do what? Disappear?" I used to mutter under my breath. She would ask me in front of the whole office how much I weighed and if I'd lost anything on my "latest diet". Then she'd hone in on me every time I relapsed and smuggled biscuits into work. If she caught me eating any contraband, she'd bring it to the attention of anyone in the vicinity, pretending to be funny. "Hobnobs? I didn't know they were low calorie?"

I quite often wanted to tell her to fuck right off, but as she was my manager, and I had a mortgage to pay, I thought that might be counterproductive.

It wasn't just her, either. My ex-husband, Darren, wasn't exactly a vision of Adonis-like gorgeousness himself, but he delighted in nagging me to go to the gym. He'd point out anything in the shopping trolley that he considered wasn't part of an acceptable diet for a fat girl. He'd nag and bully me into going on yet another diet, and when I managed to stick it out for a week, before reaching for the biscuit tin, he'd spit "I knew you wouldn't be able to stick to it. You can't stick to anything, you're useless," or some other charming proclamation that was supposed to make me feel like crap. It worked.

I even went to the doctor to try and get help once. I told him about my compulsive eating, my lack of control and increasing weight.

"You're not actually doing anything dangerous," the doctor had said. "I could refer you to the nutritionist if you like?" I swear, he hadn't even looked at me when he said it. He'd weighed me and calculated that my BMI was in the lardy range, then carried on writing something on his notepad as he patronised me.

I didn't need a nutritionist. I could have recited the fat and calories in just about anything at that point; I'd read every health, diet and food magazine ever published. .

"So what do you suggest I do then?" I'd said, angrily. "I don't know, "the doctor sighed, "but we only have a budget to treat people who are doing themselves actual physical harm. You're far too intelligent to do anything silly."

Patronising git.

This had been my life until I realised that all the obsessive dieting was actually making me put on weight, I read every self-help book on the subject and eventually made a kind of shaky peace with my body. I started the blog and realised that there were lots of other brilliant blogs written by big women who were sick of the stereotypes too.

I'd embraced the fat acceptance ethos despite Darren's reservations, bigging it up on my blog, promoting plus size fashion and commenting about how pointless dieting was, but it still sat uncomfortably with me. It had a lot of negative connotations. Was Darren right? Was accepting yourself giving up? Should you accept being less than you'd like to be? It swirled around my head sometimes like a never-ending question. Sometimes I felt feisty and determined, other times, like when I had read the nasty comments online, it reinforced all the worthless feelings from the bad old days and I would have to work really hard to not get dragged back into the 'you're not good enough' cycle. But what I did know beyond doubt was that all the diet peddling was making people fatter. The constant nagging and bitching about weight was making people paranoid. Young girls were more worried about being thin than being healthy. Nobody seemed to realise that bullying people, and making them feel bad about themselves, wouldn't make them magically able to stick to a diet. In fact, the misery was more likely to make them pig out. How come I could see this and nobody else could?

But how do you change the way people think when they've been thinking the same way for decades? I wasn't a well-known journalist or blogger. My record so far for post views was 117. I daydreamed about being able to command the attention of editors of the best-selling women's magazines. I'd woo them with my well-written and incisive social commentary on the subject of obesity, but I didn't have the confidence to pitch the ideas, instead I chose to indulge in the occasional rant about the state of the media with my girls.

My mind went into overdrive as I tried to think of ways to get my ideas into some kind of plan. Then it hit me – it was obvious. I had access-all-areas to Zoë and Lauren – a dream marketing and PR team. If I could come up with a message, my girls would know what to do with it.

Somehow I'd managed to get through a 20 minute run without even looking down at the timer. That's what happens when you're planning world domination.

It took me ages to get ready for our night out – I had weeks of non-attention to essential girly maintenance to undo for a start. I scrubbed, de-fuzzed, moisturised, covered myself in expensive body cream, sprayed myself liberally with Flowerbomb, my favourite perfume, and inhaled deeply to get a good sniff of my newly fragrant self. It had a sweet floral scent that sometimes made me think of baby lotion and other times made me feel like a mysterious seductress.

I pulled on my favourite outfit - tight-ish jeans and a purple corset-style top that gave my cleavage a personality all of their own. I straightened my hair, which was in dire need of a re-colouring - my carefully applied salon highlights were hideously out-grown, and I spent ages getting my eyeliner just right. With the addition of my very best Swarovski choker and a pair of black wedges, I was ready to face the world.

Dancing to Lady Gaga, I poured a glass of wine and gulped it back. I was actually feeling pretty good. I'd got back from the gym feeling energised and ready to conjure up words for *Glammazon* and somehow, with the help of copious amounts of coffee, I wrote over a 1000 words.

I was wasted on *Glammazon,* I could write body lotion reviews in my sleep. I needed a challenge, and right now that was walking in heels and not falling over.

I spotted Lauren in the corner of our favourite bar, fiddling with her hair and nursing what looked like a Mojito. Strange, she never came out at such short notice, and was usually stuck at the office until past nine.

"Y'alright, gorgeous?" I said, surprising her with a big kiss on the cheek.

Lauren jumped out of her skin, and I actually thought she was going to throw her drink at me. After a few seconds, she composed herself and half smiled.

"Yeah, yeah I'm OK."

"No, you're not. You were about to rip my head off a minute ago, what's the matter?"

Lauren sighed.

"I was going to wait till Zo was here, but, as Little Miss Sunshine is late, I'll tell you now, I've been made redundant. In three months I won't have a job. And there are no jobs on my level anywhere in London or around here. I don't know what I'm gonna do."

I reached over and hugged her.

"That's shit. I'm so sorry."

Lauren lived for work. I couldn't believe they'd just dump her like that.

"So, how come they're making you redundant then?" I asked. "Are they going bust or something? You're their number one account manager, aren't you?"

Lauren took a sip from her fast-melting Mojito and sighed again.

"The agency is relocating up north, to Leeds. They can't afford to stay in London anymore. They're downsizing – we've lost nearly 25% of our clients in the last six months, and the company is struggling big time. Two of our biggest accounts are in Sheffield and Newcastle, and neither of them are mine. It made sense for them to get shot of me rather than the other bloke, and he's always been such an arse-licker that they'd never get rid of him anyway."

"I don't know what to say, sweetie." I said, rubbing her bare arm. "Are you going to move back this way? Or maybe you could move in with Colin?"

"God no. I couldn't live with a man who has worse OCD than I do. I should have dumped him weeks ago but I've been making excuses not to see him so that I don't have to!"

She crinkled up her brow as if she was contemplating the awfulness of the idea and carried on, "Nah, I'll give up the bedsit, find a place outside Cambridge – maybe even in Suffolk - and try and get in at one of the local agencies. There's just no point trying to compete for jobs in London right now, there are about 200 applications for every position and the salaries are getting ridiculously low. I might even go freelance again."

Just as Lauren stopped to finish the rest of her cocktail, Zoë appeared, looking as cheerful as ever.

"What are you gorgeous girls having?" The halter neck dress she'd been waxing lyrical about looked absolutely amazing on her. Clinging to her curves, it swung as she walked, and she looked like a curly auburn-haired version of Marilyn Monroe with her huge diamante hoop earrings and crimson lipstick. Never knowingly understated, that was our Zoë.

"I'll go," I offered, so that Lauren could impart her bad news. Zoë would know what to say, she'd have come up with a four-point action plan by the time I got back to our table.

Chapter 4

Lauren's news had definitely eclipsed mine, and after a few glasses of wine I'd almost forgotten about being dumped. It wasn't as if Mark had ever made any effort to come out with me and the girls, so he was no great loss to them. He always had a perfect excuse for why he couldn't make our get-togethers, and come to think of it, I'd not met any of his friends or family either. I'm sure most of my friends thought I was making him up. He never let me take any pictures of him when we *did* go out, and I swear he only changed his relationship status on Facebook after three months of us being together because I'd sulked.

"You've changed your status," he'd messaged me when I changed mine about a month in to our relationship. I'd held back long enough.

"Yeah, aren't you going to change yours?" I'd said as nonchalantly as I could.

"I don't see why we have to broadcast our private business to the world," had been his grumpy response.

I had to actually ply him with drink to make him do it. He'd been sat there staring at his pint when I took the opportunity to mention our couple status again.

"So, you know it's only official when you change your Facebook status, don't you?"

He snorted. "Facebook again? What difference does it make? Your friends know we're seeing each other, we know we're seeing each other. Why do the people you were at school with who you haven't seen since 1992 need to know that we're going out?"

"I don't know what the problem is." I'd said sulkily, "Anyone would think you were embarrassed about me. Are you hedging your bets? Did you ever actually take your profile down off of the dating sites?"

Mark had seemed affronted at the idea I'd think he was two-timing me.

"If it makes that much bloody difference, I'll change my bloody relationship status."

I tried not to grin. Victory! Even though it was technically a bit of an argument. I'd glossed over that.

"But don't go posting any soppy stuff," he'd added grumpily.

Oh. As if I would. That was pretty much how our entire 'thing' went, one minute we'd be giggling over something we'd seen on TV and having a great time, then he'd mention Rachel, or say something that made me feel all insecure and needy. And I really hated feeling like that.

I'd read so many self-help books for single girls after splitting up from Darren, you'd think I would be a super confident Goddess of Sass by the time I actually got into a sort-of relationship again but all the wise words of the women who wrote about how to be fabulous went out the window at the first sniff of Mark's rejection. I'd managed a few dates from the better-known online dating sites before we'd met, and although none of the contenders had exactly rocked my world, I still felt a bit rubbish when the frantic pre-date texting dried up after our first meeting. To be honest, I'd found most of the serial daters online to be pretty rude. Mark had been the first man who'd bothered to follow up a first date with an *"I had a great time"* text, and the fact he was so nice to me probably made me like him even more. Until now.

So, after we'd talked Lauren back up from the depths of doom for an hour and made her drink a variety of sickly-sweet brightly coloured cocktails, she remembered there'd been something she had to ask me about.

"So, Lady, what's this about you being single again?"

I didn't want to talk about it, but the look on Lauren's face told me that she wanted distracting from planet jobless, so I obliged.

"He dumped me. By email. I haven't heard from him since." I

pulled a sad face.

"You know what? I think he's gay." Zoë interrupted, helpfully, as I was regaling Lauren with the details of our completely celibate relationship once again.

Lauren covered her mouth, but I could see she was trying not to laugh. We'd had this discussion before.

"He's not gay!" I defended, "Well, at least I don't *think* he is…"

Lauren chuckled, despite herself, and added, "He's probably so messed up that he'll never look at another woman again. You were just an experiment."

"A failed experiment." I said, dramatically. We all looked at each other. "Seriously, though, his ex, Rachel is gorgeous. She's a size ten, blonde, total gym-bunny…compared to her, I was never gonna measure up, was I? One look at my fat arse in all its glory, it's no wonder he ran off."

"Stop it!" Zoë half-shouted. "Doll, you know you're gorgeous inside and out. Don't you dare let that weirdo make you feel bad."

"It's not just him though, is it?" I pouted. I told the girls about how I'd been reading the comments on the *Daily News* website and that I was mad as hell about the way fat people were demonised all the time. They sat silently as I ranted, unable to get a word in as an almighty stream of shouty frustration came pouring out of my lipstick-ed mouth. When I stopped for breath, Lauren interrupted before I could start again.

"Whoa lady!"

I blinked and realised how unhinged I must have sounded. Lauren was looking at me intently, as if she was trying to think of something to say that wouldn't start me off again.

"It's shit, it sucks and it's all wrong" she said, carefully, "But it's always been like that. What can you do?" she shrugged. It was more of a statement than a question.

I stared at her.

"I dunno, but I feel like I want to do something though, you know? To stop this relentless tide of crap that we have to put up with. If it can make me feel bad, and I'm a grown woman with a bit of sass, how must it make teenagers feel?"

I paused. Over dramatic, me? I knew damn well how it made teenage girls feel, though, as I'd seen it first-hand. The girls knew it too. As I thought about my old school friend Jane, a wave of sadness came over me. Jane had been one of the best friends I'd ever had – until an eating disorder stripped her of every bit of personality she had and replaced it with self-hatred and an all-consuming obsession with her weight.

I also knew that Lauren was susceptible to the dieting message because every now and again she'd 'fess that she was trying a new diet, even though she was always saying she loved her curves. Zoë, on the other hand, rarely worried about her own body (she was the slimmest of the three of us and drop dead gorgeous) but she was passionate about positive body image and I thought I could hook her in that way.

"Lauren, sweetie, you are the cleverest girl I know when it comes to communications. You run awesome marketing campaigns for people, run one for me."

"A marketing campaign for what? Fat people? How's that going to work?"

"Well, I don't know. You're the guru, not me. But I'm sick of all the crap about how disgusting fat people are on telly, and lazy headlines about fat people being a drain on the NHS. You can't move for diet advice. People are being brainwashed!"

"Are you serious?" Lauren asked, raising an eyebrow.

"Yes, yes I am." As I said it, I realised I'd never been more serious about anything in my life.

"There's got to be other women out there like us, who aren't a size ten but are still fabulous. How great would it be to give them a voice? Let the world see that you don't have to be skinny to be happy?"

Before she could object, or get a word in edgeways, I turned to Zoë and said, "Zoë, you are the most positive person in the whole world. If someone like you can't help me tell the world that fat people are actually just as freaking great as anyone else, nobody can. You're fab with words and you know the audience."

If there was anything Zoë loved, it was a well-aimed compliment.

"Well yes, I do know people. But where has all this come from?"

"I'm just sick of it!" I paused for dramatic effect. "Sick of the way the media puts people down for being bigger than normal. Yeah, I'm also angry at the way they pick on people for being old, or too skinny, but this fat-hate-y thing gets me right where it hurts. I just want to DO something."

I even started to cry a little bit.

"Sorry, I didn't mean to get all emotional about this." I sniffled, "I'm fine, honest. But I really have had it up to here. You know how Darren made me feel. And now Mark with his sex ban and Little Miss Perfect wife. For years I let people make me feel like I was weak and greedy, and that I could be 'fixed' with a bit of willpower and the right diet plan. If I could just make bigger people, women, really, feel better about themselves, if I could just stop one teenage girl from going on her first diet… It would be worth it. But I just don't know WHAT to do. I have no clue!"

This was where I wanted my two besties to jump in and rescue me with their wise words. I'd done the big drama, and they were now contractually obliged to tell me what to do. Clearly nobody had told them this as they both stared at me, and each other. Awkward much?

I wiped my nose on the back of my hand. Not the best move as Lauren saw me do it and looked just a little bit disgusted. "How much do you really want to get your message out there?" she asked, overlooking my snot misdemeanour, "because if you mean it, I've got a lot of time on my hands right now, and I have some favours to call in. But are you really ready to do something, or is this just one of your drunken rants?"

How rude. But she had a point. I had been known to come up with vodka-fuelled ways of changing the world on a night out and then decide once I was sober that they were way too much like hard work. Kind of like my wine-infused promises to train with her for the next half marathon she entered.

"Prove it." Lauren said, looking at me with what can only be described as evil intent. "I reckon you should start with a YouTube video."

Now, I hadn't said anything about a video. That was super scary.

"I was thinking of something more along the lines of a blog that everyone saw due to your amazing digital marketing skills." I said, "A video…with me in it. That wasn't in my plan."

Zoé was pretending not to laugh. She knew my aversion to being on camera.

"You're either doing this or you're not, Ell" Lauren said, moving her head from side to side, "I can help you but I need to know you mean business."

"Okay, how would it work? Would I actually have to be in it?"

"Of course you'd have to be in it, you numpty!" She said rolling her eyes. "If you want to do this, you have to be the face of the campaign."

"Campaign?" I said, looking confused. "What sort of campaign?"

Lauren looked at me as if I was an idiot. "We come up with a video idea. The video gets blogged, we syndicate the blog, we Tweet, we email it to everyone we know. We create a buzz. It'll have to be smart and you'll have to decide exactly what you want to say and how much you want to do this, because if this works, it'll go viral, and you'll become an Internet superstar."

"A chubby super heroine!" Zoe added, giving me a playful prod.

I totally loved the idea of being a super heroine, but I wasn't convinced about being an Internet star. "I can't...I'd be way too scared."

Zoë interrupted. "You're gorgeous, for a start. But if you want to do this, darlin' you have to be able to walk the walk, and not just talk the half-hearted talk. I know you mean it, and you're passionate about it right now, but how will you convince anyone else if you hide yourself away behind a keyboard?"

She had a point. But I still couldn't get my head around the fact I'd be putting myself out there for public ridicule.

"Think of yourself as a modern day suffragette," she continued, clearly on a roll. "They threw themselves in front of horses to get votes for women – you're putting yourself in front of a camera to set them free from the tyranny of dieting."

I looked at Zoë, slightly stunned, and more than a bit amused. "Did you think that up all by yourself?" I laughed.

"We have to free half of the human race, the women, so that they can help to free the other half" Lauren quoted. "That was Emmeline Pankhurst."

There was no way I was going to get the girls to help me out with this unless I was prepared to step out of my comfy zone. I could feel the resistance starting to push against me, and my head was making up a million excuses to back out.

"Yeah," I blurted out, "let's do it."

Where the hell did that come from? It must have been all this girl power talk. I was just going to have to get the hell over my fear of talking to a camera and do this thing.

"Don't forget you have a writer at your disposal, too." Zoë said, sipping a Dirty Martini and pretending she liked it. One of the men at the bar had got it for her the last time she went up, and she hadn't wanted to be rude.

"Of course!" said Lauren. "You've got the contacts and a great blog following. Ellie can guest blog for you, and build up a buzz that way."

"And you're a damn good writer yourself, Ell. What about that pitching course you did a couple of years back? Have you actually pitched any ideas yet?"

"Nope" I answered, embarrassed. I'd done an e-course with a couple of well-known freelance journalists which had cost me over £200, but although I felt super-charged with great ideas when I was doing the course, ever since, I'd reverted back to being scared of commissioning editors. Clearly I was going to have to get over this if I was going to become a media personality. That, of course, was a big IF.

"Well, get on with it then. Come up with some ideas for features." Zoe ordered. "We can bombard the editors with fabulosity when you've had a bit of a brainstorm. I'll help you. I know people." Zoë was almost as excited as Lauren.

I was on the verge of backing out, yet again, when I thought about Jane. I'd lived with Jane when I first left home. We were inseparable at school, we lived around the corner from each other and because our parents were also good friends we'd been in and out of each other's homes for most of our teens. I always looked up to Jane. She was so slim and so pretty, and she looked a bit like a doll. She had enormous blue eyes, and pale skin, tiny features and a disarming smile. If she'd been a cow it would have been easy to hate her but she never seemed affected by her prettiness at all.

Jane started to panic when she began gaining weight at about 15. Some boy at school told her she had a fat arse and she believed him. She asked me to go to a slimming class with her, and although she was a little bit overweight by then, maybe about ten stone, she wasn't obese by any stretch of the imagination. I did go with her for a bit, although I didn't lose much weight and it was my first failed diet. And hers.

Jane didn't go to college with me, she went straight into work, but she got herself a flat and we ended up living together in our early twenties. Most of the time it was great fun, we were two besties in our first flat away from our parents and we got up to some mischief in that flat. It all started to go wrong as Jane gained more weight (probably down to all our alcopops and not being able to cook anything except pizza) and her dieting had turned into bulimia. I'm not sure when it started, she kept it hidden for so long that I was genuinely shocked when I caught her throwing up.

"What the hell are you doing you stupid, stupid cow!?" I remember shouting at her in exasperation and pure fear, seeing her look of guilt and disgust at being found out. She was perched on the edge of the bath, her blue eyes all red and bloodshot and an expression of horror on her face at being busted. My reaction hadn't been helpful but I was so angry with her. I was hurt she'd hidden it from me. She'd locked herself in her room after that, swearing at me until I gave up trying to get her to open the door.

Jane's bulimia became an obsession for both of us. I tried so hard to help her, but she was a complete pain in the arse to live with by then, and made herself worse by buying magazines filled with images of skinny models. She was probably around a size 18-20 at the time, and I'd point out to her, "Your throwing up isn't even making you skinny" – which was probably spectacularly unhelpful, but I couldn't seem to snap her out of it. I was sworn to secrecy and I resented that. I was way out of my depth.

Jane would go through periods where she seemed to get over it, and we'd go back on diets together to try and sort out the extra weight. I wasn't particularly big; I just went along to keep Jane company. We'd go through phases of not buying food in so that we couldn't eat it and then, of course, going on late night corner shop runs to stock up on Twix and Maltesers.

By the time we'd lived together about three years, I was engaged to Darren. I was about to move out to live with him and Jane had just split up with her long term boyfriend, James. The bulimia came back with a vengeance and she hid it even from me this time. She was depressed and I was really glad to be moving in with Darren. Three weeks before I was due to move out, I came home and found Jane slumped on the sofa. It sounds like a cliché but she'd taken paracetomol with about three quarters of a bottle of Malibu and all I can remember from the blur of what happened was that the whole flat smelled of coconut. I still can't touch the stuff, even now.

She was already dead. If she'd meant it as a cry for help then it had backfired spectacularly. I'd lost my oldest friend and I felt guilty as hell because I couldn't save her, couldn't cure her and couldn't convince her of how lovely she actually was. Darren agreed to postpone the wedding. Not least because Jane was going to be my bridesmaid. She'd been fretting about looking like a whale in her dress, and wouldn't believe me when I told her over and over again that she was beautiful, and that she would be an amazing bridesmaid. She'd been so full of self-hatred that she couldn't see how beautiful she was, and to me, no matter what size she was, she was still my gorgeous best friend Jane. I knew that it was the thought of what happened to Jane that had stopped me doing the same thing and making myself sick when I'd been at my lowest, too.

Just thinking of her brought a lump to my throat and I realised I had to do this. Enough, already.

"I don't know if I can do this on my own." I blurted out.

The girls looked at me. "You won't be on your own," said Lauren. "We'll help you. Come on, Lady, you know we get as pissed off as you do about all the anti-fat bullshit. We just don't take it to heart as much as you do. You talk the body-positive talk, but when it comes down to it, you can't walk it because you don't really believe it. Then you let losers like Mark mess with your head and blame yourself for things going wrong, when it's him with the issues. If you do this, your confidence is going to be sky high again, and you can help other women feel confident, too. It'll be amazing, I promise."

How could I refuse such an impassioned plea? I'd do it. I'd do it for Jane and for girls who felt as helpless as her. Most importantly, I'd do it for me. How hard could it be?

We'd been plotting the 'Fat Girls are Fabulous' campaign for over an hour, we were officially all talked out, so we tottered across to the cheesy 'Tropicana' bar and kicked off our shoes so that we could dance to Gloria Gaynor and Whitney Houston without spraining our ankles. Of course, Lauren had been wearing Louboutins, so we couldn't move very far from the shoe pile and one of us had to keep an eye on it at all times. You get used to that sort of thing hanging out with Lauren.

"That bloke looks like Limahl," Lauren giggled, pointing a middle-aged man with an unfortunate mullet.

"He's heading in this direction and he looks drunk," Zoë warned, "Move!"

The drunk ones always went for me. I blamed my friendly face and inability to tell them to sod off. I moved as fast as I could, while grabbing Zoë and trying not to catch his eye. Hardly a shock that someone who looked like he would have been more at home in 1982 was in an eighties cheese fest of a club like Tropicana. Still, the place was always good for a laugh.

We managed to shake off the eighties throwback and made our way to the other bar, where we managed to find a bit of floor space that wasn't too sticky. Halfway through 'Eye of the Tiger' as I was waving my arms in the air and pretending to like the song, I felt my Blackberry vibrate. I slid it surreptitiously out of my bag, hoping it was Mark telling me he'd made a mistake. It wasn't, though – it was from Jamie. I hadn't heard from him in months.

Jamie was my guilty secret – he was far too young for me, still in his twenties, and I'd met him when I was out with the girls one night. We'd been out a few times and he was always trying his luck with me but had never managed to get an invite back to my flat, despite being incredibly hard to resist. I'd heard from him a couple of times when I was with Mark, but although I'd been seriously tempted to take him up on some of the very detailed and interesting offers that he'd outlined in his texts, I'd turned him down.

I showed his message to Zoë. It was filthy.

"Do it!" She said, grinning at me.

"Really?" I shouted above the awful eighties music, "he's not exactly boyfriend material."

"Sod boyfriends, sweetheart. You need a good seeing to, and he's been chasing you for over a year now. And he's damn sexy! Go for it."

I was very tempted, and a little bit drunk. And Jamie was gorgeous and very keen. He was sporty – played football for a local team and was definitely well-toned. He had the cutest freckles I'd ever seen – and I've always been a sucker for freckles - and a smile that was so cheeky it should probably have been banned for giving him an unfair advantage. I had a sneaking suspicion that Jamie had no problem whatsoever charming women into bed, and he'd set his sights on me ages ago…probably had a thing about older women with very large boobs, I thought.

There was no doubt he fancied me, even if he did only text me when he was drunk and horny. The last time we'd been out, he'd been kissing me very determinedly as we waited for our taxis home. He'd very nearly made it back to my flat, I have to confess I was sorely tempted, but I'd jumped in the taxi and left him standing there at the last minute. He didn't look impressed, poor lad; I think he'd assumed he was going to be getting an overnight pass. I'd chickened out because I thought I'd end up fretting if he'd stayed the night and then I didn't hear from him. I was always a bit of an old-fashioned girl at heart. He hadn't texted me for ages after that, and when he did, I was with Mark. Bloody Mark.

Tonight I was feeling braver though.

"I'm out with the girls tonight. Free and single again. Are you in town?"

I waited for his reply. As usual, it took him ages. I'd practically given up when the phone buzzed again.

"On a birthday nite out. Bored. Where r u?"

God I hated text speak. I replied in my best writer-girl English.

"Tropicana. About to get a taxi home. You know where I live."

That would drive him nuts. I'd issued the invitation, laid down the gauntlet. I didn't know if he'd come over, but man, I really wanted him to.

It was 11.30 and the music in the club wasn't getting any better. Lauren had definitely had enough. She'd been standing next to the shoe pile for ten minutes, nursing a Diet Coke and scanning the room for anyone vaguely interesting. All the younger people had disappeared to *Venus and Mars*, the slightly less tacky club with the trendy DJs, but we didn't go there very often as it made us feel like babysitters.

"Listen, I'm gonna make a move" I shouted to Zoë.

"I bet you are," she giggled. "Have fun and be careful. I want to hear all about it in the morning."

Lauren rolled her eyes. "Jamie?"

I nodded.

"Just get it over with; you've been wanting to for ever."

Get it over with? That was hardly romantic. "His timing is impeccable. It's all your fault for making me feel invincible again!"

Zoë gave me a massive hug, and practically pushed me towards to door. "Go. Go!"

I went.

Chapter 5

I got home just before midnight, did a quick bathroom spruce-up and waited for a text from Jamie. I was sure he was on his way over to me, he'd been pestering me for long enough and here I was, slightly inebriated and offering it up on a plate. I wasn't going to text him again though. That would just look ever-so-slightly desperate, and I wasn't, was I?

I rummaged through my underwear drawer looking for some sexy underwear. I discarded several bits of lacy frippery for being too obvious, too tarty, or too small and settled on something just this side of sexy that I had in a matching set, a feat in itself. I put the clothes I'd been wearing earlier back on, just so that he didn't think I'd gone to any special effort. Even though I had.

I suppose I was a bit desperate, if I was honest with myself. Not desperate for sex, but I was definitely feeling a little bit needy. What I really wanted was a cuddle, and to feel desirable and sexy again. If a hot night with Jamie was what it took to cure me, then I could think of worse ways to make myself feel better. I amused myself thinking about his cute, cute freckles, his muscles, and the sexy way he'd kissed me the first time I saw him. He'd sauntered up to me, clearly drunk, and started dancing with me. I'd thought he was looking at Zoë at first, but she looked on approvingly as he grabbed my hand and led me off to the bar, to get to know me better. I seem to remember a lot of hot kissing that night and he'd expected an invite back to my place, but he didn't get one. He'd been trying to rectify that ever since, but now he had the chance, he seemed to be making me wait…

By 12.30 I was starting to get a bit narked. I made myself a coffee as I was feeling sleepy and I thumped the buttons on the machine a little bit too hard, as the horrible feeling that I was about to be stood up reared its ugly head. Feeling old, I drank my coffee, annoyed at myself for being so gullible. He'd probably met some 20-something girl in a club somewhere and decided she was a better offer than the chubby older woman who'd turned him down more than once. Then I reprimanded myself. "You're not chubby, you're voluptuous" I told myself, then had a horrible thought. What if he was winding me up?

The coffee didn't wake me up, and I really wanted to go to bed. Jamie hadn't texted, and he hadn't shown up yet, either.

What was he playing at? I decided to put something on the telly to take my mind off things, but there was absolutely sod all on. I found a repeat of *South Park* and decided it was better than nothing, although only marginally. Then I waited. And waited. I went to the fridge and poured myself another glass of wine, as the night's alcohol was starting to wear off and I needed a bit of a boost if I was going to be the confident older woman that Jamie thought I was. The cool liquid slipped down very easily, and so did the next glass. And the glass after that. So now I was a bit drunk, and even sleepier. Nice move, Ellie.

"I will not fall asleep. I will not fall asleep" I told myself, as I felt my eyes getting heavier and grittier. Sleeping with Jamie would be a bloody stupid idea anyway. How old was I? Way too old to be falling for the charms of a cute bloke I'd met a handful of times. I was letting my hormones get the better of my common sense. I didn't do one-night stands either. Never had one, the thought of the whole 'awkward morning after' made me shudder. I tried to justify my wantonness by telling myself that it wasn't technically a one night stand as we'd been out at least three times and I'd known him for ages.

What if he didn't turn up? What if he turned up, the sex was rubbish and I never heard from him again? One o'clock came and went. I was so NOT going to chase him. Sod him. Sod all men. I was going to bed and if he ever bothered to try and flirt with me again, he was going to get the wrath of Ellie. Miserably, I trudged off to the bathroom, took off my make-up, cleaned my teeth and climbed into bed. The wine had made me really, really sleepy, so I didn't brood for too long before I dozed off into a restless sleep - which was rudely interrupted five minutes later, by the sound of a text pinging on my Blackberry. I jumped about a foot in the air as the noise cut through my dream and brought me rudely into consciousness. When my heart had stopped racing, I checked my phone. It was Jamie. It was also 2.15 and I wasn't in the mood to be messed about.

"Getting a taxi now. R u still up?"

'Well I bloody well am now, since you woke me up, thanks very much', I muttered to myself. I texted back, *"I'm in bed. Go away"*

Straight away I got a reply. *"U don't mean that. Can I come over? I missed u"*

"No. I'm tired. You're too late."

"I'm sorry it's late, but I've wanted 2 c u all nite."

Against my better judgement, I giggled at that. But I couldn't let him come over now. I had bed-head, no make-up and was only five minutes off being asleep. It's hardly the glamorous image I'd wanted to cultivate, and what's more, he'd messed me about and I was annoyed with him. But...and this was a big but...I really fancied Jamie. It wasn't going anywhere, I knew that, but he was so damn cute. Lustful hormones started to overcome my common sense as the thought of being wanted again filled my sleepy, still slightly drunk head and eventually after debating the pros and cons of letting him come over, I replied, *"Go on then. But you'd better not be drunk."*

Famous last words.

I did what any sane woman would do in a situation like this. I went straight back into the bathroom, cleaned my teeth again, put some more make up on, and re-did my hair. Then I sat around in my PJ's trying to make it look as if I'd rolled out of bed looking this well maintained. I couldn't let him think I'd gone to too much effort…but I wasn't going to let him see me make up free and with bed hair. It wasn't as if we were living together. I waited…and waited. I thought about making another coffee but then decided this would be a silly idea because I'd end up needing the loo, and that's never sexy. I got my phone out and checked my emails…nothing interesting. I thought about texting Zoë for a bit of a pre-shag pep talk but thought better of it, she'd be in bed by now and wouldn't thank me for it.

I cleaned the kitchen worktops. I have no idea why I thought Jamie would even notice that there were crumbs on the worktop and a couple of dirty mugs lying around, but it occurred to me that maybe I should tidy them up. I filled the coffee machine up in case he wanted a drink when he got here. Did I have any beer in the fridge? No. Oh well, there was a little bit of wine left, he'd have to drink that.

I had butterflies in my stomach and an excited feeling. I wasn't sure if it was hideous nerves or just excitement, but it did feel good. It had been a long time since I'd felt anything like turned on, and now just the thought that something might happen was having a decidedly unnerving effect on my insides.

Eventually I heard the sound of a taxi pulling up outside and my heart began to thump. What was I doing? Could I even go through with this? Should I just pretend that I'd gone back to sleep?

My mouth was dry and my stomach started to churn. This wasn't excitement – it was full blown 'What have you done, Missy?' fear and I panicked. Then the doorbell rang. He was downstairs, waiting for me. Of course he would know I was up – the light was on. I was going to have to go through with this now. Pretending to be nonchalant, I pressed the intercom button and asked, "And what time do you call this?"

"Can I come in, pleeeease?" Jamie whined.

"Why should I let you in? It's half past two. It's rude to call on ladies at this time of the night."

"I'll be very very nice to you..."

At that point, the nerves were joined by somersaulting insides at images of Jamie being very, very nice to me indeed forming in my mind. OK, I thought, let's do this, and buzzed him in.

A few minutes later he was at my door. As was the smell of alcohol – he stank like a brewery. He was leaning against the wall outside with a dopey grin on his face, and the first thing he said was, "I've had a bit to drink."

No shit, Sherlock. My heart sank as I realised that he was absolutely plastered. Oh well. Let's do this, girlfriend..."You'd better come in. You stink of beer!"

"Sorry" he mumbled, looking contrite. Then he looked up at me, grinned and said, "You look sexy." I rolled my eyes.

Oh, but I was pleased to see him. I hadn't been stood up after all, and he was, despite being very drunk, utterly gorgeous. He looked a bit dishevelled, and I loved the way his messy dark blonde hair fell in his eyes. He was wearing a tight t-shirt and jeans, and he looked good enough to eat. Maybe it was just the alcohol from earlier, mixed with a liberal dose of sex hormones, but I was sure I'd never fancied him as much as I did right then. Even so, I felt slightly shy around him. I ignored the nervous feeling and turned to walk into the lounge, with what I thought was a seductive wiggle.

He followed me and plonked himself clumsily down on the sofa. I sat down next to him, nervously, trying to pretend I wasn't. "So, how've you been, then?" I asked, adding an air of faux-politeness into a slightly surreal situation.

"Fine, thanks, sexy. I missed you. You had a bloke, didn't you?"

"Yeah, it didn't work out. I'm single again now. How about you, have you been busy?" Well, this was awkward. I picked up the TV remote and turned the TV down. Then I moved the remote from the sofa to the table. He didn't seem to know what to say either, and he was fiddling with a strand of his hair and looking around the room. "Yeah, yeah, work's a bit mad at the moment."

Another awkward pause. I looked at him and smiled. He was so cute…and young!

"That's a nice picture" he said, pointing at one of my Marilyn Monroe portraits, snapping me out of my thoughts.

"Yes, yes it is, isn't it?" I replied.

I couldn't ignore the fact that he had started stroking my arm ever-so-gently and making me shiver. I really wanted him to kiss me, right now, dammit, but I was too shy to make a move myself. Instead, I looked up at him, gave him my best 'snog my face off, NOW' eyes and smiled. It worked, even through his drunken fog. He pulled me closer to him, stroked my cheek and then kissed me, at first gently and then harder. My insides turned to blancmange as his tongue explored my mouth and I didn't even care that he tasted of beer. I hadn't been kissed like this for a long time - I was sure Mark was just too scared to get me turned on in case I jumped on him.

Jamie's kisses were having a direct hit effect on my groin and I didn't stop him as his hands started to move under my PJs. At least they were clean on this evening… His hands were on my breasts and he squeezed them gently, making my nipples hard…I moaned quietly, which made him squeeze them again a little too hard, at which point I squealed.

"Oops, sorry!" – he exclaimed. "You have amazing boobs. I love your boobs."

"Mmmm…" was all I could manage as I pulled him back towards me. For a very drunk man, he certainly knew what to do with his hands, and he managed to get me topless within seconds, kissing my breasts and making me feel deliciously sexy. "I am a Goddess" I told myself as I stood up, took him by the hand and walked him through to my bedroom. His eyes widened as he realised he was going to be going where he'd been wanting to go for months, and I didn't have to feel the bulge in his jeans…I could see it. Oh – he was a big boy!

The nerves kicked in again, but I kicked them back out as I watched Jamie strip to reveal a very athletic, young body. Not a sign of a beer gut, and thighs that I could just bite. And that bum! I think I was watching him with my mouth open and I wouldn't have been surprised if I was dribbling a bit. Mark had been a little bit paunchy…and as for Darren, well let's not go there. But Jamie was just hot. I stared at him, and he grinned back, pulling me to him again and kissing me hungrily. He moved down to my neck and delicious little ripples of pleasure and unbridled lust travelled down my spine. I shivered and grabbed his pert little bum, pulling him even closer, which he clearly enjoyed as he took the opportunity to tug my PJs off completely, then looked at me and exclaimed, "Oh my God. You're so fucking HOT!"

Resisting the urge to reply "Who, me?" I came over all dominatrix and pushed him down onto the bed, which I'd left purposely unmade. I straddled his chest and began to kiss him, but he wasn't in the mood to be teased and before I knew it, he'd managed to turn me over and was kissing me along my inner thigh, blowing gently as he moved higher and higher. I thought I heard someone moaning loudly…then I realised it was me. Oh God. He reached the top of my thigh and started to lick me gently, driving me insane. Just as I was on the verge of letting go and giving in to a huge orgasm, he stopped and asked, "Do you have a condom?"

Oops, I'd forgotten to get one out.

I opened my bedside drawer and scrabbled under a pile of knickers for the box I thought I had in there. Thankfully, I managed to locate it, handed him the packet and deftly, he slipped on the condom and was inside me.

Oh my God. I really had missed this. I don't think I realised quite how much until now. He was building me right back up to the point where he'd left off, kissing my neck and grabbing my bum, pulling me closer to him. The sensation was delicious and

I wanted it to go on as long as possible. "You're amazing" he gasped. Drunk or not, the boy knew what he was doing.

"You're..ah...not so…uh…bad yourself" I panted, and I could tell he was trying really hard to hold on himself. So was I. I think we both changed our minds at the same point. I gave in and surrendered to an amazing, 'it's been way too long' orgasm. He groaned and collapsed on me a few seconds later, utterly knackered. Then let out a massive fart.

The fart definitely broke any post-coital bliss as I spluttered with laughter and pushed him off me. "You dirty bugger" I giggled. I was too relaxed and chilled to be angry with him, although he looked rightly mortified by his outburst.

"I'm so sorry" he muttered. "But you're good"

I blushed, although he couldn't see me. He wandered off to the bathroom to sort himself out and I lay sated on the bed, before climbing under the covers to snuggle in. I couldn't believe my luck. Jamie was gorgeous. He was also amazing in bed even when he was drunk, and he was a really good laugh and a genuinely nice guy. I wondered if now he'd managed to get what he'd been pursuing for the last year, he'd want more of it? Could a relationship with a *much* younger man work? The thoughts ran through my head as I began imagining scenarios, dates, nights out, introducing him to the girls…No, no, what was I doing? I so didn't want a full time man in my life right now. The last one had messed with my head, and I wanted *me* back. Hot as Jamie was, it just wasn't the right time.

As I was deliberating the whole wanton sex versus proper relationship issue, Jamie walked back into the bedroom and snapped me out of it. Grinning, he climbed into bed next to me and draped his arm over me. Within seconds, he was asleep, and snoring in a way only a very drunk man can. Clearly there'd be no more action tonight, and I wasn't going to be getting any sleep either if the noise that he was making was anything to go by.

I lay awake listening to Jamie snore, staring at the ceiling and replaying the night's events in my head. It had been a very long time since anyone had made love to me like that. If 'making love' is what you call sex like that. It was hot, and it didn't feel like a soulless one-night-stand. Jamie had been trying to get me in bed for so long; he must want more than just a quick shag. At the same time, I knew that he wasn't boyfriend material.

Now I was driving myself mad. Eventually I thought myself into exhaustion and dozed off around 4 am, despite Jamie's snoring not abating one bit, and the occasional fart. His, not mine. I found myself wondering whether I would hear from him again, when he was lying right alongside me in my bed. Seriously, getting laid made me think too much.

Chapter 6

I woke up again not long after I'd dozed off, and couldn't get back to sleep for looking at the man next to me. I felt a bit wanton, a bit liberated and a bit worried that I'd done something really silly, but when I thought back over the previous night's activities I couldn't help but smile. I felt like the cat that got the cream, and I didn't mind that I couldn't sleep for his drunken snoring because he'd definitely made up for it before he fell asleep. Oh man, he knew how to make me feel good.

I tried not to be Bridget Jones about it and stare at him too much. He stirred a couple of times and I pretended to be asleep, but eventually he woke up, looked at me and said, "Morning…"

"Morning sexy" I replied in what I hoped was my most alluring voice. I definitely sounded a bit husky, so it wasn't a bad start.

After that, neither of us really knew what to say. There was a few minutes of awkward silence, punctuated by yawns, and then he turned to me and asked, "What time is it?"

"It's 20 past eight" I replied.

"Shit! Really?"

"Yes," I confirmed. "Do you have to be somewhere?" My 'about to be dumped' radar kicked in and whirled at triple speed.

"Yeah, sorry, I'm supposed to be at football practice in an hour and a half. I don't suppose you've got any paracetomol? And a coffee? Black, two sugars?"

I rolled my eyes and was just about to get out of bed, hoping my make-up wasn't smeared all down my face, when he grabbed my hand and said, "I wish I didn't have to go. I quite fancy a rematch."

I had to admit that when I got a bit closer to him, thinking he was going to give me a kiss, I was hit by the stench of stale beer. That wasn't such a turn on. "Maybe another time?" I said, edging away from him and getting up to make my way to the kitchen.

"Definitely" he smiled, grinning at me in the way he had done the night before that had made my insides go all mushy. Oh God, but I still fancied him. I told myself off – I was in danger of building the encounter up to being some sort of epic romance, and Jane Austen certainly wouldn't have let Mr Darcy fart in bed or stink of stale beer when he woke up for the first time next to Elizabeth Bennet. Anyway, I was off men.

He threw on his clothes in a hurry and followed me into the kitchen. I tried to look all disapproving at his hurried exit.

"Last night was epic," he said. I wasn't entirely sure what that meant. I thought I had better try and come out with something a bit clever, but it was way too early and I was a bit hung over. I also felt a bit awkward and strangely, I wanted him out of the flat now. He was still as sexy as he had been last night but I felt a bit weird about what had happened and he hadn't mentioned coming over again yet, just a 'rematch'.'

"It was fun." I replied, trying to be nonchalant. "I don't usually do that."

Jamie looked amused, "They all say that."

"No, honest," I said, blushing. "I've never slept with anyone without knowing their surname before." I found him some painkillers, and gave him a glass of water, while I waited for the coffee to brew.

He looked even more amused now. I'd totally blown any attempt at pretending to be wordly or cool about the whole thing. "Two sugars?" I stirred his black coffee and handed it to him.

"You're so cute," he said, "can you call me a taxi?"

"Only if you tell me your surname." I teased.

He was away in a taxi back to his flat over the other side of the city by 9am. I felt slightly deflated. He'd given me a quick peck on the cheek as he left, which was pretty much all I wanted given the fact that he stank of beer, and promised to text me later.

I made myself a coffee and some toast and pottered over to the laptop, still in my PJs. I hadn't blogged anything since I'd been dumped by Mark, so I checked my figures for the last post. Hmm, I'd managed 48 views that day with my stroppy 'Weasel' post. Maybe I'd get some more hits if I wrote about my latest escapades? Let's face it, I'd just had very hot sex with a younger man, a very sexy younger man at that, and don't mind if I do blow my trumpet, thank you very much. I could justify it to myself on the basis that I was promoting plus-sized confidence - proving that a chubby girl could pull an absolutely gorgeous man. And everyone likes reading about other people's sex lives don't they?

NAUGHTY!

"I have news to report! After I was mercilessly dumped by The Weasel, I was feeling a bit low. I did what every girl should do after she's been dumped, I went out with my best girls and I had a damn good night out. Cocktails were consumed, Gloria Gaynor was danced to and gossiping was done. It was a top night out.

"I was feeling super-fabulous, working my curves and not letting my ex get to me. I even did something really naughty when I got home - with a young, gorgeous man! Being rejected by The Weasel, and the past few months of being with him, made me feel as sexy as a damp dishcloth, and I wanted to prove to myself that I wasn't completely unattractive. I've known the hot boy in question for a little while so you could say he was just in the right place (my bed) at the right time...

"I totally recommend misbehaving every once in a while. If you're a big girl, don't ever think that men won't find you attractive, because let me tell you, my toy boy was very appreciative of my curves. Men love a woman with confidence, who knows what she wants and isn't afraid to ask for it. I really loved taking control of the situation, he was there on my terms, he's gone now, and will I see him again? Who knows? But I had a great time...

"My point is, apart from showing off a bit, that you don't have to be

a size zero to be sexy. Work your curves, get out there and act confident, and you'll feel sexier straight away. Strut your stuff, girlfriend. I can't guarantee you'll end up with a hot man, but it makes you feel amazing..."

I hit 'publish' and smiled to myself. No, I was not going to get hung up on Jamie. I'd really love it if he called, because secretly I was a good girl, and even though last night didn't really count as a one night stand, it would still feel ever-so-slightly rubbish if I never heard from him again. I banished thoughts of my mum's face if she knew what I'd been up to last night – I was in my thirties for goodness sake – and replaced them with images of Jamie's dopey grin and biteable thighs. My night of lust (OK it was about half an hour but that doesn't sound nearly as impressive) had left me feeling slightly restless, but my navel gazing was interrupted by a text from Zoë.

"So?" was all it said. I knew she wanted details.

"So, he came over and he was very drunk"

"Did he stay the night?"

I toyed with the idea of teasing Zoë for a bit, which would have served her right for being so nosey. Then I remembered I would have been just as nosey if she'd gone home with someone and decided not to be so mean.

"Yes, once he eventually got here, he didn't want to leave."

"You hussy! Go you! How was it?"

I hoped she didn't want the down and dirty detail. But I wanted to share!

"It was bloody fantastic! I remember what I was missing now...Yummy."

"Are you seeing him again?"

Hmm, tricky. I really didn't know the answer to that one.

"Hope so. I'll fill you in on the details later. Do you fancy meeting up in town? I need to go shopping for undies."

The answer came back swiftly.

"Hell yeah, Missy. Wahey!"

I wandered into the city, where I'd arranged to meet Zoë and shop to improve my underwear situation. It was the sort of morning I'd usually have found an excuse to stay in bed and avoid. Drizzle, a cold wind and a city full of frowning people with umbrellas that always seemed to be at the right height to poke my eye out. Today, I didn't even want to poke the person who made me walk in the road because their brolly was the size of a small parachute. I wasn't going to let a bit of pissy rain dampen my just-been-laid rosy glow. But the thought that my new lover might be a frequent visitor to my boudoir did bring it home to me how much I needed to stock up on lingerie. I'd taken to trying to tempt fate by wearing my old grey granny pants whenever I saw Mark. Nope, that hadn't worked either. Did somebody say desperate?

I hadn't bought any new undies for as long as I could remember, and if I was going to be seducing Jamie on a regular basis, and I rather hoped I would be, I'd need some sexy lingerie. I wanted to find myself some cleavage enhancing bras, maybe a corset or basque and sexy knickers. For ages I'd wanted to be one of those women who dressed up in the bedroom. I loved the idea of being a vixen, confident enough to play around with my sexuality and spice things up a bit. I'd never been able to do that with Darren – the last time I tried buying sexy undies for him, he took one look at me in them, snorted with derision and said, "Very nice." Then went back downstairs to watch the football, leaving me standing there, feeling like an idiot, in a black corset and heels. I think I cried afterwards. I certainly didn't bother with all that again.

Jamie seemed like the kind of man who'd appreciate me making a bit of an effort though. He'd clearly liked what he'd seen last night, after all. He'd said I was hot! I blushed as I re-ran the encounter in my head.

I met Zoë outside the mall and we made a beeline for the poshest lingerie shop in the place.

"So, the sex was fantastic, was it?" She said, a little bit too loudly. I blushed.

"Shhh! Yes, I broke my drought in style" I replied, "and it was – very nice."

Zoë punched my arm playfully "You've lusted after that boy for so long. It was always going to be good. I'm almost jealous! How do you feel this morning?"

I frowned, thinking it over. "I dunno, really. I'm glad I did it, I had a great time. But I feel a little bit weird now."

"Awww, girlfriend, he'll be in touch. You were careful, weren't you?"

I rolled my eyes. "Yeees, of course. I'm not daft!" I paused. "But I did have to check the condom packet before he came over – it's been so long since I saw any action that I was worried they might have gone out of date!"

Zoë stifled a giggle. She'd been on the end of many a rant about my inability to seduce Mark. She knew just how bad things had been…

We headed into the shop. There was a stunning array of pretty smalls on display. I went straight for the beautiful red and white lace-trimmed polka dot bra, with plunging cups and a slightly 1950's style that made me think of pin-up girls and American cheesecake posters. It felt soft and seductive and I could just see myself in it.

"Oooh la la, darling, that's fabulous" trilled Zoë. "You NEED that bra!"

I had to agree with her. It was stunning, and I'd feel a complete vixen in it. I clocked the sales assistant staring at me knowingly. Either I had a very obvious 'just pulled a toy-boy' glow about me or she knew something I didn't.

I searched the rack for my size. Oh, OK. This style appeared to only go up to a DD cup, so that bra was out. The matching full knickers had a cute retro style to them but they went up to a size 16 and were also out of the question. Dammit. That must have been why the assistant had been staring at me, she was thinking "Fat arse, no chance!" I felt my heart sink.

I was wearing a full on pout, watching Zoë picking up adorable sets a couple of sizes smaller that would look absolutely fantastic on her curvy figure. Now, I'm not saying they wouldn't have looked good on my curvy figure, but I wasn't going to get a chance to find out. None of them came in anything close to my size.

"Cheer up girlfriend", Zoë said, trying to pacify me. "There are loads of undie shops in Cambridge. We'll get you some sexy smalls to seduce that man-boy of yours in."

I stuck my tongue out.

"Well, I don't think I'm going to find anything here, sweetie." I pouted.

Although there were a few styles in a bigger cup size, they didn't seem to have any matching pants. Frustrated, I put back pair after pair in an 8, 10 or 12, hunting for the lonely size 20 at the back of the rail. Either it didn't exist, or they'd all been snapped up by my fellow voluptuous sisters. Either way, it was getting on my nerves and I got out of the shop before I started muttering TOO loudly about "rubbish size selections" and "size discrimination." I forgot how much lingerie shopping stressed me out.

Luckily, Zoe tipped me off about a boutique that specialised in gorgeous bras for big busty girls. "That one would look great on you," she exclaimed. "That style is so flattering, you'd give yourself boobs you could rest your drink on and the straps won't dig in."

I was even happier when I realised that the beautiful contraptions actually came in my cup size. I picked a few up, and decided that even if the bottoms weren't big enough, if I went for one of each in black, red and white I could mix and match anyway. I looked at the price tags. Then I put two of the bras back and kept hold of my absolute favourite. It seemed that the price I was going to have to pay for having bigger than average boobage was way too much for a freelance copywriter's salary to stretch to right now. This essential purchase would have to be my 'best' bra. I winced as the slightly aloof shop girl put my card in the machine and I punched in my pin number pretending that I didn't notice the amount when it flashed up on the card reader.

" I might even remember to hand wash this one rather than chucking it in with everything else black and then getting really annoyed when the underwire starts to poke through." I moaned to Zoë, who was trying to resist the urge to splurge on a matching set she really fancied. She rolled her eyes at me, put the set back and walked out of the shop empty-handed.

"Shall we try M&S?" Zoë suggested. The black frilly bra was gorgeous but it wasn't exactly a stand out sexy seductress effort and I wanted something that would make Jamie's eyes pop out at the very least.

"We can give it a go," I agreed. "And if not, there should at least be some nice food in there to console us." The lingerie section proved to be a stupendous disappointment "What about this one?" Zoë said, over and over again, holding up bra after bra for my approval.

"No matching pants," was my reply. Over and over again.

"What about these?"

I looked up and she was brandishing the ugliest pair of granny pants I'd ever seen, in a beige stretchy fabric. "Sod off," I said, pretending to be cross with her. I snatched the offending big pants and swatted her with them. "Go and put these monstrosities back where you found them, wench!"

I sighed and pouted as bra after bra and knicker set in pink, purple or red attracted me like a moth to a flame, only for me to put it back down again when I realised I couldn't get the knickers over a size 14. I even tried colour matching from the other knickers but the shade was always just slightly out. I was clearly destined for a life of non-matching lingerie hell.

"Sweet thing, I'm sorry but I've got to go and see my sister later," Zoë told me as we made our way down to the food hall to commiserate with posh cake.

"Free lunch?" I asked, knowing the answer already.

"They think I can't look after myself, and if they want to cook me lunch, who am I to deprive them of that treat?" Zoë was more than capable of looking after herself but we all knew that she only ever had wine, chocolate and occasionally cheese in her fridge, so we often took pity on her and fed her. A cunning strategy she had been working for years.

"OK honey, well I'm probably going to go home and have a sleep anyway" I sighed. "it's time to admit defeat. I'll have to have a look online."

"It's seriously bad, isn't it?" Zoë commiserated. "I didn't realise it was so freakin' hard!"

"I'll survive," I laughed. "Go on, off you go and get your free dinner, I'll go for a quick coffee and then home for a sleep."

"That's toy boys for you," Zoë teased, "They wear you out."

I shook my head. "Go on, bugger off. I'll talk to you in the week." I hugged her and kissed her on the cheek. Zoë scurried off to her sisters and I was just about to queue up and pay for the food I'd bought to make up for lack of underwear when my Blackberry started to ring. I scrambled for it in a very undignified fashion while juggling a fruit salad, a box of cakes and a stir fry mix, hoping it was Jamie.

It wasn't.

It was Paul, my oldest boy-buddy, who I'd been seriously neglecting recently.

Y'alright?" I greeted him, as cheerily as I could manage.

I'd known Paul since our college days and he'd got me through many a broken heart in the past. Darren had been suspicious of him, as he was any man I was a friend with. He even banned me from seeing him at one point but he never actually found out about the times we did meet up or that we e-mailed each other pretty much on a daily basis and had done for years. When I separated from Darren, Paul was over the moon and we rekindled our friendship.

"What are you doing for lunch, sexy?" he asked, without bothering to reply. He always called me sexy, just because he could do it now without getting me into trouble,

"I'm already in town," I replied, "Just been shopping for underwear with Zoë, and I was thinking I might go home and catch up on my sleep."

"Underwear you say? Had a busy night?" Paul teased.

"Sort of."

I knew he wouldn't let me leave it there, and I had lots to tell him. I felt a bit bad for not having updated him sooner, but I'd been so tied up with the whole Mark thing, he kind of took second place. Bad Ellie.

"Well, why don't you tell me about it over lunch then? My treat?"

Ohh, tempting. I'd just blown the last of my spare spending money on a frivolous bra purchase and so anyone wanting to buy me food was a bonus. I figured it was a fair exchange for the amount of gossip I was about to give him.

"Meet you by Boots in half an hour." I suggested.

"It's a date!"

I meandered through the city, resisting the urge to stomp in puddles in protest at my rubbish shopping trip. Being denied pretty smalls had dampened my upbeat mood a bit. I didn't even know why I was bothering to sex up my underwear drawer; after all, I'd probably just had a one-night stand and wouldn't even need it for another six months.

"No thanks." I gave the Big Issue seller my customary brush off and felt slightly guilty as she watched me walk into an expensive coffee shop with her doleful brown eyes. I always felt guilty about not giving money to Big Issue sellers and charity collectors. Text book people-pleaser, me. At least I was always polite when I declined their requests; I'd have felt even meaner if I'd just ignored them.

I saw Paul straightaway, he was incredibly tall and his dark brown, slightly grey peppered hair was cut in a style that was instantly recognisable. He was older than me, although not much, and very self-conscious about going grey. I told him over and over again that it made him look distinguished but that didn't seem to help. He was wearing his usual black jeans, with a baggy shirt over a Green Day t-shirt, and he looked a curious mix of student and mature older man. He was a good-looking guy, who seemed to have absolutely no luck with women because he was just too kind-hearted and trusting.

I loved him to bits.

He'd already got me a coffee – he knew my favourite – and I braced myself for the barrage of questions.

"Hello darling!" Paul said with a grin, getting up to give me a bear hug and a kiss.

"Hi gorgeous." I said, sitting down. I plonked my bags on the floor, put my elbows on the table and rested my chin in my hands. I let out a long sigh and then realised I'd put my elbow in spilled coffee so sighed again as I wiped at it. Paul looked at me with half concern and half amusement.

"So, I read your blog. Why didn't you tell me things were so bad with Mark? I thought you were all loved up!"

I sighed again.

"I was. Unfortunately, he wasn't." I took a gulp of my Americano and once again launched into the I've-been-dumped story. I gave Paul the full lowdown, the rejection, the fact Mark wouldn't come near me, and the way he'd made me feel about myself. I even told him about the fact he'd still got a picture of his ex in his wallet. Paul made all the right sympathetic noises, until I started putting myself down.

"I just couldn't measure up to Rachel. She's slim and blonde and perfect –"

"But she's also a cheating bitch who left him broken-hearted for another girl! It's not all about looks, darling, and you know I think you're gorgeous anyway, but you're smart and funny and kind, and if he's too shallow and thick to see that, it's his loss and not yours."

"It's not just that." I added.

"What d'you mean?"

"I slept with Jamie."

Now Paul was interested.

"That was fast work! You've only been single a few days. I thought you'd written him off? You're old enough to be his babysitter, aren't you?"

I smacked him on the arm, "You cheeky bugger!"

Paul was smirking, waiting for me to give him the low-down. I started to feel a bit of an idiot. In the cold light of day, I realised there was no chance that Jamie and I were going to turn our night of drunken passion into a full-blown romance filled relationship. I also realised just how needy that made me sound.

Oh God. I was turning into Bridget Jones.

"He started texting me last night when I was out with the girls. Lauren and Zoë made me do it." I lied.

"You minx, I never thought you had it in you."

I blushed. "Well, I was a bit drunk. And it's not as if it was a *real* one-night-stand, is it? I've been out with him a few times, and I've known him for ages. And he did say he'd text me later even if he hasn't. But he's out being sporty. Or something."

"You don't have to make excuses for having sex, sweetie." Paul said. He knew me so well. "Do you feel better for it?"

"Well it was fun" I admitted coyly, blushing at the thought of the night before, images on Jamie naked popping up in my head.

"You've been after him for months, haven't you?" Paul asked, sipping his coffee.

"It's the other way around, actually." I said haughtily. "He wouldn't leave me alone!"

"You're just too irresistible, darling" Paul smiled. "That Mark bloke was an idiot."

I shuddered inwardly at the mention of his name. Then changed the subject.

"So, if you were Jamie, would you call me?"

"Stop obsessing, darling. It makes you look desperate and you're not. You just have to leave him alone, don't chase him, don't text him. Wait for him to call you and he will."

"It's just all this stuff with Mark, it's made me feel a bit insecure."

"Don't rely on a bloke to give you confidence, I can sit here and tell you you're great, you can let your schoolboy lover tell you how hot you are, but if you don't like yourself, you'll just be looking for the next person to make you feel good all the time. What happened to the confident Ellie I know and love?"

I hated to admit it, but the man was talking sense and I knew it.

"Mark happened. I know, I know, I shouldn't have let him get to me like that. But it's not just him, is it?"

"What do you mean, sweetie?" Paul questioned.

"After Mark dumped me I was feeling low, and started to get a bit diet-headed. I actually wondered if I should lose weight, and that made me really mad."

"Why don't you write about it on your blog?" Paul said, encouragingly. He was probably my most loyal reader, although sometimes I suspected he didn't actually read it, only clicked on it to make up the reader numbers.

"Well, you know, I've been talking to the girls about doing something to make fat people like me feel better about themselves."

Paul nodded, waiting for me to carry on. "And I thought about Jane, and what happened to her. She'd been depressed about being dumped too, she thought it was because she was fat and she got so desperate to change herself that she couldn't bear it anymore, she bloody killed herself."

"I know, darling," Paul soothed. "But what are you going to do? You can't change the world?"

"Can't I?"

He looked at me quizzically. "Well, no. The whole anti-fat thing is pretty entrenched in the media. I can see what you're doing, and I totally have faith in you, but it's a multi-million pound business and media pressure you're fighting against."

"I might not be able to change the whole world," I said, feeling a little defiant, "but I can change my little corner of it. I can challenge the stereotypes. I want a magazine column; I want to write words that move people. Oh, and the girls want me to do a video on YouTube."

Paul spluttered. "You hate stuff like that!"

"I know. They had to persuade me to do it. I'm still not sure, but then I thought about Jane, about everything she went through, the pressure she felt. And about how I feel when I feel like I have to defend myself all the time. I don't want to feel like I'm inferior just because I have a fat arse, Paul. And there's more to me than my bra size."

"Although you do have a very impressive cleavage..."

I slapped him on the arm. "Behave!"

"That's my girl" Paul laughed, draining the dregs of his second cup of tea. Sometimes I wondered why Paul and I had never got together, when he was so kind and lovely. I ruffled his hair affectionately. "You're great, you are"

"I know," he beamed.

I left the coffee shop, fired up with enthusiasm once again and feeling ready to take on the world.

Chapter 7

FABULOUSLY YOU

"I don't want to go on and on about it - but I was unceremoniously, brutally dumped recently. Can you tell it smarts a bit? And yeah, it did send me straight into the arms of a very sexy younger man, which was very nice, thank you very much, but the actual 'you're dumped' part of the scenario didn't do much for my self-esteem. I did the classic spurned woman thing and spend hours wringing out tissues while I compared myself to his thin ex. It got me thinking – why do we let men and their opinions of us affect how we feel about who we are?

We've all done it. Who hasn't been dumped by someone and blamed their weight? He told me he loved the fact I was confident, so why did I tell myself he didn't fancy me because I'm not a size ten? Going on a diet after a break-up is such a cliché, and it's so easy to fall into the trap of thinking that if we lost a bit of weight we'd be happier, more fulfilled, in a better relationship, in a better job.

The truth is, ladies, if a man's going to dump you, or not want to go out with you in the first place, going on a diet won't change that. I was dumped when I was 17 by an arsehole who told his mates (who made sure they told me) that he'd only gone out with me because I had enormous boobs, and he didn't really fancy me because I was fat. I was a size 14. In reality he dumped me because I wouldn't let him do what he was trying to do, and he felt rejected himself. But I still went on a diet.

Don't ever let another person's opinion of who you are change your opinion of yourself, and never think you have to change the way you are. Just be fabulous!"

So, I did listen to Paul sometimes, and I had to admit his idea for a blog post had been a good one. I'd been trying not to think about Mark, who I hadn't heard from since he did the 'it's not me, it's you' routine, or Jamie, who I hadn't heard from either, and instead dedicated myself to thinking about Lauren's challenge. I hadn't done anything practical yet, but I'd fantasised about becoming a media darling, landing a column in Marie Claire, going on press trips to foreign countries and meeting famous people. In reality, I hadn't got much further than looking at different types of video editing software on the Internet. As I was surfing idly, drinking my umpteenth cup of coffee and trying to muster up the enthusiasm for a page of shampoo descriptions for *Glammazon,* my phone beeped, it was Zoe.

"How about we make your first video in McDonalds?"

"I presume you're being ironic?" I replied.

"Yeah, you have a point. They might make us eat something off the menu."

The McDonalds idea was scrapped.

"How about the park?" she responded.

"I'm not standing in the middle of a park where people will laugh and point."

Lauren came up with a couple of ideas too. In between meetings she'd dropped me efficient texts with things like, *"All Bar One?"* or *"Evans?"* but then after all the reasons under the sun I could think of for not filming just about anywhere, Zoë came up with the real winner when she texted, *"Have you thought about the gym?"*

"I've thought about it, but I haven't been this week yet. Why?" I replied.

"For the video, silly"

Genius. Why hadn't I thought of that?

Filming a quick tour of the gym would be ideal, because I did actually spend quite a bit of time there, and it would be a great one for busting the 'fat girls don't exercise' stereotype.

"I'm on it." I texted back, and decided it was probably a good idea to check they wouldn't object to me and the girls messing around with a phone camera in there.

I knew the gym manager, Mel, pretty well and we usually had a laugh together, usually at my expense, when I went in for a workout. She was a super-fit fitness freak who kept trying to get me on the TRX equipment, but so far had only succeeded in introducing me to Power Plates. I'd hated the TRX with a passion ever since my first ever session on them with a young, over-concerned personal trainer. He'd repeatedly asked me if I was OK, making me determined to show him that just because I was fat it didn't mean I was incapable of doing a few push-ups. This stubbornness had resulted in me over-compensating just to prove a point, and I couldn't walk properly for about three days afterwards. I'd point blank refused to go anywhere near the harness and frame set up ever since. Harnesses and frames belonged in *Fifty Shades of Grey*, not in my gym repertoire.

"You want to do what?" Mel smirked. OK, so it wasn't an everyday request.

"I want to do a video for my blog, about being fit and fat"

"I don't see that it'll be a problem," Mel said, composing herself. "You'll have to be careful that you don't get anyone else in the picture though, unless you ask them first. I'll get into trouble for it otherwise." Seeing as I was actually at the gym, I felt sort of obliged to do a workout, so I jumped on the cross trainer and hoped for a little exertion-induced inspiration. To tell you the truth, I was still absolutely petrified of doing it. Not so much the filming, that would be fun, but people ACTUALLY seeing me. Hmmm. I hated my voice when I heard it on the few local radio interviews I'd done in the past, and the thought of people seeing me? Well…I was going to need a gallon of Rescue Remedy to calm my nerves. Or vodka. Probably both.

I'd done my research on the best length for an online video, and apparently it was around three minutes. Three minutes seemed achievable. I could manage that, couldn't I? Especially if I had new workout clothes. I went to the one shop in the city that sold plus size gym gear and managed to get myself a hot pink semi-fitted vest top and some three quarter length black leggings, which flattered my ample bum. I was ready as I was ever going to be, and decided that the best thing to do was face my fear and just do it, before I talked myself out of it. Again.

The actual filming bit was easy. I sweet talked Mel into holding the camera, but her payback was swift. "Why don't you start off by the TRX?" she suggested. I'd been planning what I was going to say, but when Mel hit the record button, it all sounded wrong. At first I had a coughing fit, then looked blankly at her, forgetting what I was meant to say.

"Big people should go to the gym." I started.

Nope, that sounded like something you'd read on one of the comments pages. Not the most encouraging intro. Scrap that.

"Ignore anyone who says you can't go to the gym just because you're big."

Too preachy.

Argh! I had my script in my head but it just didn't sound right. I felt like a newsreader. "Tonight, the Government decided that fat people should pay tax on every pound of bodyweight that exceeds their BMI" I said, in my most affected newsreader voice.

"That's it!" Exclaimed Mel. "It's ridiculous, and it will make people laugh. Start there."

"Are you sure?" I asked, not entirely convinced.

"Yes, do it, do it!"

I did it again, slightly more deadpan.

"If the answer to the obesity epidemic we keep hearing about is so simple, and all we need to do is eat less and move more, why are there fat people at the gym?" I carried on. "I'm living proof that you can be fat and fit, thank you very much."

Mel looked at me encouragingly as I faltered a bit. I caught one of the gym-bunnies with abs of steel staring at me. I flushed, suddenly feeling self-conscious. But then she smiled. See, not all super fit skinny birds are mean I thought.

I hugged the TRX pole and simpered at the camera. "I used to hate this contraption, and do you know what? I still do. Lifting your entire body weight using just a few flimsy harnesses is always going to be harder when you're overweight, there's more of you. But...I love this thing..."

I skipped over to the treadmill. Mel followed, bemused. There was someone on the machine next to where I'd stopped and I think she was trying to angle the camera so as not to include the profusely sweating man in the shot.

"Check me out, I can run and talk at the same time," I said, pressing the buttons, and trying to think of what to say next.

I got the treadmill up to running speed and took off on a flat, just as Mel angled the camera up at my face. No, not from below, it'll look like I've got double chins. Don't film my arse jiggling either.

"You see, all the crap you hear about fat people like me being disgusting, obese, drains on society is bollocks. The media would love you to believe that we're all going to die a horrible, early death, and that our only exercise... is getting up from the sofa to go to the fridge...but...that's just so they can make us miserable... by flogging diet plans that don't work!"

OK, maybe doing this video *and* running wasn't such a good idea. I was getting pretty breathless now. I turned the treadmill down a notch and regained my composure.

"They tell you...that fat people sweat...more? Well I ...certainly do," I continued, desperate to prove I could work out and talk at the same time. "But...only when...I'm working out...."

Mel sniggered. Sweaty bloke on the treadmill next to us had been eavesdropping and was looking a bit miffed. Oh sod it, I'd had enough of talking and running, I'd made my point. I hit stop and the treadmill came to a grinding halt. I wobbled a bit and took a step back, steadied myself and stepped off onto the floor.

While I composed myself, Mel turned the camera to face her, "Ellie is always in the gym, I can't keep her off the treadmill, although I WILL get her to love the TRX like I do one day. We've got a lot of bigger members here, men and women, and we tailor our plans to the individual's capabilities. I remember doing an assessment of a woman who was 19 stone, just after I'd done one for a 16 year old footballer. I nearly fell over when the woman managed more step ups in two minutes than the footballer had! Never judge anyone by their appearance."

I'd got my breath back and thanked Mel, ready to carry on with the next bit of my rant.

"Diets don't work." I said, resting against the cross trainer. "Worrying about your weight will just make you miserable. Getting fit however, that's assuming you're not already fit, will makes you feel brilliant."

I spoke directly to the camera, pulling a towel round my neck for added effect.

"If we swapped dieting and hating ourselves for doing some fun exercise that gets our heart pumping, we'd get a high that Slimfast will never give you. So do it now. Join the gym. Get the exercise DVD out, go for a walk, chase the kids around, play on your Wii Fit. Just do it."

I think I'd been getting louder and louder as the video had gone on, because there were now a few people watching me, clearly wondering what on earth I was doing.

Mel gave me a hug. "That was pretty damn good," she grinned. "See, you're not such a wuss, after all."

I think that was a compliment.

I got the girls round that evening and showed them my handiwork. I thought I'd be too busy cringing to actually watch it back, but I was pleasantly surprised when I realised I looked quite confident, strolling around the gym and pointing out my favourite bits. Lauren was frowning a bit, but Zoë was whooping and hollering.

"Go, Girlfriend!" she yelped as I got to the bit about the media flogging diet plans. Lauren shot her a look. You could tell that sometimes Zoë's effervescence got on Lauren's nerves, but I always thought it was a smidge of jealousy. Zoë was just so open and expressive, but Lauren was guarded unless she really knew someone, and sometimes I thought she would have loved to let go like Zoë did.

"I love this" Lauren said after watching the clip for the third time. "It's really…you. And I think people will connect with it, but what now?"

I was a bit flummoxed by that myself. She was supposed to be the expert why was she was asking me?

"Right now, I don't know," I admitted, "but I think I might be able to find a bottle of wine somewhere that will help us concentrate our minds."

Wine poured and thinking heads on, we got to work. "What we need is a platform." Lauren said, playing with her wine glass. "It's all very well having these videos but if they're just on your blog, they won't be seen by anyone other than your blog readers. Facebook is fine, Twitter is better, but if we want this to go viral, we need a plan."

Zoë was fiddling with her curly hair, looking thoughtful. "If we're going to plan stuff, we need paper, coloured pens and," she began, "A SWOT analysis table?" interrupted Lauren, mocking her own affinity for marketing tools. Zoë poked her tongue out, a standard response to anything she didn't have an answer for. Cute.

"What exactly does 'Go Viral' mean, anyway?" I asked Lauren.

"Basically," she said, taking a sip of her wine, "it just describes something that's got really popular, really fast. You know when someone posts a clip on Facebook and everyone shares it? That's going viral, because it gets seen by thousands, even hundreds of thousands of people, very quickly."

"How do you do it?"

"That's the tricky bit," she replied.

Zoë and I waited for the next bit of insight but it wasn't forthcoming. Lauren was deep in thought. "I'll get some crisps, shall I?" I offered.

When I came back to the room, Lauren was sitting on the floor with Zoë. I chucked the crisps at Zoë and sat down with them. Zoë was cross-legged in her usual yoga babe pose. How could anyone be that flexible, I wondered?

Lauren's expertise with social media and viral marketing was going to come in very, very useful. We sat down and constructed a plan of attack for the clip, which we were going to upload onto YouTube.

"So, we set up a YouTube account, and then we can upload it and link it to your blog" said Lauren. "We have to think of a user name."

"Curvaceous?" I suggested.

"Yuk" Lauren grimaced. "How about "Curvy Girl?"

I liked that. It sounded like a fat super heroine, which is what I wanted to be.

"Voluptuous?" Zoë added, helpfully.

Lauren pulled a face.

"How about 'Viva Voluptuous?'" I suggested.

"Isn't that what I just said?" pouted Zoë.

"Not quite. The viva bit means 'Alive' – so adding it to 'Voluptuous' gives it a bit more oomph."

"Alive? In what language?" Lauren asked. "Will people know what it means?"

"Spanish I think. Or Portuguese. One or the other. Even if they don't it sounds good, don't you think?"

Lauren chewed on the end of her pen, clearly forgetting what happened when we all did that at primary school. "Not bad, not bad..." she said, trying to think of something better. Lauren always was the competitive one.

"I like it." Zoë said, through a mouthful of Kettle Chips.

"You would, you half came up with it!"

"If I'm going to be the one on the video, I get the deciding vote," I piped up. "And I really like Viva Voluptuous."

"Alright then. I suppose it'll do," surrendered Lauren. She was clearly annoyed that her marketing genius hadn't produced anything more catchy, and I suspected that she would be going away to try and think up something else later. Zoë couldn't help but do a little victory "Yay!"

Lauren said she would set up an account for us so that we could send out email newsletters to influential media types with links to the latest videos, and I already had access to some pretty cool PR software that I used every week for *Glammazon* press releases. I'd been a very bad girl with my *Glammazon* writing and I had fallen way behind, but figured I'd be able to make the time up once we'd got this project out of the way. My deadlines had whizzed past and I'd just waved at them as they went. I agreed with Lauren that my little blog alone wasn't going to be up to the job we needed it for– we needed a better way of getting my words and pictures out there to the masses.

"It's time you got brave and put that pitching training to good use too, Madam" Lauren admonished. "You need to get the word out and get people to connect with you, and the best way to do that is to get seen. Pitch to everyone you can think of. I want to hear you've pitched at least two ideas a week, for the next month, yeah?"

I pouted. I bloody hated pitching to editors. It activated every fear of rejection feeling I knew.

"OK." I sulked.

Women with a cunning plan should never be underestimated. After polishing off wine and crisps, drawing lots of diagrams, and doodles, many of which had absolutely nothing remotely to do with Viva Voluptuous, and working until almost 3am, we had a plan in place to launch VV and the very first video on an unsuspecting public.

I'd watched the video about a hundred times before I finally uploaded it, and although there were a few bits I'd change, including my nasal voice, I was pretty pleased with the general happy go lucky, fit fat girl image I was portraying. I'd managed to do the video with no apologies for my size, not even a self-deprecating comment. I'd hopefully managed to show people that it was perfectly possible to be strong, fit, sexy and overweight.

Zoë had interviewed me for her really popular body image blog, called *Gorgeous*. We'd got a great image to go with it of me in my gym-gear, and we recorded it in her kitchen, probably because it was a very pretty kitchen. Zoë's kitchen was a reflection of her personality. There were trinkets and ornaments everywhere, an abundance of sparkly bits and pieces, and the occasional piece of evidence that this room was, in fact, used for something as mundane as eating. She rarely had any food in the house, as she was always trying new super-foods and declaring them the best thing since sliced bread…then deciding they were actually vile and throwing them out six months later when she cleared out the cupboards looking for something sweet. It was just as well she was so popular that she was rarely at home for dinner.

"So, Ellie, you've just recorded a video in your local gym, explaining how fitness isn't limited to skinny fit-birds," she started. "I've seen it and I think it's super-cool, but why did you decide to do it?"

I took a deep breath. "Voice!" was the first thing that popped into my head. Then I realised it didn't matter as Zoë was going to write this up later and nobody had to hear me. My shoulders relaxed immediately.

"I'm just so fed up with all the fat-hate I see out there. It's making us all paranoid!"

"How does it make you feel when you read negative things about fat people?" Zoe asked in her best journalist voice. Despite myself, I was trying not to giggle.

"It frustrates me. It makes me want to punch the person that wrote it, and I'm totally not a violent kinda girl! I just want to grab whoever said the mean stuff, by the scruff of the neck, take them down the gym and challenge them to a run-off on the treadmill!"

Zoë laughed. "A run off? How would that work?"

"God knows. But you know what I mean? I can't be doing with all the nasty bitchy comments about fat people. I mean, they say fat people smell bad? Have they seen how much body lotion I get through? I smell damn fine, girlfriend! And the worst BO I've ever smelled was on a very skinny man I used to work with. It's just reee-diculous. I mean, come ON!"

"Was it easy getting fit as a bigger girl?"

"I've never really been unfit," I replied, truthfully. "I've never been able to drive, I'm totally useless behind a steering wheel, and it means that I've had to rely on getting around on my own two feet a lot of the time. I've always loved swimming and walking, and I love the feeling I get from a good workout too. Ever since iPods, it's been even better, I get to go off into my own little world."

"So you're living proof that you can be fit and fat – if you don't mind me using the F-word, but what do you say to people who think that you can't possibly be happy and fat?"

I rolled my eyes, Zoë knew that was another pet hate of mine.

"I say 'do I look miserable to you?' And if I'm honest, the only time I'm miserable about my weight is when the haters go on and on about how crap I am just for being an 'unacceptable' body size. When I'm out with my mates, I am happy. When I'm with my family, I'm happy. When I'm left alone, to do whatever I want to do without being judged, I'm happy. What makes me sad is the way people are judged and found wanting because they are overweight. I had a very close friend who…" I stopped.

"You sure you want to talk about this, doll?" Zoë said, looking concerned. She reached for the box of tissues that was on top of the fridge freezer, as if she knew what might be coming next.

"Yeah, yeah, I'm fine," I carried on, pulling myself back together. "So, I had a friend who could never believe she was beautiful, when she so, so was. She had an eating disorder. Nobody saw what she put herself through trying to conform to society's standards, nobody heard her throwing up, then sobbing, and when she killed herself because she just couldn't take anymore, I was devastated. I lost one of the best friends I ever had because society told her she wasn't good enough." A sob caught in my throat as I ran through a memory of Jane and I in my head, a memory where we were arguing. She was telling me I just didn't understand that she felt fat and repulsive. I didn't understand why she couldn't see herself as I did. "You're not so skinny yourself" she'd replied, trying to wound me.

"What happened to my friend didn't stop me going through the body hatred and dieting cycle myself. I used to think this must have been how she felt, whenever I felt terrible reading another story about weak-willed fatties and skinny celebrities' cellulite."

Zoë looked moved. She knew Jane's story, and how it had affected me, but even so, I was on the verge of tears and Zoë hated to see me upset.

"So are you happy in your own skin now?"

"Mostly" I replied. "To be honest, it's always hard. You have to develop a skin that's as thick as a rhino to deflect all the negativity about being overweight. I'm not 100% on top of it all of the time and sometimes, yeah it gets to me. Like, last week when I'd had a bad day and made the mistake of reading some online comments, it brought me down a bit. Then I decided not to let it get me sad and I got mad instead. It's easy to get dragged into feeling unworthy, as if you're somehow less of a person because of your size. But that's just rubbish."

Zoë clicked the recorder off and gave me a hug. "You OK honey?" she said, kindly.

"I'm fine. How did I do?"

"Girlfriend did good!" She grinned. "And now girlfriend needs a hug for being so awesome."

So we had a video, and we had an interview. Now we just had to get them online and let Lauren work her magic…

Chapter 8

"I want to see it again."

Lauren had told me that as far as it goes, uploading a video onto YouTube and then sending the link to lots of people wasn't exactly exciting to watch, but I wanted to see the video *just* once more before she hit send, so I'd insisted we'd all got together for the event one evening.

We were all huddled around her laptop and squished up on Zoë's sofa, as I watched it once more. Lauren was pulling her best 'get on with it' face and looking impatient. "It's fabulous", Zoë exclaimed. "The interview was perfect, and the video is great, so real and so you. Just do it!"

"She's just being vain," Lauren said sarcastically. I felt a bit guilty. "Oh go on, then. Do it before I change my mind."

In a few minutes, Lauren had done what she needed to do and sent both the video and my interview for *Gorgeous* out to the masses. My words were out there, the campaign had started.

"Chubby super heroine, huh?" I said, under my breath, feeling a little bit nervous about what I might just have started.

The responses to the video started coming in faster than I'd expected. I knew I shouldn't have underestimated Lauren's powers. In less than 48 hours, the blog views for Gorgeous were going up and up, and my own blog, which I'd linked to, was boasting viewer numbers in three figures, which was a complete surprise for a girl who was happy with anything over 30. The video had been viewed hundreds of times already and although there were a few mean comments about fat people in Lycra – which were mostly mis-spelled and unoriginal as well as insulting – most of the feedback was really positive.

Reading *"Your (sic) just making excuses for yourself and you shouldn't wear that as it makes you look disgusting, have some decency and cover your fat blubber up"* made me want to hurl my coffee through the computer screen and howl in frustration, but when I read things like, *"Good on you for proving you don't have to be a size eight to be fit - you rock, and don't let people make you feel bad about yourself, because only you know who you really are,"* it did redress the balance a bit. I really loved reading all the good stuff, so I made the executive decision to gloss over all the typical 'You're fat and ugly' insults and concentrate on the lovely things that were being said.

It was hard though, I mean, where did these people get off, insulting a complete stranger just because she's fat? I couldn't imagine for a minute that they'd go up to a stranger in the street and call them 'repulsive' or 'disgusting' but it was apparently okay to abuse me from behind the anonymity of a computer screen. Morons.

I almost did cartwheels around the flat when I had a message from a 17-year-old girl who said she'd been bullied about her weight and was scared to go to the gym in case there were bullies there too.

"Watching you and your trainer talking about how many big girls there are at your gym gave me the confidence to decide I'm going to go to the leisure centre and join their cheap gym next week."

One little video was already making a big difference to somebody, and I was incredibly excited about doing more filming. Now that was something I hadn't expected.

Meanwhile, contact from Jamie, the boy wonder, was conspicuous by its complete absence. I'd been too busy with Viva Voluptuous for the last week or so to get too hung up on it, but sitting here alone, I was moping a bit, thinking I'd probably never see him again.

As luck would have it, I had an assignment for Glammazon coming up to take my mind off rubbish men, and a perfect chance to do another video - although this might have to be undercover. They wanted me to try out a brand new concept spa that had opened, and said I could take a friend. This sort of invitation always made me a very popular lady, so I decided to do a little bit of negotiating, to see if I could get Zoe to come to Glastonbury. There was no way I was going to waste the ticket I bought for Mark, I wanted my girl to come with me - with the help of a sweetener in the form of an overnight spa visit.

"No, no way, not ever, don't even ask." Zoë said, in her best "and don't try to convince me otherwise" haughty voice.

This wasn't going amazingly well, admittedly. Zoë had her 'I cannot believe you think I would lower myself to sleeping in a campervan' face on, and was inspecting her nails, willing me to change the subject. Not even a glass of expensive Prosecco had changed her mind.

"I can't go on my own. I can't drive and I haven't got a tent. Plus it's no fun without your best mate. Pleeeease?"

"Honey, I've seen pictures. Mud, dust, more mud, rain and mud. And Portaloos. It's not a place I want to be."

"But I'm trying to get us a meet with Paloma Faith," I wheedled. "I've emailed her management company and I'm sure they'll get back to me soon."

"I don't care if you manage to resurrect Amy Winehouse; I am not going anywhere near that place. Ever."

I waved another drink under her nose, and although she took it from me eagerly, she wasn't budging. I pouted. I was going to have to change tactics.

"It's not fair. I'm stuck with two tickets now that the Weasel's dumped me, and now Paloma Faith is going to be there, I have to go. And I need someone there with me if I get the interview with her. Lauren can't make it either. I'll be forever in your debt." I decided this would have to be when I played the trump card. "I've got overnight spa passes for the Goddess Spa at Rawthwaite Hall"

Suddenly Zoë was back in the room.

"Really?"

"Oh yeah. *Glammazon* want me to review the place. They have freeform yoga classes, extremely hot male Pilates instructors, and myself and a guest get one of their brand new Goddess Ritual treatments thrown in as well as a luxury twin suite, all meals and use of the spa for two whole days. But if you don't fancy it..."

"Of course I fancy it. Why didn't you say?"

"Because if you want to come with me, you'll have to agree to come with me to Glastonbury."

I could tell Zoë was struggling with this one. I'd done a bit of research and although technically I could get a refund on one or both tickets, as being dumped counted as an 'unforeseen circumstance' there was no guarantee I'd get another ticket for Zoë when the refunded tickets went back on sale again. Of course, you couldn't just transfer the bloody ticket to someone else's name. That would have been way too useful.

She knew she was taking a chance, but if there was one thing Zoë found it almost impossible to turn down, it was a free spa trip.

"OK. Buy me a Mojito and I'll think about it."

I was getting there. A Mojito was a small price to pay.

Alcohol and bribery worked and Zoë half-heartedly agreed to be my date for Glastonbury, so long as I agreed to make her my date for the Goddess Spa. She was clearly gambling on the chance that I might not get another ticket, and we arranged the spa trip.

Rawthwaite Hall was an imposing building, set into acres of countryside in Northamptonshire. There was nothing nearby apart from a few cows and sheep, and the hotel was drop dead gorgeous. The building was old but the interior was plush and modern, and when the concierge showed us to our suite, Zoë's eyes almost popped out of her head. It was amazing. Big comfy beds, a huge TV, a bathroom almost as big as my entire flat and a welcome bottle of champagne - with chocolates. So my Glammazon job had its perks after all.

I'd sneaked the camera in with me, although I hadn't asked

permission, and planned to do a bit of filming. I wasn't entirely sure about what I was going to film yet, but with a backdrop like this, I thought I'd be spoiled for choice.

I was booked in for the Aphrodite water ritual. This basically involved around two hours of being pampered beyond belief with some hydrotherapy treatments and bathing thrown in. Bliss! I changed into my robe ready to walk through the hotel to the spa – but the bloody thing hardly reached around my hips.

"Will you look at this?" I moaned at Zoë, as I tried to stretch the offending item of clothing a bit further around my hips, to no avail. I tugged it harder; trying to force both sides of the gown to meet in the middle I had to concede defeat with a heavy sigh. I flopped down on the bed.

"I know, pants, isn't it?" She sighed, "Here, wrap the towel round your waist and then tie the robe up as far as it'll go." She, of course, managed to look effortlessly glamorous even in a spa robe, with her curly hair piled up on top of her head and not a scrap of make up on.

Annoyed, I did as I was told. I felt a bit stupid, padding down through the posh corridors and reception, and into the dimly lit spa reception. I sat down, and grabbed an upmarket fashion magazine from the pile on the table, which I put on my lap to attempt to hide the strange towel formation going on under the robe. The self-consciousness of my robe/towel combo had put a dampener on my spirits, but my tantrum faded into nothing as I was called into the treatment room and melted into my spa ritual. I was bathed in the most amazing smelling warm water, anointed with aromatherapy oils, pounded with hydrotherapy jets and left to relax in a warm pool with a peppermint tea, slightly mesmerised by the multi-coloured twinkling lights on the ceiling. My feet were rubbed and massaged before I was asked to climb onto the couch and strip down to paper pants so that I could have my aromatic, relaxing body scrub. Much as I was looking forward to the scrub, I couldn't help but sigh as I tried to force the stupid little scraps of paper and elastic up to the top of my legs. They wouldn't go all the way up. I flushed as I wriggled around behind the towel that the therapist, a little scrap of a twenty-something blonde girl, was holding up to protect my modesty. The silly pants no more covered anything than being completely naked would have done, but what they did do was dig in to the flesh at the top of my thighs and leave me in mortal fear that the elastic wouldn't hold. I had visions of the flimsy elastic that held them together going 'ping' and the remains of the pants taking off at high speed towards the wall. It's not easy to relax with that image fixed in your mind, and while the treatment was gorgeous, I couldn't wait to get back to the safety of my swimming costume, damp as it was, and get out of the bathing ritual area.

Zoë, unlike me, had been having a whale of a time. She'd had a massage and was waxing lyrical about the hot male therapist who'd been working wonders on her knotted muscles. She was now off to yoga.

"I was thinking," She said as she sipped her green tea, "that more people would do yoga if they realised it's not just for skinny girls. I mean, I love yoga, and I'm not skinny. The thing is, you can get so into it that you actually forget you even have a body. You don't feel fat, thin, awkward or anything, you just feel free."

I nodded as she carried on. "It's amazing. I spoke to Leonie, the teacher, and she said she wanted to get bigger women into her classes, and was seriously thinking that she wanted to work with someone to set up a big girl's yoga class – how cool?"

"That's a fab idea." I said, "How would you do it though?"

"I don't know yet, let's add it to our list of things to do when fat girls rule the world."

I loved Zoe's lust for life. It was a good idea; I just wasn't sure how she was going to make it work. Having said that, if anyone could make an idea come together, it was Zoë. She had contacts everywhere and I had no doubt she'd be able to team up with someone if she really wanted to do it.

We went back to our suite, after a huge and very indulgent three-course dinner, and a couple of glasses of wine, to film a video about our spa experience. I was going to have to write it all up officially for *Glammazon*, but that could wait. I'd managed to liberate a pair of paper pants from the treatment room when the therapist's back was turned earlier, so it seemed like a good idea, after drinking expensive wine with dinner and starting on the bottle of bubbly we'd been left in the room, to demonstrate exactly why these items were such a rubbish idea.

I donned my swimming costume and put on an advertising-style voice as I held the offending items out in front of me.

"Paper pants. These glamorous items are the bane of any spa experience. Especially if the wearer of this functional under-garment is bigger than a size ten. Let me demonstrate!"

I was prancing around like a fool, and as I tried to get the pants up my leg, I wobbled and almost fell backwards onto the bed. I could hear Zoë sniggering and was trying desperately not to laugh myself. This was clearly serious business.

"You see? You see? Now…" I steadied myself. "I have the offending pants on, just about. If I move too quickly, they are going to either split, or spring off me and have someone's eye out. This could well be a health and safety issue, for myself, or for the therapist. Not just that, but if I were actually having a treatment, I'd now have to get up onto a treatment couch wearing these pants, clenching every muscle in my backside and trying not to breathe as I hoisted myself up there!"

Zoë was losing it and had to stop filming for a few minutes because her hands were shaking too much.

"Concentrate!" I said in my best haughty voice. In my head, this was Oscar-winning stuff. I should have gone to stage school. Zoe's laugh was infectious and soon I was laughing myself, and had to take several deep breaths and another gulp of champagne before I could carry on.

When we'd both stopped sniggering, I carried on. I demonstrated the utter impracticality of trying to sit down or move my leg upwards while wearing paper knickers, and as if on cue, the pants ripped noisily. The pair of us dissolved into fits of giggles, which Zoë mostly got on film, and we collapsed on the bed, laughing till our stomachs ached.

Chapter 9

Well, wouldn't you know it? I'd started to forget about rubbish men, whether they were crap ex-boyfriends or unsuitable toy boys, when I got a text from Jamie.

"Sorry Iv not bin in touch, work bin major busy. Wanna hook up sumtime?"

Resisting the urge to correct his atrocious spelling, I read the text back. Busy, you say? For over three weeks? Hmm. Well I can be busy too, sweetheart.

I wasn't going to give in to his undeniable charms on the strength of one text, and if he wanted to see me again, he was going to have to try a LOT harder than that. Still, I didn't delete it and it stayed there in my inbox, tempting me to reply.

I uploaded the video Zoë and I had made at the spa onto the blog, and Lauren loved it so much that she circulated it to almost everybody she knew, work wise, and Zoë did the same.

"Those pants are ludicrous" Lauren giggled, as she watched the footage of me falling over for the umpteenth time, "I'd never get them on either."

I had to agree, they were very ludicrous indeed, and my attempts at trying to get a pair on were even more hilarious.

"Saw your vid and wondered if you'd like to review our knicks?" said the tweet I'd been sent from a maker of 'bespoke spa underwear', and I was excitedly watching the number of views to my blog going up and up on a daily basis – being silly was definitely the way to go. The comments were mostly positive, with a majority of people agreeing that paper knickers were the work of the Devil.

I said yes to the spa pants although I wasn't going to inflict another 'Ell in her undies' video on the public just yet. They'd just have to take my word for it, I thought, as I replied, *"Yes please"*

I also wrote a blog post to go with the video.

KNICKERS
It's no laughing matter, despite the hilarity of the video, having to wear paper pants when you're having a spa treatment. The same goes for the robes. Some spas are brilliant and give you lovely big robes if you ask for them. This means you can actually wander around the spa without fear of flashing bits of your thigh to anyone who passes by. I love those spas.

We're thinking of compiling a list of good and bad spas for curvy women (and men, of course). Have you ever been to a spa that you've felt really catered for you as a bigger woman? Where was it? What did they do? We need to know!

Rawthwaite Hall is a wonderful place and the Goddess Ritual treatment I had there was blissful. It just would have been absolutely perfect if the lovely therapist hadn't insisted I change out of my costume at the end and put paper knickers on. I spent the rest of the treatment clenching my bum cheeks to try and keep the pants from pinging off, and lying very, very still.

If spas can't get suitable disposable underwear for larger women, why not just give us the option to roll our costumes down or even take them off and cover up with a towel? It would make the whole thing so much more comfortable, and surely that's what a spa experience is all about?"

The others agreed it was a good post and we started a 'Good Spa Guide' section on the *Viva Voluptuous* blog to try and get some interest in the campaign.

Zoë took the chance to post her own blog about her yoga epiphany, and put a shout out to people who might have a yoga qualification, to team up on a routine for women of all sizes which they could market to spas and gyms.

Lauren was preoccupied with whether or not to move out of her bedsit in London before she officially left her job, because she couldn't find anywhere she really liked and Colin was getting on her nerves pestering her to move in with him – not an idea she wanted to encourage.

"Why doesn't she just dump him?" Zoë asked while we sat around drinking tea and comparing blog views.

"She's too damn nice" I replied. "She makes out she's an Ice Queen but she'd rather boil her own head than deliberately hurt someone. I think she's waiting for him to dump her but he's not obliging."

"Seems a waste of time to me, extreme people pleasing like that," Zoë said, matter of factly. "If you're not happy, why pretend?"

"She just doesn't want to be the bad guy, I guess," was all I could really think of. I knew Zoë was talking sense but honestly, I was like Lauren, a wuss. It was probably why I'd stayed with Darren so long, and certainly why I put up with Mark blowing hot and cold for six months. Mostly cold, to be fair.

We'd booked a day in London to celebrate Lauren's birthday. She'd wanted to see *Mamma Mia* in the West End for ages, and Zoë and I had got her the tickets before she'd found out about the job. Luckily, she was in an exceptionally good mood despite Colin's sulk at her spending her birthday with us instead of him, and was up for a good time and some retail therapy before the matinee performance.

Zoë and I got the train to Kings Cross together. She was impeccably dressed in a waist-cinching fifties style retro halter dress, with a belted satin mac over the top and a parasol-style brolly. The shoes were something to behold, towering heels with big rosettes on the front. On anybody else they would have looked ridiculous, but as Zoë sashayed through the hordes at King's Cross and onto the underground, the crowds seemed to part like the Red Sea for her. I suspect they were all just admiring her style chutzpah. She didn't seem to notice, and was quite happily nattering away about yoga, *Viva Voluptuous* and how my plans for world domination were coming along.

"I'm not sure what to do next" I said, "It seems to have all been quite fast, the blogs are up, the video had a lot of people looking at it, but what now? I feel like I need to do a bit more, but where do I go from here?"

"So how many editors have you pitched feature ideas to this week?" Zoë asked, knowingly.

I looked down at my feet. "None." I admitted. "I've been too busy."

"Really?" Zoë raised her eyebrow quizzically. No way did she believe that, she knew me far too well.

"OK, you got me; I just haven't had any ideas. I don't know what to say!"

Zoë sighed. "How many times have we had this convo, darlin'? You're a kick-ass writer and you know it. Editors are only human, and they're always looking for that next great feature idea. Give it to 'em!"

If only it were that easy. "It's alright for you, you know them all! They all want to go out for cocktails with you and everything!"

"Sweetheart, I didn't always know them. How do you think I got them to meet me in the first place? I pitched the frickin' idea to them! They won't come to you. You have to get over your fear of editors."

I scowled, wanting this conversation to be over because it was too close to the truth, and that was annoying me. "I promise I'll send something out this week."

We found Lauren coveting a pair of shoes in an expensive boutique window. Covent Garden was one of our favourite places in London to hang out, as the shops were to die for. I could only really shop for clothes in Monsoon, as everywhere else was designer-type skinny.

"That's absolutely so you," Zoë trilled as I held up a gorgeous, bold print tea dress.

"You have to try it on." Lauren agreed. "It's got your name on it."

"What do you think?" I asked doing a little curtsey.

"Wow," they both cooed in unison, "buy it!"

I decided that the occasion also called for matching accessories and enlisted Zoë's help.

Lauren treated herself to a very classy skirt and jacket, making the excuse that she was going to need something for interviews.

"You don't have to make excuses for buying pretty things" I reminded her, "You're the birthday girl and anyway, you make more money than me and Zoë put together!"

"Not for much longer, unless I can find another job," she replied.

"You will. And you're not allowed to think negative things on your birthday." I reminded her, "That's the rules."

"Oh, OK then. I'd better buy something else then," she laughed. "Let's have a look in the market."

We wandered around the market and lusted over some absolutely beautiful, but way too expensive pieces of jewellery from various stalls.

"I love it here," sighed Lauren, "you can keep Oxford Street, or even Camden, this is my spiritual home."

"I know what you mean. It's so pretty. There's so much happening." I added.

The watery February sunshine peeped through the clouds, although the winter air was cold and crisp, and as I was absent-mindedly staring at a street entertainer miming while tourists took his picture, my phone pinged.

It was Jamie again. He couldn't be drunk; it wasn't even one in the afternoon!

"Hello sexy"

The boy was persistent if nothing else. I'd had a glass of wine with lunch and I was feeling relaxed, so I decided that maybe a bit of pre-show banter might be in order.

"Hi. How are you? Not drunk this time?" I sent back.

"Nope. R u busty later?"

I giggled out loud. I assumed that was a typo. The middle-aged woman standing next to me moved away from me slightly. Maybe she thought I was part of the act and was about to drag her into it?

"I'm always busty, darling. But I'm in London right now and won't be back till late, so you'll just have to manage without me tonight."

Zoë was staring at me. "What are you giggling about, missy?"

I told her I was winding Jamie up, and she rolled her eyes. She was just glad I wasn't moping over Mark anymore, so she let it go. Lauren was chatting to Colin on the phone, and he seemed to be putting even more pressure on her to move in with him. Her frown said it all.

"I've got to go Colin, we're just about to go into the theatre," she lied, and after a hasty goodbye, she sighed and cut him off.

"He's a pest." She declared, staring at her phone. "I know I have to dump him but I just don't know how to do it. He's so frigging clingy, I know he'll cause a scene, ask for another chance or even worse, try and buy me something. I don't need him right now, and his neat-freakery. I definitely don't want to move in with him. The man keeps all his shoes in labelled boxes according to their Pantone shade!"

Zoë and I laughed out loud; well aware that Lauren was exaggerating, but the thought of Colin arranging his many, many pairs of shoes just seemed so comical. They'd met on a dating site over a year ago. At first, Lauren had found the fact he had a lovely tidy house a blessing, after being married to someone who only hoovered if the landlord inspection was due. Now, however, it was more than irritating, but it did give her a lot of material on girls' nights out. She didn't love him, and found his devotion to her more irritating than endearing.

We made our way back onto the tube and over to the Prince of

Wales theatre. I was looking forward to a good sing-along, like most girls I had a real soft spot for ABBA and yes, I had seen the film many, many times. We settled in and I made sure my phone was turned off so that I didn't get any more Jamie-shaped distractions while I was enjoying the show.

Some people thought Lauren was a bit straight-laced, but the people who knew her well, like Zoë and I, knew that she was a pussycat. She was fiercely intelligent and very well-spoken, but could let rip with her potty-mouth if someone upset her. She was also unfailingly kind. The girl also knew how to let her hair down, and before long she was up with the rest of us, singing along to 'SOS' like her life depended on it. As usual, "The winner takes it all" made me cry and I forgot the words to "Does your mother know." Nobody noticed - the show was amazing, and it must have been a good crowd as by the end of the performance, pretty much everybody was up and dancing. I'd been singing along to cheesy ABBA songs for two hours and was left with a goofy smile that wouldn't go away and a bit of a croaky voice. It was a small price to pay for an afternoon of ABBA songs.

Lauren seemed to have left her cares at the door and Zoë had kicked her daft shoes off and was wiggling her backside like a pro to "Dancing Queen". I decided there and then that we didn't do this sort of thing enough. I knew Zoë was still praying to the God of Glastonbury tickets that I'd either not get a refund, or not be able to get her a ticket when the cancellations went on sale, but I totally believed that she'd enjoy the atmosphere of a festival. As long as it didn't rain – I knew she would never forgive me for a mud bath and quite possibly not come out of the camper van!

After a very expensive evening of dancing and drinking in *Tiger Tiger,* Zoë and I made our way back to King's Cross and home to Cambridge, leaving Lauren, who was planning to pack some more of her flat into boxes over the rest of the weekend, to get back on her own. We made her promise to text as soon as she got in safely. Zoë fell asleep on me on the train, and she'd kill me if I told anyone but she was dribbling on my shoulder. She was so cute I left her to it, and when we got back to Cambridge, I suggested that she stayed on my sofa rather than making her way across the city late at night in a taxi. She was quite happy to acquiesce and we stumbled in just after midnight.

Zoë went straight to sleep on the sofa, I made myself a quick late-night sandwich and checked my phone. I'd had more texts from Jamie during the evening, and now he'd most definitely been drinking as he was getting filthy again. As pleasant as his offers were, I was way too tired for a repeat performance of the last time we'd met, so I told him I was staying in London to put him off the scent and collapsed, exhausted into my bed.

Chapter 10

I was starting to feel just a little bit smug about *Viva Voluptuous*. Not only had the video had a huge numbers of views, we'd added a community area where people could join and chat about where to get good clothes, or vent their spleen about being discriminated against, and it was up to well over 1000 members now. I checked the comments on the blog. I'd been contacted by a *Daily News* journalist. Ooh!

Dear Ellie.

We've seen your video online and we wondered if you would like to be part of a feature in the women's section about obesity and health. Could you contact Helen Matthews on the Features Desk as soon as possible for more details, as we would really like to have your input?

Regards

Helen Matthews –Features Assistant, Daily News

I nearly fell off my chair when I read the message. I hated the *Daily News* with a passion of course but they wanted to interview me. This might be my chance to change that paper's attitude. I was straight on the phone to Zoë.

"Zo, what do I do? Is it worth a shot?"

"Oh God, no, they'll twist everything you say and make you out to be some militant fat and miserable skinny-basher. Don't do it!" Zoë ranted.

She was right - we both knew what would happen if I tried to speak to the misogynistic, image-obsessed hacks at the *News* about the being fat, fit, and the reasons behind *Viva Voluptuous*. I wasn't entirely convinced that I'd be able to cope with the hateful comments that I'd get either – especially if there was a picture of me with the article. I might have been Miss Curvy and Proud, but I was still smarting from the Mark debacle and I could do without being ripped to shreds by a pack of strangers over how I looked.

Ignoring the email from the *News* turned out to be a very big mistake.

Two days later, I was horrified to see my ex-husband Darren's face staring out at me from an online article about *'The worrying trend for fat acceptance.'*

It was bad enough that I was being slated for being irresponsible, encouraging obesity and ill health, along with a few other unfortunate people, but this was just mean. Where had they found my ex-husband? And what was he doing lying to the papers about me? It was bad enough that he'd gone snivelling to the papers, but he was telling outright lies. I hadn't seen him for over two years and now I remembered why.

"Ellie was obsessed with every mouthful of food she ate, and her eating disorder made our married life a living hell. I was never allowed to have crisps in the house because she'd eat a whole multipack and then go upstairs, and I wasn't supposed to mention the fact that I knew she was throwing them back up again."

The lying bastard, I'd never done that in my life. He knew that would get me where it hurt because of Jane. Talk about dragging your past up and slapping you round the face with it.

"When Ellie was being normal she could be quite fun, even though she was always trying to diet and had no self-confidence. But when she was on a binge it wouldn't have mattered what I did. She didn't notice me. She preferred food to me, and our sex life was non-existent after a while because she preferred eating whole packets of biscuits to having sex with me."

I would have to say that was the only vaguely truthful statement he'd made in the whole piece.

The News went on to slate the videos I'd made in the gym, and at the spa, and had managed to get a comment from Rawthwaite Hall, saying how disappointed they were that I hadn't seen fit to discuss my concerns about the treatment with them before posting the video. Now I'd be in trouble with *Glammazon*, too. I hadn't even mentioned Rawthwaite Hall directly in the video...but of course, I had done in the blog post and they'd put two and two together, hadn't they?

I read on, against my better judgement, with tears prickling my eyes. There was a picture of my ex and me taken years ago and one of him now, with his new wife, looking smug. I remembered that particular look of his very well. *The News* had really gone to town on me, and a few other bloggers they singled out as being responsible for encouraging obesity, and they'd even managed to get one of their favourite bitchy columnists to add her own take, picking our appearance apart (Darren had given them a picture of us where I looked incredibly miserable) and criticising me and the other bloggers for being a bad role model for young girls.

"I'm offering my support to Ellie and the other overweight bloggers, if she'd like me to help her beat her food demons. I know she claims to be happy, but let's be honest, we all know that most fat people are miserable deep down, and at an obese size 20, it's not good for her health either."

Apparently my fat behind guaranteed that I was at a high risk of early death.

Like Darren was if I ever saw him again.

It was all lies. I had never been bulimic in my life. Darren had never understood my problems with food and he couldn't understand why I stopped dieting either. He took it to mean I didn't care about looking nice for him, but in fact, it was driving me slowly mad. At one point, just before I gave up on diets for good, I was a member of three separate online weight loss websites, and I couldn't stick to any of them. I was frantic, thinking I'd never lose any weight but as soon as I started dieting, I seemed to become obsessed with food and I'd have to empty the cupboards of anything deemed 'naughty' by eating it before the diet officially started.

That never worked because by day two of the diet, I'd be back at the supermarket stocking up on TUC biscuits and pork pies. I don't even like pork pies. I'd hide them in my desk drawer, and then buy more on the way home. Darren would criticise me, asking me why I never managed to stick to a diet, or why I was eating a Hob Nob when I was supposed to be losing weight. I never lost anything, in fact I just seemed to gain weight with every diet I tried. Eventually I told him that I felt my eating was out of control and vowed to give up dieting.

He accused me of 'hiding' my eating disorder from him, and refused to accept that giving up diets was the answer. Eventually, he decided he couldn't be with a woman who defied the decree that we must all be skinny and left me for a woman at work who ate 800 calories a day. I had to laugh about that, talk about going from the frying pan to the fire. Now he had a *real* problem eater to deal with! Anyway, we'd been divorced for ages and I rarely thought about him, but the mercenary bastard had sold his story to the reporter who'd contacted me a couple of days earlier, and now I was plastered all over the news, looking fat and miserable, with a whole page of lies written about my eating habits!

There was nothing else for it. I sat at my desk, obsessively reading the comments on the article, with tears rolling down my face. I felt sicker and sicker as I read relentless unflattering comments about how I looked, and criticism of what I was trying to do. They ripped me to shreds, said I was a bad influence, was disgusting and vile, and that Darren was better off with his skinny wife than an *'ugly lard bucket who preferred chips to him'*.

At that comment, I put my head in my hands and I sobbed. I'd thought I was doing so well, I'd been feeling happier and more confident than I had done in ages since I'd started working on the VV campaign, boosting other women's confidence levels was having a massively positive impact on mine, too. I'd even been text flirting with Jamie again for the last few days. Today, I just felt like crap. That picture was terrible, but it was taken on our last ever holiday together and we'd been at each other's throats all week. Within a fortnight of that picture being taken we'd separated. The picture did tell a story, but not the one he'd painted.

Lauren took time out of her packing schedule, jumped on a train and came to see me as soon as she heard. Zoë came over too, with wine, Chinese food and tissues.

Zoë gave me a massive hug, and then I ranted, only stopping in-between foul-mouthed slurs on the *Daily News* and Darren to take another large gulp of wine or blow my nose.

"I should have given them a comment" I sniffled.

"No, because they would have just twisted it and made it look as if you'd said stupid things yourself. At least this way, people can make their own minds up, and they can brush it off as being a bitter ex-husband dishing a bit of dirt."

She was right of course. I hadn't thought of it like that.

"The people who read my blog are going to think I'm a fraud."

"That's what blog posts are for" Lauren interjected, while eating her Chow Mein. "So put the record straight. Rip him to shreds. It's not as if anyone you really care about is going to be reading that rag and believing it."

Lauren was also taking sense. She handed me a plate of Chinese food which looked suspiciously as if it was starting to congeal, and I took it anyway. Emotional crises always gave me an appetite. I thought about who would have seen the paper. Jamie, thankfully, never read the papers and Paul had already texted to tell me he'd always thought Darren was a 'wrong 'un'. Even my mum had phoned earlier to tell me not to worry, because I was better than him, and everybody knew that the *Daily News* was just a nasty gossip rag.

Even after the girls had gone, and they'd talked me back up, I was still smarting about the whole thing, and I shut myself away to lick my wounds. Of course, I didn't do any work, unless you count baking about three batches of cupcakes - the sweet scent of vanilla and butterscotch comforted me even if I didn't feel like eating any of them. I didn't dare look online. I didn't set foot outside the house for three days.

Chapter 11

"It goes without saying that although we value your input to our website, we do not approve of you using your connection to Glammazon to further your own agenda, and any spa visits or reviews in the future must be used only for Glammazon work, and not for your blog."

Oops. I'd had an almighty telling-off from the *Glammazon* bosses, who were spectacularly unimpressed at my spa name-dropping and had been forced to carry out some quite major damage limitation after my 'slating' of the Rawthwaite Hall spa in my video. I thought this was a bit mean, given that I'd been very nice about the spa, and it was only really the spa pants that had incurred my mirth and been plastered all over YouTube.

I sulked after I got a telephone dressing-down from the big boss and I knew it was serious when my favourite review editor stopped putting a kiss at the end of her emails. This was not a good sign. I needed the money so I was going to have to eat some humble pie and actually start meeting deadlines again.

The horrible article in the paper had made me feel a bit self-conscious, even though I'd had a huge amount of support from the blog.

"You look gorgeous girlfriend"

"Don't take any notice of the Daily News, they are bitter and twisted and don't like anyone who is brave enough to stand up against their body fascism." – I particularly liked that one.

"Your ex looks miserable with his new girlfriend; he's probably just trying to make you jealous."

Fat chance. She was welcome to him.

Even so, I'd still been to the gym nearly every day since reading all the mean comments about my size on the *Daily News* website. Every now and again, I checked back to see if anyone else had commented – it was like picking at an old scab, because every time I looked there was another one. I even logged on as myself and posted a few nice things, but the comments that got through the moderators had so many 'red arrows' I decided that this plan of action was likely to wind me up even more and I gave up.

Then I got an email from Mark.

Ell,

How are you? I hope you're OK. And that your paper pants aren't too tight ha ha! Wondering what you're up to as we haven't spoken in ages and I saw that thing in the paper and thought I would get in touch.

TC

Mark x

I knew my heart shouldn't have started to beat as fast as it did, and I knew I was an idiot but even so, I couldn't help it. know I should have left it at least three days before I replied, but I'm crap at game-playing and held out for about twenty minutes before replying.

"Hi,

Not wearing paper pants today, I couldn't stand the VPL. I'm good thanks despite the character assassination from my useless, lying toe-rag of an ex-husband. I'm just about getting brave enough to go out of my house now, the fear of being recognised or even kidnapped by a journo from the Daily News and shipped off to fat camp has subsided.

Hope you are OK too.

Hugs, Ell."

The old feelings started to flood back as we chatted over email. Mark had emailed me, out of the blue! What did this mean? He appeared not to have read any of the stroppy blog posts where I'd dissected our relationship, and I wasn't going to mention them just in case he went off and had a look. After we'd exchanged a few polite messages and in-jokes, he asked if he could meet up with me for a drink *'just as friends, of course'*.

My heart flipped and all thoughts of Jamie went out of my

head. I managed to leave it at least an hour before I replied to that one, and suggested we meet that evening. Well, there was no time like the present, was there? Within minutes of his reply suggesting the pub we used to spend hours in when we were going out, I was running a bath. I decided to keep it secret from the girls, because Zoë would have most definitely tried to talk me out of it, and Lauren would have disapproved. If this was going to be our big reconciliation, I wanted it to be perfect, and then I could make the big announcement when we'd sealed the deal. I knew it would only be a matter of time before he missed me.

The butterflies in my stomach had morphed into a giant Pterodactyl by the time Mark came to pick me up at 8. He looked lovely and seeing him in person just made me realise how much I'd missed him, even if I had been slating him to anyone who would listen for the past two months. He kissed me politely on the cheek and told me I was looking well. We drove in silence to the pub. It felt a bit odd, awkward even, but I'd clammed up and didn't know what to say to him. I needed a glass of wine. Right there and then.

"I expect you're wondering why I wanted to see you?" Mark said, breaking the silence.

"I thought you just wanted to catch up?" I replied, while a distinct sense of 'this isn't going quite how I wanted' creeping in.

"I did wonder whether maybe I'd get over my relationship aversion," he said, "but I really haven't. I want to be on my own for a bit, and I'm sorry if I let you down. The thing is, I still have the campervan permit for Glasto, and I realised that you'll need it to get a refund."

I could feel the lump in my throat rising to the place just behind my vocal chords where it was going to make the next thing I said sound all squeaky and pathetic.

"You, you really, um, don't want to come then?" I squeaked. So much for sophisticated. I told myself I wouldn't cry. Not in front of him, not again. I really, *really* wanted to cry.

"There's no point, is there?" Mark said gently. "I can tell you still like me, and being stuck in a campervan with me for three nights would drive you mad. Anyway, I fart in my sleep. And I snore like a wildebeest after a few beers."

I wanted to be super strong and tell him that he was being ridiculous, and of course I wasn't still into him, but he was right. I wanted to plead with him. I wanted to say *I don't care if you snore so loud the roof comes off, just being that close to you is all I need.* Instead, in a very controlled voice (because I was still trying very hard not to cry) I said, "It's fine. Just let me have the ticket and I'll sort it out."

I gulped back the rest of the glass of wine maybe a little bit too quickly. "D'you want another one?" I asked. I was going to, so it was only polite that I offered him one too. I couldn't believe I'd made such a fool of myself over this man again. The only cure for this was likely to end in a steaming hangover tomorrow morning, but sod the consequences. Mark drained his beer glass and asked for a Coke.

As if to rub the humiliation in even further, 'Love is a losing game' started to play as I waited to be served. Ain't that the truth…

"So, apart from cavorting about in paper pants, what have you been up to lately?" Mark asked as I put the drinks on the table. I told him all about *Viva Voluptuous,* Zoë and Lauren, and that I was hoping to get Zoë to come with me to Glastonbury as Lauren wouldn't even entertain the idea.

"I hope you enjoy it." He smiled.

"I hope you enjoy it?" I wanted to scream at him. Did he not know that I'd paid over £400 on those tickets? I'd spent hours trying to get them, swearing at my computer as the website crashed over and over again. I'd kind of expected a bit more gratitude, a bit more "I'm so sorry I've been a fuckwit and let you down," but nothing. In fact, I think I even caught him taking a look at his watch. "Sorry, am I keeping you?" I thought, miserably. I studied his mouth while he was talking and remembered kissing him. I wondered what would happen if I leaned over *right now* and grabbed his face in my hands, kissed him full on the lips and told him I loved him?

Banishing the idea before I did something stupid, and to make myself feel better, I told Mark that I was seeing Jamie. It might have been a little white lie but it was worth it for the flinch I saw when I mentioned his name.

"Really?" He asked, trying to sound interested.

"Yep, really." I said, and that seemed to be the end of that.

It wasn't long after my confession that Mark decided we should go home. I had a feeling it would be the last time I'd see him, and all my daft daydreams about our 'happy ever after' would have to be filed under 'not going to happen' for good. I sulked all the way home, not even trying to pretend that I was okay with this. I couldn't think of anything to say and just wanted the drive home to be over so that I could do what I'd wanted to do all night and dissolve into a sodden, tearful heap of pathetic, dumped ex-girlfriend.

He dropped me off at the flat and gave me a hug. "Good luck with the Voluptuous thing."

He couldn't even remember the name of the project that had so far, turned me into a national laughing stock.

I half-heartedly hugged him back, kissed him on the cheek, and went to flounce out of the car dramatically. My attempt at a dignified exit was thwarted by a loop of seatbelt, which caught around my heel and sent me stumbling towards the wall. Luckily, apart from grazed palms and a beetroot red face that Mark couldn't see, there was no harm done. He drove off, once he'd made sure I hadn't cracked my skull or anything, and I watched him disappear out of my road, and out of my life for good.

Once I was indoors, and feeling slightly dizzy, even though it was 11.30, in my drunken state, and with the tears starting to roll down my face, I decided to text Paul, Zoë and Lauren with *"I just met up with Mark. Why doesn't he love me? What's wrong with me?"*

One of them would bite, I was sure.

I texted Jamie, *"Get your cute ass over here, now!"*

I didn't mean it.

I texted Mark, *"I love you, you idiot man, even though you never loved me."*

The only person who replied was Paul. We had a very long text conversation which mainly consisted of me saying *"Why doesn't Mark want me? I'll never find a boyfriend"* and Paul replying, *"Of course you will darling, now go to bed and sleep it off."*

I fell asleep, fully clothed and with a heart that hurt.

Chapter 12

As predicted, I woke up with the most disgusting hangover ever.

It was one of those hangovers that's so bad you don't want to move your head, and when you take the inevitable painkillers, you sip the water really, really slowly because you know that if a whole glass of water hits your angry stomach in one go, it's going to bounce straight back up. This was not good. I stumbled into the bathroom, took one look at my face, covered in last night's streaky mascara, and winced at my reflection.

"Frigging men," I muttered, cleaning my teeth while trying not to gag. Oh boy, this was a bad one. What an idiot.

I had a Glammazon deadline to meet by the end of the day too. Drinking too much on a school night was a really bad idea. When I was younger, I used to be able to knock back drinks with very little regard to the morning after, staying out until 3am and getting up again at 7. Not now. A hangover took me all day to get rid of, necessitated several doses of fizzy painkillers, and the only thing that got me through the full horror of the morning after was usually Marmite on white toast and plenty of flat Coke.

I managed to drag myself into the shower, feeling like death on a moped, and wiped off the remains of the make-up that was smeared around my eyes. Dousing myself in hot water and washing away the last reminders of the night before woke me up a little, and I wandered back into my bedroom, and checked my phone. Oh God. Last night's text session. With a sense of 'what did you do last night, you piss-head?' I checked my messages.

It was bad enough getting a telling off from Zoë for meeting Mark in the first place, but even more humiliating was the reply from Mark.

"Ellie, I think it's probably for the best if you delete me from your phone" was his curt response to my heartfelt drunken declaration of love.

When I looked at my sent messages, I was even more embarrassed at my blatant booty call to Jamie. He hadn't bitten though - there was no reply. Thank God for that, I just knew I would have made a total arse of myself if he'd turned up all perky and expectant...and even worse I probably would have cried. Not sexy, Ellie. If he had made it over last night, it would have been the second time I'd slept with him just to silently get my own back on Mark. That was it. I decided I was definitely going to give all men a wide berth for a while and concentrate on me.

I was going to go all self-help princess and fall in love with me again. I was going to take myself out on dates, buy myself nice meals and flowers. I was going to watch all my naff 80s DVDs again, everything from *St Elmo's Fire* to *Footloose*, and go out with the girls for cocktails as often as possible. I was also going to do lots of baking. And learn Italian, so that when Zoë and I finally got back there I could at least ask for a Latte in the native language. I was SO going back to Italy.

Part one of my 'Super Ellie" plan involved getting my backside in gear and getting some copywriting done. I'd work really hard, earn lots of money and then I'd book that holiday. I could pay for both of us - it would be my thank you for her giving in and coming to Glastonbury with me. Oh, Glastonbury. I scrabbled in my overflowing 'to-do' tray for the cancellation number. I'd decided that I was still going to the festival; I could take the video camera, make some videos for the blog. Maybe scope out some hot men...

No, I chided myself, I was single, sassy and didn't need a man. I was going to go, with a reluctant Zoë, drink warm cider and shout along to any bands that took our fancy. Sod men.

After the whole *Daily News* debacle, I'd licked my blog-writing wounds and decided to come back stronger.

NEVER BELIEVE AN EX-HUSBAND

"I know that some of you have probably read the pile of pants about me

in the Daily News? Pah! It was a load of rubbish and I'm sure you're all intelligent enough to recognise the bitter rantings of a pathetic ex-husband when you read them?

In case you wondered, no, I definitely haven't ever been bulimic. I used to joke that I was part bulimic because I would eat and eat and eat but never managed to get as far as purging it, but in all honesty, I could never do that because one of my dearest friends suffered from bulimia and after I saw how it ruined her life, there was no way I was ever going to go down that route. Just so you know.

I'm a full fat, voluptuous girl with a mission, and I'm not going to be letting the twisted agenda of a Daily News hack with only a bundle of lies spouted by my ex-husband to go on ruin my fun. Viva Voluptuous is all about celebrating who you are, not what society thinks you should be, and proving you can have a great life without fitting into size ten jeans. Are you with me? Good!"

After I posted the blog, I spent ages on the phone and finally got through to the insurance company, managing to convince them that yes, being dumped by your boyfriend was in fact an extremely good reason for wanting to cancel his Glastonbury ticket, and yes, it had been an unforeseen circumstance thank you very much. I think the girl on the end of the phone took pity on me, as she didn't even put up too much of a fight. I checked the festival website to find out when the cancellations went on sale and it was in three weeks' time. Excellent!

Although I didn't really want to look at the laptop because even after a hefty dose of paracetomol and codeine my head was still hurty I clicked onto You Tube for the first time since before the *News* had published Darren's tawdry little exposé.

Oh. My. God.

My little video had been viewed 670,573 times! I had to refresh the page just to make sure I wasn't dreaming it. That was bloody fantastic! Perhaps the rubbish article had actually done us a favour?

I had a call from Zoë.

"Hey Beautiful, she chirped, a little too enthusiastically for my liking. "Are you feeling any better now?"

"My head hurts." I replied sheepishly, "sorry about last night."

"Ahhh forget it gorgeous. Listen, I have news...Great news that will make you forget Weasel ever existed. Darlin', we are getting the message to the masses. You know that article I pitched to *Candy*? They want it for May. It's a teen-girl thing; can I write something to go with it for your blog? Can you do coffee later and we'll sort out the deets?"

I told her I'd be there in an hour, hoping that the second dose of painkillers would work better than the first, and to look at You Tube on her way.

It was hard work getting into town with a hangover. I climbed gingerly onto the bus, and managed to find a seat near the back, but every cobble or bump in the road made my head pound, and I was starting to feel a bit sick, too. I concentrated very hard on a bit of unreadable graffiti on the back of the seat in front trying to avoid the urge to throw up. Eventually I got to Starbucks, which felt unbearably noisy. Why did coffee shops always seem to be full of yummy mummies and noisy toddlers? I found the quietest corner I could, because naturally Zoë was late, and sat nursing a chamomile tea and a bottle of water.

"Oh dear, gorgeous, you're not looking so good."

That's right, Zo, state the bleeding obvious.

She appeared ten minutes late, beaming from ear to ear, oblivious to my delicate state. She gave me a massive hug and sat down. "So...over 670,000 views? How freakin' fabulous is that?" she exclaimed. The thought gave me a little flutter of excitement, the first positive feeling my abused body had allowed me to feel all day.

"I know. I was thinking of packing it in after what Darren said, but I feel like we should really do this thing now."

Zoë wrinkled her nose at the mention of Darren's name. "And

what's this about you seeing Mark last night?"

I sighed and stirred my drink, which I wasn't really enjoying, waiting for the inevitable lecture. "I know. But I had to get the campervan ticket from him," I paused just to see a slight shiver of disgust cross Zoë's face, "and he really wanted to see me. I just got my hopes up."

I could tell Zoë wanted to divulge something; she looked as if she was thinking very hard about it. She didn't say anything when I finished speaking, which was most unlike her. "What's up?" I asked.

Zoë took a deep breath, paused and replied.

"Sorry, beautiful, but I've got to tell you. I didn't say anything 'cos you've been in such a bad place about him, and I didn't want to upset you even more. I saw Mark the other day with someone, and I'm sure it was his ex. They looked like they were together."

I scratched at the table with my thumbnail.

"Look, I didn't say anything because you hadn't mentioned him for ages and I didn't want to bring it up. So sorry darlin' but he really is a grade A shit-bag."

This wasn't making my hangover any better. I felt like a complete eejit. So all the 'I'm not ready for a relationship' stuff had been a big fat lie? He was back with Rachel. If only he'd had the guts to tell me, instead of making me feel like he dumped me because there was something wrong with me. I was angry with him. The stupid, stupid man didn't realise that it would have actually been better if he'd told the truth. It wasn't as if I didn't know he was still besotted with her anyway.

I let out an enormous sigh, gulped back the hurty feeling that was threatening to make me cry, and decided I was done thinking about him. Remember, you're falling in love with you, I reminded myself. No. More. Mark.

"OK, enough. So, *Candy*. What's the deal and what do you want me to do?" I said, as brightly as I could.

I think I surprised Zoë as she was expecting Mark-related

histrionics. When she'd got over her shock, she explained.

"Well, you know how it was when we were teens?"

Did I ever. Talk about never *quite* fitting in. I wasn't fat, in fact I'd been quite the opposite in my early teens, and the boys designated me the 'Ironing Board'. Later in my school life, I went from the source of their amusement and teasing to being their best mate, the one they wanted to talk to so they could find out if Jane was going out with anyone. The girls all looked so grown up and glamorous and I always felt like a swotty little girl trying to fit in. Being a teenage girl sucked.

"I sure do." I shuddered. "Horrible."

Zoe nodded, "Yeah, well it's such a major time for girls, and it's even harder now there's so much pressure on them to look perfect, be thin but with big boobs, and attract boys…all I want is a post on your blog about it, I'll write it."

I'd never written anything for that market myself but I loved the idea. If I could get Zoë on my blog to talk teenage girls out of dieting that would be amazing.

"Can you do a video to go with it?" I asked.

"Course I can, I'd love to." Zoë replied.

"Fab, in that case, you have a deal, honey." I smiled. I also told Zoë that I thought we should go back to Covent Garden and film something for the blog there, and that I was getting a refund on Mark's festival ticket. She was quite clearly more pleased about the first bit of news than the second.

"We totally should do something in Covent Garden", Zoë agreed, "but what do you want to do? Do we need permission?"

I shrugged and sipped at my fast-cooling Chamomile tea, wishing I'd got a Caramel Macchiato instead. "I think we need to get Lauren on the case. She's so bored at work at the moment, she's looking for something to do that doesn't involve closing off client accounts and sending invoices, so she'll jump at the chance of coming up with an angle for us."

"As for Glastonbury," Zoe shuddered. "If I come, and that's

still an if, I'm not going to be filmed. I can't bear the thought of appearing online covered in mud and dirt. It's bad enough not being able to shower properly for three days."

"We could just do 'Fat Girls at a festival' or something." I suggested helpfully. "Festival fashion for the well-rounded. Tips and tricks on dealing with the Portaloos. Even a bit about how being bigger means we can fight our way to the front, but makes sitting on festival boys' shoulders to watch Kings of Leon impractical?"

I could tell that the idea of barging her way through a sweaty mass of festival-goers was making her feel a bit queasy.

"Still an *if*" she said, as she finished her drink. "But I'll think about it. Your chances of getting a yes are totally multiplied by the number of cakes you buy or bake me between now and the time I have to make my mind up."

I took that as a cue to buy her a cherry bakewell muffin. I knew Zoë would give in; she was far too soft-hearted and sweet to lead anyone on and drop them. I was all fired up about rediscovering myself, getting back to the Viva Voluptuous plan and changing the world...

Chapter 13

Getting the final brush off from Mark, the lying cheating swine, had actually made me feel better about myself, although uncharitably, I hoped Rachel was still sleeping with his brother.

I threw myself into blogging for *Viva Voluptuous*.

HEALTH AT EVERY SIZE

"I just read 'Health at Every Size' and it made me angry, happy, determined and a whole mixture of other emotions. This is the science they don't tell you when you're being lectured about your weight at the doctors for the umpteenth time (and we all know you only went in for antibiotics for a throat infection). It's liberating and it's eye-opening.

There are so many ways your body tries to resist weight loss and at the same time we're misled by big business into eating foods that keep us fat, dieting, feeling shitty about ourselves and more. HAES also gives you a whole heap of figures contradicting the idea we're all going to die young because we are a size 16 or more.

You'll just have to read it for yourself if you want to get the full benefits. Women who followed the HAES advice were happier, no longer struggled with food issues (Amen to that) and improved their self esteem. But what about their health? Well there were no massive weight losses. The author says she lost a couple of stone but nothing major. But before you decide it's not worth doing and search Amazon for 2013's next diet bestseller, read on. The women who followed the HAES programme had lower cholesterol and blood pressure and were more active than before they started the plan.

The control group of dieters lost a bit of weight – but gained it back. Their activity levels, cholesterol and blood pressure all stayed the same or got worse, as did their depression levels. Half the dieters dropped out before the end of the study while only 8% of the women following the HAES plan gave up.

The dieters' self-esteem dropped. The HAES volunteers' soared.

So no, they weren't skinnier, but they were healthier and happier. And the dieters were neither skinnier, healthier OR happier. So it's a no-brainer really.

Diets. Don't. Work."

There'd been a bit more flirting with Jamie, too, I'd sworn off men, but what the hell, I was having fun with him. It seemed my drunken booty call had awoken his interest again, and he was angling for another date. When I say date, I mean 'opportunity to get me naked'.

"U R so hot babe" was about the tamest thing he managed, and for someone who usually communicated in text-speak, when he was being disgustingly rude, he used all the right words AND spelled them properly.

Against my better judgement, I agreed to a date with him. Zoë was exasperated. "What happened to 'falling in love with yourself'?" she glowered at me from the other side of the kitchen.

She'd come over to tell me that Lauren was seriously considering taking gardening leave from her job and moving back home in the next week or two, as she had sod all to do at the moment and needed somewhere less extortionate to spend her redundancy money.

I gave Zoë my best 'please don't be angry with me look' and said, "I know. But he's so damn cute. And I'm going to make him treat me like a lady. It's nothing serious, honest. I want him to date me, you know, properly."

Zoë almost choked on her coffee (decaf). "Date you properly? Listen sweetheart, he might be a cutey-pie but he's not a dating kind of guy, he only wants sex."

I was about to interrupt with "And the problem with that is?" when she said, "...and although I'd say Yay to that, and jump right in if it made you happy, you and I both know that you want a relationship with all the trimmings, not just sex."

Dammit, the woman knew me far too well.

"Actually, I don't want a relationship at all. But I'm not going to turn down a date." I retorted.

I swear, sometimes I had the mind and hormones of a 15-year-old girl and the body of a 36-year-old woman.

My sex ban met with inevitable resistance from Jamie. We'd been to the cinema and he'd even bought me popcorn. I'd mistakenly thought that as we weren't 15, this was a pretty good bet for a relatively innocent date, and I made a point of holding his hand so that I could stop it going elsewhere. "Put me down," I giggled as he spent most of the trailers trying to get his tongue down my throat and his free hand up my skirt. I think I actually heard someone behind us tutting. Well it wasn't my fault; I was *trying* to fend him off.

"Are you going all virginal on me?" Jamie pouted. I'd just told him that I was having an early night so he couldn't come back to the flat, and we were walking back to his car in the dark, hand in hand. The film had been absolutely rubbish, although it had cars and guns in it, so I think he would beg to differ.

"I'm just feeling not up for it at the moment," I said, clumsily, picking at a bit of fluff that was hanging off of my coat. "The other day was great but honestly I have so much work to do tomorrow." We got to his car and I half hesitated getting in. Why couldn't I just tell him I didn't want to sleep with him? I could feel my people pleasing gene kicking in as I tried to think up an excuse.

Poor Jamie looked a bit confused. Sometimes the age difference between us seemed like it didn't matter at all but other times, I felt like his mother telling him to tidy his room.

"Are you on your period?" he asked inquisitively.

"Yes." I lied. I know. Bad Ellie. But I was tired, and I really, really couldn't be bothered to get into a big discussion right now. The period excuse would buy me time.

I didn't hear from him for another week. It was hardly a Shakespeare sonnet when I did. *"So U want romance? I can do romance"* he texted. When I didn't reply for a few hours, he upped the ante with, *"I'll take you out to dinner tomorrow. My treat."*

Aww, cute. Yep, I could definitely do dinner.

"You'll never stick to it." Lauren said when I told her. "I give it until 8.30 and you'll have caved."

Determined to prove her and Zoë wrong, Jamie was denied. He'd booked us in for a curry at his favourite curry house and unwittingly made it even easier for me to opt for a night alone. Just the thought of his onion breath and potentially repulsive vindaloo farts was enough for me to say 'thanks for the lift, I'll see you soon' at the end of the night.

He was starting to get the idea. He'd been the perfect gentleman all night, let me choose the wine, and didn't even laugh at me when I tried to pick all the bits of onion out of the vegetable pilau.

"Am I still banned from your bedroom?" he asked as we were chomping through our curries. He looked a bit crestfallen when I said, "For now, yep. Sorry honey."

"Don't you fancy me?" He sulked.

"Yes, I really do, but…you know, it's really hard to explain. I was feeling a bit confused when you came over last time, I'd only been dumped a couple of days before, and I'm not sure I want a full on relationship at the moment. I just want to slow things down a bit, that's all."

Surely that would be enough? He was quiet for a few minutes and I thought he understood. I tore off a piece of naan and shoved it in my mouth, just as he started talking again. The waiter was eavesdropping on our conversation and I'm sure I saw him smirking. He could sing for his tip, nosey bugger.

"I'm not looking for anything serious," he said, clearly trying to gauge my mood, "It doesn't matter if you're not that into me, we're good together and we can have fun, can't we? You're so sexy, and so clever, and you always know what you want. I like that." Oh God. That look. Lauren would laugh so much if I caved in now. Stay strong, Ellie, I told myself.

I sighed and rubbed his arm affectionately. "Thanks sweetie. You're not so bad yourself. Just give me a bit of time, yeah?"

I could sense his frustration as he stabbed at his dinner. "OK, he said, clearly a bit confused as to why his compliments hadn't earned him an automatic access all areas pass into my knickers.

He didn't try anything when he dropped me home. He didn't seem to be sulking that much, and after a very nice lingering kiss, he asked me if I wanted to go for a drink with him at the weekend.. He was out with his mates on Saturday night, but he really wanted to see me again soon.

Maybe there was something in the 'treat 'em mean, keep 'em keen' malarkey I remembered reading about in *Jackie* Magazine after all?

He picked me up for lunch that Saturday and took me to a pub by the river.

"I thought this would be romantic," he said enthusiastically.

He was right – he led me to a secluded table in a corner of the pub and we sat down. There were a few other people in the bar – a smartly-dressed middle aged man reading a newspaper and drinking a coffee, a few couples, a woman absorbed with whatever was on her ipad and us. It was warm, cosy and the place smelled of log fires and pine cones. I had to give him high marks out of ten, it was a stereotype romantic pub date – well, if you've ever been on a dating site and read about people's ideal dates, you'll know what I mean.

"Pick anything you like on the menu, I'll get lunch," he offered.

"You don't have to, honey," I countered, "I can cover this if you like?"

He made a big show of getting his wallet out and putting it on the table, stared me right in the eyes and grinned. "You're worth it. I'm going to spoil you." I tried not to laugh. He was blatantly trying to impress me into bed with a pub lunch. He was so cute, and my resolve was starting to weaken, I had to admit. I was staring at that mussed up looking hair, and those sweet, sexy freckles, and thinking distinctly un-chaste thoughts when he came back from the bar with a very large glass of wine. Nice try, Mister. It'd take more than one glass though…

"Thanks sweetie, that's lovely. Lunch is my treat though." I said.

We didn't really talk much over lunch. Jamie seemed a bit distracted, and kept looking at his phone, which was buzzing incessantly.

"Anyone interesting?" I asked, after about the tenth text.

He blushed a little bit and said a little too quickly, "No, just my mate about tonight, that's all." Hmm. I didn't believe that for a minute. But hey, I'd told him that I didn't want a full on relationship, I couldn't go getting all possessive, could I?

"Fancy walking down the river later?" I suggested.

"It's bloody cold out there!" he exclaimed, looking at me as if I was completely nuts.

"It's not that cold. Anyway, I'm a bit stuffed, I could do with working some of that food off." I was lying – I'd only had a tuna baguette and a few chips, and I couldn't even finish that because it wasn't very nice. But I needed to get out of the pub, as Jamie was looking bored and whoever he was texting was clearly far more interesting than me.

"Oh, okay then." Jamie said getting to his feet, I paid up and we walked towards the river. He was right, it was actually freezing. I grabbed his hand and he looked at me slightly surprised. We walked along, mostly in silence. He really was gorgeous, and the daylight just illuminated his sexy eyes. He caught me staring at him as we came up to a bridge, and grinned disarmingly. Without any warning, he pulled me under the bridge, pushed me up against the wall and kissed me. Damn it!

My knees went wobbly. He was such a good kisser, he was making my insides do things they had no business doing at this time on a Saturday afternoon, and when he grabbed my arse and pulled me closer I was practically breathless with lust. He knew what he was doing.

'What the hell is wrong with you, woman!?' I muttered to myself as I unlocked the door to the flat later, watching him drive off. Still feeling a bit flustered, I went into the lounge. My pulse was racing, and I had to make myself a coffee and put some really dull telly on to take my mind off all the thoughts I was having. I fancied him a lot and I wasn't sure if I liked it or not.The idea for the next blog came to me while I was out on date four with Jamie. We'd been for a drink, in fact we'd had a few too many and there was no way he was going to be able to drive home, the crafty sod. I was already on the verge of caving in, even before he plied me with Strawberry Dacquiris, and he'd been very complimentary all evening. Despite suspecting an ulterior motive, I suspected that hearing, "You have the most amazing boobs" and "You're one seriously sexy lady" would never get boring.

I decided that if it made me feel good to have a man saying I was sexy, other women needed to know that not all men were obsessed with having skinny trophy girlfriends. And I was starting to believe all the things I'd read in the past about inner confidence and feeling sexy making me appear sexier than any amount of dieting or plastic surgery.

"Tell me what it is you like about me," I asked Jamie, after I'd enticed him, with very little resistance, into my bedroom. I had my arms around his neck and my head on his shoulder, while he was pressing me up against the bedroom wall. I looked up at him; he had a very naughty look in his eyes and we were both a little bit drunk. "Actually, hang on a minute, wait there," I said, bossily, before he could answer. I pushed him away gently and walked over to a chest of drawers where I rummaged, located a red Basque that I hadn't worn since I'd bought it, over a year ago, and scurried into the bathroom past a bemused Jamie.

"Where ya going?" Jamie called, confused. "I was going to tell you how hot you are!"

"I'll be right back," I teased.

Basques are never the easiest thing to get into in a hurry but I made the best of a bad job and drunk, cack-handed fingers and then appeared at the door brandishing a video camera. OK, so that wasn't the best idea, as I then had to spend the next 20 minutes explaining to Jamie that no, I was not suggesting that we video ourselves having sex, and tell him that I actually wanted to interview him for my blog. I could understand his confusion though. Oops.

So, once we'd cleared up that little misunderstanding, I sat him down on my bed, and asked him again, "What do you like about me?"

"You're sexy," he said, looking slightly shy and playing with the corner of the duvet cover as I filmed him. Oh but that was so cute. I forgot he wasn't that great with words. This was going to be a short clip. I wondered whether I should zoom in on his legs, as he'd taken his jeans off while I was in the bathroom getting into my lingerie and I thought perhaps the world needed to see just how gorgeous this man actually was. I gave in and zoomed the camera in a bit, stared at his thighs lecherously through the viewfinder, then zoomed it back out, and pointed back at his confused looking face.

"What do you mean? What's sexy?" I asked, trying to get him to spill a bit more detail. The point was that I was trying to show women that men fancied them whatever their size, and in fact some men positively adored curvy, even fat women.

"You, everything about you," he replied a bit more enthusiastically. "You're confident and you're not afraid to get naked like some girls are."

"Do you think it's a bit weird fancying a fat girl?" I asked. "Don't your mates disapprove?"

"You're not fat. You're sexy and curvy and a real woman. And my mates just think it's cool I'm seeing an older woman!"

He'd told his mates? For some reason, I was really chuffed about that. I wasn't his guilty secret, after all. "So, what would you say to anyone who told you that men shouldn't fancy big women?" I cajoled.

"I'd say that was bullshit. I've been with big girls and thin girls and I fancy them all."

"You're not fussy, then?" I teased.

He looked affronted. "Yes, I'm fussy. But I fancy girls for different reasons. I fancy you because you're soft and womanly, and you're so sexy with it. You know how to move, you know what turns a man on, and your boobs are amazing!"

Just as I was about to stop the camera, Jamie started speaking again, this time addressing the camera directly instead of talking to me. Oh, he was getting into it now!

"So, yeah, there's a lot of Ellie to grab hold of. But she has a proper woman's shape. I love the curve of her belly, the softness of her skin and her sexy blue eyes." He looked across at me for approval and I smiled, teasing him by pulling at the ribbons on my basque, which for some reason inspired him to carry on saying nice things about me.

"Ell isn't a neurotic woman who worries about the size of her bum when you get her naked. That's another thing I really fancy about her. She's got confidence and she knows what she wants. I can't stand women who get all obsessive about food and their weight.

"When you're with a big girl, it's different to when you're with a thin girl. It's all warm, soft and comfortable. I love big girls as well as small girls, and Ellie is one hot, sexy woman. She's standing here right now, giving me those sexy blue eyes, and she looks so hot I'm gonna have to stop telling you about how much I fancy her and damn well prove it..."

I was blushing and grinning like a loon. I decided he'd been a very good boy, put the camera down and rewarded him handsomely for his efforts.

I'd forgotten how much stamina a twenty-something had. Jamie stayed over that night and I didn't get much sleep. I'd promised myself that I was going to be up at six, go to the gym and then back by eight writing *Glammazon* copy (after uploading Jamie's cute little video) but at eight I was still in bed with Jamie, while he reminded me yet again how much he fancied big girls. I did the proper girlfriend thing and cooked him a bacon sarnie, sent him on his way with a kiss and skipped across the living room feeling knackered and happy.

I wanted to get back on the blog and tell everyone, but thought better of broadcasting my sex life to the hundreds of new followers I'd picked up recently. I uploaded the video clip, short as it was, and changed my Facebook status to 'in a relationship'. Jamie wasn't even on Facebook so I wasn't too worried about him freaking out. Then I changed it back, just in case.

All that sex had got my creative juices flowing, so I tapped out my next post to go with Zoë's teen self-esteem post on the blog:

STEP AWAY FROM THE DIET

"I'm fat. Not a few pounds overweight, or a bit bloated after a big dinner, I'm properly fat. When I was in my teens I wasn't fat, but everywhere around me I saw adverts for diets and pictures of skinny celebrities, and so I thought I was fat.

I went on a diet, after all, that's what you have to do when you're fat, isn't it? It was a very silly idea indeed. I couldn't stick to it, gave it up and forgot about it. Until I decided I was a bit fat again. And then went on another diet. But this time I was a little bit bigger than I had been before the first time, and I gave that one up as well. You guessed it, I stopped dieting and ate all the things I hadn't let myself eat when I was dieting. So I got a bit fatter.

This went on all through my twenties and now I'm in my thirties. And I really am fat now. But you know what – it doesn't matter. I gave up diets for good a few years ago and I haven't got any bigger! I've been married – you don't need to be thin to find someone to love you. I've had a few jobs – you don't have to be thin to get a job. I've been on holiday, been to see bands, got lots of friends and had a great time. You don't have to be thin to have a fantastic life.

The secret is to love your life, and love yourself. Love your body. Treat it well. Keep it active and feed it well. Buy pretty clothes and shoes that you love. Experiment with your make-up and hair, but don't take it all too seriously. Be the best you that you possibly can. There's only one you, and you're only here once, so put on your biggest smile, forget the people trying to make money out of you by making you feel ugly or fat, and go for it, sweethearts!"

I was starting to dream big, fired up with my new urge to make big girls feel good about their curves, and in turn, make myself feel good too. If I could pull Project Covent Garden off, it would raise the profile of the Viva Voluptuous campaign, it would also get Zoë and Lauren involved, as well as encouraging some of the lovely tribe of women I'd met through Viva Voluptuous to participate too. This called for another girl's night, some serious event planning and wine.

Chapter 14

"You're completely bonkers!"

OK, so convincing the other two that Project Covent Garden was a fantastic, inspired piece of media-savvy genius was going to take more work than I'd anticipated.

Lauren was looking at me as if I'd suggested she run naked across Midsummer Common and I could see that Zoë was considering a suitably diplomatic response. We all gathered on my sofa again, after I'd summoned them all over and promised them cake.

"I don't see what's so daft about it." I pouted. "Flash mobs are cool, and they get loads of coverage. It could be massive, and more importantly, it'll be fun!"

"You'll never get people to do it," Lauren said. "And how would you organise something like that anyway? To organise a flash mob you need to co-ordinate a huge number of people, and the logistics are just...well, they're impossible. You need numbers, you need a way of getting everyone else in on it. I just don't see how we can do it."

I didn't have the heart to tell her that I was thinking of being even more ambitious and doing the same thing, at the same time, at Westfield Stratford City and the Trafford Centre in Manchester too.

I'd had a fantastic idea. My idea was to co-ordinate three flash mobs in three separate locations, all at once. The plan was simple – everyone would turn up looking foxy, dressed in their favourite ensembles. We'd meet at an assigned place, hit the 'on' switch, sing and dance to "I am what I am," then leave. Genius idea.

It was all about confidence, feeling and looking good. There would be no point in everyone turning up in leggings or hoodies; it would have to be glam. I wanted heels, pretty dresses, sexy skirts, full on glamorama. As far as I could see, it had the potential to get us really noticed, raise the profile of Viva Voluptuous get some positive media coverage and have a whole lot of fun at the same time.

"So, will you help me do this, then, or am I on my own?"

Zoë, who'd been uncharacteristically quiet until now, contemplated the question and replied, "OK. I reckon we might be able to make it work, but I want to put it on record right here and now that sweetheart, you are officially nuts."

"What?" Lauren looked shocked, "are you serious?"

"Why not?" Zoe said. "Us girls need some fun and adventure in our lives, this might very well be it!"

Lauren shook her head, "what am I letting myself in for? Okay, I'll do it." She still didn't sound entirely convinced.

"It's going to be great. In fact it's going to be amazing. You know my friend Colette, the one who makes the corsets?"

The girls nodded.

"Well, she's trying to put together a line for curvy girls, a burlesque-style range. She'd be ecstatic if we wore her stuff to do the flash mobs. She wants to expand her clientele outside Cambridge and the free publicity would really help. She's amazing, I can give her a call, what do you think?"

Lauren loved corsets and Zoë was a big fan of Dita Von Teese. God, I'm good, I thought.

"Do you think she'll let us keep the corsets?" Lauren asked.

"I should think so." I said, hopefully, crossing my fingers that I could persuade Colette.

The idea of dressing up in the full Burlesque regalia made me feel a little bit nervous, but it was going to be for a great cause, I'd take Covent Garden, Lauren would head up to the Trafford Centre and Zoë would be in charge of Westfield City. We opened our diaries, picked a date in June, and hoped for good weather.

I had Zoë giggling as I described my vision; "I want at least fifty fat girls, and I want us all to appear at once out of Covent Garden tube station."

"But Covent Garden tube station is tiny!" Lauren exclaimed, "You wouldn't even get fifty people in there. How are you going to manage not to be noticed?"

I'd forgotten about that, but it was just a tiny detail. I'd get round it.

"I want everyone dolled up in their best party dresses and heels, fully made up, all smiling and giggling. I can see it now - we'll walk out of the station, people staring at us and wondering what's going on. I'll find us a space somewhere, press play, and..."

I cleared my throat dramatically, and began to sing, "...I am what I am...I am my own special creation..."

Zoe was transfixed as I sang the rest of the song; Lauren looked ever so slightly embarrassed. I don't think they really believed I was serious until then. Plus my singing was terrible. Lauren butted in before I could murder the entire song, with, "So what are you going to do for an encore?"

"Well, I reckon that if we manage to get away with it without being moved on I'll pick up the music, and we'll all wiggle our behinds as we walk back to the tube station, waving and blowing kisses as we go."

Zoë looked bemused, but I could tell she liked the idea, however implausible she might have thought it was. I'd have to work on them, but I thought I could probably hook them in one way or another.

"When I've finished, nobody will ever use 'fat' as an insult again!" I exclaimed with excitement.

"You're officially nuts. But we love you," sighed Lauren.

Chapter 15

The blog post I'd put up including Jamie's video had been looked at by almost 1500 people in a few days and I couldn't deny I was feeling a little bit proud of my handiwork. So was Jamie, who texted me *"Iv sent the vid to all my mates and they think ur hot too."* I blushed at that one. Twenty-something men thought I was hot. I found my lost Mojo, it had returned full force. And although I'd been making every effort to forget he'd even existed recently, a small part of me really hoped that Mark had seen the video too.

On the down side, I was sure that some miserable, bitchy people just looked out for new video uploads from me and pounced as soon as they saw one, salivating over their keyboards as they ripped my appearance to shreds and told me how fat and unhealthy I was. I quite liked the idea of making them shove their vitriol right down their throats, but I just about managed to stop myself from being just as bitchy back, taking the higher ground and placating my inner sarcastic bitch with the thought of getting the last laugh eventually when I took over Covent Garden and proved to everyone just how awesome fat women could be. If only they realised just how much a nasty comment could hurt, though.

Everyone thought I was mad. Even Colette, who I was counting on to come up with the most amazing, show-stopping outfits for Lauren, Zoë and I. She was pinning up a prom dress in her showroom when I decided to arrive unannounced and tell her all about my idea…and where she fitted in.

"I don't get it" Colette confessed, taking a pin out of the corner of her mouth and tucking it into the hem of the dress, a peacock blue ruffled effort that was going to look stunning on a 16 year old prom queen. "So, you're trying to prove that fat girls are sexy?"

"No. I mean yes, but that's not all of it. Have you seen the videos online?"

Colette said no, she hadn't had time, but after I'd explained, she seemed to get it. After making a couple more adjustments to the dress on the mannequin, she stood back, appraised her work and pulled out a stool for me to sit on.

"Sit down, and tell me what you actually want me to do for you. And while you're at it, what's all this about a younger man?"

I forgot I hadn't seen Colette since before Mark had dumped me. I got her up to speed on the Jamie situation, and then started talking dress designs. I'd never known anyone as creative as Colette. She got her sketch book out as we were talking and came up with a few ideas as I explained my vision.

"It's got to be purple." I demanded. "And I want a proper corset, with feathers, or bows, or both. And straps, or else I'll be paranoid that my boobs are going to pop out while I'm dancing."

Colette nodded and carried on sketching. "But I don't know if the world is ready for my backside hanging out, so I think I want a longer skirt. Definitely a bit 'burlesquey'. You know what I mean?"

I couldn't believe that she'd managed it so quickly, but by the time we'd finished talking, Colette had sketched out a basic drawing of an outfit, based on what I'd been telling her and a few ideas of her own.

She'd come up with a design incorporating a purple steel-boned corset with black lace detailing down the front and wide straps. It was sexy without being tarty, as the proper, boned and fitted corset was designed to hold everything in and up.

"Then, if we attach a black satin skirt to the corset, and then have soft drapes at the back that look a bit like a bustle..." Colette explained, pointing out where it would be nipped and tucked, and where all the frilly bits would go.

"You're a genius, Colette" I gushed. "I love how flattering this is, yet at the front it's all – well – out there!"

"If you've got it, flaunt it, baby!" Colette grinned.

She suggested that I accessorised the outfit with a specially made mini-top hat, purple gloves with a lace trim and of course fishnets and heels. Colette had all these bits and pieces in her studio, and I could imagine them all put together as an outfit. I'd never worn anything like it in my life. It was a bit scary, but I was up for it.

"Can I get Lauren and Zoë to come in and see you?" I asked, fired up with the excitement of seeing my idea coming to life.

"Yeah, that would be lovely, I haven't seen Zoë for ages" Colette agreed. "I know the cow is going to look stunning in whatever she wears though!"

I slapped her, playfully. "Because you're such a monster." I teased. She laughed. Colette was petite, dark-haired and slim, with an uncanny ability to customise any item of clothing and make it look like it came from a top designer. I knew she wasn't all that confident in herself though, after her husband had walked out on her three years earlier, leaving her with a seven-year old daughter and all his gambling debts to pay off.

After I'd been to see Colette, I met up with Zoe to tell her all about Colette and the fabulous costume she was designing for me - sugaring the pill because I also had to tell her the news she'd been dreading for weeks.

"Hey, gorgeous, I've got a present for you."

"Oooh! What? What?" She sounded so excited that I felt a bit cruel bursting her bubble.

"I've managed to get another ticket for Glasto, they went back on sale this morning. You're coming with me, Missy!"

"Oh…Oh! Great!" Zoë said, completely unconvincingly. I had to stifle a giggle.

"It's OK, you don't have to pretend, I know you're trying to think of a reason for not coming *right* now. But once you're there, you'll love it, I promise."

"How would you know? You've never been either," Zoë

reminded me. She had a point. Well, it might turn out to be a big mud bath, or we might just hate it, but I was going to take a chance.

"We'll be fine," I told her.

"If it rains, I'm not coming out of the camper van," Zoë moaned.

"Don't be such a pussy," I admonished. "Just get yourself some spotty wellies, and a matching brolly. You'll be perfectly co-ordinated, and dry at the same time."

Zoë sighed and pretended to be annoyed. "I won't be able to wear heels, will I? That makes me sad. Flats are not my friend."

"You'll look silly in heels, sweetie. And the stages are miles apart. And there's hills. You wouldn't want to be tottering about like a princess in killer heels while you're standing up and watching whoever on the Pyramid stage."

"You mean there are no seats?"

I think she was joking.

"So, how's the boy wonder?" Zoë asked, having got over her 'I don't want to go to Glastonbury' strop.

Jamie had texted me a couple of times and we were going out that night just for a drink, but I had a niggling feeling about it. It was the same niggling feeling I'd had about him since we first slept together, to be fair, and I was ignoring it because I fancied him so much.

"It's all good" I lied. "I'm seeing him later."

"You don't look as if you mean that. What's up?"

I made a fresh cup of coffee for myself, and some herbal concoction for Zoë, sat down at the kitchen table and rested my chin on my hands. "Zo, am I just kidding myself? He's barely 27, I'm almost ten years older than him. I didn't want a relationship, but I think I'm falling for him. Am I just being daft?"

Zoë looked concerned. We'd had this conversation before.

"You're not an idiot, sweet cheeks. But I don't think he's right for you. You needed a bit of perking up after the Weasel, and that's fine, but you need to just enjoy Jamie for what it is…a bit of fun. Don't go making the boy wonder into a full-blown relationship…"

It was with Zoë's words in mind that I met Jamie that night. I met him in the local pub, and when he arrived, ten minutes late, he bowled me over with that boyish grin and I forgot everything Zoë had said earlier.

He bought me a large glass of wine and started telling me all about his day. I wasn't really paying attention, to be honest, as I was distracted by the way his t-shirt was clinging ever-so slightly to his muscular chest, and the way his thick hair was getting a bit too long and curling at the nape of his neck…making me want to reach out and…

"Ellie! Do you fancy it or not?"

"Wha?"

Oops. Caught out there.

"I don't know – run it by me again."

He looked at me, slightly confused, and started again. "I've booked the day off on Friday, and I thought it would be cool to go shopping. I need some new jeans - we could do lunch and see what else we fancy doing while we're down there. Maybe we could even stay down that way, get a B&B, make a weekend of it? What do you think? If you can tear yourself away from the computer, that is."

He almost sounded jealous. I knew he was only joking though. Typical, he was suggesting a day out and weekend away and I'd been too busy day dreaming about his general hotness that I'd missed it.

"Yes, I'd love that. I could look for some new undies while we're there" I giggled. "How come you've decided to spoil me and take me away?"

He gulped from his bottle of beer and wiped his mouth…

"I've got to use up my holiday by the end of the month!"

Oh. Not so romantic after all, then.

"And you deserve a treat. You work too hard. I just thought it would be nice to go somewhere. Away from here."

I could have kissed him right there and then. When he went up to the bar, I surreptitiously texted Zoë, Lauren and Paul telling them I was going away for the weekend with Jamie, and within minutes, I had a hat trick of congratulations from everyone. Anyone would have thought I'd announced an engagement and a wedding in St Lucia.

Friday morning, I was up early, perfecting my hair and makeup and packing for my first weekend away with Jamie. I had no idea what to take with me because he hadn't booked anywhere. I panicked – what if we couldn't find anywhere? We'd have to sleep in the car! Resisting the urge to get on the phone and book a B&B myself and muttering "You're not his mother" as a reminder, I threw various bits of lingerie on the floor and searched for something a little bit sexy to wear. Ah, there it was, I managed to find a favourite set that I'd christened my 'lucky' underwear. In the bag it went.

I was feeling ever-so-slightly naughty as I got myself ready. There was something about the promise of a weekend away that made me tingle all over, but I knew I was starting to get a bit too attached to Jamie for this just to be the bit of harmless fun I'd envisaged. "Just go with it" I told myself. Could I do this? I was the stereotypical good girl, not usually one for flings, and I really, really liked Jamie. After Mark had left my self confidence in tatters, it was so nice to feel wanted again. Maybe it could work, even with the age gap…

"Stop it!" I said to myself as I found myself getting carried away with my daydreaming.

Jamie actually managed to turn up on time. He greeted me with a kiss and I got straight into the car, eager for our road trip to get under way. We drove to Bluewater with a really cheesy 90s indie collection playlist to accompany us. I was playing both air drums and air guitar and Jamie did his best really bad Tim Burgess/Ian Brown impression singing at the top of his lungs and shaking one fist with an imaginary maraca, while his other was on the steering wheel . After a succession of vintage Stone Roses, Blur and Suede, I realised why this wasn't something he did very often. All my thoughts from earlier came back. It felt so good, we were enjoying ourselves and we definitely felt like a couple. I looked at him as he drove, and thought to myself that we definitely looked good together. I was in a really good mood when we got to the shopping mall, and I'd even managed to juggle some money in my bank accounts and freed up £100, for shopping related activities.

Shopping with Jamie was nothing like as much fun as shopping with the girls. For a start, I wasn't allowed in the men's changing rooms with Jamie, which I thought was a little bit mean. We went in and out of every shop that looked as if it might sell some jeans that Jamie would like, for what seemed like approximately 125 hours, and I spent an inordinate amount of my precious time sitting outside the changing rooms while he tried pairs of jeans on. Then, he would either emerge in said jeans, asking me for my opinion, which was always "Very sexy", or if they didn't fit, he'd come out with a pout on his face and moan about the sizing in whatever shop he'd been denied in. I can't pretend I wasn't getting a teensy bit bored. At least you get to gossip when you go shopping with the girls, but Jamie was so focussed on getting the perfect jeans to show off his backside that there was no being distracted by shiny pretty things or expensive perfumes like there would have been with Zoë or Lauren. I could have cheered or done a little dance when he finally bought some jeans, and I got to have a look around myself.

I found a shoe shop with a sale on, and much to Jamie's surprise and relief I found some stunning heels straightaway that were the a perfect match for the purple burlesque-style corset that Colette was making me. They were practically jumping off the shelf shouting, "Buy me! Buy me!"

So I did.

Armed with my purchases, fuelled with coffee and doughnuts from Krispy Kreme, and buoyed up by my very good mood, I'd forgiven Jamie for dragging me around every single man's clothes shop in Bluewater. We giggled at the sex toys in Anne Summers – I dragged him in there trying to embarrass him but it *so* didn't work. He turned the tables on me by deliberately heading for the largest and most brightly coloured dildo in the shop and exclaiming in a very loud voice what he might do with it. I blushed furiously and snatched the offending article from him, swatting his backside with it. I could see the young shop assistant trying not to giggle.

He wasn't really interested in shopping once he'd got his purchases sorted, and I could tell he was itching to get away. "Shall we go somewhere else?" he suggested.

"Where?" I asked, hoping he'd surprise me by announcing that he'd booked us into a swanky hotel and was going to suggest a lusty afternoon of wanton pleasure.

"Have you ever been to Canterbury?" He asked. I had never been, but I knew it was not the epicentre of wanton pleasure.

"According to my iPhone it's the nearest town. Fancy it? I reckon we could find somewhere to grab a bite to eat, and then I'm going to find us a sleazy B&B and shag you senseless in it. Wearing those sexy shoes you just bought."

It wasn't quite what I'd had in mind, but hell, I did not need asking twice.

"Oh go on then."

Wandering through the city in the sunshine, I felt totally relaxed and happy. Jamie and I chatted about nonsense, growing up, first crushes and childhood memories.

"I made a mix CD for a girl I was in love with at junior school, and the teachers found it and played it to the whole class." He confessed.

"What was on it?" I asked.

"Spacemaaaaan" he sang at me, pulling a face as he imitated the Babylon Zoo song.

"That's not very romantic" I laughed. "But did she like it?"

"No, she was really embarrassed. And everyone laughed. I can't remember what else was on there. I think there might have been Wonderwall, and oh God, I'm sure there was that awful Robson and Jerome song too." Jamie looked mortified.

"I take it you never got to go out with her, then?" I asked.

"Nope. She ended up going out with my best mate, then moved to Scotland the next year," he laughed. "So, what's your most embarrassing childhood crush memory?"

"Oh God, I have too many to choose just one. I was always having crushes on boys at school, from junior school to when I left school at 16. I was so uncool."

I racked my brains for an example that didn't make me look like a complete saddo.

"I had a best mate who was in fact a complete cow bag. We used to pass notes to each other in French lessons and she asked me who I fancied. I told her I had a crush on one of the boys in her form, and she got me to write down exactly what I wanted to do to him."

I cringed at the memory, and continued, "so, being about 14, I didn't know very much. I wrote a flowery romantic daydream about a picnic and a stolen kiss in the sunshine. She kept the note. You can guess the rest..."

Jamie was grinning, "So she showed him? The cow!"

I laughed, "Yep. Not just that, she gave it to his best mate, who I couldn't stand. Who passed it to everyone he knew. By first break, everyone in the third year was asking me if I'd been on any good picnics and the boy in question had told me he never wanted to speak to me ever again."

I looked up at Jamie who clearly thought my little story was hilarious. "Oh, bless you. That's so funny. You're so sweet!"

"I was 14!!" I exclaimed, indignantly. "Anyway, he did speak to me again eventually. It probably took about twenty years though. He's even on my Facebook now."

"You'll have to point him out." Jamie smiled.

Apart from the fact that his childhood was a lot more recent than mine, we seemed to have loads in common. When Jamie found out I was going to Glastonbury he was clearly jealous. He'd been to V in Chelmsford and like everyone in Cambridge, had cut his festival teeth on the Folk Festival, but he really wanted to get to Glastonbury, it was the Big One.

"Can't you just take me instead of your mate?" he asked. As much as Zoe would probably hand him her ticket gladly, Glasto was for the girls. I liked that he was thinking ahead though. I wondered what it would be like, doing the festival with Jamie.

Maybe next year, said the soppy cow voice in my head.

"I might get tickets for next year" he said, as if he was reading my mind. I was waiting for him to ask 'do you want to come with me?', but no, he didn't mention it. It did not stop me imagining us both cosied in a tent for two together.

Despite his inability to text properly, Jamie was actually intelligent, and very ambitious. He worked for one of the tech companies in Cambridge, although he was doing an admin job at the moment, and was hoping to use his degree to actually get on in the company once they started recruiting people again. At one point, he grabbed my hand as we crossed the road, and his display of un-sex-related affection made me feel all soppy and glowy.

"They sell 200 different flavours of milkshake in here," he said, as excited as a pre-pubescent teenager, "and I really want one." I'd attempted to walk past the full to bursting candy coloured milkshake shop. I wasn't really in the mood, but he practically rugby tackled me through the shop doorway. "I'll buy you one, any flavour you like, but you HAVE to try one." I begrudgingly chose a Malteser shake, waited what seemed like forever for him to decide on the flavour he wanted, queued up for another million years to place our order and eventually wandered down the road, hand in hand, milkshake in the other, both slurping noisily.

"Let's go to the cathedral," I said, between slurps. "It's the most famous thing about Canterbury, apart from Chaucer."

"Who?" Jamie asked, studying the contents of his shake, not wanting to miss a drop.

"He was a writer and poet from the Middle Ages," I explained. Now I felt like his Mummy again. "I had to study 'A Knight's Tale' when I did my English A level, which is part of 'The Canterbury Tales'. I hated Chaucer."

"Oh, right." He said, looking confused. I couldn't be bothered to go into any more detail and decided to overlook his ignorance as he did that really hot thing when he combed his hair back off his face with his fingers.

I pointed to the 'no food and drink allowed' sign at the entrance to the cathedral, as Jamie tried to pull me through the door of the building. I signalled to my half-finished milkshake.

"You can't throw that away, I've just bought it for you," he said, pulling a serious face.

I sucked extra hard on the thick gooey substance at the bottom of my cup and the disgusting slurp noises I was making made Jamie snort with laughter, which I tried to ignore but couldn't and I laughed so hard I sprayed thick milk shake with Malteser bits over the entrance to the nave.

Oh crap. I had to go back outside. Jamie had tears running down his face and was doubled up with laughter at the sight of my hideously embarrassed face.

"I just desecrated a holy building!" I spluttered. "I think the woman selling entrance tickets was on the verge of excommunicating me!"

Jamie could hardly speak for laughing.

"Your...face" he gasped, holding onto his stomach.
"I hate you." I lied.

Chapter 16

Finding a B&B in Canterbury was not as easy as we'd anticipated.

Of course, Jamie hadn't organised anything in advance, and the frustrating task of finding somewhere to stay was largely left to me and my Blackberry 'find a hotel' app.

"Do you have any spare double rooms for tonight?" I asked, over and over again, feeling like the Virgin Mary on Christmas Eve.

"Tonight, dear? No, sorry, we're fully booked." Ah, you would be, wouldn't you?

Jamie had professed a love of tacky B&Bs so we made it our mission to find the tackiest.

"If there's a spring poking out of the mattress you can sleep on it," I whispered as we waited in a particularly dingy reception to be assisted. "I've watched nearly every episode of 'Four in a Bed' and I know what goes on in these places!"

Jamie nudged me in the ribs as a grumpy looking old woman appeared from a back room and strode towards us. "Have you seen my pussy?" I giggled.

Jamie looked at me in horror.

"Mrs Slocome?" I whispered.

"Who?" He said, wrinkling his eyebrow. "What are you talking about?"

"Are you being served?" I explained.

"Of course not I'm not," he said shaking his head at me, "she's not got to the reception desk yet."

Oh God. My old school media references were lost on him and now I sounded like a crazy cat-lover. Luckily Mrs Slocome and her pussy had no rooms for us, which was good, because it smelt like an old people's home, all stale wee and lavender, and I really didn't want to have to go over the whole 'pussy' thing with Jamie again. Seriously, what was it we actually had in common again?

We walked in to a run-down looking building with a flickering neon 'welcome' sign, except the 'o' didn't work. There was a pretty eastern European sounding girl waiting at reception.

"Can I help you?" She asked, very politely.

"I don't suppose you've got any rooms for tonight have you?" Jamie asked, almost expecting the obligatory 'no room at the inn' response we'd had for the past 3 hours and 16 minutes.

"Double or twin?" She asked, looking at her computer screen. There was a picture of Marilyn Monroe in the reception, which I was staring at absent-mindedly. Ironic, really, I thought, as this was quite possibly the least glamorous place in the world. Or at least Canterbury. Marilyn Monroe wouldn't have been seen dead in this place – even if she was being treated to a night of passion with a man as sexy as Jamie. The carpet had seen better days and an old tatty sign on the wall specified that breakfast was between 7.30 and 9.30 but the number 7 had been crossed through and it now said 8. At least I thought it did.

I hoped there weren't bed bugs.

"Double, please."

"Yes, yes, we do have a double room but only for one night, is that OK?" the polite girl said brightly, reaching for a pen. I was snapped out of my Marilyn daydream and came back to the room. We had somewhere to sleep, or more importantly not sleep, tonight.

It was very dated – the floorboards were creaky and it could have done with a bit of a re-paint but after I'd got over my snobbish thoughts and convinced myself that no, there were no bed bugs, it seemed clean enough and the bed looked very appealing. More because of the man I was going to be sharing it with than the garish orange-patterned duvet cover. Jamie had said he was taking me to a sleaze-pit so I reckoned this was a step up.

I surveyed the small, slightly shabby room and closed the door behind us.

"It'll do," I smiled.

Jamie threw his rucksack on the bedroom floor and grabbed my hand.

"Come here, sexy."

I giggled coquettishly and let him pull me towards him. I'd been entertaining ideas of playing hard to get but they'd all gone out of the shabbily painted window as soon as we'd shut the bedroom door behind us. He had that look in his eye and despite the whole spitting milkshake episode and hours of shopping, I was feeling particularly sexy. It took minutes for him to get me naked and on the bed, with his hands all over me and his kisses being rather seductively placed on my neck.

"Put the shoes on," he ordered. Ooh, kinky. I wrestled myself out from underneath him and reached for the bag with the stilettoes in. I'd always wished I was one of those women who could dress, undress and put shoes on in a sexy way, but unfortunately I made a terrible stripper. I pulled the beautiful purple heels out of their tissue paper, and in an attempt to slip them on seductively, I held onto the doorframe, wobbled a bit and hopped on one foot, while I tried, not very well, to place my foot in the other shoe.

Despite my lame attempts at seduction, Jamie was still staring at me in appreciation, so I wiggled towards him butt naked except for the shoes.

"Oh. My. Fucking. God" he exclaimed.

So eloquent. The shoes had brought out my inner dominatrix and I decided it was time that Ellie the whip cracking minx took control.

"Stand up!" I said, bossily. Jamie looked me in the eyes, I thought he might laugh, but he did as he was told. I think he might have been struck dumb.

"Get those clothes off, now!"

He was trying to stifle a giggle, and well, it was quite funny. A chubby naked girl in heels, shouting at her boyfriend - was he my boyfriend? Who knows? - to get his kit off.

"What are you laughing at? Hurry up, get your clothes off." I demanded.

He hurried. The t-shirt and jeans joined my clothes on the floor to reveal a ripped torso and a sure-fire sign of his arousal. I'd never done the bossy thing before, and now he was naked and ready for action, I was a bit stuck as to what to do next.

"Turn around." I demanded.

He complied.

"Jamie Robertson, you are a very, very bad man. I will have to punish you."

This was so cheesy. Even I was trying not to laugh now. I picked up the nearest thing I could find on the bedside table, a copy of a 'Welcome to Canterbury' magazine, and I rolled it up and thwacked Jamie's pert bottom with it.

"Ow!" Jamie yelped.

"Stop whining," I said as I thwacked him again. Clearly being bossed around turned him on, but being spanked with a rolled-up magazine didn't quite do it for him, I decided to make a note.

He turned round, pushed me on to the bed, pinned me down and started kissing me again.

"Uh oh, no you don't." I wriggled out from his clutches, pushed him onto his back and straddled him. I was trying not to put all my weight on the poor lad at once, I wanted to turn him on, not suffocate him. I worked my way down his torso with kisses. "Oh God," he moaned as I went lower and lower, teasing him and nibbling his thighs. Oh, this was fun. Those thighs...

He was wriggling and squirming around, moaning and groaning, and I'm sure I heard the words, "Oh please," at one point. I couldn't tease him anymore, he was about to explode. I took him in my mouth and sucked. Very, very slowly. Teasing him a little more, I stopped and started, bringing him to the point of no return.

Then I let go and sat up.

"What are you gonna do?" I giggled.

He soon showed me.

Afterwards, he kissed me deeply, cuddled up to me and said quietly, "You're amazing. I've never met a woman like you before."

I was totally blissed out. Oh my God. I was still tingling all over – and now he was being all cute and making my insides go as tingly as the rest of me. I shivered deliciously. It wasn't just the hormones or the fact he was ten years younger than me and gorgeous that made the time I spent in bed with Jamie so awesome. Mind you, he was certainly energetic. It wasn't even as if I was doing anything with him I'd never done before, unless you count using a magazine as a prop! It was the intense way he looked at me, the way he punctuated each of our sex sessions with exclamations about how hot, amazing and sexy I was, and how he touched me just like I was something precious. In reality, I was Ellie Johnstone, 36, and a bit on the chubby side. When I was with Jamie, I was a Goddess. I felt like the only girl in the world, and right then, I knew I was dangerously close to getting used to it.

I sighed as I thought about the cheesy self-help articles I'd read saying that confidence was what made you sexy. Until then, I hadn't believed it, but now I reckoned that a shot of super-confidence could possibly make me even sexier than perky boobs. Believing I was a super-hot sex kitten was clearly what had given me the confidence to act like a total minx with Jamie.

I nestled in and closed my eyes, breathing in his slightly sweaty smell. He smelled delicious. Against my better judgement, I was becoming ever-so-slightly smitten, and even scarier, I thought I was quite possibly falling in love.

"So, do you want to go out for dinner?" Jamie asked after we woke up from our post-coital doze.

"Mmm" I mumbled sleepily. Actually, food was the last thing on my mind but come to think of it, I had noticed a grumbling in my stomach and I supposed I had better do something about it.

"What do you fancy?" was the next question. I really didn't mind. "Anywhere" I replied.

"Italian? Chinese? Pub grub?" He pushed me for a decision.

Clearly he wasn't going to make any kind of decision himself. I was feeling a bit irritated at having to be Mummy again but chose to overlook my annoyance and just pick somewhere. It was getting on for 8pm, so it was going to have to be something quick and easy. "How about we find a pub that does food?" I suggested. "I'm not that hungry really."

He looked pleased. I didn't think he had a lot of cash left after paying for the B&B and his chivalrous nature was clearly telling him that he'd have to pay for dinner too. "It's OK, sweetie, it's on me." I reassured him.

"Oh, cool" he replied. "Thanks, sexy."

After a quick chat to the polite lady on reception about the nearest eatery, we were pleased to discover that there was a pub that did food 15 minutes' walk away from the B&B. We wandered off, hand in hand, along the main road. If this was what being in a relationship again was going to be like, I thought I could probably live with it…

Most of our time from Friday night into Saturday morning was spent making the most of the very reasonable £85 per night 'Chaucer's Retreat' B&B bedroom facilities. We bought a cheap bottle of wine on our way back from the pub and drank it out of chipped mugs while we sat in bed chatting and watching rubbish on the small and slightly out of tune TV. It wasn't glamorous, but it was pretty near perfect.

I think I must have fallen asleep before him, because I woke up in the small hours to find him sprawled across the bed, completely naked, with barely any covers covering his modesty. I couldn't stop looking at him and smiling to myself. Only a few months ago I was pining over Mark, feeling unsexy, unloved and unwanted. Now, I was here in a hotel room with one of the sexiest men I'd ever met, and he thought I was amazing. I felt amazing. I knew the girls thought I was just having a fling, and yeah, that had been the plan, but a girl can change her mind, right?

It must have been the three o' clock effect, as my mind started wandering from replaying the previous evening to pondering the age gap. I even started to wonder if Jamie wanted kids. Being in my late thirties, I was starting to panic a bit, I really wanted to be a mum one day, but couldn't quite decide whether I was panicking because I actually wanted babies or panicking because I knew that in a few years, the choice would be taken away from me. I did love kids, especially when they were at that super-cute age when they got all inquisitive and pulled silly faces. I could see myself with a gorgeous little baby girl. Or a boy – but I always imagined I'd have a girl. I imagined Jamie's delighted face when I told him I was pregnant, how he'd spoil me all the way through, be there at the birth and be a doting daddy. Agh! What was I doing!? Mentally I slapped myself, hard.

Kids were definitely not up for discussion right now as I was still being very strict about condom usage. And even though I'd known Jamie for a long time, we'd only been seeing each other properly for a little while. No, I had to put thoughts of long-term future out of my head. So much for my sassy singledom, trust me to fall for the first bloke I fancied! Once again, I thought myself round in circles until I wore myself out with all my pontificating and dozed off…

Chapter 17

I fell back asleep, but awoke to the sounds of some very vocal birds outside the window, Jamie didn't stir, after his performance the night before I thought that might be asking a bit much of even the most sex-charged, twenty-something. When he finally woke up, it was already too late for breakfast. I considered this a bit of a bonus as the greasy smells emanating from downstairs weren't exactly tempting me to sample the food on offer.

"What time have we got to check out?" he asked, sleepily. I was busy texting Lauren to tell her we'd somehow ended up in Kent - and he'd made me jump.

"Ten, I think" I replied, pressing send and leaning over to give him a kiss. "Want a coffee?"

"If that's what you can call that powdered stuff" he winced, "I prefer the coffee from your machine."

I grinned. "Ask me nicely and I might make you another one sometime." I slid out of bed and wandered across the room to make a coffee, suddenly feeling a bit vulnerable as I wasn't wearing anything. I could feel him staring at me and for some reason I grabbed the top I'd discarded on the bedroom floor and pulled it on quickly to cover my modesty.

I couldn't think of anything to say as I poured the boiling water into the mugs and stirred. I heard my Blackberry beep, and noticed Jamie had stopped watching me and was flicking through the TV channels instead. "So what do you want to do today?" I asked, a little too breezily. "Fancy exploring Canterbury a bit more, now we're here?"

"I've got to get back to my place" he replied lazily, mid-stretch, "got some stuff to sort out."

He didn't elaborate. "Oh, OK sweetie," I responded. I handed him a disgusting-looking coffee with an apologetic laugh. "Looks like puddle water – good luck with that!"

I thought I'd probably just head back and do my laundry; maybe write a blog post...or something. I didn't really know. I expected the girls would be around later and if I was honest I couldn't wait to give them a warts and all debrief of the previous day and night's events, but I had still been hoping we could spend the day together. I seemed to remember Jamie saying he had a football do that night so any more couple time that weekend was pretty much out of the question. I chided myself for feeling a bit put out that he didn't want to spend time with me instead.

We drove back once he'd dragged himself out of bed, and although he seemed in a good mood, he was a bit quieter than he had been the day before, and there was no singing this time. I was feeling a bit delicate from all the cheap wine we'd ingested the night before and I guessed he was probably the same.

"Do you want to come over sometime?" I asked, hopefully, as he dropped me off.

"Yeah, that would be great. I'll text you in the week." He grinned at me and leaned in for a kiss. I don't know what it was about that boy, I could have quite happily dragged him into my flat by the scruff of the neck, but not being the kidnapping type, I just kissed him back, and gave him what I hoped was a sultry look as I grabbed my bags from the back seat. We left it that we'd meet up at some point to be decided during the week and I watched him drive away - then bounced into my flat with all the joie de vivre of a woman on the verge of falling hopelessly in love. Even if it was against her will.

Within minutes I had a text.

"Coming out tonight, lady?" it was Lauren. I called her straight back.

"So, how the feck did you end up in Kent?" she asked.

I explained it had been something of an impulse decision, Canterbury being the nearest city to Bluewater that we'd both heard of, and that Jamie had expressed a desire to get me naked that I'd found hard to resist.

"Was it good?" She pressed. Clearly she wasn't getting much attention from Colin and was trying to recall her sex life vicariously through me.

"Hell yeah. The boy has some energy; I'll give him that. He also snores like a pig when he's drunk."

Lauren spluttered. "TMI darling. Listen, I want to hear all about it but I think this is a conversation best carried out over a few glasses of cold wine. How about Violet's, 8pm? Bring Miss Sunshine too."

"Deal. Get me drunk and I might spill the beans. I'll see if Colette wants to come too, we need to talk costumes for Covent Garden."

"We're still doing that, are we?" Lauren asked, blatantly hoping I was going to say she was excused.

"Yes" I laughed. "And you're coming."

"Bugger. OK, well I'll see you later, Miss Loved Up!"

"I am NOT in love!" I exclaimed.

"Whatever!" Lauren retorted. Was I though? God, I hoped not. I wasn't finished falling in love with ME yet.

Violet's was a new, quiet-ish bar hidden down one of the smaller streets in Cambridge. Not everyone knew about it yet, which meant that we could get reasonably cheap drinks during their three hour-long happy hour. I called Zoë and had a very similar conversation with her but promised that there would be way more goss if she dragged herself away from whatever she'd planned to watch and got herself into the city for 8. She agreed, unable to resist the lure of salacious gossip.

"Colette's coming too, you say?" Zoë asked.

"Yep. She wants to sort the deets out for your outfits," I replied, hoping I wasn't going to get another talking-to about Covent Garden being a daft idea.

"I must love you" she moaned, " you've got me dressing up

and parading myself around a shopping centre and you're making me go to a muddy, disgusting festival full of smelly people."

"Who else do you know that bakes you butterscotch cupcakes though?" I teased.

"Yeah, that is definitely a bonus" Zoë agreed. "Well honey, see you later, and mine's a vodka, lime and soda."

I thought it was a small price to pay for an opportunity to get my girls together and bore them rigid talking about Jamie.

I caught up with some of the work I had been supposed to do for Glammazon before Jamie and I went away. OK, so it was going to be a little bit late, but it wasn't *that* late. I was slightly annoyed that there was a stroppy email in my inbox from Adrian the web manager, who was questioning me over my lack of commitment and asking whether I was still *'on board with Glammazon's continuous efforts to provide excellence in beauty and spa information'* – I wasn't even sure if that was a sentence, and if it was, what it even meant. I was also a bit annoyed, to be honest, although possibly because I felt as if I'd been caught out. I hadn't been paying much attention to *Glammazon* lately, and I thought I'd been able to get away with it so far. Clearly I wasn't as good at hiding my lack of commitment as I'd thought?

I sent him an ever-so slightly grovelling email back making up a completely fabricated story about having been Broadband-less all day and promised to have it with him by Monday morning.

The email from Adrian had put a bit of a dampener on my otherwise good mood, as did the fact that instead of doing more plotting, scheming and blogging for Viva Voluptuous, I'd now have to spend all Saturday writing boring website copy. The only way I was going to get through this was with cheesy music to lift my spirits and a constant supply of coffee. I put on some ABBA, hummed along and prepared to not look up from the laptop until the work was finished.

I was feeling mighty pleased with myself by around 6pm as I

worked all day, stopping only for the occasional loo break, cup of coffee or kitchen forage. I didn't have much left to write so that left me a couple of hours to relax and get ready. Listening to ABBA had got me in the mood for some nostalgia, and with my spare two hours I thought I might as well do something useful, so to make up for missing the gym on Friday I decided to dig out my ABBA dance game for the Wii. My Wii Fit was one of those 'it will save me so much money in gym fees' purchases I'd made when I was skint, and although it definitely served a purpose, I have to confess that I didn't get quite the same buzz from stepping up and down on a Wii Fit board as I did getting a sweat on at the gym - its only redeeming feature was the ABBA game. I'd played it at Paul's house over Christmas, and while all his adult family members had joined in with great enthusiasm, flinging themselves around to 'Mamma Mia', the kids refused to take part, and had all just sat watching us with expressions that ranged from bemused to excruciatingly embarrassed.

I changed into my leggings and T-shirt, shut the curtains just in case anyone could see in, and hit the on switch. I threw myself into a gutsy rendition of Waterloo, whooping it up, clapping and wiggling, then saw off 'Fernando', 'Dancing Queen' and 'SOS' before running out of energy somewhere in the middle of 'When I kissed the teacher'. Red faced and slightly out of breath, I decided that enough was enough, and as I walked backwards to pick up the other controller, I tripped on the corner of the rug, took a tumble and landed rather unflatteringly on my bum, catching my back on the corner of the coffee table

Bugger, that hurt.

I got up awkwardly and as I twisted, there was a ping in my back. Tears sprang to my eyes as I hobbled like an old lady across the room and sat down awkwardly on the sofa. This was going to need a lot of Nurofen Plus. I couldn't believe it, the girls were going to wind me up about this, that's if they believed me, seeing as they all knew I'd been with Jamie this weekend, so any protestations about being unable to walk would probably be met with a knowing wink. I wished that HAD been how I'd injured myself; it would have made for a much better story than packing away the Wii after an ABBA session.

I gave Zoë a call, I didn't have any drugs and I needed them. Urgently.

"I cannot believe I've just knackered my back dancing to ABBA!" I moaned. "In fact it wasn't even the dancing that did it; it was the putting stuff away afterwards that did the damage. I feel like a complete arse."

"Oh gorgeous, it could only happen to you. Do you want me to bring anything over now, or can you make it into town?"

"If you could buy me some Nurofen Plus and bring them over now, you'd be my BFF." Zoë hated that term, mainly because she used it all the time writing for teen magazines. Actually, it probably wasn't the best time to wind her up, seeing as I needed her to run a painkiller errand, but she let it go, this once. "Of course I can. I'll be with you in about half an hour. Don't move!"

"I can't!" I whined.

I sat in the same position, occasionally attempting to lift myself up off the sofa and deciding it hurt too much, until Zoë turned up and let herself in. I thought I'd probably just bruised my spine, as there wasn't any numbness or tingling and everything seemed to work still – it just hurt.

Zoë was an absolute star, although she got her money's worth, teasing me with, "I had no idea you were auditioning for Mamma Mia" and the inevitable "How much is it worth for me not to tell people how you did this?"

"I'm going to tell everyone it's what happens when you spend a night with a younger man." I moaned. "At least that's a bit more exciting."

It was obvious that the night out at Violet's wasn't going to happen, so I texted Lauren and Colette and asked them to bring themselves and a bottle to mine for a change of venue. I didn't even bother trying to explain the whole ABBA, coffee table, sore back incident, I thought I'd just leave that to when they turned up and brace myself for the inevitable amusement my predicament was going to cause.

"I've hurt my back!" I texted Jamie, hoping for a bit of well-deserved sympathy from the newest object of my affections. I was testing the water, did he care about me? I thought of making a joke about it being his over-exertion that ruined me, but then I decided to leave it at the sympathy level and see if he replied.

The painkillers kicked in and I started to feel a bit better, although it still hurt to move. Lauren turned up with not one, but two bottles of Prosecco, celebrating the fact that she'd finally worked out her redundancy period and was now a free woman. Colette arrived with a sketchbook and a bottle of gin. I loved my friends.

I introduced Lauren and Colette to each other and went over the unfortunate incident of that afternoon, milking it for laughs but trying not to laugh too hard because of the pain. As expected, after they'd finished laughing, they weren't really that sympathetic to my predicament.

"Only you could hurt yourself dancing to frigging ABBA" Lauren laughed, and Colette added, "You could at least have been doing a Davina workout or using something a bit more upmarket than a Wii."

"What's wrong with a Wii?" I asked, defensively.

"It makes clumsy people fall over coffee tables." Colette giggled. I pouted. There was no way I was going to live this down.

Lauren was curled up on the sofa, flicking through a couple of magazines I'd left on the coffee table – I'd been trying to fill myself with inspiration for feature ideas earlier in the week. Zoë was cross-legged on the floor with Colette, who was showing her a few ideas and holding fabric swatches up against her face to see what would look good. I was propped up with a hot water bottle pressed to my lower back, a painkiller patch on and a bottle of wine right next to me so that I didn't have to keep getting up to go to the fridge. Zoë thought of everything. She'd have made a great nurse.

"Zo, you're so lucky, you just know that you'll look fabulous in whatever you wear," Colette sighed as she held another deep burgundy red swatch up against Zoë's perfect pale skin.

"Oh honestly, stop it. You're all beautiful, and with you making us beeyoootiful dresses, we'll stun 'em all. Who said you have to be skinny to get attention in a GOOD way?" Zoe replied, matter of factly. I could tell she was getting into the idea, although I suspected it was the fizzy wine that was making her really enthusiastic.

"Corsets look great on big girls," Colette chimed in. "There's something about a voluptuous woman all cinched in, boobs up and out there, it just shows off EVERYTHING that's good about being curvy. You'll all look fantastic."

"I bet your boy wonder will love it," Lauren interjected, waving her glass around.

"I hope so." I said, quietly. I was a bit disappointed, actually. He hadn't replied to my text about hurting myself. "Who knows?" As if to emphasise my gloom, I felt a twinge in my back and shifted position to try and alleviate it.

"So what's the story?" Zoë asked, tearing her away from the fabric swatches and Colette's sketches. "Are you two an item now?"

"Buggered if I know" I replied. "One minute he's all over me and the next he's incommunicado. We had a great time yesterday and it felt really nice. The last couple of dates we've been on, I've felt like it's going somewhere, you know? But then I don't hear from him for ages and I start getting that niggly feeling I got when I was seeing Mark."

"He's not Mark – don't go comparing them." Zoë warned. "Why don't you just enjoy it for what it is, like we said? Just see how it goes? I thought you didn't want a full on relationship anyway? And Jamie, I thought we'd established, is NOT boyfriend material"

"I don't. Well, most of the time I don't, anyway." I replied sulkily. "It's just when we're together it's great and, well, you know?" I left the sentence hanging.

As if she sensed it was probably a good idea to change the subject, Zoë picked up one of the magazines Lauren had discarded, rolled it up and swatted me with it. "He's certainly making you a bit creative anyway. Whatever possessed you to use a rolled up magazine, that's hardly sexy is it?"

Colette spluttered into her gin and I had to go over the whole story again, suitably embellished of course. "You really spat milkshake up the walls of a cathedral?" she giggled incredulously. "Really? Are you safe to be let out in public?"

We spent the rest of the evening chatting excitedly about the plans for the events in London and Manchester, and getting even more excited about the wonderful costumes that Colette had dreamed up.

Lauren, ever the sophisticated one, was going for mostly black with a hint of midnight blue, a long corset that would accentuate her heaving cleavage and give her a stunning curves. She wanted to wear a long fishtail skirt with it, and accessorise with gloves. She didn't fancy a hat, with her gorgeous, beautifully cut and conditioned hair (the cow) I didn't blame her. Zoë, who was a bit of a show-off at heart, also went for a long black corset, but with a bold pink bow around the waist, and cascading lace ruffles attached that turned it into a very short dress.

"The three of you are going to look so fantastic", beamed Colette, who was really excited and fully behind the campaign.

We were going to show them, for sure.

Chapter 18

"I don't believe it!"

Zoë called me at not much after 7.30am the following Wednesday, so excited that I thought she was going to explode.

I took a few seconds to register who it was, and where I was, as I was still highly under the influence of ibuprofen and codeine.

"I'm writing a book!" Zoe squealed, not waiting for a response from me. "I got a deal! I'm so excited!"

"You have to come over and tell me all about it. Even if I'm still in my PJs."

Getting a book published had been Zoë's biggest dream since she realised she had a talent for putting words together and making them sound good. This was a massive, massive deal for her.

"What, when, who…details please, lady" I insisted when she finally made it over, a few hours later. By then I had, at least, managed to get myself out of bed. I was still milking the sore back but in all honesty it was a lot better. I just needed a few lie ins and to look after myself a bit. I had to get myself back to fighting fitness for Glastonbury, which was approaching at speed.

"It's going to be ah-mazing. It will go hand in hand with what we're doing with the blogs and the Viva Voluptuous stuff. I'm writing a self-help book for curvy women!"

Spurred on by our campaign, Zoë had put together a proposal for a self-appreciation book for curvy girls. It was going to be full of her upbeat personality, urging women from teens upwards to be who they are and not give in to the pressures to be super-thin that were all around. The proposal had been accepted and she'd signed a contract, and I could have cried with happiness for her as she excitedly told me all about it, what the publishing house had said, when she was planning to release the book.

"I'm so happy for you, honey," I said, as I gave her the biggest bear hug I could manage.

"I have an important question," Zoë said, seriously. "Does the fact I have a book to write get me out of going to Glastonbury next week?

"No." I said bluntly.

"Worth a try, wasn't it? I'm really not looking forward to this, you know?"

"You'll love it," I said, as I handed her a cupcake. She took the cake, sniffed it, nibbled it and then then frowned.

"Won't it be full of unwashed students?" She whinged.

"Don't be daft. Glastonbury is more middle class than IKEA these days." I hunted around the coffee table, looking for the list of all the things we needed to take that I'd made earlier. "There will be unwashed copywriters and journalists, though, darling," I teased, waving a packet of baby wipes under her nose. "That's us, by the way."

Zoë wrinkled her nose and sniffed haughtily as if to underline her disgust. Much as I loved her, the comedy moaning was starting to annoy me now. Most people would have been chuffed to bits at a free ticket to see as many bands as they could fit in over three days, but despite Zoë's claim to be young at heart, and 'down with the kids', she could be a proper snob at times.

"So what are we going to wear?" Zoë finally asked, after she'd polished off her cake and composed herself, "is it all fancy dress? Don't people wear tutus and Morph suits and all that freaky stuff?"

"I've never been either, you know?" I reminded her. "I'm taking wellies. And two umbrellas. And something warm to wear at night."

"You sound like my gran," Zoë complained. "So no heels, wellies, and a cardi. I think I've aged about thirty years!"

I rolled my eyes. "Just wear whatever you want, pack loads of wet wipes, and take sun screen."

I'd managed to get onto the Glastonbury website on the laptop and showed Zoë just how many bands were actually playing. "I don't believe you've not actually looked yourself yet," I said, as she sat there looking contrite, picking at her week-old gel manicure. "How hard is it to Google 'Glastonbury line up'?"

I suspected that she might actually be looking forward to seeing more than a few of the bands, but was trying really hard not to show too much enthusiasm in case I thought she was going to actually enjoy herself.

"Did you hear anything from Paloma Faith's people?" she asked, when I pointed out where Paloma was on the itinerary. "Nah" I sighed, "There's still time but I'm not getting too excited. It would be so cool though, imagine getting Paloma on the blog..."

"God yeah"...Zoe pondered, "It would be pretty amazing. Have you got anywhere with the whole flash mob thing yet? Are you getting many people on board?"

I was actually quite excited about it as the forums I'd set up on Viva Voluptuous had been buzzing for the previous few weeks with amazing plus sized women who loved the idea of strutting their stuff, dolled up in their most glamorous ensembles, and having a laugh.

"I think we've got around 30 people so far, all saying they are up for the shenanigans in Covent Garden" I replied. I called up the forum and showed her.

"Wow, this one sounds like fun," Zoe pointed out a member calling herself Muffin_Top.

"I've got a fab outfit, heels, bling and bustier, going to get some false eyelashes and vixen nails. I LOVE Gloria Gaynor, and that song was my ringtone for ages! I'm a size 24 and I love my curves – I spent too many years on a diet and now I want to get out and sing. I'm in a burlesque group in Croydon, and I love showing off. I'm totally confident after doing burlesque and I think getting out there and shaking our tail feathers in London will be fabulous for any plus size girls lacking in

self-confidence. We're gonna be hot, Missus!"

"What about Stratford?"

I clicked through to the Stratford sign up forum. Hmm, we needed a few more to make that event as lively as Covent Garden was shaping up to be. "I could see if I can get things going a bit?" Zoë suggested. "Introduce myself, tell them about the new book and maybe tease them in with a chance of a free signed copy if they come to the event?"

"But you've only just signed the contract to write the book? It's not going to be ready by the end of June, is it?" I asked, confused.

"No, silly, I'll just put them on a waiting list. But it might get a few more people to sign up. I liked what that Muffin Top lady said – the more women we can get into it, the better it will be - and hopefully the more we can boost fat women's self confidence levels when they FINALLY realise they are just as sexy as skinny girls."

"It's a great idea" I mused. "So, when do you think the book will be out?"

"Not till the end of the year," replied Zoë, animatedly. "It's going to take me a good six months or so even if I write like a demon for the next few months. Some of it's already written in the form of past blog posts, it just needs to be prettied up and all."

She explained a bit more about the book, how it was going to be a how-to guide, with lots of practical tips and interviews with inspirational women. "You have to let me use the interview I did with you for the blog – is that OK?" she asked. "Course it is, sweetie. But you'll have to sign me a copy," I teased.

Zoë grinned. "You got it." Catching me looking at my Blackberry and frowning, she guessed I'd been looking to see if Jamie had emailed me. He hadn't.

"So, how's it all going with Jamie?" she asked, aware from my frown that it could have been going better.

"He wants to come to Glasto with us," I replied, "but doesn't understand that you can't just swap a ticket or get one at the last minute. Glasto has so many layers of security these days it's like Fort Knox."

Zoë didn't seem surprised. "Is he giving you grief about it?" she said, pushing me to admit that yes, in fact he had been acting like a petulant teenager and was sulking. "I do really like him" I admitted, "and sometimes I think we could work – but when he's acting like a big baby he does my head in."

"Aw, but you secretly wish he was going to be in that campervan instead of me, don't you?" Zoë asked, knowing the answer. "Not at all." I lied.

Chapter 19

The day of reckoning came, and although it was a bit dull and grey, it didn't actually seem too bad. It was warm, and part of our plan had been to go as glam as we possibly could do, despite the fact we wouldn't be able to wash properly for three days. We'd packed our most glamorous flats and sandals (I drew the line at attempting to navigate Glastonbury in heels) and some killer outfits that made a change from the usual festival fashion. We knew we'd stand out but we didn't care.

I really wanted to try and get backstage with Paloma Faith but repeated attempts at contacting her management had all come to nothing, and so I'd given that up as a bad idea.

I was so glad when the sun started to peep out from the clouds as Zoë drove us down to Somerset. We'd left it until the Thursday night, as there was no one we wanted to see on the Wednesday, and besides, I didn't want Zoe to have to be there longer than she needed to be, I wasn't sure I could handle the earache. I hoped we'd get a decent space ready for when the festival officially opened on Friday morning.

"You can't possibly need another wee!" Zoë grumbled.

"Sorry honey, I think it's the excitement." We'd stopped four times in three hours for me to go to the loo, and Zoë had been getting annoyed. At least the traffic wasn't too bad. I shuddered at the thought of the time I'd been stuck in a long traffic queue on the way to Edinburgh with Darren, and been forced to get out and go in a field because I couldn't take it anymore. My tiny bladder was legendary.

"Can't you just use the chemical loo in the van?" she complained. "Surely that's what it's there for?"

"What, and risk you braking suddenly? Or someone seeing me?" I shuddered again.

"Nobody can see you. And it would mean I could get on with

driving and not have to try and find yet another services." I was so glad it wasn't raining, Zoë's usually sunny disposition was clearly being tested by the prospect of three days in a field and inclement weather would have put her in an even worse mood. We found somewhere to stop and I placated her with a green tea and a flapjack. I had to keep on her good side; there's no escape in a campervan…

After a four hour drive we followed the signs to the campervan area, parked up, and began the precarious task of trying to put the loo tent up. The campervan didn't come with facilities; it did have water but no toilet except for the stinky chemical loo. Disgusting as this was, we'd agreed beforehand that the outside tent would be our toilet of choice for any overnight bathroom needs and we'd have to make do.

Two women with no camping experience attempting to erect a tent was always going to end in tears, and a lot of bad language. We tried and tried to get the stupid thing up, but every time we thought we were almost there, we realised we'd put one of the plastic rods in the wrong way and had to take it out and start again.

"It doesn't go there," I insisted. I had hold of the tent while Zoë did her best to feed the bendy rod through it in a direction it plainly didn't go. We'd been spotted by a group of men who were watching us with amusement. Determined to get this thing right, I sat down on the grass, studying the instruction leaflet again, leaving Zoë huffing, puffing and swearing. One of the men came over to see what was going on. "What seems to be the problem, ladies?" he asked. I wasn't sure whether he was being helpful or patronising, so I gave him the benefit of the doubt.

"This instruction leaflet seems to have been written in Swahili" I moaned, waving it at him for emphasis. "And we can't get our tent up!"

"Why do you need a tent when you have a campervan?" he asked, not unreasonably. Zoë peeped out from behind a drooping canopy, looking bad-tempered, and scowled, "It's our bathroom." The tent was now leaning precariously over to one side and our mystery man, who introduced himself as Dave, put his arm over to prop it up. "Do you want me and my mate Steve to have a go?" he asked, kindly.

"No, you're alright." I replied. "We can manage."

"I bet you can't" Steve laughed as he came to see what was going on. I wasn't sure I liked Steve. He was holding a can of Stella and seemed a bit drunk. The challenge seemed to spur Zoë on, and as Dave stepped away from the droopy tent, she called out, "Here, grab the other end and we can get this one through!" More huffing and puffing ensued, and the rod was in place. "Yay!" I cheered, as it became blatantly obvious where we'd been going wrong. "Who needs men?" Zoë said triumphantly as the last rod went in and we hammered the pegs down.

"It's a work of art," I declared, looking at the tent.

We sat in the campervan with plastic cups filled to the brim with warm wine and the sound of music thudding from down the bottom of the hill. This was going to be our home for the next three days. "Where are we going to sleep?" I asked, glancing around the van and not seeing anything remotely bed-like.

"We'll have to toss a coin" she replied, pointing up at the van roof. To get any sleep, one of us was going to have to pull the shelf down and climb up onto a precarious looking bunk bed. Whoever lost the toss was going to have to put the driver's seat down and attempt to sleep on that. "It's not glamorous, is it?" I noted. "It was your idea!" she snorted back, gulping the cheap wine and wincing. There was a sink and running water, the fridge didn't work and there was one very small mirror in which we could do our make-up. It wasn't glamorous, but it was bearable.

"Shall we explore?" I suggested. She agreed. I could almost sense her bracing herself for it, as she sauntered out of the van, tossed her auburn curls back like a drama queen and walked across the bumpy grass to find her bearings. "Remember there's a huge Welsh flag three caravans down" I pointed out. That would be useful when we came back later, in the dark, trying to remember where our camper van was. I should have brought some bunting, or something, I thought to myself. Either way, we'd still be able to look out for that flag, and we were definitely on the right, towards the back of the field. We'd be fine.

We trundled down the hill and made our way through the gates, and what felt like about six layers of security. It was busy already, and there was so much to take in.

There was a fenced off area with some kind of circus going on – I could see women in skimpy sequinned leotards swinging on hoops and trapezes high above the ground. Just the thought of being that far off the ground made me shudder but they were leaping from swing to swing, catching each other mid-air and somehow turning round and landing on the net beneath them gracefully. We could hear muffled laughter and strange noises from a marquee a bit further in. Zoë grabbed my hand and yanked me across to see what was going on. "I didn't know they had this sort of thing" she said naively, "I thought it was all indie music and cider."

We peeped around the entrance to a marquee. It wasn't very full, and the comedian at the front seemed to be dying on his feet, although there was the occasional ripple of laughter. He had some kind of ventriloquist act going on, with a turtle. I'd never heard that sort of language coming from a turtle before. Clearly he wasn't going down very well, and we weren't the only people who decided to go and find someone else to watch.

"Are you hungry?" I asked as we walked along, trying to work out where we were on the map. The smells coming from the nearby food court were making me salivate. If we'd expected to have to make do with a few burger cans and a chippie, we were pleasantly surprised. "I don't know what I want – there's too much to choose from!" Zoë mumbled as we took in the vast selection of foodie choice ahead of us. Gravitating towards the delicious-smelling veggie van, Zoë skipped over to get herself a falafel or something else with chickpeas in (she was having a vegan phase) and I headed for the hog roast, because it smelled divine. We found a slightly sticky plastic table to sit at while we devoured our food. "I think this is going to a very expensive weekend," Zoe complained, licking her fingers.

"I think you're right," I said. "That hog roast roll cost me £5!"

Zoë looked right at home, actually. She was sitting back in the chair with her best Gucci sunglasses on, a big floppy hat and a gorgeous maxi dress. The dress was in a kitsch 1950s red, black and white floral pattern that a lot of women would have found difficult to pull off, but on her it looked amazing. She had low wedges on, with big red bows on the front. Her hat was adorned with a huge red flower. So much for the body confidence book, I thought, she should have written about fashion or become some rich woman's personal shopper or stylist.

I wasn't looking too bad myself, with my skinny jeans, some cute jewelled flip flops and a very low cut patterned top that showed my cleavage off to its best advantage. Yes, I did say skinny jeans. I loved wearing them, and leggings; despite the snarky comments I'd seen about them only being for slim women. When you're blessed with a bodacious bum and a smallish waist, you don't want to cover up in baggy tent tops and the worst fashion crime of them all – baggy boot cut jeans! I looked good in fitted outfits and skinny jeans, and I wasn't going to let an intern on a fashion magazine make me feel bad about it, thank you very much.

The sun had gone down, and I was starting to feel a bit chilly. Even though the only wine we had back at the van was going to be warm, I still fancied it. "I'm knackered" I sighed, "And there's not much on tonight. Fancy going back to the van and chilling out?"

"I thought you'd never ask," Zoë replied. "It is getting dark."

We headed on out and up the hill to the camping fields. With a sinking feeling, I turned to Zoë and asked, "Have you got a torch?"

"No, why?" she replied.

"Look."

There were no lights beyond the first field. And we were in the field right at the back. Our clever plan to look out for the Welsh flag had fallen flat on its face as my night vision was ropey and we had nothing except a couple of tiny mobile phones that emitted any kind of light at all. I tottered carefully, trying to avoid tripping over anything as we went into the next, dark field.

"Whose bloody stupid freaking idea was this?" I heard Zoë mumble as she followed behind me.

If anyone was going to get her foot stuck in a pothole, it was going to be me, wasn't it? As we were getting more and more frustrated at our lack of navigation skills (and vowing to buy a torch the next morning, even if they were extortionately expensive) I suddenly disappeared from view, and found myself on my backside on the grass. For some reason, Zoë found this incredibly funny and doubled up laughing as I indignantly dusted myself off. My ankle was throbbing a bit but I didn't think it was serious. "I'm glad it's dark." I said, trying not to laugh myself. "At least nobody saw that."

"Nobody except me." Zoë sniggered, holding her hand out to help me up. "You daft mare. I hope we find the van soon, I'm dying for a wee and there's a box of warm wine with both our names on it."

We eventually found our way back, and relaxed in the van. The unmistakeable aroma of cannabis was wafting from a nearby tent, and we could hear some unidentifiable sixties hippy-style guitar playing coming from another one. There was noise all around, from the thumping bass of the music at the festival, people walking past talking and laughing, and even two people having a drunken argument about where they'd left their caravan. “At least it’s not just us” I thought.

For some reason, the combination of warm wine and being tired left me feeling melancholy. I was missing Jamie, against my better judgement, and at the same time I couldn’t help daydreaming about what it would have been like if I’d been here with Mark, like we’d planned. He’d seemed really keen on the idea – until I’d presented him with the tickets, like some sort of fait accompli. It was probably about the time he withdrew from ‘us’ even more and started cancelling dates as well as thinking of excuses not to come in when I asked him. I sighed deeply. I missed him, sometimes.

“Wassup?” Zoë asked sleepily.

“Nothing” I lied, went back to my daydreaming and attempted to get some sleep. She’d won the toss and was up on the bunk with her Kindle, trying to read because the noise outside meant she couldn’t sleep. I was really uncomfortable; the duvet I’d brought with me kept sliding off and there was definitely something digging into my back. I switched my phone on, just to see if there were any messages. There was a missed call from Jamie. Oops. Well, I’d just have to call him in the morning.

Chapter 20

I was unlucky enough to feel the need for the toilet very early the next morning. I blamed the wine, and the fact I'd been too scared to leave the campervan and go for a wee in the middle of the night. The rumours about the loos at Glastonbury were all true.

The nearest portaloo was small as well as smelly and not built for an ample bottom. I'd had the same problems with the campervan, everything was small and with my size 20 hourglass frame I just felt as if nothing fitted where it should do.

"Living in a thin world" was going to be the theme for next video blog, and we were doing it right here, outside a long line of disgusting Glasto Portaloos. First, we had to find one that wasn't already 'blocked up'. There was no way I was going to film that, the mere thought of standing too close to it made me want to heave up my morning bacon roll. We hunted down some loos that were a bit out of the way and found some that hadn't been desecrated yet. Zoë held the camera and the door while I walked backwards into the cubicle to prove a point about how small it was.

"This…is my bum." I said, turning round and pointing at my behind for comedy effect.

"This is a lesser-spotted Glastonbury Portaloo. A rare sighting at the festival as it's not yet overflowing with smelly things that make a girl's nose wrinkle."

We had an audience now. Clearly they wondered who the fruit loops were filming themselves in the toilet.

"Just another example of fat people fitting awkwardly into a thin world," I continued. "This loo is so small that when I sit down, my elbows touch the sides of the cubicle. As I turn round to reach for the loo roll…"

Oh crap. There wasn't any, was there? Nobody told me that there was no toilet roll in these things. I was very glad I was just filming and not using the facilities. Note to self – we needed loo roll as well as a torch.

"OK, there is no loo roll, so that's what you might call a moot point. But anyway, every single Portaloo here is likely to be exactly the same size. It's uncomfortable and awkward. The world is designed for slim people, and if you're fat, you deserve to be uncomfortable, right?"

"Yes!" Shouted an idiot from over the other side of the crowd that was forming around us.

We had a joker. I had no contingency plans for hecklers.

"Oi! Smart arse!" I shouted. "Want to come here and explain why we deserve it?"

At first I thought he was running scared, but then a weasel-ly looking man with long hair and a bald patch, skinny legs and a t-shirt stretched across his belly with 'Super Tramp' written on it appeared looking defiant.

"Well, you did it to yourself." He said arrogantly. "We're trying to help because if the world was too comfortable for you, you wouldn't need to go on a diet would you?"

"I don't need to go on a diet, sweetheart." Zoë interjected. Oh, this was going to be fun.

"I didn't say YOU needed to go on a diet" he whined, "but if you're too fat to get in a Portaloo, you need to cut down on your pies, love."

A few people laughed. Even more had come to see what was going on now.

"Don't 'love' ME, Super Tramp man." Zoë retaliated. "It's naff, out of date, stereotypical assumptions like yours that make life so miserable for women who don't fit into the Heat magazine perfect woman mould. It's creeps like you that can make perfectly lovely women feel small and worthless just because they have a bigger number on the label in their knickers than Megan Fox. Does it make you feel good to put other people down? Does it make you feel like the big man with all your mates?"

He looked absolutely terrified.

"Alright, keep yer hair on love, I was only having a joke."

"I am NOT your love. Now go and crawl back into your hole, or your Portaloo, whichever you came from, and don't come out until you've grown an opinion of your own."

At that point, people started clapping. I was grinning from ear to ear, Zoë was a bit pink in the face but otherwise triumphant. Mr Super Tramp skulked off and we had a fantastic video for the next blog.

"I never thought we could have got so much drama out of a toilet!" I giggled as the crowd dispersed.

I was surprised at how much Zoë got into the spirit of Glastonbury. She picked out some bands she really wanted to see, mostly the obscure ones I'd never heard of, and we wandered off to laze around on the grass and sit in the sunshine. Florence and the Machine were on later and we both wanted to get a good place for that, so we were just ambling around most of the day, taking it easy.

I wasn't supposed to be checking my emails, but when I switched on my phone and snuck a surreptitious look at them while Zoë was searching for something to eat, I actually squealed out loud.

Zoë came back with a concerned look on her face and pitta bread stuffed with chips and hummus in her hand. "What's up?"

"We've got a backstage pass to meet Paloma!"

"Aaaaaggghhhhhhh!!!!" Zoë jumped up and down, which sent chips flying in all directions. "No way! When?"

"Tomorrow! We need to get press passes, so we'll have to find security before tomorrow. Oh my God, a proper backstage pass and we're meeting Paloma ...I think I might wet myself!"

Zoë looked at me as if she wasn't sure whether to believe me or not, but she was grinning from ear to ear. "Is the bar free?"

"I don't think so – but you never know who we might bump

into." I said mysteriously, going over it all in my head and trying to come up with insightful, witty things to ask Paloma. I don't think either of us could have been any more excited.

"Where do we go to get the passes?" Zoë asked. "We have to find security" I replied, "Her manager's going to put our names down on a list"

"Can we see if we can meet Florence too?" she continued, dropping what was left of her chip-stuffed pitta in an over full bin and clearly getting over excited.

"I think we might be pushing our luck, but you never know" I laughed. Right now, my mission was finding out where to get our precious press passes from, and not missing out on interviewing someone I had a bit of a girl-crush on. We hadn't been promised an interview exactly, but we could have a chat with her and get it on video, and it would be amazing for the blog. And for me!

"I can't believe Paloma Faith has seen my little blog" I said, a little bit drunk, swigging cider. We'd managed to sort out the passes so we could get backstage and no longer had to use the really smelly loos. We also got to mix with the proper journo types who were all busily typing up their reports of the day's acts, as well as pretending to be ever so important. I hadn't seen anyone I recognised, although I was keeping my eyes open. It had been quite an afternoon – there'd been an impromptu secret Foals gig right over at The Park, and swarms of us made our way over there. We couldn't see a thing and my feet and ankle were killing me by then, but we had to be there because it was secret. How anything with that many people involved could ever be described as secret I'm not sure, but in the end I sat down and just listened, while Zoë stood up, swaying in the sunshine and singing along to the songs she knew, pretending her feet didn't hurt and that she wasn't wishing we'd brought the picnic chairs after all.

There was a person dressed as a Rubik's Cube chasing

someone else who was dressed as Iron Man round and round a tree, and at one point the Iron man attempted to climb the tree and the Rubik's Cube tried to grab his foot and pull him out again. It was all very surreal. We left Foals before the end, as we couldn't see anything anyway, and walked all the way back to the Pyramid stage where Florence was about to start. This festival malarkey definitely involved a LOT of walking.

"We can't see much," pouted Zoë. "We'll just have to make do with the screens" I suggested. Florence was packed out and when she came on stage, ethereal in her floaty dress and bare feet, and launched into "Lungs" the crowd erupted and she looked visibly thrilled. A group of inebriated lads in front of us started to ogle Zoë. "Wanna get up on my shoulders darlin'?" one of them asked, with a cocky grin on his face. He couldn't have been older than his early twenties. His mates were all jeering at him, swigging from a bottle of disgusting blue liquid. "OK then!" Zoë replied.

The boy looked scared to death – he'd obviously been expecting a rebuff. I stifled a giggle as he stooped down so that Zoë could get on his shoulders. "Anything for a decent view" she yelled at me, although I could only just make it out over the noise of Florence and the crowd, by now singing along loudly to "Shake it out". I switched my phone on quickly and took a few pictures of Zoë waving her arms around on some stranger's shoulders, having the time of her life. And this was the girl who didn't want to come to Glastonbury?

Later, we wandered slowly back to the camper van, this time with a torch, arm in arm.

"Ellie Johnstone, I bloody love you." Zoë slurred happily. "And I love this place. It's not full of smelly old hippies at all..."

"I love you too, you old lush." I replied, thinking that today couldn't possibly have got any better.

Chapter 21

Neither of us got much sleep that night. It wasn't just the heat or the noise, or being incredibly cramped, but neither of us could quite believe we'd managed to blag backstage passes, and Zoë wouldn't shut up, chattering until dawn started to break. It seemed like question after question and my exhausted brain and body didn't know where she could possibly have got her enthusiasm from at that time of the morning, after two sleepless nights. I mumbled sleepily as she asked; "So do you want me to do the filming while you ask her the questions? What are you going to wear? Do you think we'll bump into anyone else? Do you think she can introduce us?"

We both dozed off eventually, once Zoë had realised there was absolutely no point trying to get a sensible answer out of me until I'd at least attempted some sleep. When I finally woke up, I yawned, stretched and caught the duvet as it slid off me once again, then realised it was gone 11. Oh bugger. I sprung up off of the makeshift bed and into some semblance of life.

"Oi! Sleeping beauty!"

I picked up a cushion and aimed it at the dozing Zoë, who started in her sleep and promptly went back to her dream. Trust her to want to sleep now when we had precisely an hour before we were due to meet Paloma Faith in the hospitality bar.

I tugged at her duvet and she groaned, mumbling something incoherent under her breath.

"Get up, sleepyhead. We've got an hour, and it takes twenty minutes just to get into the festival from here!"

Suddenly there was a sign of action from beneath the covers and a bleary-eyed Zoë sat up, looking panicked. "Shit!" she exclaimed.

So much for prepping and making ourselves look our best. We had about half an hour to get dressed, get our make up on and get out of the campervan. Taking turns to nudge each other out of the way of the world's smallest mirror, we somehow managed it, although we weren't looking so hot. Two days without a proper shower and hardly any sleep had left even the ever-glamorous Zoë looking a bit bedraggled, her fabulous curly hair looking decidedly frizzy, and I didn't even want to know what I looked like. I consoled myself at the thought that everybody was in the same slightly unwashed and sleep-deprived boat.

"Have you got the camera?" I called after Zoë as she strode down the hill.

"Yes, doll," she said breathlessly, rushing as fast as her slightly impractical wedges would let her.

"Is that whatshisname from Muse?" Zoë asked, breathlessly, as we made it into the hospitality bar with minutes to spare. I looked over to where she thought she'd seen Matt Bellamy. "Nah. Don't think so."

I was definitely a bit star struck as I waited for Paloma to appear, and going over all the things I wanted to say in my head. I knew Paloma had admitted to having a few body image issues of her own – and she was gorgeous. If someone like that admitted to not owning a full length mirror, and having to lose weight because of unflattering camera angles, what did she think of people like me, trying to crusade for fat women in a world where they were rendered either invisible or objects of ridicule? I was so excited.

"What if she turns out to be a cow?" I said out loud, when I'd really meant just to think it. Zoë was walking towards me with a glass of wine, to 'calm my nerves' and looked surprised. "Don't be daft," she said, "she's adorable. Anyway, one of my friends on *Candy* interviewed her last year, and said she's exactly as you'd expect her to be, kooky but lovely. She's pretty honest, too, she doesn't sugar coat anything." She was also 15 minutes late. "I hope she's still coming" I fretted. "Are you ready with the camera?"

Zoë rolled her eyes. "Yeees" she drawled, "Now calm down. You're a shit hot professional journo, remember? Not a star-struck amateur!"

Right on cue, I saw Paloma walking towards us, flanked by the woman I assumed was her manager.

Zoë sprang into action, switched on the camera and winked at me.

I took a deep breath, put on my confident face and smiled.

"So sorry I'm late, you're Ellie, right?" Paloma held her hand out.

I reached out and shook her hand – my, but she was so dainty. Then she leaned towards me and air-kissed both my cheeks as if we were old friends, "Really, really sorry…"

"Don't worry about it," I gushed, "It's so fabulous to meet you – you're a bit of a hero of mine! I'm so glad you could make it, you must be really busy?"

"Yeah, it's a bit mad" she smiled, "But I just love it, the whole festival vibe, the buzz, all the great people. I'm having a marvellous time." She stopped for a few seconds and then carried on, "You're the girl who did the paper pants thing online aren't you? That was so funny."

I smiled; she'd instantly put me at ease. "Yup, that clumsy oaf was me. And this is Zoë Ellis, my friend, journalist and blogger. She's got a book coming out soon on body confidence you know?"

Zoë blushed.

"That's wonderful," said Paloma, "a woman after my own heart! Everyone needs to feel beautiful."

Zoë was clearly chuffed to bits with this and decided to get in on the action. "I love what Ellie's doing too," she interjected, "she inspired me to come up with the book idea. We need an antidote to all the crap in the media about how women should look."

"Oh, God yes we do" Paloma enthused. "I get so cross with

the pornification of women, like we're all expected to have flat tummies, big round boobs and fake everything. Real women have cellulite, wobbly, jiggly bits and look like crap when they get out of bed in the morning!"

"Especially after two nights in a campervan with no sleep and no showers," I agreed. Zoë pulled a face. I carried on. "So, Paloma, if you have a message for all the women out there, what would it be?"

"Embrace your body." Paloma replied, after thinking for a few moments. "You are what you are and it's so depressing we live in a society where we think other people will treat us better if we're thinner or have less wrinkles. We're all beautiful. Oh, and if you need anyone to big up your paper pants campaign, just say the word, those things are a menace."

I blushed, "They are silly aren't they? How can you relax if you're worried that your knickers are going to roll down or ping off you for the whole time you're being massaged?"

"Exactly!" giggled Paloma. I spotted her manager looking at her watch and realised she was about to be dragged away. "Are you coming to see me later?" she asked. "Course we are!" Zoë interrupted before I could get a word in. "Wouldn't miss it!" I added.

"I hope you enjoy it – I left the balloons at home this time though," she grinned. "Oh, and absolutely LOVE what you're doing! Viva Voluptuous!"

"Oh thank you"…I stuttered, star struck again. "Thank you so much…"

With that, Paloma Faith tottered away.

We'd been in her company for less than five minutes but I was smiling like a loon. And we had another brilliant bit of video for the blog. And technically, she'd endorsed Viva Voluptuous. I couldn't have asked for anything more and I thought it was unlikely I'd be able to get the grin off of my face for at least a week. Zoë was going to eat her words with an extra dollop of humble sauce if she ever complained about me taking her to Glastonbury again.

I squealed and jumped up and down on the spot. Yes, I really did. Zoë was grinning all over her face, and I couldn't stop smiling either. We'd only got a few minutes of footage but it had been worth the exorbitant cost of the tickets just for that few minutes. We walked over to where the crowds were already gathering for Paloma's set, and we were nowhere near the front, although we had a great view of the big screen to our left.

"I can't believe we just did that, girlfriend" Zoë laughed. "And I've interviewed Gary Barlow."

"Have you? When?"

"Oh it was years ago for a teen mag. He was loooovely."

"Would have preferred to interview Robbie," I giggled. "Preferably in a hot tub. Naked."

Zoë rolled her eyes and playfully punched me on the arm. "You know what, now I've actually done my first festival, I've decided I kinda like them."

"Told you so," I retorted, deadpan. Admittedly, I was very glad it hadn't rained, because a wet Zoë wouldn't have been anywhere near as amenable to schlepping around in a field for three days.

Paloma Faith came on stage and put on an amazing show. She wasn't wearing helium balloons this time, like she had done a couple of years before, probably because the logistics of being attached to helium balloons on a windy day had almost resulted in her flying off the stage. Zoë and I joined in, singing along at the top of our voices, and when she played 'Me and my cellulite', Paloma introduced it with, "This is for the fabulous Ellie and Zoë, for inspiring women to be happy and be themselves. Mwwwahhh!"

Chapter 22

I hadn't charged my phone up for over 24 hours by the time I got home. I thought we'd probably be able to get by on Zoë's and had relished the freedom from the dreaded flashing red light on the Blackberry anyway. So when I did charge it back up, I was a little bit worried to see about five missed calls. They were from Jamie, apart from one from Adrian at Glammazon on Friday. I'd really missed Jamie, after all my protestations that we were just having fun. I wanted a bit of a flirt, maybe I could get him to come over and see me soon?

It was late, so I thought I should probably text Jamie, as he'd not been helpful enough to actually leave a message when he'd called. I hoped he was OK.

"What's up? Did you miss me??" I sent.

Surprisingly, he texted straight back. *"Yeah but u didn't miss me did u?"*

So he WAS feeling a little bit jealous! Ha! For some reason I was quite heartened by that tiny admission. I quickly asked *"Do you want me to call you now?"*

"Busy now." came back a few minutes later.

I wasn't expecting that. It was late. Who was he busy with? I felt my jealous girlfriend alter ego kick in as the tables turned on me.

"Oh? What are you up to?" I pestered, hoping he was going to say he had a mate over for X Box games and beer.

"With Lisa." Ouch. Lisa? His sister's name was Suzanne. I didn't know who Lisa was. I was beginning to get a sinking feeling.

"Who's Lisa?" I keyed in, nervously.

He didn't reply. I had my answer right there.

How dare he? I was absolutely exhausted after the excitement of the last few days, and a long drive home. But I felt the adrenalin kick in and a sense of righteous indignation taking over. He knew I couldn't talk to him while I was away – we were in a field in the middle of the countryside. OK, it might have been one of the biggest music festivals in the world, but there was still nowhere to plug in a mobile charger in the campervan. I'd told him that before I went. Stupid arse. Bloody men, why were they so contrary? Was Lisa the person who'd been texting him all the time when we were out the other day, before I went away?

I scoured the fridge for anything chocolatey. There was nothing. I hadn't been shopping for ages and all I could find was a leftover chunk of Edam that had gone slightly hard around the edges, some eggs and an out of date yoghurt. It was too late to ring for a take away. I didn't even know why I wanted to eat anything, it was stupid o'clock and I wasn't remotely hungry. That didn't stop me from hunting through the kitchen for a sugar hit. I struck lucky and to soothe the rising feeling of rejection I stuffed down a whole packet of chocolate chips intended for baking. They tasted sweet and cloying but they still disappeared in a blur of "How very dare he?" I slumped on the sofa and sighed. Now I felt sick. Thoughts of Lisa, whoever she was, being younger and prettier than me, filled my head. So much for my post-Glastonbury and Paloma Faith induced high. I was too tired to cry, and fell asleep with a frown on my face.

The following morning, I left it as long as I possibly could for fear of being accused of stalking, but I still managed to catch him just before I knew he was about to leave for work. The call was short, tense and to the point. I skipped the niceties – he'd see right through a description of Glastonbury. He hadn't texted me back all night, and I was not happy - to say the least.

"So. You're up then? Has Lisa gone home?" I spat, sarcastically. This wasn't going to be pretty.

"What's the matter with you? You were in Glastonbury, and you weren't answering my texts." Jamie responded sulkily. It sounded as if his bottom lip was out so far he could have tripped over it.

"My battery was flat! And I wasn't out shagging other men while I was there! And anyway, I was busy interviewing celebrities" I said, deliberately showing off.

Jamie didn't bite. "Well I didn't know we were supposed to be exclusive." he retorted, pushing all my buttons. I was pacing the living room, my voice had gone all high and squeaky and I thought I was about to cry, although I was desperately trying not to let on. I didn't want to give him the satisfaction.

"So you've been seeing other women the whole time?" I asked, not really wanting to know the answer.

"Well, only one." My mind went back to the day we'd been for the walk by the river, and the constant texts he'd been sending. I bet that was her. I could feel a lump in my throat. What an idiot.

That was supposed to be OK, was it? Make me feel better? It didn't. That actually made it worse, it felt as if he'd just been two-timing me with this Lisa all along and I was the last to know. I was just an experiment in pulling an older woman. I'd been such an idiot.

"One less now!" I said, dramatically. "We're done."

I couldn't help but wonder if Lisa had seen the YouTube video of Jamie telling everyone how sexy he thought I was? No, she was probably thin and hadn't even heard of Viva Voluptuous.

I hung up on him with a dramatic flourish of the phone, flung the offending thing on the sofa and burst into tears.

So that was it, then. The Boy Wonder and I were no more, Canterbury had meant nothing, and the girls (and Paul) had been right. It wasn't really a big surprise; it hadn't ever really felt right from the beginning. I was going to have to go back to my 'falling in love with myself' plan, swear off men – again – and concentrate on Viva Voluptuous and the flash mobs, which were in a couple of weeks. I mentally kicked myself for going 'off plan' in the first place. It was being dumped that made me decide that I needed to give myself some TLC in the first place, and wasn't it typical that as soon as I started to come around to the idea of letting a man back in, he let me down instead?

I wasn't in the mood to tell anyone that I'd just dumped Jamie yet, so I just gave myself the rest of the morning off, snuffled a bit, surfed the Internet and ate biscuits. Don't knock it, it worked for me.

After I'd sulked enough, I decided to cheer myself up by adding the two Glastonbury videos to the blog and writing a blog post.

GLASTONBURY SHENANIGANS

If you'd told me this time last week that I'd be brushing shoulders with Jessie J, Ellie Goulding and drinking cider in the same bar as Cara DeLevigne, I would have rolled my eyes and laughed at you. But that's what happened to me when I was at Glastonbury. Oh, and watch this space if you want to see a fabulous interview I did with the gorgeous Paloma Faith.

We managed to get our hands on backstage VIP passes to meet Paloma Faith and we had a fantastic time celeb-spotting. The things you need to know about Glasto, the vital things are:

If you don't get a VIP pass, you'll have to use the Portaloos or the long drops. Take it from me; go for the long drops every time. If you're bigger than a small child, moving around in a Portaloo is seriously compromised, and if it's warm, three days of sunshine on a plastic cabin filled with – well, you know – is not good. The long drops are open but more bearable. Oh and two more tips: loo roll and hand sanitiser spray are ESSENTIALS.

Remember to take a torch. Lighting is not good.

You won't get to see everyone you think you want to. The festival is HUGE and it takes ages to walk between just the Pyramid and Other stages, let alone the smaller ones. Pick out a few absolutely unmissable acts and then just see where you end up.

Everyone else is just as unwashed as you. It really doesn't matter.

Just take baby wipes and hope for the best.

You won't be able to charge your phone anywhere, except the O2 tent, where the queue will be horrendous. Embrace the silence. Everyone who matters will be at Glasto anyway J

It was brilliant - Glastonbury is a really chilled out festival. We saw men dressed as women, people in giant Womble costumes, Smurfs, an army of people dressed as Slash, and a group of nuns. I bet they were hot under there. It was refreshing not to feel like I didn't fit in there, because there were no rules, no dress code, and everyone was there to have a good time."

Lauren was full of news when I met her for coffee. She didn't even give me a chance to tell her how Zoe and I had got on at Glastonbury, and "I've dumped Colin!" was the first thing she said to me as she handed me an Americano. We walked across to the nearest table, only slightly sticky, and I digested this welcome news as I put my coffee down.

"At last!" was my considered reply. "When? How did he take it? Is he waiting outside your front door with flowers every day? If you had a bunny I'd be hiding your saucepans."

"Ha!" snorted Lauren, "He's not quite that bad. He was all upset, but I told him a little white lie and said I was just too busy trying to find a new job, and that it was too difficult to maintain a relationship while I was living with my parents. He offered to let me move in with him, again, but I said I needed my space. He doesn't like it one bit, but he was seriously starting to get on my nerves."

"Starting to?" I said, raising an eyebrow.

"Yeah, yeah, OK. He's been doing it for months."

I stirred my drink purposefully. "Well, we're both going to be single and on the pull, then." I admitted.

"Really? I thought you were Miss Loved Up with Jamie? What's he done now?"

I sighed deeply for dramatic effect. "Oh, just sleeping with some other girl the whole time we were seeing each other.

Apparently you have to ask someone if they want to be in an 'exclusive' relationship these days if you don't want them shagging around as soon as you go away for three days."

"What an arsehole." Lauren replied, with a concerned look.

"I've been an idiot haven't I? The funny thing is, after a bit of wailing and copious carbohydrate ingestion this morning, I actually feel OK. It's like I knew he was just a fling, even if I didn't want to admit it."

"So we won't get any late night 'nobody loves me' rants by text then, like we did with Mark?" "I can't promise anything." I grinned. "I'm embarrassed more than anything. I let my hormones get the better of me."

"I wouldn't mind a dose of lust-fuelled sex myself, to be honest." Lauren pouted. Her descriptions of Colin's pre-sex routine had Zoë and me in stitches more than once. He had to shower, make sure the bed was clear, fold everything up on the chair by the window and lie on his side of the bed before any action could commence. It hadn't exactly been wildly passionate.

"Lust ain't all it's cracked up to be. Although when it's wrapped up in a very cute package that's ten years younger than you and covered in cute freckles, it can be quite distracting..." I said wistfully. "Anyway, it will free me up to do more work on the blog, pitch ideas for articles and maybe even do some more work for Glammazon."

That was when I remembered I still hadn't called Adrian back. Damn. Oh well, I'd give him a call later. There hadn't been any narky emails from him in my inbox when I got home, so I assumed everything was OK.

"I've been looking at houses," Lauren said, "but I think I'm going to have to go for outside the city, as I need somewhere big enough that I can rent out a room. The rents in the city are heinous, I have no idea how you afford your place."

"I can't, really," I admitted, "but I'm just about keeping my head above water and the landlady at bay. I'm waiting for a miracle, a lottery win or something to give me the money so I don't have to stress every month about my disappearing savings account!"

"I've got my redundancy money to tide me over for a bit, but I need something or else I'll get bored" Lauren mused, as she checked her phone. "I'm waiting to hear back from a couple of agencies but nothing doing yet." She seemed distracted, and didn't seem too interested in hearing about Glastonbury, apart from the Paloma Faith interview.

"How did you manage that?" she asked when I showed her the footage. I don't think she believed I had it in me. "I'm in with the stars," I lied. She'd seemed faintly disgusted at the Portaloo debacle, although she'd agreed it was funny when Zoë kicked off. "She's feisty, isn't she?" Lauren laughed as she watched Zoë put the Super tramp man firmly in his place. I left her watching the rest of the videos and went up to get more drinks in. I could tell Lauren needed something to do, she wasn't herself. I texted Zoë while I was deliberating whether to have a chocolate twist or an apricot pastry with my second latte, *"Can you get to Costa? Impromptu flash mob meeting."*

The queue wasn't moving fast at all, and Zoë had texted back before I'd got to the front of it.

"I'm on it, be there in 20. On a bit of *a Glasto comedown"* I sniggered to myself. How ironic.

Zoe arrived, dropped her oversized bag on the floor, tucked her shades behind her ears and looked at me expectantly. "So what did I miss?"

"We've got to get organised. We need more people or we're just going to look daft. It's all hands on deck." I bossed.

"Someone get me a green tea and I'll get my thinking head on." Zoë said, pulling a chair from the table next to us and smiling sweetly at the couple who were sitting there, having a bit of an argument. Lauren dutifully went over to the queue, while I stared at my cooling coffee waiting for inspiration, or Zoë, to come up with a way to attract hordes of people to next week's event.

"How about we set up a Facebook group? Invite Viva Voluptuous members? Tempt them in with lots of descriptions about how much fun it's gonna be. A day out in London or Manchester...shopping opps, maybe getting on the telly...?" Zoe suggested.

"Really? Do you think that would work?" I asked. I wasn't sure about the logistics, we wanted lots of people but there was no point making it really public – the whole thing about the flash mob was supposed to be the element of surprise, surely?

"Well, it's worth a try, isn't it? We can set up an event for all three mobs, and invite group members. That way we can work on 'em all and try and build up a bit of a buzz?"

"I think it's a good start," Lauren said as she handed Zoë her tea. "Most people are on Facebook. Invite them all to join a private group and they'll be intrigued. Then invite them to an event and you'll make them feel special. We need someone to come up with brilliant descriptions for each event though, get people all excited."

Both women looked right at me. "That means me, then?"

"Well it was your idea," Zoë smiled sweetly. "Anyway, you're brilliant at flowering things up. You can think of something, and we'll set up the groups. There are people on the forum already who're really into it, get them involved too."

We had a week. Was Facebook going to be enough? "OK, I'll do that but how about this – why don't you two make a video with dance moves for the girls to copy, so they can learn it for the big day?" Zoë looked horrified, and Lauren looked as if she thought I'd gone stark, raving nuts. I took this opportunity to get in before they could come up with a reason why they couldn't do it. "Look, most people know the song. All we have to do is come up with a sort of YMCA-style dance so that we're all dancing from the same...hymn sheet?" I explained, hurriedly, and choosing to ignore the complete mess I'd made of my clichés.

"I can't dance!" Lauren wailed. "That's why I can't do it!"

"You think I can?" pouted Zoë, "I think I can when I've had a few glasses of wine but really, darling, I am not the best person for your dance video."

I sighed. "Don't you see? That's the point! You don't have to be any good. I'm useless too. It's all about having a laugh, right? If we get that across, that the whole thing is about having fun, laughing at ourselves, and looking foxy while we do it, it's going to get way more people in than if we're all serious and proper."

They couldn't argue, although the look on Lauren's face told me she was trying very hard to think of a way to do just that.

"Look, I'll do the descriptions. I'll video you two prancing about like nutters and we can upload it all at the same time we set the groups up. Maximum impact. What do you think?"

"Nope, not doing it." Zoe said in her very best "Don't try to persuade me" voice.

"Aw Zo..." I said miserably. "If you're going to do it on the day, what's the difference anyway?" Lauren was still keeping very quiet. She liked people to think she was buttoned-up and sensible but to be honest there was nothing she enjoyed more than letting her hair down and I'd seen her dancing on many a podium in the past.

"Alright. For you, I'll do it." Lauren said, clearly uncomfortable about the whole idea. "Just so long as we film the video indoors, yeah? Not outside." She turned to Zoë, who was scowling ever-so slightly. "You're better than me at this sort of thing, Zo. I couldn't choreograph my way out of a paper bag. Let's get onto YouTube and see if we can find some inspiration."

"You're evil, Ellie Johnstone," Zoe mumbled.

"But you love me?" I replied. She didn't confirm or deny...

Chapter 23

The morning of June 30th dawned and it was fantastically sunny. I was so beside myself I could hardly contain it as I got myself ready for the event we'd been planning for months.

So many people had been looking at the blog since I'd added the Paloma Faith clip. I was getting messages from people all over the world - including Venezuela, Estonia and New Zealand, and I was particularly proud of one that had described me as a comedy genius. Everyone was predictably falling in love with Zoë too, and she was becoming a bit of a celebrity in her own right, with people asking on blogs 'Who is this woman?'

The girls' dance video was predictably hilarious. I hadn't been allowed to see them filming, "It will put me off" Zoë moaned, but the result was comedy gold and when I uploaded it the comments came in thick and fast.

"Those two are gorgeous"

"Makes me feel better for not being able to dance"

"I'll be there on Saturday!"

Zoë pretended not to be bothered, but secretly she loved every minute of the attention she was getting. As a result of all the positive press, we were getting loads of people to the website and if everyone who had joined the event on Facebook and said they were going to turn up for the flash mobs actually did, it was going to be absolutely amazing.

"Oh my God, are we really going to do this?" I said to Zoë, while we waited at Cambridge station for our respective trains. "I'm so excited I think I'm going to wet myself" she giggled. "Not in that lovely outfit," was my stern reply.

"Have you got everything?" I asked about a zillion times. I'd gone over everything in my head, we'd synchronised our phones and we'd gone over the plans for each event over and over again.

Lauren knew the Trafford Centre pretty well as she often

frequented the designer shoe boutiques, so she had her route all planned out. She called me as I was on the train.

"I've done the walk, let alone that stupid dance, in my head about 50 times this morning. I'm meeting the rest of the girls in the car park and we're all going to walk down the walkway and into the mall together. It's fine. Don't panic!"

"I'm not panicking!" I lied.

I sat on the train to London done up in my over the top burlesque-style regalia. I was too scared to get a coffee in case I spilled any down my cleavage, which was somewhere up around my ears in the tightly-laced corset I was wearing. Surprisingly, nobody really stared at me, although my boobs did attract a bit of attention from some of the men on the train. Maybe they were just afraid? I did spot a couple of other beautifully-dressed larger ladies on the train to Kings Cross but didn't want to ask them if they were heading for Covent Garden in case they were just going to a show...

Zoë had already been up to the shopping centre at Westfield Stratford City to check out the layout and she knew where she was going to assemble her gang.

"I've given all my girls my mobile number just in case things go tits up" she'd assured me earlier that morning.

My heart was racing as I got off at Kings Cross and made my way to the Tube. I did feel a bit of an arse, but I was so happy that this was happening I didn't care about the funny looks I was getting. This is London, I thought to myself, get over it! *"Are you there yet?"* Lauren texted

"Just getting on the Piccadilly Line" I replied.

"I'm here. Looking good. Got butterflies. Being stared at by small child." She sent back. I tucked my phone in my bag as I headed underground. Oh crap, the platform was heaving and it was going to be a 'mare getting on a crowded Tube train in this get up. Oh well. I barged my way through onto the first available train and felt my boobs squash even further towards my face as I

was backed into a corner by a cross looking old man. I could see a few big girls getting on a few carriages down, but there was no way I could attract their attention. I hoped I'd just catch up with them when I got off the train.

I hate the underground at the best of times and it was really busy that morning. The butterflies in my tummy were driving me crazy, as I ran over and over the plans in my head. Get everyone together. Get to Covent Garden for 11. Music on. Dance. Run for it.

On Facebook I'd told everyone to come and find me at Patisserie Valerie, which was behind the Market Building in Bedford Street. I pushed my way off the train, made my way to the lifts and then through the station, out into the gorgeous sunshine and fresh air. Well, we'd picked a good day for it. It was only five past ten, we had ages. The place was absolutely packed though; everyone had come out in the sunshine. I couldn't see the girls I'd spotted earlier, but hoped they'd find me by the café.

Three beeps on my phone alerted me to Zoë's arrival at Westfield. She was ready to go. *"I can't see many people"* she texted, clearly stressing a bit. I wanted to give her a call but it was way too noisy. There was a band playing right where I'd hoped to be…I crossed my fingers that they'd bugger off by 11.

"How many are you expecting?" I texted Zoë back, as I headed away from the noise and people to the relative quiet of Bedford Street.

"At least 35" was her answer. It wasn't that many but it was a small mall anyway, so I guessed the main thing was that she had a few people turn up.

I waited nervously outside Patisserie Valerie, and was more relieved that you can imagine when my first two ladies arrived a few minutes later. "I'm Karen," said the first woman, who had really gone to town and was wearing a long dress with Marilyn Monroe style white gloves and heels.

"You look stunning!" I exclaimed, "Thank you so much for

coming!"

Her friend, Katya, was very large, and she worked it. Accessorising her stretchy pencil skirt and striking hot pink lace tunic top with the most enormous flower in her hair, she towered over me in platform heels. She had a killer smile and long black hair which she'd put up in a ponytail high on her crown. She really did look amazing. I wanted to hug them for just turning up.

By 10.30 there was a crowd of impeccably turned out women forming in Bedford Street, and I felt immeasurably proud looking at them all. So many gorgeous women who all looked amazing. Most of them were wearing dresses; some had gone the full hog and dressed in corsets, ruffles and bows, and sexy skirts. There were a few prom dresses, some vintage style outfits and plenty of bling. I even spotted one or two tiaras.

The next half-hour passed so slowly that I felt like I was counting the minutes. I popped into the shop and bought a coffee, against my better judgement. I was gasping!

"Is there a carnival or something?" said the kindly man who served me, as he looked me up and down.

"We're performing in the square a bit later" I said, mysteriously, handing him the money for my drink.

"Oh, right. What sort of performance?" he enquired. "Dance!" I laughed. Well, if you could call it that. I took my latte and walked out of the shop, giggling to myself.

"So why did you decide to do this?" one of the quieter women asked me, as I walked back to the girls, "It's a brilliant idea, but you must have to be really confident to set something like this up."

"Not at all" I laughed. "I'm just fed up with the way fat people get such bad press, and I wanted to get out there and do something about it!"

"Do you think this will really help?" the girl, called Linda, asked. She looked slightly dubious and I felt as if she wasn't really sure why she'd signed up to this.

"It isn't going to change things overnight. But it'll be fun and we might change a few people's minds." I replied. I felt like I wanted to find out more.

"What made you come along today?" I asked.

"I've just split from my husband," Linda said quietly. She continued, "We were together for sixteen years and all that time I got fatter and fatter. He was horrible about it, called me a fat bitch and refused to sleep with me until I lost weight. Most of the time he was OK but I thought I deserved it because I couldn't stick to a diet. Anyway, it turned out he was sleeping with a woman at work, and that was the final straw. I found you when I was looking for a slimming club, believe it or not. You seemed so confident and happy with being fat and I thought, why not?"

I could have cried. Viva Voluptuous had saved someone from slimming club hell!

I did wonder what I thought I was doing though, as I walked up towards the market at 10.55. My heart was beating like crazy and I was trying to take a few deep breaths while I pretended to be Miss In Control. What if we couldn't set up because the band were still there? I couldn't hear them and I thought they'd gone. Why didn't I check? I was stressing now. Trust me not to be organised. I'd look a total idiot if we had nowhere to stop.

Thankfully, there was a bit of space where we needed it. "Go!" I half-shouted and everyone headed for it. We were just about in place when on the dot of 11, I set the box down on the ground, in front of the Market, surrounded by the VV tribe and pressed play. After a slight delay, when I started to panic that the stereo had died on me, Gloria Gaynor kicked in with "I am what I am…"

Gloria took me over as I sang, flung my arms around and wiggled my backside in time to the music. I completely forgot the agreed routine, although some of the girls seemed to have got it off by heart. I was grinning like a loon as I belted out "Life's not worth a DAMN until you can shout out I AM what I a-a-a-a-a-am!"

I twirled round, wiggled, almost caught Linda, who was standing next to me, with my elbow, and lost myself in the overwhelming feeling of happiness that had hit me out of nowhere. I was loving it! Perhaps I was a natural extrovert after all. Just give me some cheesy music and off I go.

The sight and sound of 60 or so voluptuous women, dressed up to the nines and singing their hearts out to Gloria Gaynor seemed to stop the very busy market in its tracks, just for a couple of minutes. The adrenalin rushed through my veins as I carried on singing at the top of my voice, complete with theatrical flourishes and wiggles.

"There's one life and there's no return and no deposit, one life so it's time to open up your closet." It was obvious that not everyone knew the words, but buoyed up by the spectacle, some of the crowd were clapping and joining in too. We seemed to attract a few more people as the song went on, not all fat, just wanting to have a bit of a sing. It made me smile.

Some of the girls could hardly sing for laughing, and others were getting right into the flow and singing every word like they meant it. I knew we were being filmed on several mobiles, and hammed it up deliberately as I caught a group of Japanese tourists with their video camera.

One woman, Nicole, a good size 24, had gone all out and was wearing a full length crimson evening dress with a faux fur stole, which she waved dramatically in time to the music. She looked a little bit unsteady on her stripper heels, but as far as I was concerned she deserved ten out of ten for effort and was having a fabulous time. The sun was out, there wasn't a cloud in the sky and it was getting pretty hot now, but we carried on regardless. The sizes of the ladies ranged from barely a 16 to the larger end of the scale, but without exception, they were all dressed up and looking glamorous. What's more, everyone looked like they were having the time of their lives!

The song goes on for longer than you might think, and I had a funny feeling we might get moved on at some point. As it happened, we got away with it and managed to perform the full 5.57 and even got a huge round of applause. I did spot a couple of PCSOs in the crowd but I think they might have been laughing too much to stop us in full flow. As Gloria faded away I took a bow, swept up the music box, flounced off and shouted, "Come on ladies!"

They all followed me in the general direction of the tube station, posing for photographs as they went, curtseying, bowing and waving. I was on a massive high. It had worked! We'd pulled it off! Paul, who'd foregone his football and come to cheer me on (while hiding around the corner) gave me a massive hug and called me a genius. I called Lauren first, still on a massive high.

"So…tell me, Lady, how did it go?"

"It was brilliant" Lauren told me, "We had over sixty people I think, and the crowds were a bit bemused, but they stopped and started, and I know I saw loads of people with cameras. I think a few of them were joining in and singing along, and some of the shop staff came out for a nosey as well. I think we pulled it off."

Good old Lauren, I knew I'd be able to rely on her to organise her end of things.

"You're a star. Yay to us!!" I said, appreciatively.

"That's not all," she carried on. "Guess who managed to tip off the local press about five minutes before the event? We didn't get a massive response but one of the local rags sent a reporter down just to see what was going on, and even better, she was a plus size girl herself. She was LOVING it."

"No way! Fan-freaking-tastic!"

"Yes, way. She stopped me after we'd finished, as the rest of the girls went back to the car park. Everyone was clapping and it was just, oh I dunno, just so lovely. And the reporter asked me all about VV and what we were doing, so I gave her a few really good quotes about you, the campaign, and even mentioned Jane, but I didn't give any details about her. She thinks you're amazing."

"I think you're amazing, Lauren Greene." I said. Because she was.

I filled her in on how Covent Garden had gone, and then after we'd compared notes, she said, "I think you'd better call Zoë." She said with a hint of laughter.

She refused to elaborate, so I hung up after telling her how amazing she was again and called Zoë.

"I've been trying to call you!" Zoë exclaimed. "Have you spoken to Lauren?"

"Just got off the phone from her now" I said, "It went really, really well. How did Stratford go?"

"Ummm…." She began…"Pretty good, well, mostly. Except the being thrown out by arsey security bit."

"Security? What did you do?" I said, slightly concerned.

"They came at us like we were a bunch of terrorists, grabbed the stereo and switched it off!" She said, clearly disgruntled. "I was mortified!

"It's not so bad, though," Zoë said, trying to make the whole thing sound a bit less disastrous, "I managed to get a decent amount of people there, loads of people were pointing and laughing, we got a big ol' crowd going and one of them works for a PR firm in the city, so she's offered to help us out if we need it."

"Did they tell you why they were so mean?" I asked, feeling Zoë's disappointment.

"They said it was something to do with health and safety," she replied. "Whatever."

"That's crap. They're just killjoys." I moaned. "There aren't any plus-sized shops at Westfield are there?"

"Not that I know of," Zoë agreed, "they probably just didn't want fat people cluttering the place up." I could tell that my friend had felt a bit let down, but I pointed out that none of this had been her fault; she'd just been a bit unlucky. She'd done a brilliant job getting everything organised, and although I hadn't seen the pictures yet, her descriptions of some of the outfits made it sound as if everyone had gone to a lot of effort to dress up and get involved.

All in all, I think we could call that a success.

Chapter 24

FLASHMOB AT THE SHOPPING CENTRE!

"If you'd gone down to the Trafford Centre at the weekend, you'd have been in for a big surprise – as were the shoppers who found themselves regaled with "I am what I am" by a group of beautifully-dressed plus sized women. The group, who appeared from nowhere at 11am, danced and sung to the 70s disco classic, led by Lauren Greene who explained what the flash mob was in aid of when we caught up with her after the event.

Lauren told us, "The flash mobs are all part of a campaign started by Ellie Johnstone, creator of the Viva Voluptuous website. You might have seen some of Ellie's videos already – she interviewed Paloma Faith at Glastonbury recently, who is a supporter of the campaign too. We're fed up with the way that fat people – mainly women – are portrayed in the media, and the obsession with thinness that's ruining so many women's lives.

We want to promote positive body image – and when we say that, we don't mean the silly 'Real women' nonsense that gets trotted out by people who want to make thin women feel as bad as fat women already do. No, we want to promote body confidence for everyone. We're ALL real women, and we all deserve to look and feel good."

Lauren certainly proved her point with a stunning display of plus sized women, all glammed up to the nines and having a fabulous time. Apparently there was a similar event in London's Covent Garden as well as a slightly less successful attempt in the mall at Westfield Stratford City. "

We couldn't possibly have predicted the furore that our flash mobs created. Quite apart from the article in the local news, beautifully set up by Lauren, the website community was getting more and more members; we'd made it onto three news websites and of course Lauren made sure that she email-bombed just about everyone she knew telling them about it.

Which is why when I got the call from the *Daily Recorder,* a down market tabloid specialising in 'exclusives' about Katie Price or reality stars, I wasn't suspicious.

"Of course I'll do it" I agreed when the assistant ran the idea past me, "What do you want me to do?"

"It's an opinion piece. You and a fitness type, you get to tell readers why you think you can be fat and happy, and then the other person gives their opinion."

It sounded harmless, even fun. "We'll sort out make-up and hair, and if you let me have your dress size I can organise some clothes to choose from too?"

I liked the sound of it.

When I got there, the shoot wasn't anywhere close to being glamorous; it was in an old warehouse in the middle of nowhere. They sent a taxi to pick me up from the station. I'd turned up looking like I'd just fallen out of bed, looking forward to my glamorous makeover. When I arrived at the warehouse it smelled damp and musty. There was a camera and lights set up in one of the corners, and a middle-aged man was loitering around, fiddling with the lights and tutting to himself loudly. I knocked on the door to get his attention and he jumped.

"Hello?" I started, nervously, "Am I in the right place for the photo shoot?"

He gestured towards the kit in the corner and said, sarcastically, "Yes, love. You're a bit early."

I wasn't. I was bang on time by my reckoning, but I didn't want to argue with him. "I'll wait," I said nervously.

I busied myself texting Zoë and Lauren, telling them I wasn't sure about this. A glamorous, petite blonde appeared a bit later, perfectly made up and looking amazing. "Please tell me that's the makeup artist", I thought to myself. Of course, it wasn't. That was my opponent. I thought I might as well be friendly so I started chatting to her and hoped someone would arrive soon and tell me what the hell was going on. We talked quite amiably about the shoot. It turned out that Tracie, or Rapunzel, as I nicknamed her, was a personal trainer with her own business. Not to mention a part-time model. She had to be no more than a size eight, and she was disarmingly nice, too.

Eventually, the shoot coordinator arrived, looking flustered.

"Sorry I'm late" she called cheerfully, "Stuck in traffic! Shall we get started?"

What do you mean, shall we get started? I panicked. My hair wasn't done, I had no makeup on, and I was dressed in my comfy train clothes. A loose top and yesterday's leggings. There was absolutely no way I was going to be photographed next to Rapunzel wearing my tatty leggings, not to mention with a bare face and hair that had been left to dry naturally because I thought it was being styled.

Unfortunately, that was exactly what I ended up doing.

I was posed next to the model, who smiled seductively and worked the camera as I shuffled awkwardly; following the photographer's instructions to crouch down, lean back, move a bit to the right, turn my head to the left and the rest. I'd managed to dig out an emergency lipstick and some concealer but other than that, I was as nature intended. Rapunzel, on the other hand, looked like she'd just walked off the cover of a magazine. If I could have escaped right there and then I would have walked out of that damp warehouse and gone home. The only problem was that I didn't have any taxi numbers and I wasn't entirely sure where I was. Not clever, Ellie.

I couldn't believe I'd been stitched up like that. I was utterly furious. Thankfully, the article wasn't out for a week or so, which gave me a chance to warn people in advance, and write a blog about the disgusting way I'd been stitched up. Hopefully I wouldn't be misquoted in the interview as well, that would really be a pain in the butt. I called the girl who'd set the whole thing up when I'd finally managed to get out of the warehouse and back on the train home. When I asked her where the stylist and makeup artist had got to, she at least had the decency to pretend to sound sorry and surprised that she hadn't turned up.

"I'll look into it and get back to you," she promised. Would she hell, I thought. I was so angry that I blogged about it as soon as I got home.

DASTARDLY TACTICS

I have been right royally stitched up by a horrible low-rent tabloid. You've heard of The Recorder? Apparently, for some reason it's one of the most popular newspapers in the country. Don't believe everything you read, is all I'll say.

I went up there for a photo shoot today and was promised a full on glamorous look to go with the interview, but I turned up au naturel and was met with…nothing. Except a model who just happened to be in full make up. Complaining about fat people looking a mess.

Do you smell a rat? I smell a whole lab-fuil of them, and I'm so angry. This is the sort of shitty treatment fat people get. Right now, there will be a few smug people having a right laugh at how they got one over on the fat girl who thought she was something special.

You know what? I am special. I'm a better person than any of their editorial team, or the mean person that thought up this hilarious prank, because I'm trying to help people feel GOOD about themselves and they are just trying to reinforce dull, boring stereotypes that are designed to make people feel BAD.

It's the last time I trust the press. And I haven't even seen the interview yet."

Once I'd got that out of my system, I sat down and quietly congratulated myself on the things that had gone right. The video of the Covent Garden flash mob had gone viral, turning up on blogs everywhere. It was amazing to see the whole thing filmed from start to finish. I could hear people muttering, "what's going on?" as we all walked up to the Market together and someone shrieked, "Euw, they are all fat birds!"

What an idiot. I hadn't heard that on the day, and almost wished that I had because I'd been in such a freaking fabulously good mood that I would have come back with something clever for a change. I carried on watching - I hadn't been able to take it all in as it was happening, so it was lovely to get the chance to see the amount of effort that everyone had gone to, to dress up for the event, which only amounted to a few minutes after all. I heard an American man comment and whistle as a girl in a cute prom dress wiggled, giggled and flashed her thighs coquettishly in time to the song. I heard someone saying "They look amazing, where are they from?" In fact, most of what I heard was positive, although one teenage boy pretended to vomit and a twenty-something skinny girl tutted as she walked past and said that if she ever got that fat she wouldn't go outside, let alone make a show of herself in public. We had a long way to go.

I lost myself in watching the video, feeling so proud of myself, Zoë and Lauren, and the wonderful women who'd made such a massive effort for my little campaign and me. It would take more than a stitch up by a grotty tabloid to derail me now. As I uploaded the video to the Viva Voluptuous blog, I felt a huge wave of happiness, as I realised that after all the crap I'd gone through earlier in the year, the rubbish men and even the lies Darren had told the *Daily News* about me, I was feeling more confident now than I ever had done in my life. Now I just had to harness that feeling. It was just at that moment that my email pinged and I got the news I wanted – all three of us were going to be on TV…

Chapter 25

"Relax, they're both lovely."

The girl who was applying industrial levels of stage makeup to my face was trying to calm me down. I smiled, and replied, "Thanks – I've never been on TV."

The interview on the One Show had to be one of the most nerve-wracking things I'd ever done. It rated alongside my first ever smear test and all of my three driving tests in the terrifying scale, and although Zoë and Lauren were pretending to be cool with it, both being way more media-savvy than me, I could tell they were nervous too. Zoë kept fiddling with her nose stud, which as well as being a disgusting habit, meant she was getting stressed. Lauren had just gone quiet, and Lauren didn't do quiet as a rule.

Somehow the makeup artist had managed to make huge amounts of slap look almost natural. We were all done up in the outfits we'd worn to our various flash mob events, and we'd told everyone we knew to look out for us on TV. My mum had also told just about everyone she knew and so the weight of a lot of people's expectations was definitely on my shoulders here.

"OK, let's do this!" I glanced at Lauren, who was looking amazing, and at Zoë who was still playing with her nose. I hoped she wasn't going to do that when we were in front of the cameras, as she'd beat herself up for ages if she did.

My mouth was dry and my heart was racing as we were led through to the studio for our slot. The thought of messing up my one and only ever TV appearance was bringing me out in a cold sweat. I was so glad I had the girls with me to charm the presenters!

I felt incredibly exposed as I walked out in front of the cameras and sat down on the famous One Show sofa. They were running the clip of the Covent Garden event as we took our seats, the same one that had appeared everywhere and gone viral. I couldn't help myself giggling, especially when I heard the skinny girl's comment at the end again. Alex smiled at us.

"Ellie Johnstone, Zoë Ellis and Lauren Greene have been in the news recently after they staged three flash mobs in locations in Manchester and London. The girls each turned up at shopping centres surrounded by groups of very well-dressed plus sized ladies, and sang and danced to a Gloria Gaynor song in front of amused crowds, to show the world that it's fine to be fat."

Alex turned first to me and said, "Ellie, you and the other women at Covent Garden look like you're having so much fun on that clip, So go on, what was it that inspired you to put on a show like that – and why three?"

I took a deep breath.

"It was fun, and thank you! Why did we do it? It's a long story. Viva Voluptuous is a positive body image campaign. I was fed up with reading all the negative rubbish about fat people that seems to be everywhere in the media. I was feeling a bit fed up one day, and I read some hurtful comments online saying that all fat people were ugly, lazy and greedy, and I got angry and started blogging..."

I stopped for a breath. I may have said that all very fast indeed. But I carried on regardless.

"I was angry because people are so judgemental. I'm big, and so are these two gorgeous girls" (I gestured to Lauren and Zoë) "and we don't fit the pie-eating, sofa slob stereotype. We all have our own businesses, work hard, look good and even work out. So I thought it would be a really good idea to try and make fat people feel a bit better about themselves by getting a gang together of fabulous, fun, plus-sized women who felt and looked great, enjoyed life and wanted to prove the idiots wrong."

Before she could stop me, I added, "And I had a very close friend when I was younger who died thinking she wasn't good enough because she was fat. If I can stop one woman from feeling that bad about herself, making a fool of myself on TV will have been worth it." Alex politely waited for me to finish and said, "I'm so sorry to hear about your friend, and what you're doing here is just fantastic", then asked, again, "But why a flash mob? And why the three locations?"

Oops, I'd forgotten that bit during my mini rant.

"It was because we wanted to get publicity, really. Doing something people wouldn't expect, something a bit daft and funny would get attention. We hoped it would be filmed by people on their phones and uploaded, emailed and seen by people all over the world."

Another breath. Ellie, you're gabbling again…

"We chose the three locations because of how busy we thought they would be on a Saturday morning in June. Covent Garden was for tourists, and the other two were for the shoppers. We only got moved on from one place so I reckon it was a result, don't you?"

Alex laughed, and turned to Zoë. "Zoë, you were in charge of the Stratford singalong, weren't you?"

Zoë nodded.

"So, how did you feel when the security staff moved you on?"

Zoë sighed, "Well I had a bad feeling about it right from the start, actually. The atmosphere there was quite weird and I spent the whole time looking around to see if security were coming to get us, so I must have had a premonition, as they did! At least we got past the first chorus before they turned the music off. They said we needed a license and they couldn't let us carry on 'cos of health and safety. Spoilsports."

"Spoilsports indeed," Alex laughed, "You all looked amazing on the day, and I see you've got your outfits on that you wore on the day, too. We all want to know where the fantastic costumes came from?"

Lauren, who'd been asked the question, replied, "We had the specially made by a brilliant seamstress in Cambridge, called

Colette Richards. She's designing a completely new range of burlesque costumes, and her corsets are absolutely amazing. The best thing about her is that she knows how to dress a curvy woman, and so we knew that she'd make us all look fantastic."

"You've been the victim of some unfair media coverage in recent months, haven't you, Ellie?" Alex began, with a sudden seriousness, and I could tell she knew she was on dodgy ground as she gave me a look that seemed to say, "Don't worry, I'll be gentle with you."

"How did it make you feel, being exposed like that?"

"Ummm....well. Um, all I can say is that, um, it was all lies - I've never been bulimic in my life, and although I've always struggled with my a weight problem until I gave up dieting for good, I've never had a serious eating disorder. I think it was cruel of my ex-husband to say what he did to the media, not just because it was rubbish, but also because it belittles people who do have eating disorders. Still, people do all sorts of strange things for money, don't they?"

If I'd said what I'd really thought about him, I'd have been bleeped. I thought I'd done remarkably well not to lose my cool there and silently congratulated myself.

"I understand" Alex sympathised. "It must have been upsetting, and if you've never had an eating disorder, I can imagine you were really angry."

My silence indicated that I didn't want to talk about Darren's lies any more.

"There are people who believe that the negative press obesity gets is necessary to encourage people to lose weight and get healthy," continued Alex, changing the subject. "Do you agree that there is a problem with obesity in the UK? And what would you say to people who think they are doing the right thing by highlighting the health risks, people who might say what you're doing is irresponsible?"

Lauren interjected, "I ran a half marathon last year, but I'm a size 18. Am I fit, or unhealthily obese?"

"Good point" Alex agreed. I continued, "Overweight people might be put off going to the gym, thinking that it's full of skinny people, judging them. Constantly belittling and insulting obese men and women doesn't do them any good. It makes them feel worthless, and in a lot of cases it can send them straight to the biscuit tin to comfort eat. I know I've been there!"

Alex and Matt laughed at that. I didn't think it was that funny, but still.

By now I was gesticulating, waving my hands about and getting quite worked up. I saw Zoë flinch out of the corner of my eye as my right hand went flying in her direction. "Encouraging overweight people to get fit without the emphasis on losing weight, improving their self- image and making them feel good about themselves is much more likely to work than nasty comments about being fat. Someone who actually thinks they are worth looking after is much more likely to take care of their body than someone bullied into weight loss and made to feel less than human"

I was definitely on a roll. I could hear people starting to cheer and clap. Oh boy.

"And me, Zoë and Lauren all prove that you don't have to be slim to be fit. I'm at the gym three times a week, Zoë is a yoga-bunny and Lauren's already told you about her half marathon. None of us are a size ten, so where does that leave the critics?"

"Wow!" exclaimed Alex. "You're really passionate about this, aren't you?"

"We all are" Zoë interrupted. "We set up a website, Viva Voluptuous, with a blog, and a community for plus-size people, so that we could give the plus-size community a voice. We're not the only big women, or men, who are sick of seeing all the nastiness about obese people. It's like a socially-acceptable prejudice, the one 'ism' that people are allowed to be open about. You can't insult anyone based on their race, religion, gender or sexuality, and that's a good thing, but you can say whatever you like about a big section of the population, on the excuse that it's in their interest. Sorry, but why is that acceptable?"

More people were clapping. We'd hit a nerve. I was really enjoying myself now, and it looked like Lauren and Zoë were having a great time, too.

Alex looked thoughtful. She replied, "That's a very good point. I never thought of it that way. I know that some people do turn to food when they are feeling upset, so it makes sense that upsetting them wouldn't help; it would just make them comfort eat even more. That does make a lot of sense. So, are there any more plans for dancing in the street?"

I laughed. "Do you have any idea about the logistics of organising something like that? It was an absolute nightmare! It was great fun though. We all have plans for the future – Zoë is writing a book, I'm trying to grow the online community and keep up with the blogging. Lauren is the brains behind the outfit, and she gets us all the attention, too. Oh, and look out for an interview in the *Daily Recorder* soon, where I'm talking body-acceptance with a part-time model and fitness trainer!"

"It sounds like you're all going to be really busy. Thanks so much for coming to talk to us, ladies, it's been a pleasure. And good luck with all your projects!"

We all smiled graciously, stood up and walked off to cheers and claps. I think we'd managed that one. I didn't even trip over any of the camera cables as I made my way to the exit at the back of the studio.

As soon as we were out of the way, we all squealed and hugged each other. "I can't believe we just did that!" I yelped. "We were on the telly!"

"We're damn famous as well as damn gorgeous," Zoë said pulling an exaggerated pout. "I hope I managed to get that on Sky Plus" Lauren laughed, "Would be just my luck if it forgot to record it." We wandered through to hospitality, hoping to meet a celebrity, but then it dawned on us – there wasn't anyone famous...we were the celebrities for a day! People knew who we were, knew what we did, and wanted to talk to us. All at once I was very humbled, very excited and just a little bit scared.

Chapter 26

"Fat versus thin – who's the healthiest?"

Well, that was a crappy headline for a start. I'd been on a high after the One Show, which we'd all agreed had been a massive success.

I'd almost managed to forget my embarrassment at being stitched up monumentally by The Recorder until I saw exactly what they'd done with the article and the unflattering images that went along with it.

"Oh my God" Lauren said seriously, when the girls took me out for a coffee to commiserate. "That's not a good look, is it?"

Zoë had tried to be nice, but no amount of positive spin could make what that horrible newspaper had done to me into a good thing. "You don't look that bad," was the best she could do. She handed me a piece of carrot cake in a desperate attempt to pacify me. I didn't want it. Sugar and carbs weren't anything like enough to make this injustice feel any better.

"Nobody is going to be looking at the words when they are all too busy laughing at the state of me," I moaned. I could hardly bear to look at the double page spread, Rapunzel on one side looking glamorous, me on the other looking like I'd been dragged in off the street.

I hadn't been expecting myself to look amazing, given the circumstances, but in the biggest picture, the one which included both of us, Rapunzel/Tracie was pulling a standard model pose, showing off her toned tummy and legs and still managing to look casual. Her smile lit up the page and she just looked amazing. I, on the other hand, looked a hot mess. Great.

"What the freak did they do to your hair?" Zoë asked, incredulously, studying the photo while she sipped her elderflower tea. She was trying to pretend she wasn't drinking coffee again but I knew she'd been up late all the previous week trying to get some work done on the book, so she wasn't fooling me.

"Nothing. That was the whole point. There was meant to be a stylist, remember?" Although I'd done my best with the comb in my handbag, my hair looked dull and lifeless. It had dried slightly wonky and my fringe wasn't sitting quite straight.

"You were right royally stitched up, weren't you?" said Lauren, stating the obvious.

"That's what I told you, remember?" I sulked. "I wasn't just making it up for sympathy! I bloody hate newspapers. If they aren't digging up creepy ex-husbands to tell lies about me, they're taking pictures of me that make me look like a bag lady."

The others were concerned, but I didn't feel they were treating my misfortune with the seriousness it deserved, and I'm sure I saw Zoë trying not to laugh.

I looked at the pictures again and sighed dramatically, looking for sympathy. I looked huge in the picture, as the top I was wearing was baggy and unflattering. I also looked ever-so slightly angry. That wasn't a complete surprise as I think I clenched my teeth in fury through the whole thing. I could have cried. Now I wanted the carrot cake.

The interview wasn't much better. So much for Miss Sweetness and Light and her kind words about size not being everything. She'd ripped into obese people, describing them as lazy and gluttonous, weak-willed and a waste of taxpayers' money.

"What a bitch" Lauren sniffed, "I thought you said she was lovely?"

"She was, to my face!"

She took the opportunity, of course, to ferociously plug her own fitness courses, and insultingly, even issued me a challenge, asking me to go along to her classes so that she could, "whip me into shape." Silly cow, I could have swung for her! At least my interview had been minimally tinkered with and I sounded mildly sensible. I also thought, smugly, that I sounded like a

MUCH nicer person than Rapunzel.

Meanwhile, the congratulations we'd been getting on our One Show performance had been coming in from all over the place. I'd even had a message from ex-husband, Darren.

"Saw you on TV Ellie. Sorry about the News. You're looking good. Melinda and me aren't together any more. Hope you're OK."

Sorry about the news? Oh God, he meant the quotes he gave the paper. I didn't know whether to reply or not, then decided that the best thing to do would be pretend he hadn't upset me.

"I'm fine. Thanks. Don't worry about the paper, I didn't."

I didn't want to waste any more time on him. Or add that I was sorry he'd split up with his girlfriend. I wasn't sorry at all.

Paul had been super-proud of his best girl-friend, and had helpfully showed the video to most of his mates, including the single ones. He was practically pimping me out to every half decent single male he knew, and I had to call him to explain that I appreciated his help, but actually I wasn't interested in a boyfriend right now. I was having fun being single and all the trouble I'd had with men in the past six months had well and truly put me off the idea of coupling up for a bit.

It was nice to hear their compliments – even though rather a lot of them seemed fixated on my cleavage.

Yet again, the *Daily News* had done a complete character assassination, describing us all as 'roly poly' and making up some daft article around obesity figures being 'worryingly high' due to people like Lauren, Zoë and myself advocating that 'fat women just carry on eating'. They were calling us 'leaders of the new fat-loving movement' – now that wasn't quite how I'd have described us, but trust the *News* to make a good, positive thing sound negative.

They'd illustrated it with the typical 'headless fatty' photo, this time of two very large women on a wall, eating chips. The only good thing about their vicious article was that it gave us a bit more publicity, and included that media clip of Covent

Garden – a few thousand more 'likes' on that would be very welcome, thank you very much! I didn't even read the comments to the article. I actually couldn't be bothered to find out what some over-opinionated idiot sat behind the safety of his screen thought of me. No doubt I'd have absolutely no desire to ever appeal to any of the gutless men that posted badly-spelled bile about fat women on that website anyway.

As I read what they'd written, although I was hacked off beyond belief to start with, I realised what a difference a few months had made. When all this started, just after Mark dumped me, I hadn't been feeling that good about myself, but now I felt great…and look what had happened! I'd been in the papers three times and none of it had been good for my image, I'd been dumped and I'd been duped into having my picture taken with a model to be compared unflatteringly. But even though it stung a bit to read nasty things about myself, I wasn't going to let other people's negativity put me off my mission. The others would never forgive me if I gave up now – every time I asked Zoë for anything in the weeks after the flash mobs she replied, "I danced. On a video. For you," before agreeing to it. I'd come too far and even though it was a bit scary putting myself out there, I couldn't imagine going back now. I had to carry on – even though I wasn't quite sure where I was going to take Viva Voluptuous next.

Every time I had a message, email or comment from someone who told me they'd been inspired to give up diets and just 'be' it cancelled out all the snidey bitchy news comments. And to be fair, the *Daily News* had called us 'leaders' – that had to be good, right?

The newspaper article was like the elephant in the room when I met Zoë, Lauren and Colette for dinner in the tapas restaurant the night it was published. They'd got there before me and deliberately lined up platters of all my favourite tapas along with a large glass of wine. But although I was a bit annoyed at being played by the tabloids, I was dealing with it all with a shrug and a "So what?"

"How are you feeling?" asked Colette, timidly. It wasn't like Colette to be timid.

"I'm absolutely fine" I replied, picking an olive from the bowl on the table and popping it into my mouth. After chewing for a bit, I added, "although if I ever come across Rapunzel again, she's going to get a copy of the *Daily Recorder* shoved up her tiny backside."

"Yeah, she doesn't do a lot for female solidarity, does she?" Lauren said scathingly. "It's just typical though, the whole pitching fat women and slim women against each other."

I rolled my eyes. "Tell me about it. It's so bloody frustrating that women have to pull each other to pieces all the time. Classic divide and conquer. I really believe that society likes to keep us women in our place by making us turn on each other and spend way too much time hating ourselves. If women just woke up and realised what was going on, we'd damn well take over the world!"

Zoë clapped theatrically. "Well said girlfriend!" she exclaimed.

We all tucked in to the delicious food, and knocked back wine as we caught up on each other's news. Colette was treating us to the meal as a thank you for our plugging the studio on TV for her. She was beside herself with excitement, "I've been flooded with people wanting corsets and I've got absolutely no idea how I'm going to get them all made!" she enthused.

"If you want any help with the design, babe, I'm your girl," offered Zoë, helpfully.

"And me!" I added.

"Don't forget me, either." Lauren chimed in.

It looked as if we all wanted in on that particular project.

Lauren had some news for us – in the last few days she'd been for another two house viewings and she'd finally found a gorgeous three-storey place not far from the City that wasn't too expensive,

"I just need some sucker to move into the spare room and help me pay for it."

I'd have offered but I loved my little flat so much – it was small but the location was fantastic and it just felt like me. I couldn't see myself moving out for a while, unless the money ran out anyway.

Zoë was happy where she was too. I couldn't imagine her and Lauren moving in together either – if it weren't for me, they'd probably never have been friends. Zoë's ditsy-ness and disorganisation drove Lauren, who was used to having things scheduled, arranged and planned well in advance, absolutely nuts. She'd come to love Zoë in small doses but I couldn't imagine them sharing a house.

"No offers, then?" Lauren said ruefully. I don't think she'd actually expected any.

"Sorry honey, I'm not giving up my views across the common for anyone, not even you." I laughed. Colette had a twelve-year-old daughter at school on the other side of town to Lauren's new place, and she was a single mum, so the chances of her wanting to move in with Lauren were remote.

Zoë remained diplomatically silent. She had been uncharacteristically quiet lately, as she'd been working really hard on getting some more words written for her book. She'd also been on a few dates, with perfectly nice men, but just not felt anything for any of them, so she'd decided that rather than wasting her time on men she didn't really like that much, she was going to wait for Mr Perfect. Lauren and I laughed a little bit too loud when she went into detail about her latest 'finding romance' theory.

"What?" she mock-whined, "There's got to be someone out there for me. I've put my request in to the Universe, done a little love ritual, and now I'm just going to sit back and wait for Mr Amazing to be delivered."

"Does he come ready-wrapped with a big pink bow?" I teased. She pretended to sulk, and I said, "Oh come on, it's funny. There's no such thing as cosmic ordering, and if there was, I'd be rich, living in a massive villa in Italy and having my pasta cooked for me by Johnny Depp. Oh – is that too much information?"

Lauren giggled again. "Can you conjure me up a real man, please, while you're waving your fairy wand? I don't want another man with more shoes than me and a cleaning obsession; I want a rugged, muscular bit of rough who's going to treat me like a princess."

"No. You have to do it yourself. Write it down, exactly what you want. Send it out to the Universe. Keep the page you've written it on, and you'll see. One day, you'll get what you asked for."

"Whaaatever." This might just have been one New Age theory that was too far-fetched for me.

We had a great girl's night out, planning world domination via You Tube and corsetry, talking about going away for a weekend somewhere, and congratulating ourselves on what we'd achieved so far. If we were going to go abroad, or anywhere in fact, I'd have to work really hard and get some work done for Glammazon. I hadn't heard from them since I'd sent my last batch of copy across, and that was…before Glastonbury. Then it dawned on me with horror. I still hadn't called Adrian back…

Chapter 27

I finally got around to calling Adrian, after putting it off way too many times.

"I was going to send you an email," he began, somewhat sternly I thought. I was standing in my kitchen, freshly brewed coffee in my other hand, bracing myself for the worst, "but you've saved me the time." He continued. "I'm afraid we're going to have to let you go, Ellie."

It was what I deserved. It still wasn't what I needed though. Panicking, I decided bribery might be a good way to salvage the situation.

"I'm so sorry, Adrian. I can catch up with the copywriting, I'll work evenings and weekends until it's finished if you like. And I'll throw in a few free days' work too? Just to make up for any problems we might have had with workflow recently? It won't happen again, I promise."

"I don't think that will work. We've already had to assign the project you were working on to another copywriter, and because she's had to start from scratch, it's cost us more. Let's be honest, you haven't really been interested in Glammazon since your *other* commitments took over, have you? We had to undertake some serious damage limitation after your comments about Rawthwaite Hall became public, and although we've been happy with your work until recently, we don't think it's tenable to keep you on as our resident copywriter."

Well that sounded formal. I gulped, and tried to compose myself. If all else failed, I thought, I was going to have to go for the undignified approach. Begging.

"Is there anything I can do to change your mind, Adrian? I really need this job."

"I'm sorry, Ellie. We can't afford to support you while your loyalties clearly lie elsewhere. I'm really disappointed that it's come to this, but there really isn't anything else to say. We'll send you what we owe you for your last batch of work."

I didn't know what to say. 'Thank you,' seemed inappropriate. So I went for the childish option and hung up on him.

I wandered into the kitchen to make myself a coffee. I noticed I was getting low on my favourite coffee pods. "You're going to have to go back to instant now," said the nagging voice in my head. That was just the first of a whole list of cost-cutting measures that my oh-so-helpful brain started bombarding with me when the realisation that I was now officially jobless hit me.

No more girls' nights out. No more impetuous makeup binges. No more expensive highlights. No holiday with the girls. I couldn't even be bothered to cry. I knew it was all my own fault, because I'd been so blasé about *Glammazon* for so long. I'd been arrogant enough to assume that my writing was so good and I'd been with them for so long that I couldn't be replaced, and now I felt like an idiot.

Good, regular and reasonably-paid copywriting jobs were hard to come by. Now what was I going to do? I had the money from the sale of the house to fall back on – well some of it – but that wouldn't last me long and I was supposed to be keeping that for when the economy got better and they started pushing cheap mortgages again. At this rate, my ever-dwindling deposit wouldn't buy me a tent.

I sat, dejected, trying to think positive thoughts, but none were coming. Realistically, the money I had left in the bank wasn't going to last me very long. Maybe I could write a book? Maybe I could sell stuff on eBay? Or take a course in something at the adult education college and retrain? I could do beauty therapy, I knew all about beauty, after all.

But I didn't want to be a beauty therapist. I was a writer. A writer with nobody to write for. I'd still not done any pitching, despite all my promises to the girls. I'd done it in the past when I'd been feeling optimistic, and before the economy went to pot and there wasn't a surplus of unemployed feature writers going freelance for their old editors on the cheap, but even then I'd only ever managed to get about three articles out of a pitch to a magazine in my entire journalistic life.

Lauren was the first person to call me and commiserate when she got my *'what am I gonna do now?'* text message – but she wasn't going to let me wallow.

"It's a bummer, but you've got the perfect angle now. These people know who you are now, you can introduce yourself to all the editors who turned you down when you were unknown on the back of everything we've done, and offer them opinion pieces. Use it to your advantage! "

Lauren was right. I'd been ignored or rejected time and time again when I sent ideas to magazine editors in the past, but that was when I was sending random ideas and hoping for a bite, I was a complete unknown. Maybe they would be interested now I was recognisable and had already been in the media with the campaign? It was definitely worth a try. I vowed to email as many editors as I possibly could in the next week or so, and try to convince them that they really needed my irrepressible brand of positivity and wit. Or something. This time I had no excuse.

Whenever I got stressed, my creativity took a plummet and right now, I was stressed to the extreme. I decided that a workout in the gym wasn't going to cut it today, even a long stomp on the treadmill would probably just leave me feeling more wound up. I needed de-stressing, and for that, I needed to get out in the sunshine.

It was a beautiful day.

There was a slight breeze on the common, which made the trees rustle every now and again, and it was gorgeously warm outside, without being too hot. I took a long walk along the river, following the towpath that ran alongside the common. There were a lot of people out enjoying the summer sunshine that day. I watched the mums with their buggies, gossiping while cute toddlers ran around, exploring and finding everything fascinating. One little boy was chasing a harassed-looking family Labrador with a piece of bark. It looked as if the dog might have been in that situation before. I saw an elderly couple walking hand in hand together, and sighed inwardly. Maybe that would be me one day. I seriously doubted it, given the quality of mankind I'd come across in my thirty-odd years of being on the planet. There were a couple of teenagers just wandering around, probably waiting for some others to join them as they looked at their watches every few minutes.

The river was calm, with occasional ducks, geese and swans floating by. I often likened myself to a duck – in part because I had a slight waddle to my walk, but because of the way we looked as if we were gliding along with no effort but if you looked underneath we were paddling furiously to keep afloat! It was how I felt at that moment. To anyone looking over at me, I was just wandering down the towpath, but in my head there was all manner of stress and paddling going on.

I stuck my ipod on and walked in the sunshine. It really was beautiful in this part of the City, and I felt incredibly lucky to have all this so close to my home. There was absolutely no way I was going to give my flat up without a fight.

When I got back to the flat, I went straight to my laptop and began searching online for people to pitch my column ideas to. Armed with freshly-made coffee – I hadn't totally embraced the idea of instant just yet – and a big bar of comfort chocolate, I researched, browsed like a mad woman and made note after note about readership, voice and the current columnists of some of my favourite target magazines in my tatty old pink notebook, trying to create ideas, angles and loop everything in with what I'd seen on the news recently. It felt like hard work, but I plodded on, resentful that *Glammazon* had put me in this position and angry at myself for being dumb enough to make it so easy for them.

I had to come up with a way of making my semi-notoriety pay.

There was no Marie Claire column on the horizon, I was going to have to work really hard on coming up with feature ideas, but I did have a website that had lots of members and a message that more and more girls seemed to be agreeing with. Could that be the answer?

Chapter 28

"Sorry darlin', I've put myself under house-arrest 'til I've got to the end of my first draft."

Zoë was playing hard to get ever since she'd been writing her book.

"There's no way you could spare me a few hours? Not even if I throw in a cake?"

"I'd love to, honest I would," Zoë said, clearly still typing as I could hear the keys clicking in the background, "but I really can't …sorry babe."

Ah crap. At least Lauren had agreed to come and play, being a lady of leisure now. I was especially glad as I wanted to run a few ideas past her.

I'd missed Lauren when she moved to London and started working silly hours, so I thought the fact she'd moved back in with her parents again now and had loads of spare time would be good for our friendship, too. Lauren was such a great person; she was really kind-hearted and generous as well as having a dry wit and sharp intelligence that made her a fun person to be around. We'd drifted apart slightly since she'd been working and living in London, and Zoë and I had spent so much time together lately that I felt as if I'd shut Lauren out.

I'd actually known Lauren a lot longer than Zoë, since college in fact. She vaguely knew Paul, too, and they got on reasonably well when they met up, but she'd been studying Media and Business Studies while I'd been the arty farty one studying English. She carried on and went to university, while I went straight to work in an office, then moved in with Jane, putting all my dreams of becoming a writer on hold to deal with insurance quotes and renewals. It was a big mistake that led to many years of make-do jobs.

Lauren was the successful one, and even though she'd had to

admit defeat when her events company started losing money, she had just sold it to someone else and moved straight into a brilliant job in marketing within weeks. I'd gone from one rubbish job to another, got married, moved house a few times and eventually ended up working as a freelance copywriter when my temping options had run out and I decided it was now or never.

We had always managed to keep in touch, meeting up as often as we could, even when we were both married, and I'd secretly slightly envied her with her high-powered job and designer lifestyle. My ex, Darren, had never liked her, mainly because she didn't suffer fools gladly and he was an idiot. He also resented the fact that she made more money than he did. I knew she worked hard for it though, and to be honest, without a job, Lauren seemed a little bereft. She'd definitely lost some of her sparkle, although she said she was enjoying the break.

The fact she'd been hunting for marketing jobs online already told me a different story though.

Working together on the plans for Viva Voluptuous would be a brilliant way of perking my friend up, as well as making money and growing the brand. Growing the brand? Yes, that was what a day in Lauren's company, talking about business did for me. It made me talk like a grown up and a potential businesswoman instead of an amateur farting around.

"I want to make some money from Viva Voluptuous – I was thinking of running ads – what do you reckon?" I asked Lauren, hardly giving her time to sit down.

"I don't think you'd make much from ads at the moment, hun," she said.

"Really? How do other people make shit-loads of money with websites then?" I asked, wondering where all these dot.com millionares had come from in the early naughties.

"Porn!"

I laughed. "I don't think we want to branch into chubby porn, do you?"

"I can't think of many things worse." Lauren confirmed. "Ells, you're just going to have to woman up and start coming up with ideas for articles, sending them to editors and doing what you know you're good at. You're a fantastic writer, why does it scare you so much?"

"I don't know." I admitted. "I've tried everything to get my head around pitching ideas. I did it a lot when I started out but I didn't get any replies and it just knocked me back. I think I've just got it into my head that I can't do it."

Lauren drained her mug of every last drop of coffee, put it down on the table and reached into her Gucci bag. She was the only person I knew who could afford one. I thought as she did it that if I had a Gucci bag, I'd probably put it on a shelf and stroke it occasionally, but never take it out.

"Here," she said, handing me a notepad and a pen she'd picked up on her last spa trip. "Write down some ideas. We'll brainstorm."

"I can't."

"Why not?" Lauren was looking exasperated.

"I just can't conjure up ideas out of nowhere." She clearly didn't understand, this was my big problem. Rubbish ideas, no imagination, and I didn't know where to start.

"Look around you," Lauren gestured. "People watch. Make up stories about these people, get inspiration from them. See that girl over there?" She pointed surreptitiously at a very slim teenager who was pushing a piece of blueberry muffin around a plate. "What's her story? If she picked up Cosmo, what would be the headline that caught her eye?"

As if it were that easy, I thought to myself. "How should I know?" Lauren looked as if she wanted to slap me. I can't say I blamed her, despite my general positivity, this pitching article ideas to editors thing had become such a hurdle in my head that I just didn't want to know.

"OK," Lauren continued, trying to prove a point. "She's 18, she's just been dumped by her first boyfriend because she won't shave all her body hair off like the women he's seen in porn films."

What was her obsession with porn today? Had she been bored and having a cheeky surf, I wondered?

"What would I know about all that? How does that come into what she'd read in Cosmo?" I was being deliberately obstructive because I knew full well what she was getting at.

"She wants to feel better. She wants to read something validating her decision to stick to her guns. She wants a confidence boost. So…if there was a magazine with a cover line, "Painful Sex – the beauty rituals of the sex industry" or something like that, she could find out all about what strippers, porn stars and escorts have to go through to get work." She was furiously writing all this down as she spoke, and I had a feeling she was going to give me the piece of paper when we left the coffee shop, as homework.

"The pain and hassle of all the waxing," she continued. "The surgery, the amount they spend on make-up. The check-ups at the STD clinic. Then you'd have a bloke's point of view, of course, saying that he prefers women au naturel, and a 'normal' woman will win out every time over surgically-enhanced. You get someone to say he prefers body hair. Bingo, you've made her day and probably a lot of others, too."

She made it sound so simple. "How did you get all that from just watching that girl with her Frappuccino?"

"I made it up. And that's why you've got to do. Use your imagination, and don't tell me you haven't got one because we all know that you have."

I was picking at my cuticles now, feeling under pressure. Lauren slapped my hand. "I don't know anything about the sex industry though," was my last feeble line of defence.

"You're a bloody journalist. Find out."

I left the conversation hanging there. I really didn't have any more excuses.

I got back to the flat later that afternoon, armed with Lauren's piece of paper. I hadn't read it, but as I procrastinated, waiting for my laptop to spring to life and making myself yet another coffee, I glanced down at her list of instructions and ideas, and noticed that at the end of the list, she'd added, *"You can do this. Love you!"*

I sat down at the laptop, opened up a blank Word document and stared at it for a few minutes. Lauren's words were rattling around in my brain. She believed in me, and so did Zoë. I could do this. I decided I wasn't going to get up from the computer until I'd come up with a fully formed article outline based on Lauren's idea, and emailed it to an editor. Three hours later, I'd fleshed the idea out, come up with ideas for case studies and emailed it to *Glamour.* Well, fingers crossed, I thought. I was ridiculously proud of myself, and texted both the girls with, *"I'm a proper journalist! I pitched an idea!"*

Both girls replied within minutes.

"At freakin' last, Missy! Well done you!" from Zoë.

"Told you so" from Lauren.

We teased Zoë out of her self-inflicted house arrest later that week, as I wanted her to sell her books on VV. Zoë was thrilled that I'd asked her and suggested we created a few guides and workbooks for the site too – my personal favourite being *"How to be Prom Queen every day of the year"* which I wished had been around when I was 16 at end of term discos. I think I only ever got asked to dance once, and there was an evil rumour for weeks that he'd only asked me for a bet.

Zoë had a way of writing that teenage girls related to, bubbly and light-hearted, but the message was always the same – 'Be yourself.'

We decided to celebrate our creativity with wine. We put Adele on, God only knows why, and, as we often did after a few drinks, we found ourselves getting tipsy, a bit melancholy and talking about men.

"I'm so lonely," sighed Lauren. She was staring into her wine glass and swilling the liquid round and around as she spoke, almost as if she was expecting the answer to her problems to appear at the bottom of the glass.

Zoë and I looked at each other in surprise. This wasn't like Lauren; she was always so upbeat and independent.

"Hey…." I put down my glass and hugged her. "Why, Duchess? You've got us, and you're an amazing, beautiful woman."

"But I'm still lonely. I see people my age with a husband and kids, and I think; I want that. I love my job, well, I did love it. Not working for a while has just made me realise how dull my life is. I've got nobody to come home to, not even a lodger yet, and I feel like I'm going stir crazy in that big house. At least when I was living in the shoebox I could hear the neighbours arguing through the wall."

She managed a laugh at that point. I didn't really know what to say to her. It was so unlike the Lauren I knew to feel sorry for herself.

"You'll get that, sweetie. Really, you will." I didn't know what else to say. I had no idea she was feeling lonely and now I felt even guiltier for spending so much time with Zoë.

"Girlfriend, you're hot, you're sassy and you're too much of a catch to be single for long. I'm surprised you haven't had any offers since we were on telly." Zoë joined in. I knew that she'd had quite a few propositions since we'd been on the One Show but Lauren hadn't mentioned anything.

"Thanks honey, but I'm still single now, and the only offers I've had since that show have involved parts of my anatomy I don't usually reveal to strangers."

Neither Zoë or I knew what to say to that – we'd both had those messages too. But Lauren continued, "Am I just too fussy? Colin was a nice guy. He still texts me every day. I kind of miss him now."

"NO!" Zoë and I both said at once. We couldn't have our friend settling for second best, she was awesome!

"There's always dating sites," I said, trying to be helpful. Lauren raised her eyebrow at me. I forgot, that's where she'd met Colin. And where I'd met Mark. OK, moving swiftly on...

I thought maybe it was time to be honest, too.

"You know what...I want kids. Really, really want kids. So much so that I almost didn't insist on condoms when I was with Jamie."

Lauren looked at me as if I was a halfwit.

"It's OK, don't worry, I was a good girl. But there was still that little bit of me that wondered what would happen if I 'accidentally' fell pregnant. I could SO be a single mum. I'd even adopt. I want kids, and I'd love to find a man who wanted babies with me. I'm running out of time!"

It was true. My biological clock was ticking so loudly I couldn't ignore it if I tried. Cute babies on TV adverts made me want to cry at certain times of the month, and whenever I congratulated yet another friend who'd posted images of their first baby scan, or adorable new born on Facebook, it was always with a tinge of jealousy.

Zoë gave me a cuddle. "You'd be an amazing mum, honey. There's someone out there who'll want to be an amazing dad to your babies. And you're a spring chicken, lady; girlies are having babies in their forties and all now. Don't give up."

I knocked back the last of my wine and burped.

"She's not going to pull a baby daddy if she keeps doing that." I heard Lauren say.

"Actually, it will make me a better mum if I can show my baby how to do it properly." I giggled. "But it's OK, I'm potty-trained." I added.

"So, Little Miss Sunshine. What's your secret? Are you going to make any confessions tonight?" Lauren asked Zoë, before the conversation degenerated into toilet humour.

"Not really." We could both tell she was hiding something. She wouldn't look either of us in the eye and was picking at the crystal that was stuck to one of her bright fuchsia nails.

Lauren pressed for a bit more, "There must be something."

"Well…."

Lauren and I waited, as Zoë teased us a bit more.

"I think I might have met my Mr Right…"

Chapter 29

Zoë's admission stopped us in our tracks. She blushed, coyly and I couldn't think of what to say. Eventually, I managed "You sneaky little vixen!"

"How did you manage to keep that quiet??" Lauren asked, incredulously. We both thought she'd been working on the book, and all this time she'd been busy falling in love with someone we didn't even know about.

"Do you remember I spoke to that instructor about a class for big girls when we were at Rawthwaite Hall?" Zoë began, "Well, I've been emailing her ever since, and it looked as if I was going to get the go-ahead to work with them on a franchise for them, and a few other spa gyms around the country. It was mega-top secret or else I would have told you before. I'm still supposed to keep it under wraps but I think I can trust you two?" She looked at us. We nodded.

"The only trouble was, I didn't have anyone to do it with. I couldn't just rock up and tell them I'd invented a yoga routine because I don't have all the right pieces of paper. It's all to do with insurance and qualifications. I don't have time to get qualified, so I put the word out on some of my forums, and a guy called Chris messaged me."

She paused theatrically; anyone would have thought she wanted a round of applause. When she didn't get one, she took a swig from her glass of wine and carried on.

"So, anyway. Chris. He's a yoga instructor from Brighton, he's 45 and he's a real man. He's absolutely gorgeous. Just freakin' adorable. We've talked on Skype every night for the last three weeks, and he's been up to see me twice too. We did lots of kissing but because he's such a gent, he insisted on sleeping on the sofa."

A gentleman too? Now I was jealous.

"He wants to work with me on the yoga classes, and we're talking to the spas formally about it this week. He's fully qualified and we've made a video of the routine we've come up with, especially designed for curvy girls and bigger men, which we're going to put online after we've showed it to the guys at Rawthwaite. It's only a mock up but you can have it afterwards for the website if you like, too?"

"When are we going to meet this wonderful specimen of a man?" I asked.

"Does he have a brother?" pouted Lauren.

"Oh and that's fantastic news about the yoga!" I added, realising I'd completely forgotten Zoë's other news in the excitement about Chris. He sounded perfect for her, she always did love her spiritual types, and there weren't many of those around.

"It's not definite yet, so shhh…but thank you!" she said, coyly. "I can't believe all this is happening so fast. I know you think all my Law of Attraction stuff is ridiculous, but I asked for all this, baby, and I got it. Although I have to say the TV coverage helped too. Apparently they saw us on telly, thought I was photogenic and decided I'd be the perfect girl to present a curvy-yoga DVD!"

Well, duh. It almost sounded as if she was surprised by this revelation. Actually, she probably was, as Zoë appeared to be the only person on the planet who didn't realise how gorgeous she was.

"Oh my God, lady, it's all happening for you, isn't it?" Lauren said slowly. I could detect a tinge of envy as she spoke, although that was hardly surprising after her revelations earlier. "Well done."

"You're amazing." I screamed, enveloping Zoë in a massive bear hug. "I'm so proud of you. I have to meet Chris!"

Zoë beamed, clearly relieved to have been able to blurt out her secret at last. I was pretty amazed she'd managed to keep it to herself for so long, as she was normally useless.

"I've got an idea," Lauren piped up. "I'm going to take us all to Brighton for a weekend, for our girl's holiday. We get a weekend away from this place, and we also get to have a nosey at Mr Wonderful. And I don't want any arguments from either of you, because we all deserve it. Don't worry about the money, it's on me."

"You don't have to, darlin'" Zoë objected. "I love the girlie holiday idea, don't get me wrong, but you don't have to pay for it all, honest."

"You two are always skint", she said, rolling her eyes theatrically, "and I've got loads of lovely redundancy money, so if I can't treat my two best mates in the whole world now, when can I treat them? And it's only a few nights in Brighton, it's not a week in the Maldives…"

She had a point.

I wasn't going to argue. I needed a holiday and there was no way I could justify shelling out for one right now, so if Lauren wanted to spoil us, I wasn't going to stop her.

"You can warn the wonderful Chris that we're coming to check him out" I laughed. "Give him time to find an excuse to be out of the country."

"He's not like that" Zoë said, defensively. "He's actually very sociable. He works as an instructor at one of the chain gyms in Brighton, and we both agreed that the classes they have in most gyms just follow the same format, the same franchises run everything and so there's really no variation in the way it's taught. He's into being more creative with the poses, like I am, so that they can be adapted by bigger people and nobody feels left out. It's all about feeling your way into the poses, not following the rest of the class and trying to make your legs go where they don't want to."

I couldn't help it. "So, has Chris been feeling his way yet, then?"

Zoë threw a wine bottle top at me. "He's been very respectful.

I'm not sure how much longer that will last though. I fancy him so much. I never thought I would fancy a man ten years older than me, but he's so sexy, so fit and toned and he has a voice like warm caramel, that just makes me want to…well, you know."

We knew.

"And there's something else." Zoë said, quietly.

Lauren and I waited, impatiently, for Zoë to continue.

"He said the 'L' word."

"No!?"

By my reckoning, they couldn't possibly have been seeing each other for more than three weeks. That was fast work, even for Zoë.

"Yes!"

Lauren snorted. "And he wasn't trying to get into your knickers? Does he know you haven't got any money?"

"Don't be mean!" I admonished. "Some people are just romantic. So..." I turned back to Zoë, "When did he say it? Was it really romantic?"

"Yes, but in an unromantic kinda way. He came to see me last week, and we were just sitting on the sofa, eating chips from the chippy. I dropped a bit of chip down my cleavage, and it was still really hot, and I was hopping around trying to get it out as it had lodged itself right down inside my bra! He was on the sofa, laughing so much he could hardly breathe, and when I'd fished it out, I threw it at him. He said "Oh Zoë, I do love you." I said, "Why, because I can store enough food for a week in my underwear?" Then he just got all soppy and serious and said, "No, I just love you.""

"Did you say it back?" I asked.

"I did. I've never said it so fast. Never felt it so fast. He's The One. I just know it."

"Aww." It was so sweet. My bestest friend was besotted. I was happy for her. Why couldn't I find a man like Chris instead of commitment-phobics like Mark and Jamie? Maybe there was something in all this 'ask and you shall receive' nonsense that Zoë was always chirping about. I vowed to ask her if I could borrow one of her hippy books and find out what she had to do to pull this ideal man of hers. Without making it look too obvious of course.

Chapter 30

"I think we should take our costumes to Brighton."

Zoë was full of bright ideas. I had to giggle though. She'd come up with that corker of an idea a couple of days before we left.

"You really want us to dress up in all that regalia and strut our stuff while we're away?" I asked, ever-so slightly sarcastically. My bad mood was still lingering as we planned the trip and the other two sensed that I needed cheering up. I'd had nothing back from any of the people I'd sent feature and column ideas to, and I'd been fretting about money.

Lauren and I had already planned to go slightly wild while we were away, let our hair down and forget the business and our stunning lack of man action.

"Who needs men anyway, lady? We're going to be the belles of the ball in our pretty frocks." Lauren laughed.

"I don't believe you just used the words 'belles of the ball' and 'frock' in the same sentence." I joked. "Were you being ironic?"

"Did you pack the gin?" Zoë asked, interrupted our mock bickering. "I think so" I replied, unzipping the mini case on the floor of the car, and ferreting around furiously to try and locate the rest of the bottle we'd started the other night.

Lauren stuck her finger up at me in the back of the car as we drove along. The thought of turning myself into my burlesque alter-ego helped to kick my backside out of my funky mood .

How Lauren had managed to find us such great rooms in the middle of tourist season I don't know, but they must have cost a fortune. Somehow she'd managed to find a B&B with a family suite that comprised of a double room and a single adjoining room. The theme was 'Romeo and Juliet' and the décor was unashamedly over the top, with no expense spared. There was an enormous king-sized bed with satin throws and heart-shaped cushions, velvet drapes, pictures of Verona and the Italian countryside all over the room and amazing antique-style furniture that gave the whole room a really quaint feel.

There was even aromatherapy – the room smelled of a blend of lavender and rose and I would have loved to have known how they did that because I never did work out where that scent was coming from. It was gorgeous.

"I want the big room, it's my holiday!" Lauren pouted playfully, pulling rank after we were shown to our rooms and realised that one of us was going to have to go in the adjoining room, the furthest away from the bathroom.

I ended up in the small room. At least if I snored they wouldn't be able to wind me up about it in the morning.

Brighton was packed, and very lively. Everywhere we went, we were handed flyers for clubs and bars. "It's like Ibiza with giant sea gulls," exclaimed Zoë.

"Oooh! Shoes!" Lauren veered off towards a designer shoe shop with some beautiful specimens in the window, sorely tempting me into trying on something I knew I couldn't afford.

She was straight in there, trying on something uber-sophisticated from Kurt Geiger. I had my heart set on a strappy pair of heels that I knew I wouldn't be able to walk in after ten minutes, but they were so damn sexy I had to try them on.

"What d'you think?" I said to the girls, posing in the heels after we'd admired Lauren's Kurt Geiger beauties and agreed that she couldn't possibly have resisted them.

"Winner" was Lauren's response.

"Abso-frickin-lutely!" chimed Zoë. My internal bank manager was apoplectic with rage as I handed over my card, reminding me in no uncertain terms that I didn't actually have a proper job at the moment, but I chose to ignore the voice of reason in the name of beautiful footwear.

Zoë managed to find herself some gorgeous tops in the sales, but there wasn't anything much for me, as usual. I sulked a bit at the lack of decent clothes, but cheered myself up with gorgeous body lotion while I was in one of the organic shops, silently kicking myself for coming to a place where spending money I didn't have was going to be so deliciously easy.

"I don't know why they never have my size out in the shops," I moaned at Lauren, who was eyeing up a gorgeous top in Coast.

"They've probably sold out," she replied, distracted. She put the top back and huffed a bit. It was expensive. VERY expensive.

"But I've had this argument with some of the shops before." I said, browsing through the hangers and looking at the sizes. "They'll do our sizes online but they don't have them in stock. You have to ask for them to order the size you want in. I don't want to have to go up to the assistant and announce my size to the entire shop, I want to be able to try things on and buy them on the spur of the moment like anyone else."

"Why don't you say something then?" Lauren said. She's heard this rant before; she was entitled to not be listening. I thought a change of subject might be in order.

"Have you ever been down The Lanes?" I asked Zoë. I knew that Lauren had been, and I loved the place.

"No, let's have a nosey," she replied. We left the arcade and wandered down to the Lanes. I'd shut up about the size issue and was just enjoying the sunshine, the sea air and being away from home and the craziness of the last few months.

"Did you know I had a tattoo?" Lauren said, as we walked down the narrow passageways and admired the amazing designs in one tattoo artist's shop window.

Zoë looked as if Lauren had just bitten her. "Where?" She asked, indignantly. She'd wanted to have a tattoo for ages but didn't know what she wanted, and in all honesty admitted she was too much of a wuss and couldn't wait until they found a way to just stick them on instead.

"Top of my hip. It's one I designed myself when I got divorced."

Of course, we all had to have a look, when we found enough room and a secluded corner to have a good nosey. She pulled the waistband of her stretchy jeans down slightly and there it was, a very pretty, professional-looking design that featured a phoenix rising from flames, hearts and crossed swords.

"Well, Lauren Greene, you dark horse!"

We did all the touristy things; we went to the Brighton Pavilion and had a good laugh at 'Brighton through the ages', headed up along the pier and ate hot doughnuts straight from the bag until they made us feel sick, and walked along the pebbled beach looking for talent – and a man that wasn't obviously here on a romantic break with his boyfriend. Well, Lauren and I did. Zoë was still excruciatingly loved-up, and looking forward to introducing us to Chris later. We'd agreed to meet him in one of the quieter bars so that we could interrogate him properly. Of course, I mean 'get to know him.'

The sky darkened and I told the girls I could smell rain coming.

"You can't smell rain!" Lauren argued as I suggested we hit the nearest coffee shop.

"Wanna bet?" I retorted as the first tiny drops hit. It was typical south coast summer weather, one minute it was hot and sunny, the next minute the clouds were rolling in off the sea and threatening to ruin our fun. The gulls were getting fretful and I sensed a storm, I had one of my 'heads'. We ducked into a Starbucks and sat gossiping over lattes for a while. It had been such fun, just wandering around together, shopping and chatting, and I felt slightly guilty about the resentfulness I'd been feeling earlier in the week.

Zoë got quieter and quieter as the time we'd arranged to meet Chris got closer. I could tell she was nervous; it was a big deal to her that we liked him

"Don't worry honey, if you love him, we all will." I reassured her as we walked up towards the bar where we'd arranged to meet him. The storm had come and gone, and the sun was peeping out from behind the remaining dark clouds.

She needn't have worried. Chris greeted us as we walked through the door, bounding up from the seat he'd been in, next to the window, and beaming. First things first – he enveloped Zoë in an enormous hug and said, "Hello my darling" before kissing her, passionately. Wow. He was clearly as smitten as she was.

When he'd put her down, he turned to Lauren. "You must be Lauren?" he asked, taking her hand and kissing her cheek. "Pleased to meet you Chris, she replied, "yes I am, and I've heard all about you."

"I hope the reports were good?" He smiled. He did the same to me, kissing me on the cheek and adding, "So you must be Ellie. Wonderful to meet you at last."

"Likewise," I replied, blushing furiously. Blushing? What was that all about? I had to confess I could have developed a crush on Chris quite easily. He was stunning. He was about six feet tall, with close-cropped dark hair that was just beginning to show signs of grey. He had amazing blue/green eyes, a slightly crinkled smile and a very neatly trimmed slim goatee beard. What's more, he had muscles you could see through the surfer-style t-shirt he was wearing and a flat, toned stomach that wouldn't have looked out of place on a man 20 years younger. He may have been 45 but whatever he was on, I wanted some of it because he could pass for a lot younger.

He asked us all what we were drinking, and disappeared to the bar to get them in. I turned to Zoë. "Are there any more like him where you found him?" I gushed, "Because he's gorgeous!"

"I know darlin' and he's all mine…I am a very lucky girl."

"So how exactly have you allowed this man to sleep on your sofa when he's been to see you?" asked Lauren. "I think that's a crime!"

Zoë didn't reply.

"He wasn't on the sofa last time, was he Madam?"

"A lady never kisses and tells," was Zoë's response. Just at that moment, Chris appeared with a tray of cocktails and we had to stop grilling her. Although it was fairly obvious, given her slightly exaggerated dignified silence on the subject.

Chris turned out to be great fun as well as gorgeous. He was divorced, with a young daughter, and on good terms with his ex-wife. I wondered how people managed that, as I would have cheerfully murdered Darren.

He'd only been a yoga devotee for about eight years, but he said it had saved his life. He'd been working in an office as an IT manager, stressed to the max, drinking 10 black coffees a day and drinking too much wine every night. He'd stumbled across yoga by accident when the wife of a friend set up a class and desperately needed members. To cut a long story short, he loved it so much that he started to embrace a holistic lifestyle and not just the yoga. He cut out alcohol, gave up drinking coffee and eating red meat, got his health back and decided to train as an instructor. He'd completed all the right certificates to teach in health clubs, spas and gyms, but was looking for a new challenge. That's where Zoë came in.

"It all sounds way too perfect to me," I thought, slightly uncharitably, as I sipped my Pineapple Daiquiri. They both seemed blissfully happy though. Chris couldn't seem to take his eyes off of Zoë for a minute and she was staring adoringly at him, taking in every word he said. It was like watching two teenagers!

I felt ever-so slightly jealous of their obvious closeness. It had been such a long time since anyone had been smitten with me. If, in fact, they ever had.

It almost seemed mean to drag Zoë away for our night out, but we had to get ready. We agreed to meet up with Chris before we left the next day and tried not to call out "Get a room" as the lovers kissed each other goodbye.

"She'll be moving to Brighton by the end of the year," Lauren commented.

I didn't like it, but I thought she was probably right.

We made our way back to the B&B and got ready for our night of drunken debauchery,

"I reckon we should really glam it up tonight, girls." Lauren said, "Because there aren't many other places we could go where we could get away with it." Lauren, the expert, had decided in advance that we should hit the gay bars, mainly because three women dressed in silly heels and burlesque costumes would feel right at home in a bar where the DJ may apply lipstick and work 6 inch heels better than all three of us put together.

"I don't think I've ever worn this much make up in my life," I laughed, as I lined my eyes. I was always trying to do the perfect flick with my eyeliner, but as usual, after three attempts and three really bad, wonky lines, I gave up.

"Come here, silly" Zoë laughed, watching me wipe my eyes with make-up remover yet again. "I'll do it for you."

I sat really still as Zoë drew on a perfect winged line complete with a dramatic flick. It looked fabulous with my glittery eye shadow. "You'll do!" She exclaimed.

The hassle I went to attempting to attach false eyelashes with diamante on them would have merited an entire blog post all to itself, but eventually after a lot of fussing and preening, pulling each other's corset ribbons as tight as they'd go and deliberating over whether we'd be able to walk in our vertiginous heels for more than ten minutes, we were ready to hit the town.

We rocked up expecting fun, frolics and disco music, and instead we found a half empty bar complete with a very grumpy barman who I swear changed the music from the hi-energy chart dance tracks to Erasure's greatest hits as we stepped in the room. After one drink, we moved on. It was like walking into a pub and everyone looking at us because we weren't 'one of them'.

"I thought Brighton was meant to be lively?" Zoë said,

wrinkling her nose in disdain as we walked out of the bar.

"I think someone forgot to tell them that going out for the night is supposed to be fun." I laughed. "I've never seen such a bored-looking bunch of people on a night out before."

"You never went out with me and my ex, then…" said Lauren, "So where to next?"

"How about that place?" Zoë spied a deceptively muted looking exterior that was playing loud dance music and was rammed full.

"Go for it" I agreed. Lauren followed us in, with some trepidation, and I'm sure I spotted a few people laughing at us as we made our way up to the bar. I was starting to feel slightly self-conscious now. I hoped we weren't in for another dose of what had happened in the last place and was ready to turn round and walk straight out, but Zoë wasn't having any of it. Flashing her customary megawatt smile, she strode up to the bar defiantly. One of the bar men stood straight to attention as soon as he spotted her, and asked her what she wanted.

"What do you recommend?" She asked. Flirting with gay men was another one of her specialities; I don't think anyone was immune to her charms. The bar man picked up the cocktail menu and suggested a 'Pink Flamingo' –a house concoction with the consistency of runny blancmange which involved rather a lot of vodka, strawberry liqueur and some sort of cream. It was a lurid pink colour and Zoë's eyes lit up as he handed it over.

"That's ah-mazing!" She exclaimed.

Within half an hour, we were 'adopted' by a group of absolutely wonderful men, a fantastic crowd who wouldn't let us buy a drink all the time we stayed there. They even insisted on requesting 'Big girls you are beautiful' and 'Bootylicious' for us when we got up on the dance floor.

"Aren't you the girls off the telly?" Kevin, one of the men who'd 'adopted' us asked me, looking at our costumes in recognition. "You could say that" I confirmed, slurping my second

Pink Flamingo and starting to feel a little bit sick. Those babies were SWEET.

Of course, once he realised we were almost-famous, he went straight over to the DJ and the next song was announced "for the big girls off the telly who sang in Covent Garden" – and we were expected to get up and sing along to Gloria Gaynor once again. 'I am what I am' – not only the anthem of gay men, now the anthem of these three curvy girls too.

"I could get used to this." Lauren shouted over the music, swaying slightly on her heels due to the effects of the cocktails we'd been treated to all night. My attempts at drinking orange juice or water to try and steady myself were met with "Don't be silly" from every person who insisted on buying me a drink and I was drunker than I'd been in a long time.

"Have you got any Rihanna?" I yelled at the DJ, who nodded and yelled back, "Just for you!"

Within minutes Lauren, Zoë and I were in our customary positions for "The only girl in the world," singing along at the tops of our voices, waving our arms about and probably all imagining someone as we sang it. For some reason, as I yelped along drunkenly, all I could think of was Jamie. Because for a while, back there, he'd made me feel like I was the only girl in his world. My mind went back to Canterbury and the B&B…I shook myself out of it. Jamie was history.

"I want to go hoooome," I whined. "My feet huuuurt."

It was past three, and we had all been in agony with our impractical shoes and done our usual and kicked them into a big pile by the side of the dance floor.

"Who's idea was that Jager Bomb?" groaned Lauren, looking decidedly worse for wear. "I never drink shots. Evil things." We'd been drinking Jager Bombs when we got fed up with cocktails, not something I did very often, and the energy drinks much have kicked in so that I didn't get my usual midnight slump and want to go back to the B&B, choosing instead to wave my arms about a lot and dance in exactly the same way to every tune that came on. Even so, the effects only lasted so long and I was flagging now.

"Where's Zo?" I asked, looking around.

"On the dance floor over there" Lauren replied, hobbling as she slipped her shoes back on and pointing to where Zoë was still dancing with a group of men.

"You're gorgeous!" shouted one, clearly in awe of this powerhouse of a woman who was wiggling and strutting to Beyoncé and asking every man in the house to 'put a ring on it'.

"Thank you very much!" She yelled back, grinning all over her face. People were so drawn to Zoë, it was fascinating to watch her in action. She tossed her auburn hair, which she'd left down for the night, backwards and forwards as she shimmied and whooped...Lauren and I were exhausted just watching her. I'd already hit a wall, and like a party pooper, I pouted at Lauren and demanded, "I have to go to bed. Now"

Lauren didn't look too upset, as the shots she'd been knocking back appeared to be wearing off. She grabbed Zoë, who could probably have carried on until sunrise quite happily, and we left the bar. It wasn't far from the bar to the B&B, and we were back in our room within 15 minutes, limping, ears ringing and heads not quite feeling right. It had been a great night. I just hoped someone had remembered to pack the painkillers...

Chapter 31

"I have got the mother of all hangovers," I whined.

I wasn't alone, Zoë was even paler than usual and looked like she was about to throw up and Lauren wouldn't put the TV on because her head was hurting too much. We hardly said a word to each other as we packed our stuff back up.

"Do you want breakfast?" Zoë asked, clearly praying that Lauren and I felt as awful as she did, and would say no to a greasy fry up.

"Hell no." I replied, looking at my slightly grey face in the mirror as I walked past it. "I don't think I want to eat anything for a while. And I'm never drinking again."

"Neither am I." Lauren moaned, hiding her eyes behind large sunglasses. The sun was out, it was hot already and we were going to have to force ourselves out into daylight at some point. I just wanted to go back to bed.

"I felt a bit like a celeb last night." Zoë said as she attempted to put her make up on. "It was a wicked night. How did you feel when they recognised us off the telly?"

I had to admit I'd got a little tingle of excitement. "I loved it!" I exclaimed. "I could get used to it!"

"You might have to if we keep this up," Zoë smiled. "I have to admit it was fun. Even if I feel like death this morning, it was worth it for last night. Now I know what it's like to be on TOWIE!"

I rolled my eyes. Zoë knew my feelings on that programme.

We'd promised to meet up with Chris before we drove home, so staggered off to a nearby coffee shop and drank double shot Americanos and cappuccinos to try and make ourselves feel a bit more human. Even Zoë had a coffee, so she must have felt terrible.

Chris appeared, full of energy, looking enthusiastic and

cheerful. Much as I liked him, I just wanted him to go away and let me feel sorry for myself in peace. My head hurt every time I moved, despite a dose of painkillers, and I had a queasiness that taunted me with the thought that throwing up would be the only respite from the hideous churning noises my angry stomach was making. I must have looked like I'd been run over in the night, even a shower hadn't made any difference. I was definitely not at my best.

He took one look at us and almost visibly backed off. He was probably picking up on our damaged auras or something. He practically tiptoed up to Zoë and gave her a kiss on the cheek, very gently.

"Hey, baby" she smiled, despite herself. "How are you?"

"I think I probably feel better than you do, darling," he replied. "What time did you get to bed?"

"About four."

"Ooh nasty. Should I be talking very quietly then?"

"Yes, please" Zoë groaned.

I had to feel sorry for the poor man – he didn't really know what to say, and none of us could be bothered to talk. We were a walking reminder to teenagers of the evils of drinking too much.

The journey home was conducted mostly in silence, after we'd managed to tear a besotted Zoë away from Chris. It was like something out of Brief Encounter.

We got home to find that there had been yet another attack on us by our favourite newspaper, the *Daily News*. It was clearly a slow news day, because they'd devoted an unfeasibly large amount of space in their Sunday supplement to ripping the whole concept of Viva Voluptuous to shreds. Oh, and joy of joys, they'd dragged out the unflattering image my darling ex-husband had sold them, as well as the one from the other rag that had stitched me up! I was never, ever going to get a boyfriend again if he saw those gorgeous pictures first…

This time, the paper had really gone to town, and as well as their 'Diet Doctor' telling me that I was at risk of diabetes, heart disease and all manner of other things due to my unhealthy weight, I also had a sanctimonious cow of a columnist telling me that I couldn't possibly be happy at the size I was. The columnist was a well-known tabloid 'stirrer' who could always be relied upon to get lots of people commenting about her articles. She had a very elevated opinion of herself as well as a way of offending people by deliberately being 'provocative' so that people would comment on her badly written articles. It was so predictable that she'd have a go at me, as the tide had been turning recently and with the TV coverage and the success of the flash mobs, people were warming to us. I'd even seen us mentioned in a couple of magazines, in body image articles. I just knew that at some point, the great British 'drag them down before they get too big for their boots' would happen, especially as we were big women and big women were definitely not allowed to be happy or successful.

I disliked Linda Williams, the columnist, intensely even before she'd had a pop at me, but there she was, insulting me, Zoë and Lauren, poking fun at my pictures, *"Look at the bags under Ellie Johnstone's eyes, does she look happy or healthy to you?"* and calling the campaign *"deluded, dangerous hogwash, which can only undermine the medical profession's efforts to deal with the obesity epidemic."*

The article went on to slate us personally, saying, *"These three women in their tacky fancy dress costumes think that they are empowering fatties everywhere. Well, let me tell you, these deluded pantomime dames – or should that be the three ugly sisters – are damaging the health and well-being of all the women they so smugly claim to be representing, and for that they should be ashamed."*

She claimed to weigh herself daily, and if she went more than a pound over her ideal weight, she would hit the latest faddy French diet until that pesky extra pound was gone. This apparently made her healthy and happy. I thought it made her an obsessive narcissist with too much time on her hands, but it was clear I was in the minority, because as usual, the commentators were out in force, saying insufferably rude and insulting things about me, and unfortunately, my two best mates as well.

I thought back to the way that comments like that had made me feel when I first decided to start Viva Voluptuous, and it hit me that they didn't hurt anymore. Well maybe a couple of the really nasty comments stung, how could they not? And the whole article annoyed me because it was so negative, but I felt so much better about myself now that the usual pathetic personal insults thrown at me were bouncing off me. It was as if Viva Voluptuous was my shield, protecting me from the vitriol of complete strangers. I could get my head around that fact that they weren't being rude about me; they were just typing rubbish about some random stranger they'd been encouraged to insult by a hateful newspaper columnist. I knew that everything we'd been doing since the beginning of the year had changed the way I felt so massively that it could do the same for others, too, and despite feeling a bit deflated, it just made me vow to carry on regardless.

I thought about Robin, a girl who'd been so down on herself that she'd put up with a rubbish job for years rather than put herself out there and apply for a new one. With some encouragement from the girls on the Viva Voluptuous forum, she'd finally applied for a job she really loved the sound of, and we'd built her confidence up so much that she'd actually got the job! She was so happy she gushed, *"I'm amazingly grateful for Viva Voluptuous, your message and the wonderful women who talked me into going for that job. Without this forum I'd never have had the guts to even apply for the job!"*

Another woman, Eloise, had started wearing colours after sticking to black, grey and brown for years. It sounded silly, but she was so excited about experimenting with fashion and clothes that she wrote, *"I feel like a completely new woman, and I haven't had to lose any weight to do it!"*

Comments like that made it all worthwhile. Not to mention the people who'd admitted they'd been too nervous to go to a gym because they were fat, watched the original video and given it a go. I felt proud of what we were starting to achieve and it would take more than a few bitchy comments to take that away from me.

"Just as well the snarky cow didn't see what I looked like this morning," I thought to myself as I closed down the news website and opened up Facebook instead.

I took a couple more painkillers to try and knock out the last of the headache, and head still thumping, I sat down at the laptop.

I'M NOT GIVING UP!

"Some of you have probably seen the latest character assassination the Daily News has done on me, I'd suggest that if you've got the print version, use it to line your cat's litter tray or something equally useful, because it's a load of ill-informed crap.

Linda Williams says that trying to boost women's self-esteem is 'deluded and dangerous'. I think it's way more dangerous to bully people into trying to conform to a fashionable stereotype that just makes them miserable and can harm their mental health. My friend, Jane, died because she didn't think she was good enough. She'd been admired all her life for her looks, but became obsessed with them when she started putting on a bit of weight. Because of this, and some other things that were going on in her life, she ended up with uncontrollable bulimia. She couldn't live with herself, and committed suicide. Tell me, Linda Williams, who is the more dangerous? Viva Voluptuous for trying to make fat people feel good about themselves, or papers like yours who humiliate women (and men) and incite self-hatred?

Will anyone who hates themself ever make the effort to take care of themselves? Why would they, they've been conditioned into believing in their own worthlessness. Only by giving people a sense of worth, the permission to love themselves as they are, and the tools they need to build their self-esteem will they ever realistically be in a place where they can lose weight if they need to – and it won't be through sticking them on a 1200 calorie diet or banning carbohydrates.

Isn't it just as deluded to assume that you're healthy just because your weight never inches over eight and a half stone anyway? Does Miss Williams know what's going on inside her? Doesn't she know that some people store excess fat internally, around their organs, and that it's much more dangerous than having a fat bum?

Maybe she'd like to come to the gym with me and we'll see who has the most stamina. She might even like to come to the doctor's with me, so that we can compare resting heart rate, blood pressure and cholesterol? I doubt she would be up for that challenge, she probably knows I'd win. But that's enough about her; let's talk about us.

When I started this campaign, I wasn't very happy with myself. It wasn't about my weight; it was about how other people, mostly men, had left me feeling. I was confused and susceptible to believing the type of rubbish that Linda Williams writes about fat people. I knew in my head and heart that I wasn't that fat, gluttonous stereotype that gets trotted out all the time – and I knew my best friends weren't either. I'd still feel wounded when I read pages and pages of Daily News comments about fat people though. I felt despised, hated, and ridiculed.

Everything I've done with Lauren and Zoë on Viva Voluptuous has made me feel better. Nothing's changed, I don't think my weight is any different, and I still eat the same way I did and go to the gym as often as I can. The only thing that's changed is my sense of self-worth. I was dumped by the Boy Wonder when I went to Glastonbury and it didn't even merit a mention on the blog because (a) I wasn't surprised and (b) I didn't let it get me down too much. I can't pretend I was happy about it, but he wasn't boyfriend material and I knew that all along. It was fun while it lasted and hey, he gives good video!

Six months ago, if I'd read an article about myself that was as nasty as the one I've read today, I would probably have cried. I might have headed into the kitchen to bake muffins or cupcakes too. I would have taken it to heart and tried to think of a way that I could change myself.

Today, I stayed out of the kitchen (partly down to having been out on the town in Brighton last night and the thought of food making me feel physically sick) and there have been no tears, just a sense of 'here we go again'. And I don't want to change myself; I want to change the world!"

After posting the blog post, I decided to add a few pictures we'd taken the night before at the club in Brighton. There were some amazing pictures of the three of us with our arms around random men, and each other. Some were of Zoë, dancing like a loon while Lauren and I had been standing on the side-lines nursing blisters and aching feet. There was one of Lauren posing with the DJ and staring down at his crotch – I had no idea what he'd just said but she was obviously finding it very funny.

We'd just had the best girl's weekend ever. Despite my aching head and an overwhelming desire to go to bed that hit me around four o'clock, I wouldn't have changed a second of the weekend, even down to the last couple of Jager Bombs, which would account for why I was feeling so rough. I wondered whether Zoë would move down to Brighton if things carried on going so well with Chris. I didn't think he would want to move up to Cambridge, not with his daughter being at school in Brighton and the two of them being so close. I hated the idea of not being able to see Zoë all the time, but at the same time I could tell that she was so in love with Chris, and he adored her. I couldn't imagine they'd leave it long before wanting to move in together. Looking on the bright side, it would mean plenty more girl's nights out in Brighton, and that could never be a bad thing.

Both girls had sent me texts bemoaning the state of their heads since we'd got back, and swearing about the unflattering newspaper coverage. I'd tried to placate them with clichés like 'there's no such thing as bad publicity' but really hoped they wouldn't take any of the bitchy comments to heart. Zoë was a sensitive soul, and underneath the confident exterior, Lauren wasn't as tough as she liked people to think, either. But we were all up for public scrutiny now, and if we were going to be making the campaign even bigger soon, I guessed they'd just have to take the crap that was inevitably going to be thrown at us along with the good bits like being on TV and getting bought lots of drinks in gay bars in Brighton. There was a lot of work to do if we wanted to get the website off the ground, and start really making a difference.

But not until after I'd caught up on my sleep. I crawled into bed, and treated myself to a very early night.

Chapter 32

Dear Sarah,

Thanks for sending me your idea. It's great, but it's not really what we're looking for right now. Thanks for thinking of us, and please do get in touch with any other ideas you have."

Regards

Davina - Features Assistant, Best Magazine

I sighed and deleted the email. I'd spent ages writing that pitch and I couldn't help feeling a bit tearful as the sting of rejection hit me once again. Lauren had convinced me I was onto a winner and had been so excited for me when I told her I had finally pitched an idea, even if technically, it was hers.

"See, I said you could do it, lady," she'd said, giving me a hug. "You just need to keep on coming up with ideas. Remember how easy it was to find that one?"

I'd started to believe that I could do the pitching thing, after my pep talk with Lauren that resulted in the sex industry idea. She wasn't even a writer, she was in marketing, and she managed to come up with an idea just like that. I'd put all my eggs in one basket though, after sending the pitch off, rather than trying to do the same thing again and come up with a few entertaining ideas of my own.

I didn't really want to tell the girls that the pitch had been rejected. I could always send it on to another editor, and I probably would when I'd got over my sulk, but right now I was going to make another coffee and text my words of woe to everyone. I texted the girls, and Paul, and put a sad face at the end for extra effect. I was looking for a bit of sympathy here, Goddammit!

"Send it to Cosmo!" Lauren replied straight away. I knew that's what she'd say. She was a bit obsessed with seeing me in Cosmopolitan, a feat I thought quite unlikely for a fledgling

writer that nobody had heard of.

Paul replied with *"Sorry hon - Would a pizza night cheer you up?"*

"Yes, I think it might," I replied. I didn't have plans for most of the week, and I hadn't seen Paul in ages, it was about time we had a catch up. The last time he'd come to see me, I'd been in the middle of a baking session. I don't think that was a coincidence.

I'd invited him over to sample my handiwork. He never could resist my baking. Paul was a great person to have around if I ever had any leftover food, because he loved my cooking and was guaranteed to take it off my hands. True to form, he'd munched several brownies, drunk my fridge free of Diet Coke, and made himself feel sick with a sugar, butter and chocolate overdose. His advice had been clear though.

"You've got to focus your mind on what you want your website to do, honey. Is it to be an inspiration to other curvaceous women, or is it to make money?"

"I want it to be the first place people go when they're looking for anything to do with being plus-size. They've got to feel at home there, feel like it's a welcoming place."

Paul's advice had been "You have to go with your heart," and "I loved what you wrote on your blog the other day, you need to do more from your heart, girl," which hadn't been exactly useful at the time. He'd been cheering me on with the pitching as well, and when I'd told him that I wished I was one of those prolific writers who could pitch three ideas a day, he'd hugged me and said, "There's nothing to be scared of. You're just out of your comfort zone and it's a bit nerve-wracking. I know you can do it. You can make the website whatever you want it to be, help loads of women, and then do even more if you can come up with some ideas and get them out there where everyone, and not just fat people, will see them."

Paul always seemed to have complete faith in me. I don't know why, as he'd been the one there with the tissues, picking up the pieces after yet another mishap, on many occasions. He'd also been there cheering me on whenever I had a tricky decision to make, giving me a non-emotional point of view. He did have a way of making me think I was invincible.

We made small talk while we waited for our starters, and I was just telling him about my weekend in Brighton with the girls, when he interrupted me, rudely, to ask about my love life. What he actually said, was, "So, are you getting any at the moment?"

I frowned. "Mind your own business."

He laughed, which annoyed me because I was sure he knew that I'd been single since Glastonbury and no, I had most definitely not been 'getting any.'

"So you haven't heard from your schoolboy lover then?"

"Will you shut up? He was 27. You make it sound like I'm some sort of weirdo. Loads of women prefer younger men. Old men don't do it for me."

"Cradle snatcher" he teased. "Have you been back on the dating sites then?"

"Nope. They all want skinny girls." I sighed, twirling my spaghetti with my fork and wishing I'd worn a darker top as the tomato sauce splashed me. I stared into my spaghetti Bolognese, thinking how nice it would be to be having a romantic dinner with an adoring man.

"Don't be daft. Not all men are shallow you know?" said Paul, interrupting my daydream.

"Most of them are." I replied, sulkily. "My love life is non-existent. The only attention I've had recently is from gay men."

"Well you're not going to get any other sort of attention if you go to gay bars, are you, you daft mare?"

I ignored him.

"Dating sites are for young, skinny girls and people who want to cheat on their other halves," I complained. "I actually had someone tell me that he couldn't be seen out with a girl over a size 12 once."

"His loss" Paul sympathised, concentrating on his garlic bread, which was about to drip butter all down his t-shirt.

"Yeah, whatever." I definitely needed to talk about something else. "So, what do you think I should do with the site then?"

After sucking his fingers to get rid of all the butter that had oozed out of his garlic bread – boy was he going to stink later – he wiped his hands on his jeans and replied with a shrug, "I don't know. If not adverts, I don't know how people make money. You either have a money-making site or you have something that's going to be all warm and fuzzy and make women feel good. I don't see that you can have both."

"That's not a great help, sweetie," I pouted.

"I'll finish, shall I? OK, you were making the observation that all dating sites are for skinny girls, and here you are, a writer looking for ideas, as well as a campaign to improve self-esteem for big girls. Do the words 'two birds, one stone' mean anything to you? Write something about plus size dating!"

I had to admit it was a good idea.

"I think there are already dating sites just for curvy women. They call them BBW dating sites and it's all about being big, fat and proud. I did join one once but I think I was actually too small for them as I didn't get any interest at all!" I laughed.

"Well, you could pitch some ideas to magazines for a feature on the rise of plus size dating" he suggested, "you could talk about how seedy plus size dating sites are, or how hard it is to find a decent, normal man on one. You could also go on everyday sites too and compare the responses you get?"

It was a good idea, and I had a tingle in my belly as I thought about it. I hadn't seen anything like it anywhere else, I guessed nobody wanted to go on a plus size dating site if they weren't plus size. For a change, the big girls had the advantage. Maybe I could even scout out the best places for Viva Voluptuous members to join, get them a discount…my mind was running away with me.

"Paul Clarke, I think I love you."

He blushed.

"Are you having a dessert?" he asked, hoping for a yes, judging by the look on his face.

"Definitely. I think this calls for the gooiest, most disgustingly calorific dessert on the menu, don't you? And another drink to toast your genius idea with."

A smile spread over his face as he grabbed the menu from me and studied it.

"I was hoping you'd say that," he grinned.

Chapter 33

Big Hearts – Dating at any size

Paul's little nugget of inspiration had turned into a really well-written pitch and I sent it by email with my fingers firmly crossed. This one would be the one that broke the drought. I could do this! And I hadn't even needed to be nagged into it this time.

I had to do a bit of convincing when it came to Lauren and Zoë. We'd all had our fair share of dodgy experiences with dating sites in the past, and although Zoë was firmly off the market now, her relationship with Chris was new enough for her to be able to remember what it was like. I had no such qualms though, and ever the optimist I'd dived straight in and started having a window shop of available men. Just for research purposes, you understand?

"Are you sure?" Lauren had wondered, when I told her what Paul had suggested.

Lauren had met Colin online and my last foray into online dating had produced six months of being with a man who was still in love with his ex-wife. Perhaps we weren't the best adverts for online dating. Still, I wasn't actually looking for love; I was just seeing who was out there and reporting back on it dispassionately. Well, that was the plan.

"I don't believe you're actually doing this," she frowned as we Googled plus size websites. I rejected a fair few of them outright for being just TOO much. "I might be a fat bird but seeing naked fat women with their backsides in the air doesn't actually hold much appeal for a straight girl," Zoë giggled as I couldn't resist showing her one of the more lurid sites on my laptop.

Lauren pointed at a huge advert with a very large naked woman on it, and some strategically placed hearts. "Would you trust your love life to a website with adverts this tacky?" she laughed. She had a point, and there was no way I was going to take my chances on joining a site like that. Some things were way beyond the call of duty.

I got rid of the offending page and shuddered. I felt like I needed to wash my brain after seeing some of the grotty pages devoted to 'BBW dating'. And why was it always women? There was nowhere to go if you had a thing for chubby men? I quite liked a man with a bit of chunkiness to him.

I was getting quite into nosing around some of the better dating sites, and although I'd intended just to chat and not actually meet up with anyone, there were a few men that looked and sounded lovely. I added my own profile, using an old picture that hopefully nobody would recognise, as well as no mention at all of Viva Voluptuous. I described myself as a freelance writer, looking for friendship and maybe more, and there was absolutely no mention of sex. Just to be on the safe side, I used an old email address - I didn't want perverts sending dodgy pictures to the account I used for work email.

I decided that I wouldn't make the first contact; I'd wait and see who messaged me.

Within less than 24 hours I'd had responses from a few semi-literate men who were asking me to show a bit of cleavage or tell them my bra size. Jesus, was this as good as it was going to get?

I'd had messages from a man whose selling point seemed to be that he had never had a girlfriend and was still living with his parents at 43, and a couple of men who'd started off OK then descended into trying to guess my bra size and ask me what I liked in bed. "Not you" was my answer.

"Hi, lovely pic, tell me more about you" started one of the nicer messages, from a man called Ben. I messaged back straight away with:

"Hi Ben, I'm Ellie. I'm 36, live in Cambridge and I've been single for a while. Looking to get to know a few people, but dating sites are a minefield. Tell me more about you."

I quite liked the sound of him. His profile didn't tell me much, although he did say he was an 'acquired taste' and had 'a bizarre sense of humour'. Interesting!

Ben emailed me straight back with, *"Nosing around a minefield isn't a great idea. What do you want to know? I ran away and joined the circus but they sent me back because I was scared of clowns. Now I work in mental health. And I can cook a mean spag bol."*

His massage made me snort out loud. We swapped instant message details and sat for hours that night talking nonsense to each other about all sorts of trivia – especially music tastes and embarrassing record collections.

"I love the smell of vinyl and used to collect rare, obscure punk singles" he informed me.

"So you're a bit of a music nerd then?"

"Yeah probably. Cheeky mare. What was your first ever single?"

I had to think about that. I didn't know whether pretending to be cool and saying Blondie or something was the way to go, or admitting to something really, really bad. I went for the latter.

"Remember you're a Womble," I admitted, sheepishly, if you can be sheepish over an instant message with the camera off.

The next thing I saw was the emoticon that was rolling on its sides, holding its tummy and laughing. Oh well. At least he hadn't run away…

"You've been on the telly, haven't you?" He said in one of his messages. I was impressed – he actually recognised me from the TV whereas nobody else had, so I sussed him out as being a bit cleverer and more perceptive than some of the others. *"I saw you on the One Show with your mates, you seemed really fun. I've always liked curvy girls. I thought it was really sweet when you mentioned your friend, too, but she didn't really let you talk about it, did she? What happened, if you don't mind me asking?"*

I told him, without going into too much detail, about Jane. His reply was, *"Oh my God, that's terrible. You must have been devastated. I hate the way the media try to make everyone conform to such a narrow idea of what's acceptable, and make anyone who doesn't fit in feel bad, I love what you're doing to change things, your thing at Covent Garden was class."*

I blushed, even though he couldn't see me.

The only other interesting guy was called Rick. He'd messaged me straight away with a confident, *"Hi Gorgeous"* and began flattering me with *"Your pic is fantastic, what a cleavage, do you have any more?"* and *"Your job sounds really interesting, what do you write about? Wanna write about me?"*

Rick was confident and chatty, worked as a personal trainer and looked quite nice. He was also very forward. I liked him immediately, even though he made me feel a bit nervous.

"Wanna talk on text, sexy?" he'd asked me after a couple of days of swapping messages. Despite my reservations, he seemed really fun, and forgetting Lauren's words of advice when we went into the project, I gave him my number and we started texting each other.

"Send me more pix of you," he texted late one night.

I was being sucked in by his constant attention. He was so complimentary, although he seemed to change the subject whenever I asked him about himself. I didn't know if he'd ever been married, had kids or anything except where he lived and that he was into fitness in a big way, drove around selling books, and liked football. Oh, and boobs.

"Your cleavage is just fantastic. Send me a close up," was a typical request. One day I searched online and took a picture of a topless woman, cropped it to remove the head and just show the top of her cleavage, and sent it to him to see if that would shut him up.

"OMG!" I got back almost immediately, *"Just wanna bury my face in those"* I was annoyed that he was so obsessed with my boobs, but there was part of me that was flattered.

Apart from Ben and Rick, I'd also had a contact from a nice enough sounding guy while I was out shopping, and looked at it briefly on my phone, thinking I'd reply later. When I got home, I had a missive from the same man, saying, among other things, *"I know you've looked at my message, you rude bitch, why didn't you reply? I hate women like you, think you're too good for me, do you?"*

I replied with a curt, *"Well, actually I looked at your message on my phone while I was out, and I'd fully intended to reply. But I don't think I'll bother now."* I duly blocked that one.

Although I was chatting to Ben most days, he was quite laid back. He made me smile and I was beginning to look forward to his messages. I was trawling the websites and making a note of some of the icky messages I was getting too, for the potential feature.

"If u want hot sex no strings txt me" was one. No thanks. Even with strings.

"Feeling horny, wench?" asked another. It took everything in my power not to reply with, *"No thank you and I'm not your wench, tosser"* and delete him instead.

Clearly some men thought that just because I was fat and on a dating site I must be desperate.

Rick started calling me all the time, and his constant attention was flattering. He blew hot and cold though – some days he didn't contact me at all, texts went unanswered and if I tried to call him, even at a time we'd agreed, I'd just go straight to voicemail. If I asked what he'd been up to, his reply was always the same.

"With a client."

I told Lauren about him over a coffee.

"I thought you weren't going to meet anyone?" she said, concerned, raising a just-plucked eyebrow.

"I know, I know, but he's so charming! He wants to meet me when he's next in the area." I said excitedly.

Lauren frowned, "What do you know about him?"

"Well, he's a personal trainer," I said, trying to remember everything else he'd said, "but he also has another job where he travels around the country selling books, I think. He's 40, six feet three, dark hair and glasses. He looks cute, and he says he wants to settle down. He wants to go to the Ice Hotel in Norway, too! I've always wanted to go there, and he says he'll take me one day. He's even climbed Kilimanjaro for charity and he wants to do the Himalayas next."

"Sounds too good to be true," Lauren snorted.

"I said that to him the other day, and he sulked for ages!" I laughed. "He told me off for judging him."

Rick had called me and been so charming; I told him that he was just telling me what I wanted to hear. That was how it had felt – it sounded almost as if he was saying anything I wanted, just to please me. It was a bit creepy really. He had been very annoyed with me when I suggested it though. I'd ended up feeling awful about doubting him, and apologised.

"So you haven't actually met him, then?" Lauren asked.

"Not yet. He promised to the other day but then cancelled," I admitted.

"I'm hearing alarm bells," Lauren said, with the concerned look on her face that usually preceded a lecture. I didn't look at her. She was going to try to talk me out of meeting Rick if I did, and I was enjoying the attention.

If I was honest, Rick did sound as if he could be a bit of a player. But I wasn't in this seriously, so it didn't hurt to flirt a bit, right? He flattered me so much, telling me how much he fancied big girls, I couldn't help but respond. So what if his flirty-ness was getting a bit crude, it was just a bit of fun, wasn't it?

So I was all set to meet up with him. He'd promised to take me out the next night, and had been flirting hard since the early hours. He was getting pretty full on, and when I told him off for being presumptuous, he responded with, *"Send me a pic of ur amazing tits"*

"No!" I replied, annoyed.

Well, after that, Rick refused to reply for hours. Clearly, the fact I was point blank refusing to give him any masturbation fodder was annoying him to the point that he wasn't even going to reply, let alone take me out that night.

I decided that plus-size dating sites were obviously full of complete losers, and consoled myself with the fact that I was supposed to be researching them, not getting myself involved with yet another waste of space.

The only thing that cheered me up was a completely daft conversation with Ben, who appeared to have some spare time before he went into work later. He started with.

"So. Who do you think would win in a fight? Orinoco or Uncle Bulgaria?"

The stupid arse. From that opener we ended up discussing the merits of various children's TV characters until he decided he was late for work and had to get a move on. He seemed like a really lovely, funny guy, but he hadn't asked for my phone number or to meet me yet.

I was keeping a note of all this for the fabulous feature I was planning in my head. I couldn't stop fretting about Rick though. I felt as if I'd offended him – and I was worrying myself round in circles about it, constantly checking my email.

While I was obsessively checking, something popped up from *Gracious* – the weekly lifestyle and fashion magazine I'd been trying to pitch to for about five years with no success whatsoever.

Dear Ellie

Thank you so much for this idea. I think it could work as a double page in Gracious – or maybe even stretch to three if we can get enough case studies. Could you confirm that you'll be able to provide us with at least two unique case studies, with images too, if possible?

I saw you on the One Show recently and I'm really pleased that you contacted us, as we've been thinking of covering more plus-size features and fashion for some time, but we've been looking for the right angle. This feature should be great – most people don't realise the pitfalls of plus-size dating so anything you can give us will be great.

Regards

Laura

I let out a little squeal, read the email about three times just to make sure it said what I thought it did, and then picked up my Blackberry.

"I'm going to be in *Gracious*!" I blurted down the phone to Lauren, the first person I could get through to.

I couldn't be bothered to wait for replies to texts; I was practically dancing around the flat by the time I'd got to the end of the email for the third time.

"Someone wants me to write an article for them!" I squealed. "A proper magazine! Woohoo!"

"You clever girl!" Lauren was so pleased, I think she'd started to believe I'd never do it, and she was pretty relieved that her constant nagging and pep talks had worked. "You got a pitch accepted. Oh my God! I'm so proud! Which one? And what article?"

I'd told her that I re-pitched the sex industry piece to Cosmo, but although I'd sent it, I hadn't expected a reply to that one, and I hadn't got one, either.

"The features editor absolutely loved my idea for a feature on plus-sized dating, and she's seen us on telly, so she really up for it." I gushed.

I couldn't get through to Zoë; her phone was turned off so I suspected she was either with Chris or writing furiously.

The deadline for the article was unbelievably short so I was going to have to turn this around pretty fast. With my recent experiences, I thought I should have a lot of material. I decided to put Rick and Ben out of my mind for a bit, and get on with writing my first ever *Gracious* feature instead.

Chapter 34

At first I thought it was my alarm, but as I came to, I realised that my phone was ringing, it was after midnight, and it was Rick. I almost sent him to voicemail, as my thumb hovered over the keypad, not really wanting to get into a conversation with him when I was half asleep. In the end, curiosity got the better of me and I picked up.

"Hello," I said in my most disdainful voice. "So how are you?"

Oh my, did he sound pathetic. "I'm OK," he replied slowly, "although I hurt a bit and I'm on painkillers."

"What happened?" I asked, concerned.

"I don't want to talk about it" was his response. The sensible voice in my head was telling me that he didn't want to talk about it because he was playing games, but not wanting to have an argument at that time of night, I tried to get him off the phone.

"I don't think this is going anywhere, do you?"

"No, neither do I. I can't be in a relationship with someone who doesn't trust me."

Who said anything about a relationship? This guy was unbelievable! I wanted to get him off the phone now and get back to sleep.

"Right, well…OK then. Let's just be friends?"

"I can come over now if you like?"

No way was I having him here this late at night.

"No, let's leave it. I'm tired. We can meet up for a coffee in town sometime."

"OK, well are you sure I can't come over now? Just for a chat, to sort this out?"

"Yes. I need my sleep, I'm tired, and I'm not in the mood. I'll speak to you soon."

"Please can I come over?"

"No. Night, Rick." I had visions of him turning up on my

doorstep, a bit like Jamie had done that night. The difference being there was no way I was going to let Rick into my house. Eventually I got him off the phone, and tried to get some sleep.

My restless sleep was interrupted at about 7.30am by the sound of my phone going off again. I was spectacularly annoyed when I saw Rick's name flash up on the screen. Now he was starting to get on my nerves.

"What time do you call this?" I growled, in my sleepy state.

"I'm doing a delivery around your way about 8 and I wondered if I could pop in for a cuppa on my way past. I really wanted to talk to you."

"Can't we just meet up in town?" I asked.

"I've got to go to Norwich after I've been to Cambridge. I just wanted to see you; we need to sort this out."

I didn't really know what exactly we needed to sort out.

"There's no point. Anyway, I'm going out."

Annoyed, I hung up on him. He called a few more times but I didn't answer. Eventually he seemed to give up.

He turned up about ten past eight. Luckily I was dressed. I have no idea what made me let him in, but he sounded so pathetic and I felt a bit guilty. I pressed the buzzer to let him up and before I had time to change my mind he was at the front door. My God he was huge. He was also pretty good-looking in the flesh, although the picture on the website was clearly at least a few years old, and very flattering.

"Do you want a coffee, then?" I asked, grumpily. "I have lots to do, you can't stay long."

"Please." He replied, looking around nervously, and was fiddling with his keys. I really didn't trust him. The sooner he was out of my flat, the better. I had a nervous feeling in the pit of my stomach that wouldn't go away.

He followed me into the kitchen and before I knew it, his arms were around my waist from behind me and he was kissing the back of my neck. I shrugged him away, and glared at him.

"Aren't we supposed to just be friends?"

"Yeah but you're gorgeous, can't we start again?"

He carried on, pulling me closer and then turning me round to face him. I have to admit it felt good, but unwelcome thoughts were interrupting the flow, trying to get my attention and tell me that this wasn't a good idea. I wriggled away again but he got hold of my arms and steered me to the sofa, where he carried on kissing me, and telling me how sexy I was. I was thinking of ways to extricate myself from the situation, but hoped he was just a bit over keen and that if I just didn't respond he'd get the hint. Then his hand started to stray to the button on my jeans. I moved it away.

"Rick, I'm not going to have sex with you."

He pulled back. "OK" he said, and carried on kissing me. His hand started to move up under my top instead. I pulled away and said again, "I'm not going to sleep with you; I'm not up for that."

He ignored me this time, kissing my neck and shoulders, pinning me down to the sofa. "You know you want it. You're a sexy lady." he insisted, reaching again for my jeans. I couldn't move, and he wasn't stopping. I started to panic as I tried to turn my head away from him, but he was kissing my neck, my face and his hand was undoing my bra as I tried to squirm. This wasn't happening, was it?

No it damn well wasn't. Mustering up all my courage, I decided that brute force wasn't going to work but outsmarting him might. "Do you want to take this to the bedroom?" I said in a shaky attempt at a seductive voice.

His eyes widened and he released his grip on me a bit. I pulled myself away from him completely, jumped up off the sofa, grabbed my phone and ran to the door. He looked confused.

"Get OUT!" I shouted. "Get out of my house NOW!" Rick sat there looking stupid. My heart was beating fast and I was in two minds whether to run outside, leaving him in my home, or just hope he would leave now I'd got away from him. I was on the verge of tears but trying to look defiant and feisty.

"Did you hear me? I want you to go."

Rick stood up, angrily and I thought he was going to hit me so I got out of his way. He strode towards the door, spitting the words "Frigid bitch" and left, not even looking at me as he went.

I slammed the door behind him and locked it, just in case he tried to get back in.

Chapter 35

I was still shaking half an hour later, even after scrubbing myself down in the shower for ages. While I was in there, I missed a call from Laura, the features editor at *Gracious*. Luckily she left a message; she wanted to make sure I had case studies for the feature.

If only she knew. Did I have a case study for her? I hadn't intended to end up as an example of what could go wrong when you date online, but at least, and I'd really rather not, I'd got some first-hand material now. I could have kicked myself for letting myself get into that situation. Why did I have to be such a 'nice' girl? Why couldn't I have just told him I wasn't going to let him in? I was my own worst enemy.

Lauren and I had always had a deal; if we dated anyone for the first time, we let each other know, and checked in while we were on the date to let each other know we were OK.

I hadn't had a chance with Rick; he'd just weaselled his way in.

I shuddered at the thought of what might have happened.

I ignored a few texts and calls from Lauren and Zoë over the next few days and spent most of the time on my own, brooding and baking. There was enough confectionery in my flat to stock up a tea room, with experimental muffins sitting alongside the flapjack I'd made earlier, and a particularly interesting batch of cupcakes which I'd decorated with silver balls just because I felt like it. I hadn't even looked at the feature for a couple of days, and the deadline was the end of the week. I just couldn't seem to muster up the enthusiasm to write about dating sites when I'd just had such a hideous time with someone I met on one.

Lauren wouldn't let it drop, Ben was sending me cheery messages that I was ignoring and Paul was wondering why he hadn't heard from me in days. Why wouldn't they leave me alone to sulk? I lied to Lauren and told her that I hadn't replied because

I was working so hard on the *Gracious* feature. I just ignored Ben's messages.

Paul knew I was covering something up, and as I munched my way through three silver-ball festooned cupcakes one by one, I decided that I might have to 'fess up to him about my stupidity. I could also make him feel guilty – as far as I was concerned, the whole thing was his idea in the first place, so I could give him a kind of guilt-by-proxy. Of course, Paul would also be able to help me get rid of all the baked goods that were in my kitchen, because I was running out of boxes to keep things in and if I ate any more sugary things I was going to be sick.

He'd invited me out for a drink but I didn't feel like going out, so I told him he could come over and see me instead. After a bit of resistance, he agreed to come over and I braced myself for a really big lecture.

I wasn't prepared for the, "What the hell happened to you?" though.

Paul was looking at me with genuine concern written all over his face. OK, so I was wearing manky leggings that I'd had on for three days and a t-shirt that had evidence of three days baking down it. I hadn't bothered with putting on any make up or straightening my hair. I didn't actually realise I looked that bad though. If anything, I thought I might have looked as if I'd had just a bit of a baking frenzy. Paul had an ability to see right through me sometimes, and he could clearly see there was something wrong.

"You've been baking again. What's up?" he asked, looking worried.

He was being so nice that I just flung myself at him and burst into tears.

Paul steered me towards the sofa, sat me down, and stroked my hair as I sobbed and snorted. I couldn't even manage to get any words out, as I let go of all the tension I was feeling. Eventually, the sobbing gave way to snuffling, and I sat up, wiped my face on my top, looked at Paul and stuttered, "I've had a bit of a bad experience. That Rick bloke came over out of the blue, I shouldn't have let him in – I thought he was going to rape me!"

I don't think I'd ever seen Paul that angry before. The colour really did seem to drain out of his face as he took in what I was saying. "Are you OK? Darling, why didn't you call me?"

He got up off the sofa, and started pacing around the room, muttering. "I should have looked out for you…this was all my idea"

"Paul, sit down honey, please…" I pleaded, "I'm OK."

He did as he was told and gave me a hug. "Do you want to talk about it, darling?" Despite his kind words, he was furious, and he looked as if he was about to explode.

"Yeah, I guess." I started. "But you'll have to calm down."

"Sorry sweetie. I promise I'll bite my tongue. Just tell me what happened."

I told Paul about Rick, from start to finish. To his credit, he didn't actually interrupt, tell me I was an idiot or make any comments about my naiveté. I think he was just scared that I might cry again and I'd already ruined his t-shirt with my mascara.

"I think I'd rather forget about the whole thing, and forget all about dating sites. Hateful things."

"No, no, you can't let one bad experience ruin your plans, Ellie. And you mustn't blame yourself for this. He manipulated you, made you feel sorry for him, and then caught you when you weren't expecting it. Men like that are sly, and that's probably why he's on a dating site for bigger women, because he thinks all bigger girls have low self-esteem and will be easy to manipulate."

He paused for a minute, then carried on, "That's another reason you have to carry on. You're trying to help women who might have felt crap about themselves before, feel more confident. That'll stop them falling prey to assholes like him. And your article will highlight the way some men prey on insecure women."

He gave me a big cuddle and I just sat there, head on his shoulder, feeling safe. I didn't actually want to say anything. Luckily, I knew Paul so well that I didn't actually have to. I don't know how long we sat there, TV on in the background, in total silence.

Paul stayed with me till late that evening, and somehow managed to talk me reluctantly into carrying on with the feature. He also managed to see off a fair number of muffins and cupcakes.

Once he'd gone, although it was late, I thought I'd better reply to the girls too. I sent them both exactly the same text, "*Sorry I've been anti-social but had a really horrible experience with Rick and wanted to hide away and lick my wounds.*"

Lauren had obviously gone to bed but Zoë called within minutes and I had to go through the whole thing all over again. Thankfully, this time it was without the waterworks. She wanted to come over to make sure I was all right, but I talked her out of it. I did get a bit of a lecture for breaking the number one dating rule though; always let your mates know when and where you're meeting a man for the first time.

I knew I'd been an idiot. It was my pride that was wounded more than anything and I'd get over it. It just made me so angry that men like that were able to get away with treating women like crap. I wondered how many other women he'd done it to. I was even more determined to keep on with Viva Voluptuous though; somehow it had strengthened my resolve. Even with my newly-found confidence, I'd still fallen victim to flattery and let a pest get the better of me, even if he didn't get what he came for. Women needed to be strong, be empowered and not fall prey to creeps like him who would take advantage of them because 'fat women were always grateful.'

I couldn't sleep, with ideas and thoughts buzzing around my

head. I checked my email and there was yet another message from Ben.

"Are you OK? I haven't heard from you in a while, are you seeing someone? I can take the rejection, I'll just go back to the circus."

I smiled at his persistence, despite myself. I toyed with the idea of deleting it, but chose just to ignore it. He was going to have to wait, though. I just wasn't in the mood for talking to men. I started work on the article. The words for the case study seemed to flow out of me, as I typed away, getting angrier and angrier. Taking all my frustration out on my long-suffering keyboard, I typed harder and faster until I'd managed to get it all out of my system and into a perfectly crafted anonymous case study.

I went for a last wander into the kitchen, in search of sweet things. Tomorrow, I decided, I was going to think positive, get my head together and get back onto the Viva Voluptuous campaign.

Tonight, however, I was going to eat more cake and go to bed.

Chapter 36

Any intentions I might have had of wallowing in self-pity were nipped in the bud by constant calls and visits from the girls, texts from Paul and the promise of a birthday weekend away. It happily coincided with a PR launch for a new brand of tights that Zoë had managed to wangle us invites for.

I managed to drag myself out of my doldrums and let myself get excessively excited about the whole thing, not just because I loved York almost more than anywhere else in the country, but also because I loved tights, and getting a decent pair of funky tights above a size 16 was like finding a doughnut at a slimming class. It just didn't happen, and if you did by some miracle manage to find one, it was invariably a disappointment.

This brand was a plus-size range, and they had everything from soft woolly tights to glitter-ball styles, funky patterns and sexy fishnets. About time! I was going to blog the hell out of this and I wanted to get in with the PR girls for the brand so that I could try and wangle a discount for Viva Voluptuous.

I'd managed to write the *Gracious* feature, I'd written my little heart out, and in a twisted way, what had happened with Rick had made it easier. I'd managed to write a good contrast between the sleaziness and desperation I'd encountered on the few plus-size dating sites I'd joined up to, combined them with the competition with 'normal' dating sites and argued the case for a mainstream version of that for plus sized people, and their admirers. It was almost like an advert for something that didn't exist yet!

We were booked into a swanky hotel in the centre of York, which was close enough to The Shambles and all the shops and bars. York was my go-to place whenever I felt like I needed a bit of a boost, even more so than Brighton, which was always great for a shot of sea air and decadence. I was really looking forward to spending some time with the girls, as between my hermit-like behaviour and Zoë writing and disappearing backwards and forwards to see Chris or the yoga DVD people at Rawthwaite Hall, we just didn't seem to be seeing that much of each other. Lauren had been busy moving and also managed to find herself a lodger, which was great. He was a rugby player and quite a bit younger than her. I wasn't sure what he did as a day job, because as far as Lauren was concerned, 'Rugby Player' was enough. She hadn't admitted it yet, but I knew she had the hots for him.

This weekend had been planned for months, and it was just what I needed.

However, I wasn't quite sure who came up with the idea of walking all the steps in York Minster, while being filmed, just to make the point that fat girls can be just as fit as skinny girls. Oh, actually, that would have been me. Silly Ellie. There are 275 of them, in a spiral, the staircase is incredibly narrow, and it's dark in there. Very dark. Probably too dark for the film that Lauren tried to take, I thought as I clambered the stairs, to even come out properly. It was definitely one for the blog, as we had to keep stopping, and trying not to laugh as I grabbed hold of the ropes along the side of the stairs for dear life, yelping "But what if I fall down?"

I was convinced that I was going to slip on the stone steps, even in my most sensible shoes, let go of the ropes and take the other two girls out as I went tumbling to my doom. My panicked face alone would have made for a good video. Zoë was sniggering all the way up while Lauren was telling me off for being such a wuss, and it was definitely a comedic moment. We all managed to get to the top eventually, and I'm not going to lie, we were all out of breath.

"Last one to Betty's buys the Fat Rascals." I said, between gasps of air.

We filmed ourselves being given our certificates for climbing all 275 of the steps, and declared the expedition a success. We also got some stunning film from the top of the Minster, as we got our breath back.

Zoë and Lauren treated me to a birthday tea in Betty's, complete with scones and jam, Fat Rascals and Earl Grey tea.

"So how are you feeling?" Lauren asked me, as I munched my way through a plate of clotted cream covered scones.

"My legs are still a bit wobbly." I laughed, "But the cakes are helping."

"I didn't mean that." She said, and then I realised what she was talking about. My heart sank.

Zoë cottoned on and shot her a warning look. It didn't stop Lauren though.

"You haven't really talked about what happened, honey. We just want to make sure you're OK."

"I don't want to talk about it." I said sternly, continuing to shovel scone and cream into my face in the hope that Lauren would drop it.

"Have you heard from him since?" she persisted.

I sighed as a blob of cream fell off the scone and dropped right down my cleavage. Scooping it out with my fingers and eating it, I braced myself. She wasn't going to let it lie, and it was my birthday. Not fair.

"No."

"Have you heard from the other one?"

"Ben. Yes. Once or twice. But we're just friends."

Zoë put her fork down and looked at me, expectantly. "Ben?"

Guiltily, I realised that I hadn't even told Zoë about Ben. Mind you, there wasn't really anything to tell.

"He's the only other person I made contact with while I was on the other fat girl dating site. Seems like a nice guy but I'm just not interested."

Suddenly I didn't want any more cake. I pushed my plate to one side, sulkily. "I had a bad experience, and I just about got away with it. I'll be blogging about it as soon as I'm up to it, just warning girls to look out for the kind of man who thinks a fat girl should be grateful for any attention she gets, and therefore allow him to do whatever he wants to her. It's made me realise just how sleazy some men are. Now can we change the subject?"

"Not yet," Lauren said, sternly. "It's not just about one sleazy bloke is it? It's you, and your inability to say no, in case you upset someone."

"I don't know what you mean" I lied. Now I was fiddling with the frill on the edge of the table cloth and avoiding looking at either of them. Why did I feel about 12?

"Yes you do!" Lauren continued, on a roll. Didn't she know she was supposed to be nice to me on my birthday? "You're always worrying about what other people think of you, and you always have done. You think if you don't do what people want, they won't like you. How do you expect to deal with the flak you get for being a fat girl advocate if you don't toughen up a bit, Missy?"

"That's different. I believe in Viva Voluptuous." I said, defending myself.

"Well, you should believe in YOU!" Lauren said, raising her voices in exasperation. I looked around to see if anyone was listening to our argument. Lauren carried on, "You have to believe that you're OK as you are. You don't have to be, say or do what other people say you should, just to be accepted. You're absolutely bloody wonderful the way you are, you silly mare."

I didn't quite know what to say. I was tearing up. I knew she was right. I was a people pleaser and it was time I started standing up for myself. "OK, OK, you're right. But I really don't want to talk about it at the moment. I want to talk about something fun. So, how's the yoga DVD and your hot yoga lover?" I said to Zoë, in an effort to change the subject and break the tension.

She visibly seemed to light up at the mention of Chris. Lauren sighed and looked at her watch.

"He's just so freaking HOT – I can't believe my luck!" Zoë was grinning all over her face.

"So, does the yoga, you know, help?" I giggled.

"Ummm…let's just say the man is flexible and leave it right there."

"I do believe you're actually blushing, Miss Zoë." Lauren teased. She was clearly a bit annoyed that Zoë's love life had interrupted her lecture, but I really didn't want to talk about it anymore, so I was very glad to have got the conversation back onto something more fun.

"I'm totally head over heels about the guy," smiled Zoë. "I've never met anyone like him. We've had a few, shall we say, creative issues with the DVD, but he just makes me laugh whenever I get cross with him, and I can't argue with him."

"So do you know when the DVD is coming out?" I asked.

"We're looking at a pre-Christmas release, to hit the shops in time for all the New Year fitness DVD action. The classes are already being trialled at Rawthwaite, Chris has done a couple and run a few training days for other instructors. It's going into *Being Active* health clubs in the next month, and they'll be doing a PR push on it, 'cos they really want to make some dosh out of the pudgy pound right now."

"So obesity is finally fashionable then?" Lauren exclaimed, laughing.

"Ha! Well I wouldn't quite go that far, but we're definitely making a difference, girls. We've got a kick-ass website, we've been on TV, I'm in *Gracious* and we're getting big people into yoga and fitness. And we've been on telly! We're officially leaders of a movement, according to the *Daily News*. We're just freakin' awesome!"

"We most certainly are!" I agreed, holding up my hand to high-five Zoë.

"Awesome!!!" we both exclaimed, with a high-five. I turned to

Lauren and did the same.

The waitresses looked amused and the table of OAPs next to us looked slightly scared.

"Alright, birthday girl," Lauren said, affectionately, "scoff up the rest of that scone and let's get ready to party!"

Chapter 37

I'd been to PR launches before. I'd met a few celebs, sometimes I'd even been star-struck enough to get a sneaky picture taken of myself while I'm with them, but this launch was a cut above the usual. I had no idea why they chose to launch in York, because big swanky parties like this were usually the preserve of London. Someone told me that the company director was a local and hated travelling down to the capital, so maybe that was why she'd decided that the best place to unleash her fabulous new hosiery on an expectant world was York city centre.

They'd hired a really big, very nice wine bar and had it decorated with images of 1940s and 50s film stars. I wasn't sure what the relevance was between funky tights and film stars, but it sure as hell looked good.

"Isn't that what's-her-name from Hollycaks? You know, the blonde one?" I said to Lauren, pointing at a giggly, over made-up woman I vaguely recognised.

"They're all blonde on Hollyoaks," Lauren replied sarcastically, "you're going to have to elaborate."

I thought I saw a few people from the TV doing the rounds and swiping canapés, and I was sure I spotted someone I'd seen on X-factor a few weeks ago holding court with a couple of photographers as well.

I was looking pretty hot, even if I did say so myself. Not only was I kitted out in my highest heels, but Zoë and Lauren had got together with Colette to create a gorgeous corset, for my birthday. It was a deep midnight blue, plain but absolutely beautiful. I was wearing it with a black pencil skirt and I felt amazing. Zoë was decked out in a curve-hugging red halter neck dress and shoes that were so high she had to concentrate before she walked anywhere. There was no way she was getting tipsy that night. Lauren was more understated, in a sophisticated and very expensive wrap dress accessorised with bold jewellery and of course, her trademark Louboutin heels. We all looked the part.

The PRs had really gone to town with the goody bags at the launch – there were samples of the latest Lancome fragrance and Chanel skincare, a bar of expensive-looking artisan chocolate (a very small bar) and vouchers for pairs of the new range of tights. They hadn't even unveiled the name of the range yet, it was all still a big secret.

"Is that Angelina Jolie over there?" whispered Zoë.

"Don't be daft," I replied. Although to be fair, the woman resolutely ignoring the food and smiling enigmatically definitely looked like Angelina. But there was no way Angelina Jolie would be at a press launch for tights. I mean, come on. She doesn't even have any fat friends, why would she have been interested in plus size hosiery?

"Maybe she knows Ivy McCauley?" Lauren suggested. Ivy, the owner of the company, had been a model until ten years ago, and it was quite possible that she had celebrity friends. Maybe Zoë had spotted a real, live A-lister?

"She's heading into the ladies'" I whispered to Zoë. Although I'm not entirely sure why I was whispering, as nobody could have heard us over the noise of 200 plus people and a PA system blaring out Girls Aloud. Girls Aloud? Whoever was responsible for the playlist probably needed a bit of instruction on what 'the young people' were listening to.

There was nothing else for it, one of us was going to have to follow Angelina into the toilets to see if it was actually her or just a very convincing impostor. I got the short straw.

I sneaked in, hoping that nobody thought I was only going to the loo because Angelina Jolie was. Even if that was, in fact, exactly what I was doing. I was going to have to get in and stare at her, without her realising that I thought she was Ange. And what's more, part of my challenge was to get a picture of her on my Blackberry, if it actually was.

I could almost hear the other two sniggering as I took up the challenge.

I managed to follow the mystery woman into the ladies' but by the time I got in there she'd disappeared into a cubicle. Damn! I decided that the best plan would be to pretend I was touching up my make up in the mirror, get my phone ready, and wait. Listening out for sounds of her calling Brad on her mobile (because that was going to happen, of course) I stayed as quiet as I could, listened for the sound of the loo roll dispenser and then the flush, and got ready for Angelina's exit. In my head I was making up very silly headlines for the blog.

"Angelina Jolie doesn't wash her hands after the toilet - shock."

I turned to look in the mirror at her as she stood next to me by the sink. She was looking down at her hands, but then I caught her eye and...of course it wasn't her. She smiled at me, probably wondering why I'd been staring at her so intently while she was washing her hands, and I smiled back. There goes that headline, anyway. She did look just like Angelina, though. I wasn't going to tell her that...I suspect she already knew. She left the loo and I hung back a bit, just so that I didn't look like I was stalking her.

I walked out to find Zoë and Lauren doubled up laughing at me.

"Can't believe you fell for that one!" Lauren giggled, while I looked on, confused. The rotten cows had been winding me up and hadn't thought it was Angelina Jolie for a minute. No fair! I blushed and then reached for my drink.

"I knew she wasn't, really." I lied. "I was just playing along with you."

I could tell neither of them believed me.

So we enjoyed plenty of free wine and champagne at the launch, they'd put on a burlesque show with dancing girls, all very curvaceous, but wearing a pair of the new tights as part of their costume. It was very clever. After the show, and more canapés and drinks, there was a Q&A session, and then time for interviews with the creator of the range herself, Ivy McCauley. The only thing I wasn't entirely sure of was the name they'd chosen for the tights; 'Razzle'. I know it's catchy, but wasn't that the name of a smutty magazine?

I really wanted to have a chat with Ivy. Ideas for the website had been coming to me thick and fast just lately and I'd been thinking about how fantastic it could be if I managed to link up with some exciting new fashion brands.

I managed to get my time and dived in for a quick chat with Ivy, away from the party. She was very glamorous – quite obviously plus-size but she wore her curves well, and nobody would be able to tell her that big girls weren't sexy. She was wearing a super-glamorous shift dress in a muted shade of blue, and some understated heels. Her long, blonde hair was piled up on her head into a messy up-do and she looked at least ten years younger than the 54 she was reported to be in the tabloids.

"Please, sit down," she gestured.

As I sat down, attempting to be elegant, she stared at me intently. "So, it's Ellie Johnstone, isn't it?"

"Yes, that's right. I run the Viva Voluptuous website."

"Oh!" A flicker of recognition crossed Ivy's face. "I know you – you were part of the Covent Garden flash mob, weren't you?"

I grinned. I loved being recognised. "Yes, that was me! Seems like a long time ago now"

Ivy smiled. She was an intimidating woman, but I sensed that she quite liked me, so I was probably OK.

"Yes, I remember, and you were on that evening show, too? I like that. You were dressed up in burlesque outfits, yes, and it made me laugh. So, Ellie. What did you want to ask me?"

I took a deep breath.

"I wondered whether you would be interested in working with me, and Viva Voluptuous?" I gabbled. I was scared she was going to say no, after all I was just a glorified blogger and she was a semi-celebrity, ex-model and well known for not suffering fools gladly.

"What's in it for me? What did you have in mind?"

"I was thinking perhaps we could design a VV range of tights, which we'd also sell through our website? I can give you our membership figures and all the techie information later, but I just wanted to run the idea past you."

"I don't usually do promotions with websites," Ivy said, "but I might be able to make an exception. I do love what you girls are doing, and I don't think it would hurt to be associated with you. Can you send some ideas and figures across to my PA? We can discuss it tomorrow?"

"Thank you, Ivy." I almost sung, grinning from ear to ear. I couldn't believe it had been so easy! Obviously I had to convince her it was worth her while, and the offer might not have been that great, but she wanted to work with us. And she'd heard of me. I was actually getting to be well-known, enough that someone reasonably famous knew who I was.

Zoë and Lauren were waiting outside, excitedly, clutching the last glasses of free champagne.

"So?" Lauren asked, impatiently. I tried to pretend to be disappointed but I was rubbish at hiding my feelings and couldn't contain my grin any longer.

"I think she's in!" I exclaimed.

"OMIGOD!" Zoë gave me a massive hug and a sloppy kiss on the cheek, leaving hot pink lipstick marks on my face. Lauren hugged me too. "She knew who we were, and she likes what we do." I explained. "How cool is that?"

"Pretty damn cool, lady." Lauren replied. She managed to procure me another glass of champagne and we toasted the evening's success, downing the glasses in two gulps. And burping. Well, I did. So uncouth, I know.

And at that moment, something happened that I would have never in a thousand years have expected. We were papped. Out of nowhere, as we were downing drinks and belching the bubbles, someone took a picture of us.

We didn't know who it was, where they were from or what was going on, but there had been plenty of people around taking pictures of the girls in the Burlesque show, Ivy presenting the range, and various D-list celebrities enjoying the freebies and the chance to get in the tabloids. But we weren't expecting them to recognise us!

"Did that really just happen?" Zoë giggled. "Did someone just, you know, PAP us?"

"You know, I think it did." Lauren laughed. "Oh My God. We're actually famous. I mean really, properly."

"Why did they have to get a picture of me knocking back free champagne though?" I moaned, " My mum will give me so much grief for not being ladylike."

Zoë smacked me. "It's your birthday, silly. And you've been given free champagne all evening, got Ivy McCauley in on the website AND got us papped. I don't think anyone's going to be too upset at you drinking to that!"

I had to admit that she had a point. I sneaked off to the loo again, and decided to check my email while I was waiting. Clearly the free champagne had started affecting all the women at the party as the loo was choc-full and the queue was out of the door. There was an email from Ben – I hadn't heard from him in ages. He'd obviously kept the email address I'd sent him, and for some reason that made me smile. A lot.

"Hi Ellie, how are you? It's your birthday today, isn't it? Happy birthday! I hope you have a wonderful day. I don't know what the situation is with you, you're not online on the site anymore so I thought maybe you'd got together with that other guy. If you did, I hope it's going well. If not, well my luck could be in, couldn't it? Let me know before I'm forced to undergo intensive therapy for my clown phobia so that they'll let me back in the circus ring with the elephants. Remember you're a Womble - Ben xx"

I was far too drunk to reply, and I wasn't sure if I should. I felt like putting the whole dating site experience behind me and never going there again. I ignored him, despite giggling at his message.

Everyone was leaving the bar now, apart from a few stragglers, and the three of us decided we'd probably better stagger back to the hotel. Against her better judgement, Zoë had got herself very, very drunk and we had to help her back, taking an arm each to stop her getting her heels stuck in the pavement and falling flat on her face. It was Zoë's special move after a few too many.

We got back to my room and there was yet another bottle of free champagne waiting. This time, from Chris, who had sent it for me to share with Zoë and Lauren as a birthday gift. That man was way too good to be true. I decided to save it – even I wasn't dumb enough to think drinking any more was a good move. Zoë fell asleep draped across the end of my bed, after a few choruses of, "We got papped, we got papped!" and Lauren went back to her room. I was just glad we didn't have to check out until eleven...

Chapter 38

It still shocked me to see my picture in *Hot*. Of course, they got me at an unflattering angle, pulling a face while I was necking champagne. The caption was terrible. I even showed up in the *Daily News* sidebar of shame, with Lauren and Zoë, glasses of champagne aloft and grinning inanely. It seemed that the launch of Razzle Tights was a huge media occasion and the very fact that we'd managed to secure an invite and get an audience with Ivy McCauley was pretty impressive.

I'd told everyone about the event and blogged all about it on the website, where we'd also added the video of us climbing all the steps of York Minster tower. Just to make it worth doing, we'd suggested before we went away that we used the challenge to raise some money for Cancer Research and set up a page for donations; after we'd got back from the weekend we checked the page and found we'd been sponsored over £2000. So our red faces and breathlessness were worth it.

I posted links to the online *Daily News* and *Hot* magazine to show that we'd actually been papped at a celebrity event. I didn't really care that the pictures were less than flattering; they were proof that people knew who we were and what we stood for. I was also enjoying the attention and showing off a bit.

I'd sent some figures and a proposal to Ivy McCauley as she'd asked me to, and I was still waiting to hear back from her about the Viva Voluptuous tights idea. Zoë and I had already come up with some funky designs.

It seemed as if the three of us were working really hard on various projects. Zoë had been busy working with Chris on the yoga, and her book had come back from being edited, so she was busy writing it for the umpteenth time and adding in all the bits she forgot the first, second and third time around. This book writing business was definitely hard work and sometimes I could tell she almost wished that she'd never suggested it. The research she'd had to do in the first place, the interviews and then actually pulling it all together and writing it all in her own style – it was hard-going and Zoë had put in many a late night and early morning when she'd been stuck on a chapter.

"I can't do this anymore...it's too freakin' hard" she'd complained one day, after sitting up until almost 4 am trying to get one of the chapters just right. She'd been working on rewriting that chapter for ages, and she just couldn't get it to sound how she wanted it to.

"Keep at it, sweetie, get it perfect and you'll have a best seller on your hands. Remember, the world needs you!"

That seemed to pacify her but I could tell she was really starting to stress out over getting it finished on time and off to the publisher. They wanted to cash in on all the publicity we'd been getting and were pestering her to get that manuscript finished so they could rush the publication through the system and get it out there while body confidence was still such a massive hot topic.

Everything was going in the right direction and it was feeling good. I even relented eventually replied to Ben's email.

"Hey You, I had a lovely birthday, got very drunk at a celeb party and got papped. That makes me sound way more famous than I am, but I like the sound of it anyway. I'm not seeing the other guy, I'm still a free agent, but I think you should have therapy anyway. Being scared of clowns could cause major issues for you in the future, and develop into a fear of men in big shoes too. You can't be too careful."

Despite my reservations I was starting to look forward to hearing from him. Later, he replied:

"Hey Miss Ellie,

Well today I met up with an old friend of mine, and I told him I was talking to one of the girls who was on the TV dressed up in the dancer's costumes in the summer. He wanted me to get your autograph!"

Mister Ben"

He'd taken to calling me Miss Ellie, after the matriarch from Dallas, following a long involved conversation that took us through kid's TV, eighties telly and even as far as El Dorado and Only Fools and Horses. I'd told him my favourite old TV had to be Howard's Way and The House of Elliot (for the dresses, you understand).

"I used to sneak downstairs and hide behind the sofa to watch Dallas when my Mum thought I'd gone to bed," he admitted. "And I loved Miss Ellie because she reminded me of my Nana."

I thought that was such a cute anecdote that I didn't really mind him renaming me Miss Ellie. And it seemed only right to call him Mr Ben, too. *"As if by magic, the mental health nurse appeared"* I'd say, every time he popped up on instant message.

One thing I didn't expect was that our celebrity appearance in the media would have such a great effect on Viva Voluptuous. Within a few days, we'd been contacted by companies who wanted to know if they could advertise on the site. It was hard to say no when the offer from a big diet company came in but we stood our ground. No way was I letting a diet club advertise on VV.

Paul was convinced that we should start offering a dating service too, and that I should meet Ben.

I'd been putting Ben off for a couple of weeks, scared of getting into another situation like I'd been in before. I'd been very, very careful not to get into any conversations that could be interpreted as being a come on, but even so, he'd asked me out twice.

"Do you fancy meeting me then, Miss Ellie?"

I did...but I didn't. I had to think on my feet.

"When?"

"Any afternoon this week? I'm on nights but I'm around until 5ish"

"I'd love to, but I can't do this week, I'm really busy."

"What, all week? You can't even escape for a teeny weeny coffee with a very strange man?"

I giggled to myself. I was tempted, but nope, I was standing strong. Not going down that road again.

"I'll let you know if I can manage to get away, but probably not this week…"

"OK, how about next week?"

"I'll keep you posted, OK?"

Each time I'd told him I had too much to do with the website, and I had a horrible feeling he knew I was telling fibs. Paul, ever the logical one, sat me down one evening and asked me, "How long are you going to blame yourself for what happened with that other guy?"

Always to the point, was Paul.

"I don't blame myself. But I'm just not up for anything." I lied.

Paul rolled his eyes at me and gave me his best Paddington Bear style hard-stare. "Really?"

I couldn't look him in the eye. I hated being nagged. I hadn't mentioned Rick for weeks and I'd banned the rest of them from talking about him as well, so Paul was pushing his luck making me go there.

"Really." I lied again.

"Come on, Smellie. I don't believe you."

I thumped him. He knew I hated that nickname and so he used it when he wanted to wind me up.

"What's wrong with this Ben bloke? He sounds like he really likes you."

"I told you, I don't want a relationship at the moment. I'm dating myself."

"Crap!" Paul was smirking. He thought the idea of dating yourself was a whole lot of self-help mumbo jumbo. "You have to get back out there and take a chance. You've been single for months, since that little boy you were going out with…"

I hit him again. "He was 27!"

Sometimes I hated Paul, even though I also loved him dearly. He knew me too well, and he was usually spot on. He was this time, too.

"If you're nervous, just meet him for a coffee, as a friend. Not even a drink, just a coffee and a cake, in the town, somewhere neutral. Have a chat with him, suss him out and then decide if you want to go on a real date with him. You don't have to agree to everything a man says, you know? You can tell him you want to be friends."

I sighed. I wished Paul would stop being so…right.

"I'll think about it. But I'm not going to promise anything."

Paul knew I was a stubborn cow when I wanted to be. But he'd also hit the nail on the head, just like Lauren when she'd had a go at me in York that afternoon. I'd been guilty of that with my ex-husband, Darren, too. With Mark I'd tried to mould myself into what he wanted me to be, to make him love me back. With Jamie I'd let him decide whether he saw me or not. I'd accepted that he would turn up drunk, whenever he felt like it, and want sex. I let him think it was OK to see other women, and been too scared to admit to him – and even myself - that I wanted more. I gave him the go-ahead to avoid any kind of commitment and so I was as much to blame when he didn't think it was a problem that he was sleeping with God only knows who else. I told myself that this was all I wanted because I was scared of getting hurt again.

I was a doormat, and that's why men were taking advantage of my nature and not treating me properly. I felt as if the sun had come out in my head. No more Miss Super-Nice Lady.

I knew a lot of fat people were people pleasers. It was almost a case of "I know I'm fat, but if I'm nice to you, maybe you won't notice." As I looked back I realised that it had been my problem for a very long time. Even with Jane. I'd looked up to her, idolised her even. I'd started dieting with her when I was only slightly overweight, just to keep her happy, and got sucked into hating my body because it wasn't magazine perfect. Finding out that she was just as screwed up as everyone else really knocked her off the pedestal I'd put her on. She, in turn, had been built up to look perfect, everyone loved her and she was so bound up in her beauty that when she thought she was getting fat, she couldn't cope with it. That was how she pleased everyone and she felt as if she was letting herself and everyone else down.

Then I thought about Zoe, who was universally loved, but usually pleased herself. She didn't have any airs and graces but she was genuinely happy with herself, her body and who she was. People were drawn to her, and although she was undoubtedly beautiful and genuinely nice, her complete lack of self-obsession and genuine interest in other people was probably one of the things that made them love her so much. She never complained about her size, she was just Zoe. Take it or leave it.

Paul and I sat in silence for a good twenty minutes while I processed all the thoughts he'd churned up. He didn't mind; I'd been extra specially kind and decided that I was going to let him watch the football anyway. Part of me felt such an idiot for letting people treat me the way they had. I couldn't blame it on my weight – it was me, pure and simple. I'd always thought I had to be unselfish, put everyone else first, and while that was fine with the people I loved and trusted, because they wouldn't take advantage of it, it gave the rubbish men in my life way too much power. It was so obvious. I needed to stop being nice, listen to my heart and head, and not take any more crap from anyone who didn't have my best interests at heart.

Chapter 39

It didn't take Ben long to ask me out again.

I had to give him full marks for determination. We were in the middle of another long, involved discussion about the pros and cons of daytime TV, and I was ranting as best I could over Instant Messenger about how most of it, especially the talk shows where unfortunate people were baited into swearing at each other because they didn't know who the father of their unlucky offspring was, made me want to put my foot through the TV.

He caught me off guard with, *"So what are you doing after Jezza then?"* and before I could think of an excuse I'd agreed to meet him for a lunchtime coffee.

I changed my mind about three times, sent endless text messages to Zoë

"Should I do this?" I fretted.

"Do you want to meet him?" she replied.

"Yes, I think so…"

"Well, are you sure?" Zoe questioned.

"Yes, he makes me laugh." I texted back.

"What's the problem, then? Where are you meeting him?"

"In Starbucks, just for a coffee."

"You'll be fine. Let me know how it goes. Text me and let me know you're OK"

She was very patient with me, even though she was in the middle of finalising the details of the cover for her yoga DVD. While I was texting, I tried on just about everything in my wardrobe at least once. There were jumpers on the bedroom floor, jeans, leggings and shoes. The place looked like it had been burgled.

Of course, then I went back to the first thing I'd picked out, which was jeans and a jumper. My best jeans, of course.

I was stupidly nervous, even though I'd made it really clear that we were just meeting as friends. The poor guy couldn't have been nicer about it. I found myself on a bus into the city centre about half an hour too early. Nerves rattling around in my stomach (which was already growling because I hadn't eaten anything all day) I walked round a couple of shops to pass some time, sneakily looking out of the window to see if anyone who looked like Ben arrived. I wanted him to arrive first, so that if I chickened out I could make a run for it and he'd never know. I know, that was pretty mean of me. It was only a last resort.

I saw a man walk slowly up to the coffee shop, looking hesitant. He stopped, looked around and looked directly in the window of the jewellery shop I was hiding in. I caught a glimpse of him…what a disappointment. He was a lot shorter than the 5 feet 10 he'd given as his height on the dating site, he was wearing a t-shirt that looked as if it had seen better days and I'm sure he had more hair in his profile photograph. I couldn't see his face properly as he'd turned around again, but I could feel my heart sinking. Never mind, I told myself, we can still be friends. He did make me giggle. It was nearly time for the date so I wandered out of the shop, slowly, bracing myself for a closer look at the man I'd been getting so excited about.

Just as I walked towards him, I felt a hand on my shoulder.

"Ellie?"

"Wha…?" I turned to see a slightly flustered, very cute guy smiling at me. He had an adorable, cheeky grin and the most gorgeous eyes I'd ever seen. Oh my God. It was Ben. He had dark, curly hair, and looked a lot younger than his 42 years, dressed in loose jeans and a navy jumper, with trainer boots.

"Ben?"

"Sure is." He leaned towards me and gave me a massive hug. It was lovely.

The relief was immense as I watched the stranger I'd thought was Ben walk off down the road, munching a pastry from the coffee shop.

"You smell like my Mum," was Ben's next statement. Confused, I stared at him, trying to think of a witty reply.

"It could be worse. I could smell like your Nan."

"True." He exclaimed with sheepishly. "Sorry, that was probably the worst introduction EVER, so now we've got that out of the way, are we going in for a coffee? My treat? And I can even stretch to a cakey thing if you'd like?"

"How could I refuse?" I smiled back.

I needn't have worried about getting on with Ben. We chatted for what seemed like hours. "So, where have you been for the last few weeks? I thought I was never going to get a reply from you," he asked. I felt a bit mean.

"I've had a lot on – been to York with the girls, and been working a lot too." I said, truthfully. I thought I'd leave the bit about not wanting anything to do with men for a bit out.

"I haven't been to York in years. I'd love to go back." Ben grinned. "I love Betty's Tea Shop."

"Oh God, me too!" I exclaimed. "I can't go to York and not go to Betty's. It would be a complete waste of a visit."

"You're a girl after my heart" he smiled. "Talking of Bettys, which makes me think of cake, would you like something cakey? I'm going to have something."

"Mmm, yes, talking about that place always makes me hungry too," I said, thinking of Fat Rascals. "I think my blood sugar levels are calling for carrot cake!"

Ben didn't give me anything resembling a disapproving look as I ate up every last crumb, forgetting to offer him any. Maybe it was a bit too forward to start eating food from each other's plates anyway.

By the time we'd seen off three coffees and I'd made two trips to the loo (damn you drinking coffee on an empty stomach) we'd just about exhausted all the people-watching possibilities and felt like a change of scenery. "Do you fancy going somewhere else?" he asked, innocently.

Still touchy after the Rick incident, I wasn't sure whether he was angling for an invite back to my place, and even though I really liked him, I wasn't going down that road again.

"Do you fancy a walk in the park?" I suggested.

"It's freezing!" He replied. "But as it's you, I'll do it."

We walked out of the city and towards the park, which was populated with a few people walking their dogs and that was about it. The chill of early autumn was putting people off today and I was glad I'd worn a jumper. Poor Ben didn't even have a jacket and I realised he must be freezing. We crossed the main road towards the park and as we walked, Ben grabbed my hand.

"Are we on a proper date, Miss Ellie?" He asked, playfully, "Or are we just friends? Your call."

I didn't take my hand away. I guess that told him all he needed to know. "What do you think, Mr Ben?"

He smiled and squeezed my hand. My heart did a little somersault. I hadn't expected to like him so much.

We walked around the park, chatting about all sorts. I told him about my childhood, growing up on the south coast and then moving to Cambridge when I was in my early teens and meeting Jane.

I told him the basics about my marriage, although when I started he interrupted, "I think I get the picture, I read that piece in the *Daily News*, where your ex said you used to throw up."

I went cold. "I didn't, you know? You do know that was all lies, don't you?" I was so embarrassed.

To his credit, he said that he thought Darren sounded like an arsehole. "He is." I agreed. "He wanted a skinny wife; well I was slim when we met. Jane was ill back then and even though I was barely out of my teens, I was dieting, but I wasn't fat. He knew Jane had an eating problem but he still pressurised me for years after she died, and was always suggesting I went back to a slimming club. One year, he actually bought me a slimming club membership for Christmas!"

"Bastard! No way!?" Ben actually laughed out loud at that one.

"He did. A gym membership wouldn't have been so bad, but no, he had to go one step further and buy me a slimming club membership. For ten weeks. I felt obliged to go, and sit through all those women yakking on about their weight and how many biscuits they'd eaten, every week for ten weeks."

"I can't believe that he'd do that. It's even worse than an ironing board!"

I giggled. I could talk about it now.

"It is, isn't it? His excuse was that I joined every year after Christmas, which was true back then, so he was trying to be helpful and save me money. Last of the great romantics, hey?"

Ben still couldn't believe anyone would buy their wife a slimming club membership for a Christmas present.

"And I thought my mum's annual Christmas jumper was bad."

Ben also told me a lot about his past. I knew he was a mental health nurse, which was how he'd managed to see me during the day at such short notice. I already knew that, but I didn't know what had made him choose that as a career.

"I haven't always been in this sort of job," he confessed. "I worked in offices for years, and hated it. I went through some bad times about ten years ago, went into a massive depression after I broke up with a long-term girlfriend and she wouldn't let me see our daughter. It turned out that she wasn't even mine and she'd been having an affair with someone she met at work."

I felt so sorry for him – I could see it was painful dredging all this up. Instinctively, I took his hand. Well, it was cold!

"I was already starting to get depressed, I don't even know where it came from. But when Louise left me, I couldn't function. I started drinking and that made me even worse. I'd drink myself silly at night and try and get through a day at work, then smoke weed as well when I got home. I was a mess."

I gave him a hug. It was brave of him to be so honest. He carried on.

"Then everything just seemed to spiral. I had what the medical profession used to call a complete nervous breakdown, although now I think they call it a 'major depressive episode'. I couldn't go out, I couldn't work. I lost my job, I stopped washing and if it hadn't been for one of my oldest friends forcing me to go to the doctor, I would probably have killed myself. I was paranoid – I thought the neighbours were spying on me and that if I left the house I'd be kidnapped. It was mad!"

He was laughing at himself. I had to smile too. He clearly didn't take himself too seriously.

"So how did you get over that?" I asked.

"Slowly," was his reply.

It turned out that his friend, Angela, had frogmarched him stinking and shaking, to the doctor, who'd had him admitted to a psychiatric clinic. With a lot of medication, time and attention, he slowly recovered, and after a few weeks he was well enough to go back to his flat again. Angela had been to see him almost every day as he recovered, making sure he ate properly, keeping an eye on him and supporting him. She sounded like a diamond. I must have liked him already, as I was almost jealous of the way he spoke about her.

He skipped over a lot of the gory details, but after he'd fully recovered, he decided that he wanted to do something useful with his life and with some help from a loan from his parents, went back to college to do a nursing degree. He desperately wanted to become a mental health nurse, and eventually he qualified and found himself a job locally. "So, I've been working as a nurse for two years and I really, really love it" he enthused, "but it's really stressful, I'm knackered a lot of the time and the money's crap."

"Apart from that, it's great?" I laughed. "Yeah," he said sarcastically, "and I get to steal happy pills out of the medicine cupboards."

I rolled my eyes. He'd already told me that he was still on medication, as doctors wanted to keep him 'level', but in his own words, he was "content and happy."

I thought he was amazing. Not only had he managed to drag himself out of a debilitating depression and breakdown, he'd turned his life around and dedicated it to helping other people in a similar situation to the one he'd been in. What a man.

We sat down by the pond, and watched a few bored looking ducks trying to salvage morsels of food from the greenish algae that was starting to form around the side of the pond. I was still feeling a little overwhelmed by Ben's admissions. I didn't think any less of him for his mental problems, if anything I felt in awe of him for being so, well, normal after he'd been through such a trauma. His problems with his ex, the daughter that wasn't his and what followed made my silly problems with men and money pale into insignificance. I really, really liked him.

He was sitting very quietly, watching the ducks and holding my hand. I thought he might be mulling over what he'd just told me. I wanted to reassure him that I wasn't going to run a mile just because he hadn't led a charmed life. I shuffled in a bit closer to him and said, "Thank you so much for telling me that. It's so brave of you."

He shrugged. "I'm not brave," he sighed, "I just didn't want to let the crap beat me. You only get one life."

"It must be your turn to ask me stuff now." I said, "So, go on, is there anything you want to know?"

Ben looked thoughtful.

"Hmm...." He said, as if trying to think about what he could say. "There is one thing I'd really like to know."

"What's that?" I asked, expectantly.

"Can I kiss you?"

I gulped. I took a deep breath. Then I replied, "Oh go on then."

So he kissed me.

Something told me I might have picked a good 'un but I was still scared. Ben ticked all the boxes though; he was a gentleman, he was gorgeous, he was funny and intelligent, and man could that guy kiss. I replayed our pond-side snog in great detail over and over. I was definitely going to be taking this one slowly.

I was straight on the laptop, Googling 'major depression', and trying to get as much information as I could about what I might be letting myself in for. He was on meds, so I didn't think we'd have a problem. He was also having regular check-ups with the doctor to make sure that his medication was still working, and he was absolutely religious about making sure he went to them, because he didn't want to go downhill, find out he couldn't cope and then lose his job, which he loved.

"I had a lovely time today, Miss Ellie" Ben texted when he took a break from his shift.

"Me, too…must do it again sometime?" I replied hopefully.

"You bet. Didn't think we'd ever get to meet!"

"Why?"

"You didn't seem that keen. And then you met that other guy. What happened to him?"

"Long story." I replied. I didn't really want to get into all that.

Even though I had such a good feeling about Ben, the shadow of Rick was still hanging over me. I'd really liked Rick when we were just talking and messaging each other. Could Ben be too good to be true as well? I didn't think anyone who could be so brutally honest about his past, and his problems, could possibly be trying to manipulate me – depression and mental breakdown aren't exactly a selling point, are they? All these thoughts went round and round in my head like a never ending spin cycle of worry, until I finally dropped off to sleep in the early hours of the next morning.

Plus Size Lonely Hearts

Oh my God.

There it was - my article over three pages of *Gracious*, and with all the case studies, including the anonymous one I'd written about what happened to me with Rick. I was so excited. I had texts and calls from everyone. My mum called, sounding so proud that I was instantly guilty about not having seen her for three months.

"I knew you could do it, if you just kept at it," she'd said excitedly. It was lovely hearing my mum sounding so pleased for me. I loved her to bits but as she had moved back to the south coast a few years ago and I was still in Cambridge, getting to see her and dad was a real pain. "I'll just put your father on" she said, as a familiar voice said, "Well done, you."

I knew dad had always wanted to be a writer himself, and if anyone had pushed me into writing, it had probably been him. He was clearly impressed, far more than he had been when he'd seen me on the One Show. I don't think he'd really got the whole Covent Garden making a spectacle of myself thing.

When I read back what I'd written, I was really pleased with how it sounded. I was a real writer! I'd managed to get my first ever article in a high-end fashion magazine, and the by-line said 'Ellie Johnstone, founder of Viva Voluptuous and face of the new positive body image movement" Oh. My. God. I was so proud. When I looked at the *Gracious* website, a few people had already commented on it. Some of the comments were a bit mean – well of course I was writing an article about experiences of plus-sized women in a fashion magazine.

"What's a story about fat people doing in a FASHION magazine?????"

"I don't want to see oversized women, I want to see models and people I can admire"

"If getting a date is so hard for these women, perhaps they should go on a diet?"

Same old, same old. They could say whatever they liked – I was the one grinning from ear to ear because I'd just had my first article published in *Gracious*, and nobody, even snarky fat-haters, could take that away from me. Leader of a movement, that was me. A fat suffragette, a chubby Che Guevara, emancipating women from diets everywhere.

Lauren called, partly to congratulate me, and partly to fill me in on the latest – the crafty minx had got her claws into her lodger, Will, and they were, in Lauren's words, "Sort of seeing each other."

"You mean you're in and out of each other's bedrooms?" I laughed.

"It's so good," she gushed. "With Colin everything was so, well, planned. And it never felt very passionate. And I always had to do the work! But Oh. Em. Gee, Will is full on. The man's an animal. And he's got a buff body, too."

"He's a rugby player, of course he's going to be buff, honey" I laughed. "So you're glad you got a sexy lodger then?"

"Hell yeah. I'm even considering letting him pay me in kind for the rent so that I can legitimately keep him as my sex slave."

"Ha! If he does housework as well he could well be the perfect man…" I mused.

I was in a really good mood as I munched my toast, and read the congratulatory texts as they came through. Until I got one from Mark. I have no idea why, but every time I thought of him, I still felt just a little bit sad, and slightly cheated. I clicked through to see what he had to say for himself.

"Hey Ell. Well done on the mag. Wondered if you fancied a drink and a catch up?"

I didn't know what to do. I'd come so far since he'd dumped me earlier in the year, and it was probably his brutal dumping and the way he'd made me feel that had given me the kick up the behind to start the blogs, the videos and everything else I was now working on with the girls. I wanted to smack him for going back to his ex-wife, but at the same time, maybe I owed him for giving me the inspiration to get my Mojo back?

I texted back, although I left it for a good two hours because I didn't want him to think that I actually wanted to see him. Even though part of me really did.

"I'm a bit busy but I could probably see you tonight for an hour or so."

Did that sound desperate? I suppose there was some seriously unfinished business I had to get off my chest, and if I left it too long I would have chickened out. Why did the thought of that man always set me right back?

I agreed to meet him in the pub we used to drink in almost every week, just for old time's sake. Funnily enough, I never went in there with anyone else. I think it just reminded me of him too much, and the way I used to sit there, staring at him and thinking, "Why won't you just kiss me?"

Towards the end, he'd avoided even giving me more than a quick kiss goodnight, presumably in case I got ideas. Paul genuinely thought he'd been struggling with his sexuality, and that he was going to 'come out' when he dumped me! I remembered telling Paul that unfortunately, not all men had such a high opinion of me as he did. I knew Mark wasn't remotely gay. Just because he didn't fancy me, that didn't mean he fancied men…

He arrived, late as usual, and I was pleasantly surprised that I didn't get the butterflies I'd grown so used to when we used to meet before. I thought he'd lost a bit of hair and he was looking quite tired. I didn't actually fancy him anymore. The relief was amazing.

"Would you like a drink?" He asked. "The usual?"

He remembered what I drank! "No thanks" I said, just to be awkward. "Could I have a vodka, lime and soda please?"

He returned with his customary pint of lager and my drink. I noticed that his hand was shaking as he put my glass down. How odd. He didn't seem to know where to look or what to say. Well, this was awkward.

"How've you been?" I started, breezily.

"I'm good, yeah, things are good." He replied, awkwardly. He really didn't seem to be able to look me in the eye.

"Glad to hear it." I lied. What I really wanted him to say was that his life was a pile of steaming turd and it had all started since he'd dumped me. Then I could tell him how great my life was and make him feel terrible. Fantasist? Me? Perish the thought.

More awkward moments. This wasn't good. I thought I might as well come out and say it.

"So, why are we here, Mark?" I asked. "I haven't heard from you in months, and it's all a bit out of the blue. You can't tell me that you saw the article in *Gracious* and were suddenly overcome by an overwhelming desire to see me. What do you want?"

Mark looked embarrassed. He took a large gulp of his beer and wiped his mouth. I was waiting for the burp, but he started to talk instead.

"I just wanted to explain."

"Explain what?"

"I read your blog. I know I wasn't very honest with you and I feel really crap about it. I wanted to tell you that it wasn't you."

"I know."

Now he was taken aback. He stared at me, not quite sure what I knew or what the best thing to say was.

"What do you know?"

"I know that you were in love with Rachel the whole time we were seeing each other. I know that you were going out with me to take your mind off her but that you couldn't bring yourself to show me any affection because you thought you were betraying her. I also think you wanted her to get jealous and ask you to try again. Am I right?"

"Sorry." Mark swigged at his beer nervously, unable to look me in the eye.

"It doesn't matter. I just wish you'd been honest with me back then. I thought it was me. I thought you just didn't fancy me, and my confidence was shot when you dumped me. I spent months trying to change myself to be more like Rachel but how could I? She's nothing like me."

I was impressed with myself. I hadn't got upset, angry or even emotional. I actually didn't care anymore. My feelings for Mark were gone! All it had taken was meeting up with him and realising he actually wasn't all that after all.

He didn't really say any more about the subject. I didn't really want him to.

"Well done on the One Show thing. I saw you on there and I thought you looked really good."

"Thanks – well I have been pretty busy since you dumped me" I said bitchily. I chased the ice around my drink with the end of the straw as I waited for Mark to say something. As I looked up I swear I caught him picking his nose. Gross!

"I watched it on YouTube too. Couldn't get over how much you'd changed." He mumbled.

"You mean I actually looked confident? It might have been the fact I was having a good time, and oh, maybe the fact I had a 20-something boyfriend put a spring in my step too." I said, determined to twist the knife. I thought I saw him wince.

"You deserved it," he said, eventually. "I shouldn't have treated you like I did. I'm glad you're happy now."

I sensed that he wasn't happy. I asked him outright, "Are you still with Rachel?"

"Yeah, for now," he said, miserably. "She wants us to have kids but I think it would be a mad idea. Still, what Rachel wants, Rachel gets."

He was still suspicious about her and while he was working all hours, she was spending his money and had even applied for credit cards in his name and run up debts she was never going to be able to pay. He didn't think they would be able to afford children, but he was obviously scared to death that if he didn't give in to her demands, she'd have another affair and he'd be left alone again.

I actually felt sorry for him now. We said our goodbyes and I wished him luck, giving him a polite kiss on the cheek. There was no electricity, no longing, and no regret. He was actually quite pathetic. I knew I'd never see him again…because I really didn't want to.

I walked home from the bar feeling happy and content. All was good in my world…

Chapter 40

Buoyed up by the success of my *Gracious* article, which had been trending all over Twitter, I decided to chance my luck with my new best friend and pitch another idea.

"Sorry I'm fat"

Stereotypically, fat people, especially plus-sized women, are drawn into a cycle of people pleasing and expected to be grateful for being accepted, especially in the dating world. I'll look at the issue, how it's affected many women and the things they've been expected to do to 'fit in' or keep men because they've felt inadequate.

I'll also talk to plus size women who have overcome this and are genuinely happy, don't take any messing around from men – or other women – and are living life on their own terms."

I can also find a body image expert who can give us tips on how to stop being a people pleaser and please yourself, no matter what your size."

I emailed that off to Laura at *Gracious*, crossing my fingers superstitiously as I pressed send.

I got up to make a drink, and as I was walking towards the kitchen with my lucky mug in my hand, I heard the ping of an email arriving in my inbox. I practically threw the mug down and sprinted to the desk, where I saw a message – from Ben.

"Hey, Miss Ellie, how are you? Really sorry I haven't been able to sort out seeing you again yet but I've been roped in to cover loads of shifts this last week...but, but I do have a window in my busy schedule for tomorrow, and I wondered if you fancied going to the pictures tomorrow afternoon? I'll even throw in popcorn and let you pick a film. As long as the male lead isn't prettier than me."

"OK sweetie. It's a date. Don't work too hard and keep your paws out of the medicine cupboard!" I replied. Fabulous, I was really glad he'd asked me out again.

He met me outside the cinema, looking absolutely gorgeous.

The late autumn sunshine was making him squint and he was pulling a really strange face, then grinned at me, grabbed my hand and kissed it like an old fashioned gentleman. With a smile, he said, "Come on then, torture me with a chick flick. But if it's a period drama, I'm gonna talk all the way through it and annoy you SO much that you'll never ever want to take me to a period drama again."

I grinned and rolled my eyes at him. "Really?" I said, with an exaggerated sigh, "and there I was thinking you were going to let me see anything I wanted?"

He held my hand all through the film, which wasn't a period drama, so I couldn't actually eat any of the big bag of popcorn he bought us. I reckon he did that on purpose as he munched through the bag like a starving man, and managed to ferret out all the crunchiest, sugariest bits anyway. I didn't take much notice of the film, because I was daydreaming through most of it, furtively looking at Ben when I thought he couldn't see me, and thinking about just how nice it was to actually go on a proper date again. He caught me looking once, and instead of asking "What are you staring at, weirdo?" he just winked at me.

On our third date, we went back to the park during the day and wandered around, hand in hand, talking about absolutely everything. There was hardly anyone around that afternoon, it had been raining the day before and the ground was just the wrong side of squelchy. I'd put my best boots on but regretted that decision as soon as I'd started the walk and was doing my best to dance around puddles and muddy patches, while Ben strode through every bit of mess he came across, engrossed in our conversation.

"I still haven't heard back from Laura about the article idea I had" I told him.

"It's only been a few days, though, hasn't it? Not even a week?" He asked, "How long do these things usually take?"

"I don't know" I said, kicking at a pile of leaves, temporarily forgetting my boot situation, "I've only ever had a couple of them accepted, usually they just ignore me!"

"Awwww…" said Ben in mock sympathy, "are we feeling a bit sorry for ourselves?"

He was so funny, and he was incredibly attentive, asking me if I was cold, if I wanted to go somewhere else, if I wanted a coffee and generally making me feel like he really liked me. I found out about his family, who all lived a long way away. He'd only moved here to be with his cheating ex, Louise, and so his family hadn't seen him at his worst. Angela, his best friend, was no threat, even though he told me how much he loved her. She was happily married and had been for years – they'd met in his last office job. She'd since left to have kids and he was close to both her sons and even went out drinking with her husband occasionally.

"You know she'll love you?" he told me.

I blushed. "Oh really?" I said, fishing for compliments. "Why's that?"

"She'd love anyone who makes me happy," he smiled. I melted. Me? Making a man happy? We'd only been on a few dates!

I was really enjoying myself. It was freezing in the park that day, and as we were so close to my flat, I decided to bite the bullet and ask him in. It was getting dark, even though it wasn't yet 5pm. Hot chocolate back at mine seemed like the way to go, and I thought a cuddle on the sofa would be the perfect way to end a lovely afternoon.

"Are you sure you don't mind?" he asked, cautiously. I hadn't told him about Rick, but he knew I wanted to take things slowly.

"Of course not," I replied, breezily. "It's bloody freezing out here and it's lovely and warm in my flat. Plus I'm sure I have some Come Dine with Me on the planner I haven't watched yet."

He pulled a face. He loved reality TV as much as I did but while I drew the line at shouty chavs, he hated cooking shows with a passion. Well, we couldn't agree on everything. He walked back to the flat with me, anyway, the thought of a dose of rubbish TV not putting him off at all.

"You've got a lovely place." He said as he looked around. I must admit, I'd tidied up before he'd come over, just in case I was brave enough to invite him in. It looked and smelled lovely, and I did have an eye for interior design, and lovely retro posters.

"It's home," I agreed. "So, do you want a coffee, a tea or a hot chocolate? I might even have some Baileys to put in the chocolate..."

He groaned... "I'd love to take you up on that but I have to work a bit later. Maybe when I have my next day off?"

I made two steaming mugs of chocolate and handed his to him as he stood next to me in the kitchen. "Do you want cream on that?" I asked, innocently.

For some reason he found that question hysterically funny, or perhaps he was laughing at me, standing there brandishing a can of squirty cream with intent. His giggles started me off and the pair of us were soon in hysterics over absolutely nothing, and laughing until our sides hurt.

"You're a stupid man, Mr Ben!" I managed to say between giggling fits.

"Stupid about you, Miss Ellie."

He grabbed me in a bear hug and I thought he was going to squeeze me to death. I kissed him, and he pushed me up against the kitchen worktop and kissed me back. We stood there in the kitchen, just kissing and holding each other, for what seemed like hours, until the kissing became more insistent and his hands were under my jumper, then under my bra, trying to unhook it.

I couldn't complain, my hands were down the back of his jeans, groping his bum and pulling him closer, and my heart was beating at a rate I wasn't used to, half through unbridled lust and partly with fear. As he undid my bra and started to move his hands underneath to cup my breasts, I had a flashback to Rick.

I froze.

"What's the matter?" Ben asked, confused. He moved his hands away quickly, realising something wasn't right.

"I'm sorry…I'm sorry…I just can't."

I'd gone from feeling great, thinking I was going to end up in bed with this amazing man, to feeling scared and angry again. Rick had ruined my afternoon and probably the whole relationship. Ben was going to think I was a tease, and that would be the last I'd see of him. Tears sprang to my eyes.

"What's wrong, Ellie. Did I hurt you? Have I done something wrong?" he looked so worried. I had to tell him about Rick, even though I hadn't so much as mentioned his name in weeks. Oh crap.

"Come and sit down. I've got something to tell you."

I led Ben over to the sofa, where he sat next to me, leaving what can only be described as a respectable distance between us. I really hoped I hadn't just screwed everything up.

I told him what had happened with Rick, how he'd manipulated me, managed to get into my house and almost forced me into having sex with him when I'd told him I didn't want to. I told him how scared I'd been, how I felt like I'd brought it on myself for letting him

"Oh Ellie. Miss Ellie," was all he could say. He looked at me sadly.

"I'm sorry. I don't know what to do. I thought I was OK, but as soon as we started getting close, I just had horrible flashbacks, and I went cold. I'm so sorry."

Ben took my hand.

"It's fine. Well, no, it's not fine. You've been hurt and I hate him for what he did to you. But I'm not him, Ellie. I'm not the kind of man who would force you into anything. I'm a bit disappointed that you couldn't tell me, but I guess it's not easy to go over all that again is it?"

I shook my head.

"Maybe it's too early, Ben. Maybe I'm not ready for a

relationship after all. Maybe we should just be friends," I said sadly. My heart hurt. I'd just made a complete fool of myself and upset lovely Ben in the process. I just wanted him to go, now, because I thought I was going to cry. Maybe this was for the best.

"If that's what you want?" he said, sounding slightly irritated.

"Do you want to just be friends?" I asked.

He looked a bit annoyed at that, and thought for a minute or so before replying, quietly, "What do you think? Don't turn the decision back on me. I really like you, but I'm not going to make you do anything you don't want to do, and I don't want to feel like every time I touch you, you're thinking about him and what he did. I don't know what you want me to say. It's your call, Ellie."

Typical. He didn't really get it at all, did he? My heart sank as I realised I was just going to have to let him go, no matter how much I liked him. I just wasn't ready. Paul had been wrong.

"I really like you too. Can we just be mates?" I said, not entirely sure that I meant it.

Ben seemed crestfallen. I felt guilty now, on top of all the other emotions I was dealing with. I hated making him feel bad but there was no point leading him on, was there?

He sighed, and replied "OK Ellie. Keep in touch, yeah?"

Ben got up off of the sofa, and I followed him to the door. He turned to me, gave me a friendly hug, and a kiss on the cheek.

"I will, I promise."

I meant it. Maybe, when I was ready, Ben would give me another chance. He left, and I flopped on the sofa staring at Come Dine with Me but not watching it. I felt numb. Had I done the right thing?

Chapter 41

I moped around the flat the next day, not really wanting to talk to anyone. I hadn't heard from Ben since I'd unceremoniously chucked him out of my flat and I had a horrible feeling I'd blown it.

I'd planned for the kitchen to be my sanctuary for the day, as I pored over my cookery books, looking for the elusive recipe that would turn me into a Domestic Goddess, and make me forget about yesterday's disaster. I found a couple of slightly complicated recipes that involved me going out and into the city to try and find ingredients I didn't have in the cupboard, and braved the driving rain to try Waitrose first. If I couldn't find what I needed there I should at least be able to find some fancy crisps. I also decided to treat myself to some flowers. Who needs men when you can buy your own pretty things?

I trudged through the busy streets in a world of my own, stopping occasionally to check my Blackberry for any texts. Nope, Ben was definitely steering well clear.

Half-heartedly checking my email, I realised I had a message from Laura at *Gracious*.

"Hi Ellie, we love the feature idea, and I'd like to talk to you about commissioning that. We've also had such an amazing response to your first article that we'd like to talk to you about further opportunities at Gracious too. Can you give me a call when you have a minute, please? Have a great day, Laura."

Oooh! That sounded promising. I scooted off down a reasonably quiet alleyway to call her straightaway.

Laura sounded pleased that I'd called, always a good sign.

"Can you get into London this week at all?" she asked. "I really want to call you in for a meeting with me and our Editor, Sheena, but her diary is pretty chocka. I can get you in on Thursday morning?"

I could feel my heart thumping. Me, meeting Sheena Edwards from *Gracious*? I'd walk over hot coals to get there on Thursday if I had to.

"Yes, I should be able to get in, what sort of time?"

I was trying to sound casual but grinning all over my face at the same time.

"Can you get in for 9.30?"

Oh crap, that was going to mean a very early start. But for Sheena Edwards, I'd do it, even if I had to attempt to put my make up on while I was on the train.

"Yes, yes I should be able to do that. What's the meeting about?"

"Well, we loved your writing style and we think we could use you as a regular writer. We also think you'd be amazing as an ambassador for the plus-size fashion movement. Plus size is where it's at, at the moment, and with everything you're doing, you'd be the perfect person to really give our campaign a voice."

"Campaign?" I said, curious to know what she had in mind.

"Yeah, it's top secret so keep it to yourself, but we want to be one of the first magazines to really push plus size fashion to the masses. It's potentially a massive market and it's woefully ignored by all but a few of the good designers. We want to champion it, and hopefully get in there first before all the other magazines jump on the bandwagon."

"Me? Really? That's amazing! I couldn't be happier. I'd love to." I was aware I was sounding a bit gushy, and I reined myself in. Decorum, Miss Johnstone.

"OK, I thought you might like that idea! It's not definite - Sheena would have to meet you first, but it's looking good."

We made arrangements to meet and I practically danced into the supermarket and picked up my baking ingredients. Then I decided that some clothes shopping was in order if I was going to impress a fashion magazine editor.

Short-notice fashion emergencies had never been one of my

strong points. Trying to find smart clothes in plus sizes isn't the easiest thing in the world at the best of times, and to get anything a bit more upmarket than leggings and a nice top usually meant scouring websites for something and hoping that it would fit you when it was delivered. I didn't have time to take chances though, this was my one chance to impress one of the biggest names in magazine journalism and I couldn't just wait around and keep my fingers crossed something would fit properly.

I wandered around from shop to shop, hoping to find something. It might have only been October, but the shops were all crammed full of Christmas party dresses.

What was I going to do? The high street just isn't set up to cater for a big girl having a wardrobe emergency. I had a look in the first shop I came to that sold anything over a size 16. It was a complete dead loss. Unless I wanted a sequinned monstrosity in a garish colour, or a plain pair of leggings, anything in between was cheap, loud or both. I picked up a jacket in a cheap material that was massively overpriced and looked over at the assistant, who to her credit had the decency to look apologetic. I flounced out of the shop, feeling annoyed. I didn't think Sheena would be knocked off her feet by my curvy girl fashion savvy if I rocked up in a cheap looking suit that made me look middle aged.

Maybe Next would be an idea? I liked their clothes and they did most of them in size 20. Again, the racks were crammed with party dresses, mostly too small. Over in the corner there were a few formal bits and pieces, I said a silent prayer to the Fat Fairy and investigated the 'office clothes' section. Unfortunately, if there was anything over a size 18 in the shop, it wasn't on this rack, and despite finding a nice top that would have looked good with a plain pencil skirt I seemed to remember was lurking in my wardrobe back home, it was out of the question. There was a sign by the till saying that if I couldn't see my size, they could order it, but I just didn't have the time to fanny around with ordering. I needed something now.

I ended up in a department store, checking out the designer ranges. Lucky for me, there were a couple of designers that catered for a size 20, and although there weren't many things that would have flattered me, I managed to find a heavy jersey fishtail skirt that made me look at least two sizes smaller, and a really gorgeous patterned tunic top, with a very subtle peplum that skimmed my curves and looked totally on-trend at the same time. I skipped into the changing rooms, braving the horror that is the changing room mirror, just to make sure that they looked OK. Yes, they'd do. I swished the shirt around like a little girl in a princess outfit and imagined myself impressing Sheena Edwards. Happy with my outfit, I thought I might as well accessorise, and I went on to spend even more on a pair of amazing heels that would probably prove to be a big mistake when I got home from London, and some chunky jewellery. My hair needed doing again but I decided I'd spent far too much money already and headed off home with my bags of goodies.

Thursday came, and I hadn't heard anything from Ben. I couldn't let it upset me, though, could I? I wondered whether I should contact him instead. Oh sod it, I thought, and fired off an email as soon as I woke up.

"Hi Ben, hope you're OK. Sorry about the other day, I hope I didn't upset you. I'm fine - just thought I'd let you know that I'm off to see the editor of Gracious about that article…anyway, take care, Ell xx"

I dragged myself out of bed and to the station to catch the train into King's Cross. It was still raining, that horrible fine rain that seems to make you wetter than any other type of rain, and realised the shoes were a bad idea when I got on the train and found there were no seats at all. I was going to have to stand in silly heels on a mucky train floor for the next 45 minutes. There was only one thing for it, dirty floor or not, I took the heels off. Well, if I had to choose between grubby feet and hobbling like a little old lady into Sheena Edwards' office, then grubby feet were going to win hands down. Or feet down, if you're going to be pedantic. I ignored the funny looks I got from bored and grumpy looking commuters, and gritted my teeth for the whole journey. Luckily I'd had the time to put my face on before I left.

As I got into London, my Blackberry beeped with messages from Lauren, Zoë and Paul, all wishing me luck. I was so lucky to have such amazing friends. I decided to take them all out for a big dinner when I got home. Still nothing from Ben, though.

I got a taxi over to *Gracious'* offices, which cost me a fortune, but meant I was able to wear my killer heels, and signed in at reception. I got a little thrill from telling the very glamorous receptionist that I was here to see Sheena Edwards, although she'd obviously heard it so many times that she didn't bat a perfectly mascaraed eyelash.

I was shown into the lift, which was as big as my flat. It mirrored all the way around. I looked at my reflection critically. Would I pass the Sheena Edwards test? She would have known I was a big girl from the media coverage she'd seen, so I didn't think she'd be too taken aback at my size. I did look good, the outfit I'd bought fitted me perfectly and even though my hair was in need of a 'do, I'd managed to straighten and style it so that you could only really tell from behind.

I sat in the waiting area, feeling ever-so-slightly as if I was going to see the dentist. The butterflies in my stomach appeared to have morphed into very large moths, and their gentle fluttering had been replaced by a very insistent gnawing that was making my stomach come up with some very loud, uncomfortable rumbling noises. Of course, I hadn't eaten yet. I'd been way too nervous and in too much of a hurry to so much as chow down a banana and now I was wishing I had. I tried to take my mind off things by glancing around the waiting room. Pristine, bound copies of *Gracious* were scattered around on designer coffee tables, and there was a drinks machine in the corner that I was too scared to use. There was a folder containing media packs and magazine information, and the room felt strangely efficient and not at all calming or relaxing. Perhaps it was just me, focussing on the strange noises my stomach was making.

Suddenly I was hit with a griping pain in my lower abdomen. Oh no…that meant only one thing - I had to find the ladies, and fast. My appointment was still five minutes away, but the place seemed empty and there was nobody around to ask where the loos were. I stood up, slowly, clenching my muscles tightly, and tottered over to the door in my silly heels. Making my way carefully along the deserted corridor, I spotted the ladies room, and dived in with great relief. It was, thankfully, empty. I'd always been plagued by IBS when I was really stressed or nervous, and if I'd thought about it, I would have taken a tablet before I came out. I didn't have any in my bag, so I was just going to have to get on with it. This wasn't going to be pretty.

The toilets were fragrant and a bit posh. There were fresh flowers and little baskets of expensive hand wash lined up along a huge spot lit mirror. I raced into the cubicle and shut the door behind me with utter relief, sat down and did what I had to do. The sound effects were particularly unladylike, and I cursed myself for forgetting to take a tablet before I came out. I had about two minutes to get back to the waiting room and hope Sheena wasn't early.

As I emerged from the cubicle, I heard another door open next to me. I thought I'd been alone! I didn't want to look up, and acknowledge that I was responsible for the horrible smell that was emanating from the cubicle behind me, but as I approached the sink and looked up, I realised with horror that the person who'd witnessed my embarrassing moment was none other than Sheena Edwards. I could have gone home there and then. I smiled politely, washed and dried my hands and walked out, giving Sheena one last glance as I went. I could have sworn she was smirking.

At least I knew I'd be there before she was. I made it back to the leather sofas just as a pretty, twenty-something woman appeared.

"Ellie Johnstone?"

"Hi, yes, is it Laura?"

"Yes, lovely to meet you, Ellie. Come on through."

Laura was just how I'd imagined her – tiny, with artfully scraped back blonde hair and that 'made up to look like I'm not wearing any make up' look. She was wearing a pair of extremely skinny black jeans and a little top which accentuated her perfect, perky boobs, and a pair of ballet flats. If she hadn't been so nice I could have hated her for looking so perfect!

I stood back up again "Come on through, Ellie" Laura said kindly, "It's just fabulous to meet you! I loved your article, I had no idea what it was like for…" she faltered, looked at me and then carried on, "fat women."

I tried not to laugh. She didn't want to acknowledge the elephant in the room, the fact that I was a chubby girl. It was sweet, really. "I don't suppose you would!" I grinned, breaking the tension. "It's not so bad. But it could be better!"

Compared to the rest of the place, the meeting room seemed quite plain, and the table we were sitting around seemed unnecessarily big for just the three of us. Laura poured me a glass of water and I attempted to compose myself, waiting for Sheena to appear. Despite having just had to rush to the ladies, my stomach was still churning and I really hoped I didn't have to excuse myself again.

Ten minutes later, Sheena walked in. I noted the lack of apology for her lateness, but didn't think it would be a good idea to mention it.

"Nice to meet you, Ellie," Sheena said confidently, extending a beautifully-manicured hand. No trace of amusement at our earlier meeting. I stood up and shook her hand. "Likewise" I replied, "Thanks so much for meeting me. I've been a Gracious reader for years."

Sheena smiled, I cringed. It was Paloma Faith all over again. I kicked myself, and decided to try and be at least a little bit cool.

"So, Ellie, you know that first and foremost Gracious is a fashion magazine? We loved your Plus Sized Lonely Hearts feature and I was exceptionally pleased that it garnered so much media attention. You write very well, and I also think that the Don't Hate Me article could work. But I wanted to run something else by you."

I gulped. "Yes?" was all I could say. I was so excited, my throat and gone dry, and I took a quick swig of water.

Laura was smiling at me, and taking notes. This looked important.

"We like the idea of being the first quality fashion magazine to really cater for plus sized markets, and we've been looking for someone with influence to spearhead our campaign," Sheena explained. I was trying not to stare at her because I couldn't believe I was in the presence of someone so influential. And that she'd just heard my bowels being incredibly irritable and still wanted me to write for her fashion magazine. Influential? Me? I think I almost wet myself on the spot.

"We'd like to trial a plus sized section in Gracious. We'd do all the call ins, get the samples and arrange photo shoots here of course, but what we'd want you to do is the comment, interviewing designers, critiquing the plus size offer on the high street and everywhere else. I'd expect you to do some research, we might send you to find out what was happening in the plus size markets in say, New York, or find new designers and comment on general plus size issues as you have been doing so far."

I was trying to act nonchalant but nothing was going to stop the grin from spreading across my face, and I felt as if I was going to cry. In a good way. Compose yourself, Miss Johnstone, I told myself not for the first time that day. I think I took a little bit too long trying to calm myself, and Sheena looked at me expectantly. "Well?" she asked, "Is that something you would be interested in taking on?"

"Yes, yes it would, thank you so much for the opportunity" I gabbled. "I would love to work on a project like that with Gracious."

"That's great news," Sheena smiled. "We can sort out the finer details later but I just wanted to talk to you about it, as we've been thinking of covering plus size fashion and issues for some time now, and you caught my eye when you were cavorting in Covent Garden."

Laura giggled and Sheena added, "Loved those outfits. You know, if I had a cleavage like that, I'd be out there shimmying to Gloria Gaynor too!"

Sheena wasn't as scary as I'd thought. And she'd just offered me the opportunity to write for *Gracious* every week on plus sized fashion, on a three month trial basis. At that point I was frighteningly close to hugging her but I thought that my new role as plus size ambassador for *Gracious* might not survive manhandling the magazine's editor. The rates she offered me to write for her were so much better than I'd been used to as a dogsbody copywriter for *Glammazon* that I didn't even bother to haggle. The whole meeting took less than an hour, and I waited until she'd left the room to take off my heels and walk around on the plush carpeted floor, just because I could. I couldn't believe it. Me, writing for *Gracious!*

"Thanks so much, Laura!" I grinned.

"You're so welcome" Laura replied, offering me a biscuit from the plate on the table. "It's nice to be doing something different, and Sheena's given me this project to oversee, so it'll be me you deal with most. You'll have to come up again when I'm not on deadline and we can go for lunch?"

"Yeah, definitely. I'd love to!" I said, taking a biscuit. Laura was lovely and I quite liked the idea of spending time with media fashion types in London. Now THAT was something I never imagined myself saying.

If I hadn't been wearing such daft shoes, I would have skipped back to the station. Unfortunately though, I had to get another heinously expensive taxi instead, but I was so happy that I didn't care. To make the day even better, I managed to get a seat on the train home, where I sat happily sipping my coffee and planning my first column. Ellie Johnstone had some serious work to do…

"Oh my GOD darlin', I'm so happy for you!" Zoë squealed when I told her my news. I'd called her from the train and I think that the people on the other side of the carriage could probably hear her hollering. "I'll tell you everything later but I just wanted you to know." I said, "I have to call Lauren …yay!"

"You're a freaking legend, lady" Zoë continued, "and this calls for very expensive bubbles!"

"I know…I'm so excited!" I gushed back. "I'll see what I can sort out with Lauren and Colette, we have to have a proper girly get together. Me? I mean, me? She wants ME to do this, Zo! Aaagh!"

I could hear Zoë giggling. "OK, darlin' go and call the others, and let me know when we can get together and drink to you being the face of plus size fashion for *Gracious*!"

Next, I called Lauren. "Told you so, lady" was her response. "You just needed a kick up the backside and you'd be on a roll. I'm chuffed to bits for you. When do you start?" She was also very keen on the idea of drinking to my success.

I couldn't get hold of Paul, and my call went to voicemail. I texted *"Got the job"* knowing he'd be straight on the phone as soon as he could get away from whatever work meeting he'd been trapped in. Two *Gracious* features, a successful blog, a TV appearance, and now a job as a columnist for *Gracious*. Could things actually get any better?

Chapter 42

It would have been a big lie to say that I hadn't been thinking about Ben. He hadn't replied to my tentative email about the meeting with Sheena, and I'd composed so many emails and texts since then, trying to apologise, explain or just see if I could get him to reply, but I deleted every one before I hit send, scared that if he ignored me again, that would be it. I'd hoped he would have been in touch, even though I'd sent him packing. I know, I was being very contrary indeed.

In my own twisted way, I wanted him to prove that he really liked me, because if I never heard from him again after I rejected him, it would have meant he was like Rick, and I would have got him all wrong.

I went over and over the events of that afternoon in my head. We'd had such a lovely time, he'd told me all about himself and we'd really connected. I thought back to when we were in fits of laughter in the kitchen and smiled, despite myself. I really liked him. But I was too stubborn to actually contact him, in case he didn't feel the same way.

I hadn't mentioned it to the girls, because I wanted to bask in the glory of the success with *Gracious* and we were all working so hard on getting things in place for the dating site. Zoë asked me if I'd seen Ben, but I just evaded any further questioning by saying we'd had a nice time but his shifts were all over the place so I didn't know when I'd see him again.

So when the email pinged up in my mailbox, I wasn't quite sure what to expect. I hesitated before I opened it, went to make a coffee, read some more Twitter, and eventually decided that I couldn't ignore it any longer, I just had to woman-up and read it, even if it was going to be a big fat disappointment.

"Miss Ellie" was the title. Not giving anything away, there.

I opened the message and started to read.

"Mr Ben formally requests the company of Miss Ellie at 8pm tomorrow evening, for dinner, drinks and intelligent, witty conversation. Mr Ben will be treating Miss Ellie to dinner, at an establishment of her choosing, along with drinks and any dessert that she so chooses.

Mr Ben will be ready with transport to the venue at 8pm.

RSVP as soon as possible."

I had to smile. Bless him he hadn't actually given up on me after all. Not a word about how mean I'd been to him, just an invitation to dinner. The fact that I'd been thinking about him ever since we'd been on our last date was a pretty enormous clue that I didn't really want to just be friends with this man. I really, really liked him. I didn't even bother playing hard to get or making him wait. I replied straight away.

"Dear Mr Ben. Miss Ellie would very much like to accept your kind invitation to dinner. She would like to also warn Mr Ben that she might also accept his offer of a very naughty dessert, which will probably result in the phrase "I feel sick now" being uttered at some point in the evening, probably after she has attempted to eat the entire thing despite her better judgement.

Mr Ben has Miss Ellie's permission to surprise her with his choice of venue, but will be waiting outside her place of residence at 8pm."

I sent the message with no hesitation. I was going to see him again after all. He didn't hate me.

I was really looking forward to seeing Ben again. I could just picture that smile, those eyes – I swear his eyes changed colour with his mood, like those novelty rings you used to get. I spent absolutely ages getting ready, put some purple glittery nail polish on, showered, and slathered myself in expensive body lotion and then perfume. I decided to go fairly casual with the outfit, opting for skinny jeans and a clingy top which really showed off my cleavage and skimmed over my bum. I'd noticed that Ben seemed to be a boob man, as he'd been trying very hard not to make it obvious that he was staring at my chest a few times when we'd been together. He'd failed miserably of course and I'd caught him out more than once.

I added my favourite boots, which had survived our afternoon in the park, and chunky jewellery, spritzed some more perfume and straightened my hair. I still needed a haircut.

I was ready by 7.30, even though he wasn't going to pick me up until 8. Trying to watch Eastenders to take my mind off the nerves I was feeling, I fiddled with my phone and went back over some of his old text messages. He was so daft, and funny. He never used text speak; he was just the perfect match for a writer. We'd had long conversations about text speak and how modern culture had ruined the beauty of the English language – I couldn't remember ever having a conversation like that with any of my exes. He knew what the word 'flounce' meant and I could never catch him out with long words.

He was caring as well, telling me bits and pieces about his day at work and how much he wished he could help some of the patients more, but the staff situation being so bad that he just didn't have the time.

I knew he had some issues, but then it was my issues that had caused the biggest problem with us so far. He'd been so understanding about it, what could I say?

True to his word, Ben pulled up outside the flat just before 8. He looked gorgeous and he smelled absolutely divine. He'd put on some jeans with a crisp, white shirt, which he wore under a loose jacket. He stepped out of the car, walked round to the passenger side and opened the door for me. "Please, Milady," he said, mock-seriously.

I did as I was told and got in the car. We drove out to a gastropub in a nearby village, quiet and secluded. He led me to a table right near the fire, which was a good move as I was freezing, and he pulled my chair out so that I could sit down.

I giggled. "What a gentleman you are, Mr Ben."

"Why, of course I am, Miss Ellie." He replied with a sly smile. "A gentleman is what the lady wanted, so a gentleman is what the lady shall have."

He ordered a bottle of wine, which as he was driving, was probably meant almost entirely for me. It wasn't cheap wine, either. He was making some serious effort to win me back round here, and little did the daft sod know that he didn't have to.

We made small talk while we waited for our starters, and I sipped at my wine, resisting the urge to down it in one to calm the nerves I still felt.

I hadn't eaten much all day and a belly full of wine on an empty stomach would have just made me talk complete nonsense until it wore off.

"Ellie," Ben started, nervously, "I just wanted to say that I'm really sorry about the other day."

I reached for his hand. "Don't be. I just freaked out, it was my fault."

"No, I shouldn't have assumed...."

He went quiet for a few moments, thinking about what to say next.

"The thing is, I think you're amazing. I've never met anyone who makes me feel the way you do. You're gorgeous, you're smart, you're funny and I just want to be with you all the time. I kept away from you when you said you wanted to just be friends, hoping that if I gave you a few days, you might miss me. But when I didn't hear from you, I thought I'd better make the move, because if I didn't try again I would probably regret it for the rest of my life."

"Didn't you get my email?" I asked, confused. The rest of his life? That sounded serious.

"What email?" he questioned, as he screwed up his face in confusion, cut off in mid flow by a waiter who put our food down and walked away as slowly as he possibly could, obviously trying to eavesdrop on the conversation a bit longer.

"I emailed you to say I was meeting the editor of *Gracious* about some more work, last week." I explained. If he hadn't got my message, then that would explain why he hadn't replied…he didn't think I was a flake, he just didn't think I wanted to talk to him! I couldn't be bothered with messing around any longer. Sod playing it cool. I took a deep breath and went for it.

"Ben – I haven't been able to stop thinking about you. I felt like such an idiot after you left that day, and I really thought I'd blown it. I haven't told many people about what happened with that other guy, and I've been bottling it up for so long now that when things got a bit heavy, I got all confused. I shouldn't have done that to you."

He squeezed my hand and smiled. "Shall we start again?"

"Mr Ben, I think I'd really rather like that."

He grinned that crinkly-eyed grin again and I knew I was doing the right thing. "So, the *Gracious* thing. Did you get another article out of them, then?" he asked.

"Oh, I think I got more than that!" I replied, unable to stop beaming, and told him all about the meeting, and my new job.

I was so happy I completely lost my appetite. It didn't stop me making a pretty good effort to eat my dinner, though, or valiantly take on the challenge of a chocolate and fruit sundae. Ben had to help me with it; there was no way I could have managed that on my own. He took a picture of me with the mountainous dessert and uploaded it straight to Facebook, just to wind me up. I kicked him under the table. I finished up most of the wine myself and felt just a little bit tipsy when we left the pub and the cold air hit me.

We talked all the way home as if nothing had happened, and when he dropped me off, he kissed me goodnight, gave me a huge hug and then reached in his pocket for something.

"Here," he said, handing me what looked like a CD. "I haven't done this since I was at school, but when I was sitting at home thinking about you the other night, I made up a playlist with songs that made me think of you. I thought you might like to hear it."

Nobody had ever made me a mix tape when I was at school. I thought it was quite possibly the most romantic thing he could have done. I kissed him again, took his face in my hands and said, "Ben, thank you. I've had a lovely, lovely night and I promise that I'll listen to your CD before I go to bed tonight, even though I am just a little bit tipsy."

"You're funny when you're drunk." He grinned. "I hope you like it."

"I will, I'm sure."

I got out of the car, walked up to the front door of the building and felt Ben's eyes on me as I opened it, turned round and blew him a kiss. He waved, and drove off. Of course, the first thing I did when I got in was play the CD. It was lovely. He'd found some beautiful songs – 'Song to the Siren' by This Mortal Coil, 'I'll be your mirror' by Velvet Underground and 'Grace' by Jeff Buckley. He'd put a couple of jokey tracks on there, something by The Wombles and 'Kooks' by David Bowie, but I was still overcome by the effort he'd made to put the songs together. I listened to the entire playlist, then texted, *"Thank you xxx"*

I was stunned when he texted me straight back with, *"I think I'm in love with you."*

Chapter 43

Nobody had told me they loved me in so long that I'd forgotten what it felt like.

Even so, I wasn't sure what to do. Was I in love with him? I think I'd forgotten how that felt, too. I didn't love Jamie, although I did care about him a lot. I was besotted with Mark, but that wasn't love. I'd held something back with both of them. With Darren, I couldn't remember how it felt to be in love, although I must have been at some point. I didn't like the taste of wedding cake enough to get married without at least thinking I was in love.

I played it safe and replied, *"I think I could quite easily fall for you, too xx"*

I couldn't sleep that night. I didn't hear any more from Ben, but he'd probably just gone to bed. I knew he was working during the day and had an early start. I looked at the clock – it was almost midnight. I wondered if Paul was still awake. I sent him a quick, *"Are you still up?"*

A couple of minutes later, the phone buzzed and he'd replied. *"Yes. Watching Family Guy and eating crisps in my pants."*

"That's too much information, sweetie. And why do you have crisps in your pants?"

"Very funny. Bedtime snack. What's up?"

"Saw Ben tonight. He says he's in love with me."

"Whoa, that's quick. How do you feel?"

"I think I might really like him."

"Do you think you could fall in love with him?"

"I think so."

"Well, what's the problem then, you daft mare? It's about time you had some luck!"

Paul didn't know I'd already thought I'd messed it up once. I'd managed to keep that to myself as I was so embarrassed – which was unusual for me.

"I know. D'you think it might be a bit fast though?"

"It's a bit unusual for a bloke to be that honest, but you know the man, what do you think?"

I thought for a bit. *"I think he might actually mean it."*

"Should I get a hat?"

That made me giggle.

"You look funny in hats."

"Point taken. Get some sleep, Missus, and I'll come round at the weekend for a catch up. Happy for you."

"OK. Night sweetie xx"

I still couldn't sleep. Emotions were swirling around in my head that I hadn't felt in a very long time. I started to write my first *Gracious* column in my head. I didn't even have to send it in for a fortnight. I composed blog posts in my head. Then I went back to "Ben loves me" again.

I tried to meditate. I only ever attempted to meditate when I couldn't sleep, which was probably why it never worked because the reason I couldn't sleep was that I couldn't get rid of the same annoying thoughts that invariably interrupted my attempts at being serene and emptying my conscious mind. Zoë was always yakking on about the joys of meditation but to me it just seemed like too much like hard work. I'd been on a meditation retreat once, as a freebie for *Glammazon* and found it really hard. The retreat started off with an introduction to meditation techniques that was illustrated by the conscious appreciation of a raisin. We had to touch, hold, smell and then taste the raisin. We had to put the said raisin in our mouth and roll it around, feel it, taste it…guess who accidentally swallowed hers?

And then the woman with the cough started to annoy me. And I started thinking about the write up I was going to give the retreat. I do remember my head dropping a couple of times in the 'real' meditation classes, as I consciously relaxed every part of my body according to the teacher's instructions. Only he'd told us to try not to doze off. Bugger. I couldn't win. Really.

I was the same with yoga. Yeah, I know Zoë and Chris swore by its restorative powers but really? I just couldn't get the yoga class at the Ayurvedic clinic out of my head, which was full of old people who shouldn't have been instructed to relax their muscles quite so much. I think you get my drift?

I tossed and turned for ages, and eventually dropped off, exhausted but just a little bit happy.

I must have slept well, because when I woke up, I'd missed three messages from Ben, and one from Zoë. Zoë wanted to meet me for a drink – not even a coffee – in town, and bring Lauren. We hadn't had our celebratory *Gracious* column related drinks yet, and it was unusual that she wanted to meet us this early. Ben just wanted to know how I was. I suspect that was probably because of the amount of wine I'd drunk the night before and of course his declaration of love last thing before bed.

"*Morning beautiful*" was the first one.

"*Are you awake yet, sweetie*?" was the second.

"I *haven't put you off, have I?*" Was number three.

When I did finally wake up and reply, I thought it was sweet that he cared. Obviously it wasn't just me that worried about these things… I texted him back with.

"I'm fine, Mister Ben. Just overslept. And no, you haven't put me off at all. I'll call you later xx"

I made arrangements to meet up with Zoë, even though the last thing I really wanted after a restless night and a gut full of wine was more alcohol. I got dressed, feeling a bit wobbly. Zoë was being very cagey about what she wanted to talk to us about. Maybe she was getting married? She'd been spending a lot of time with Chris lately and it wasn't all because of the yoga project, which was pretty much sorted now. I knew she was expecting the DVDs to be ready by Christmas and I was already plotting a New Year offer on those to get more people on the site. Zoë having the endorsement of Rawthwaite Hall, and one of the biggest fitness chains in the south, meant that the DVD was almost guaranteed to be a success.

I walked into the bar where Zoë was waiting, with Chris of course, and beaming all over her face.

"I got my book, I got my book!" She was clutching a purple, glittery covered paperback which had the word 'AMAZING' written on it in silver letters. It was just SO Zoë.

"You sneaky mare!" I exclaimed, snatching the book from her hand to get a closer look at it. "I didn't even know you'd sent it to be published!"

"I know, I decided to stop talking about it and just write the thing. And rewrite it. And edit it about three times. That's why I was so quiet for so long. I know you all thought it was because of Chris and me, but even when I've been with him, I've been writing. I've worked so hard on this, been up late at night doing edits and worked through weekends. I've honestly never, ever worked this hard in my whole life… and I'm so pleased with it. I thought it would be fun not to tell you, so I could surprise you with it when I had my copies! I'm so excited! It's really my book! I wrote it! I made it! All my lovely, lovely words in a pretty purple booky."

She hadn't even ordered any drinks yet but Zoë was so excited that she was almost singing the words. Chris gave her a protective cuddle. "I'm so proud of you," he said, lovingly.

"Thank you baby," she replied, grinning happily. "You're my inspiration."

I pretended to throw up.

"I'm going to get some fizzy down me, d'you want to help me?" Zoë chirped, "and where's Lauren? I wanted to tell you both together, but I got a bit too excited and couldn't keep my trap shut."

"She's coming…she should be here by now."

Chris went off to order the champagne. I decided that fuzzy head or not, I could probably force a glass down me given the situation.

"I'm proud of you too, y'know?" I told Zoë. "I know I wind you up about being ditzy but you're amazing. You've done so much in the last year – the book, the DVD, the classes. You've done loads for me, and you've been there to pick up the pieces whenever I've screwed up again. You're the best!"

"Aww, thanks doll." Zoë gave me a hug. "I'm just so happy. It's been a fantastic year. How about you? It's been ages since we had a real girly chat. I'm so excited about *Gracious*, you've really made it! You deserve this, gorgeous, you really do."

"I didn't tell you, did I?" I said with a smile.

"What?" Zoë took the book back from me and put it down on the table, carefully, making sure it wasn't near any wet patches. She was all ears and watching me expectantly.

"I've seen Ben a few times now."

"Ben? The cute one who you met online? Yay! What's he like? How's it going? Spill, lady!"

I started to tell the tale, and I might have mentioned how sexy and how lovely he was a couple of times by the time Chris came back with a big, expensive bottle of champagne. Right on cue, Lauren walked in, looking a bit flustered.

"Sorry I'm late!" she trilled, air kissing us both. "Mwah!"

"Where've you been?" I laughed. "Did you hear the sound of a champagne cork or something?"

Lauren pulled a face at me.

"What's all this in aid of, then? Who's getting married? Or is this in aid of our new fashionista?"

Then she spotted Zoë's book on the table. "Is this your masterpiece, Zo? I didn't know you'd finished it!"

"Neither did I," I interjected.

"It definitely is," said Zoë, still as excited as ever, and sipping her champagne. "And I wanted to invite you all to the launch party in November, too. OK girlies, get a glass of fizz in your hand and we're going to toast…us!"

"Sounds like a plan." I agreed, lifting my glass up to the other two and exclaiming "To us!!"

"Launch party?" Lauren said thoughtfully, "I'm gonna need new clothes."

"We're great we are." I added. "We're a movement, remember?"

"And you're the face of *Gracious'* new fat fashion section!" Zoe said excitedly. "Go, you, Missus. You're bloody amazing!"

"So…You're not getting married are you?" Lauren asked, changing the subject, after taking a large gulp of bubbly.

"No," said Zoë. "I just wanted to get us all together, to show off my book, and to see you all before it all goes a bit nuts next week with launch party planning and all. And to congratulate Ellie for the fantastic new job, and getting it on with a half-decent man!"

"Did you get it on with Ben?" Lauren asked, keen to make up for missing out on this snippet of gossip.

"Well, we've been out a few times now. I saw him last night and he made me a mix CD. Then he texted me and said he thought he was in love with me!"

Zoë squealed. "Ellie's in lo-ove"

"A mix tape? How quaint." Lauren said sarcastically. I chose to ignore her. I thought it was romantic.

"I didn't say I was in love with him!" I exclaimed. The pair of them looked at me. "It's written all over your face, woman!" they laughed.

I blushed. "Well he is adorable."

"When are you seeing him again?" Chris asked. He'd been staying out of the conversation but in reality he was just as nosey as the girls were.

"Well, tonight, I think. I just have to get some blogging done and I'm good to go."

"Keep us posted, Missy." Zoë said. "I'm so excited! I haven't seen you so loved-up since, well, ever!"

I blushed again.

"I suppose I should 'fess up." Lauren said quietly. "I'm kind of going out with Will." I pretended I didn't know already, Zoë hated being the last to know anything.

"Your lodger?" Zoë asked.

"Err. Yeah. He's just so fit! He loves rugby and I've been to watch him play a few times. It's so sexy. He's actually really sensitive, but he's built like a brick shithouse and he makes me feel like a Goddess."

"Is that why you were late?" Zoë questioned.

"I'm afraid so," Lauren giggled. "He wouldn't let me get out of bed."

I shook my head in mock disgust. "Good girl" Zoë said wickedly. We clinked our glasses again and chorused, "Cheers!"

Chapter 44

Ben and I arranged to meet up for a drink in the city that evening. I'd been playing the CD he made me over and over again, and every time I heard it, I think I fell a little bit more in love with him.

I'd been working really hard on the website all afternoon, as well as the blog.

FAT FASHIONISTA

"Watch this space everyone, the world is getting a new fashionista. Only this one's plus sized. I can't say too much yet but I'm going to be writing for a magazine soon (did you see my article for Gracious by the way?) and covering everything you need to know about plus size fashion, designers and trends, as well as issues that we all identify with.

I'm so excited, I can't tell you. It's been an amazing year and I've come a long way from being dumped at the start of it to appearing on TV and being papped at a celebrity PR party. And now I've got my dream job and I'm writing a fashion column! I just wanted to say a big thank you for all your support with the blog, the videos, and of course the flash mobs.

It's not all about me though. I started this because I was so fed up with the bad press that plus size people were getting, and I wanted to redress the balance a bit. I had absolutely no idea that it would be this successful, maybe I tapped into a zeitgeist? But there are so many amazing, gorgeous big women out there that one day we were always going to fight back. I'm just privileged to be one of the people leading the fight.

...Viva Voluptuous!"

I spent just as long getting ready for this date as I had done the last one. I wanted to see him so badly, and it was more than just lust, I loved being around him. I'd never felt so comfortable with a man before, especially not this early on. He made me feel as if I was perfect just as I was, and that he wouldn't change anything about me. Nobody had ever made me feel that way before.

I was on a bit of a high as I walked into the pub where I'd arranged to meet Ben. God, he was gorgeous, and he was there early with a large, cold glass of wine waiting for me on the table. He got up from the table and gave me a hug and a kiss. "Hello gorgeous." He smiled. My knees went wobbly.

"Hey sexy," I replied, cheekily. "Had a good day?"

He told me all about his day, and as he described what he'd been doing, he waved his arms around animatedly. He told me about the patient with serious, debilitating OCD who he'd been trying to work with. It was a partial success, "The poor guy thought that if he didn't chew his food 65 times, his family would die. He also spent a very long time in the shower as every time he washed the soap off, he convinced himself that he wasn't clean and needed to wash again."

Ben had managed to get him out of the shower in less than ten minutes, which was a definite result.

I told him all about my day, Zoë and her fabulous book, working on the blog and then I also confessed that I'd been listening to his CD on repeat all day. He looked slightly embarrassed but pleased. "You liked it then?"

"I loved it, sweetie," I replied. "It was probably the loveliest thing that anyone's done for me, in years."

"Really?" He smiled, looking right into my eyes, "Well, you deserve better. And there's plenty more where that came from. I can't stop thinking about you! What have you done to me?"

I laughed out loud. "Turned you into a great big soppy old git?"

He punched my arm, playfully.

"I've got a day off tomorrow." He said, hesitantly. "I wondered if you wanted to spend it with me?"

I really did want to hang out with Ben, but I had a lot to do with the deadline for the first *Gracious* column looming.

"Why don't you stay the night?"

Ben looked confused. "But I thought you weren't, you know, up for anything just yet? Don't feel like you have to do anything you don't want to."

"I want to." I said quietly.

"Well, let's get out of here then," he said, drinking his vodka and coke down in one. Turning to me with a grin, he added, "If I'd known a bit of Velvet Underground would have that effect on you, I would have played it for you sooner."

I smacked his backside.

Back at the flat, I felt suddenly shy and self-conscious again. It didn't last long, as Ben sat me down on the sofa and kissed me gently. He stroked my hair softly and whispered, "You're lovely, Ellie. I never expected to meet anyone like you."

He kissed my neck and shoulders softly and it made every nerve in my body tingle deliciously. I couldn't resist him any longer, turning to him and kissing him back, harder. I didn't feel afraid at all. It felt perfect, and I was going to let what happened, happen. I wrapped my arms around him and pulled him closer, and he took it slowly, teasing me and stopping, just to make sure I was still OK with it. As his hands moved under my clothes, I felt more than OK, sliding my hands under his t-shirt and feeling his hot skin under my palms. He smelled delicious again, and he felt so good.

We must have spent nearly an hour on the sofa, kissing, cuddling and more. Now I knew the meaning of the phrase, "Hot and bothered". I realised that Ben was leaving everything up to me, but I still felt a little bit shy. Eventually, dishevelled and wound up to the point of no return, enough was enough. I stood up, took his hand and led him into the bedroom.

"Come here, you." I said, in what I thought was my best sexy voice.

He didn't need telling twice.

It was everything I'd hoped it would be, even though at one point I think I elbowed him in the face in the throes of passion. But it was still fantastic. He kept telling me I was beautiful, and sexy, and gorgeous, and for ages afterwards I laid in his arms as he stroked my hair. Just before we fell asleep, with the moon shining on us through a gap in the curtains, he kissed the top of my head and said, "Ellie Johnstone, I bloody love you."

"I love you too, Ben Andrews" I replied. And I meant it.

Chapter 45

I woke up next to Ben feeling very pleased with myself. He was snoring gently but looked gorgeous, all dishevelled and bed-headed. I didn't regret a thing, I'd kicked the ghost of Rick right out of my head and replaced it with memories of Ben telling me how beautiful I was and kissing me so much he left me with a stubble rash. I hoped I'd be able to cover that up!

"Morning, beautiful" he said sweetly when he woke up. He looked so cute. "You look just like a little mole" I teased. "Would you like a cup of coffee?"

"Have you got any biscuits?" He asked, before pulling me back towards him and adding "for afters…"

He stayed with me until about lunchtime, after getting up eventually, insisting on watching Jeremy Kyle and shouting at the telly, and then realising that I really needed to get on with work and leaving me to it. I went over and over the night before in my head; it really had been lovely, and I was smitten.

After he left, I had a call from the marketing department at one of the biggest plus-sized fashion retailers in the UK, wanting to know if they could partner with the website in some way. I couldn't believe it, they wanted to link up with Viva Voluptuous and offer exclusive deals in return for a reduced ad rate. I was so excited, I couldn't believe we'd managed to get them on board, although to be honest I'd been emailing them and tweeting them and basically doing everything I could to get their attention for weeks. The thing that clinched it was probably that I just happened to mention that I was going to be *Gracious'* new columnist and for some reason that seemed to wake them up, and they were straight onto it. I wasn't afraid of a bit of name dropping.

That night, Lauren and Zoë came over for with Colette for a catch up.

"Did you see Ben last night, gorgeous girl?" Zoë asked. I blushed, and that was all they needed to know. "How did it go?"

"I saw him this morning, too." I said enigmatically.

Lauren winked at me. "I'm so pleased for you. I was beginning to think you were going to be one of those awful women who pretends she wants to be alone and doesn't need a man, but then stares at your boyfriend like he's her last meal."

"Cow!" I joked. "You can keep your rugby player, and I'll stick with my sexy nurse."

"And I'm very happy with my bendy yoga dude," added Zoë." We clunked our coffee mugs and all three of us silently hoped for the best…

Chapter 46

It was the official launch party for Zoe's book that saw Zoë, Lauren, Colette and I all making our way up to London together on the train, chattering excitedly. I'd managed to cover up my embarrassing stubble rash quite well, although the teasing I got from the girls about it was relentless.

"Aren't pash-rashes a bit teenage romance?" Zoe laughed as I looked at my reflection once again, hoping the embarrassing rash had calmed down a bit.

"I don't know what you mean" I blushed, "It's not a pash-rash it's an allergy!"

Ben had texted me promising to get up on the train after his shift. He hadn't managed to get out of work completely but he managed to get someone to cover the afternoon so that he could race up to London and be with me. Chris and Will were also under orders to dress up smart and be by their girlfriends' sides.

We got to the venue mid-morning, and the event organisers had done an amazing job. The whole place had been decorated in shades of crimson and violet, with drapes and lanterns and even a borrowed chandelier or two. It didn't look like a boring provincial bar anymore; it looked vaguely like a Parisian night club. I loved it.

The three of us wandered around, inspecting everything. They'd gone with the purple theme all the way through, with chair bows, purple balloons and glitter everywhere. There was a pile of books on one of the tables, and, "Oh my God, you've got a bloody purple throne!" – only Zoë could actually pull off a padded purple throne trimmed with silver hearts and not look a complete idiot.

They'd put together some fabulous goody bags for us, mostly food-related but with a couple of make-up samples as well and a copy of a brand new book called 'Girl Power' by a new author who wanted to promote herself on the site.

"Oh wow - Just look at that!" Lauren pointed at the cupcake towers that were standing pretty and proud on one of the tables at the end of the room.

"They've done an amazing job" I said enthusiastically. Zoë smiled, "It's always good to know the right people," she said enigmatically as she inspected one of the goody bags.

We were expecting over 200 people, nibbles, drinks and then music. The organiser's niece, Theresa, was going to be singing. She was adorable – she arrived with no makeup on, looking about 15, but by the time she'd got dressed up, made up and ready to go, she looked glamorous and very sexy.

The party was due to start at 3pm, and people started milling around just before then. The men had managed to get to us on time, and were having a great time getting stuck into the free booze before anyone else arrived. We were too busy fussing around, checking and rechecking, to worry about them draining the bar dry before the party got going.

The music started, the guests started arriving, and the venue filled up with people. Everyone seemed to want to talk to Zoë and she was loving it. There were people from some of the most fashionable women's magazines asking me all about Viva Voluptous – it wasn't common knowledge about *Gracious* yet - and we had tabloid press there asking us all sorts of intrusive questions about the site, even though it was Zoë's launch day. I spotted Zoë out of the corner of my eye, half dragging someone towards me. Uh Oh, I thought, what's she up to now?

"Ell, this is Denise from the *Daily News* – She wants to talk to you about Viva Voluptuous," she said with a wink, clearly glad to palm the hapless writer off on me. I agreed to be interviewed by her in private and decided I was really going to let her have it. A few glasses of champagne can do that to a girl.

"So, Ellie, can you tell me why you decided to start your crusade for fat women?" was the journalist's opening line.

"I'll tell you why." I said, dramatically, buoyed up with free booze and bravado. "I was sick to death of reading about how disgusting, repulsive and lazy fat people are. I had a friend who killed herself because she believed her weight made her unworthy of even being alive – how can that ever be right? I read your newspaper's constant slating of overweight people, men and women, and it made me angry. I wanted to show people, and the media, what fat people have to go through every day, the things we have to put up with that thin people don't even consider.

"I also wanted to prove that just because we're fat it doesn't mean we are miserable, unhealthy or ugly. I think what we've done has proved that beyond all doubt, don't you?"

I could almost hear the cogs in her brain start to whir as she processed what I'd just said. I knew full well that whatever I said would be twisted beyond all recognition, but I didn't really care.

"Don't you think that it would have been easier to just lose weight?" she carried on.

"Have you ever been on a diet?" I asked back. "Around 95% of dieters put all the weight back in five years, usually with a bit more for luck. Not only that, but in 2012, one of the biggest weight loss companies in the world, the one that advertises on your website, sent a representative to the all-Party Parliamentary Group on Body Image, and she actually admitted that people on their diets shouldn't expect to lose more than 5% to 10% of their body weight. They don't tell you that in their expensive adverts do they?"

"I'll take that as a no, then," sighed Denise. "Do you see yourself as some sort of underground fat acceptance movement?" was her next shot.

"We're not underground," I answered, "but if you want to call us a movement, go right ahead! In the last year, there's been a shift in MOST of the media towards including men and women of all sizes and questioning the accepted idea that only thin people can be happy, healthy and even desirable. I can't claim full responsibility for all of that, but yes, I do think that Viva Voluptuous has played its part in getting the message across. It's OK to accept and love yourself if you're fat. It's possible to be healthy and fit, and find love."

The interviewer muttered something to herself about being delusional and carried on with her one-sided interrogation.

"Is it true that you were bulimic a few years ago?" was the next, predictable question. Given that her gossip rag had started that rumour, I guess she had to do her best to keep it going.

"Absolutely not!" I replied. "I developed a binge-eating problem years ago, after a stressful time. The constant dieting I'd been subjecting myself to, even though I wasn't obese and was barely overweight, kept me on a tight leash, but as soon as my life got stressful I couldn't keep dieting anymore and all I wanted to do was eat the food I'd denied myself for months, if not years. The problem was, I couldn't stop. The bingeing went on for a few years, with diets in between that led to more bingeing. I only got better when I gave up dieting, learned to accept myself as I am and started treating myself properly."

"Have you lost weight since then?"

"I have no idea," I replied, truthfully. I'd even refused to look at the scales when the nurse weighed me after my last smear test. I just didn't want to know.

"Do you think that helping people stay obese is irresponsible, given that there are more and more obese people causing a drain on the NHS?"

"How can empowering people be irresponsible?" The questions she was asking me were so pathetic, I could hardly even be bothered to answer them.

"It's not empowering anyone, is it?" she said haughtily. "It's letting people think it's OK to be fat, when it quite clearly isn't."

Her prejudices were showing up loud and clear. I was about to have some fun with her.

"Soon, there will be more fat women and men than thin ones. Are you going to tell the majority that they are in the wrong, that they are disgusting and lazy and greedy, when they are all bigger than you?"

She didn't know what to say to that. I carried on, "And don't think for a minute that because we're fat we can't run after you and take you out. I think if you look at my first video on YouTube, sweetheart, you'll realise just how much exercise I do, and how fit I am. Lauren has run half marathons and have you SEEN Zoë's yoga? It's stealth fitness. We pretend to be unfit and unhealthy, just so that we can catch you out and take over the world."

Denise was not amused. I don't think she'd managed to crack a smile yet. Miserable cow.

"As a fat woman, do you find it difficult to find love?" was her next shot. OK, I suppose that was a reasonable question for someone who'd been plastered all over Twitter writing about dating experiences.

"No more than any other woman." I answered.

"How about your love life?" She carried on. "You're single, aren't you?"

"Actually, I am in a relationship. But I'm not prepared to talk about my personal life, thank you."

I didn't want to drag Ben's name into it. I'd only been seeing him a few weeks and I didn't see why he needed to be in the papers just because I was.

"Well, thank you for your time, Ellie." She finished "Good luck with your venture." She shook my hand weakly and walked out of the room, clutching her goody bag and her voice recorder. I couldn't wait to see how she was going to twist my words and spin the interview to fit the *Daily News'* narrow agenda. I didn't really care, I was getting used to tabloid tactics now and I would soon get my own back with my *Gracious* column. I just wished I could have told her about it right there and then, to see the look on her stuck up face.

The rest of the party was fantastic. I chatted with loads of people, and lost count of everyone who told me they wanted to work with us. Zoë was quite happy about Viva Voluptuous being another focus for her book launch, she was having a whale of a time signing books and charming all the journalists in sight anyway. Theresa's dance routine was spectacular and very erotic. The men in the room were giving her their full attention for the 20 minutes she performed, including Ben, Will and Chris.

"Oi, you, you're only supposed to have eyes for me!" I joked. Ben looked so guilty; I just had to put him straight, "It's OK. You'll be seeing enough of me, later..."

His eyes lit up.

Colette came bouncing up to us, beaming, and announced that the massive plus-size fashion retailer who'd asked to work with us also wanted Colette to design a range of sexy burlesque-inspired clothes for them, which they would market in their catalogue and on their own website but under Colette's own name. She was hugging all three of us, and I'd never seen her so excited.

"I'm going up to London to meet their creative team next week!" She said excitedly. "I've got so many ideas, and they're going to let me pretty much come up with all the ideas around their theme. I can't believe it…it's all because of you lot. And that barmy dance you did."

She seemed a bit overcome with emotion, or maybe a bit drunk. Either way, she was very, very happy.

"It's not because of us, you daft mare" I corrected her, "You did this all by yourself. If you hadn't come up with those amazing costumes for all of us in the summer, you wouldn't be here now. Everyone saw them, and they loved you. It's all your own work…"

"I am quite clever, aren't I" Colette grinned. "I love you girls…"

We stayed until late, soaking up the atmosphere and talking to as many people as we could. The book launch had been a huge success. Zoë had pretty much guaranteed herself a serialisation in the *Daily News* and my interview was going in too, although I was expecting it to be as unflattering as usual. With their readership, we were bound to get noticed, and hopefully that would get more people advertising with us, so we'd start making money too.

With Viva Voluptuous I'd created a place where people could go, find all sorts of ways to feel great about themselves and have a good laugh at our video blogs. I'd done what I set out to do, even in my own little way, by making people think about their preconceptions – and if that made one person think twice about coming out with a tired, boring stereotype then it was a success. Now I had an even bigger platform – I was going to be in a top magazine bringing fashion and advice to plus size women everywhere, and I was going to do my level best to make curvy girls feel damn good about themselves.

As I looked over at my amazing friends, and then at Ben, who I'd overheard at least three times telling people, "Yes, Ellie Johnstone is my girlfriend, isn't she amazing?" I thought about Jane. I knew she would have approved of what I'd done. I only wished she'd been around to see it.

Silently I raised my glass and thanked my late friend. "I love you," I whispered...

Epilogue

The *Daily News* write up was predictably mean, but it led to a huge surge in numbers for the website, and a whole lot of sales for *Amazing*, Zoe's book.

The DVD went on sale just after Christmas and made the Amazon Top 10 for fitness. Zoë and Chris started looking for a house to rent in Brighton soon afterwards.

Lauren decided to set up a freelance communications agency, spurred on by her success with Viva Voluptuous. She and Will carried on living together, although technically she was still his landlady.

Colette's business went into orbit after the Viva Voluptuous launch, she opened a bigger shop and took on three staff members. She sold the rights to her burlesque designs to *The Plus Sized Diva* after spending hours keeping their marketing manager topped up with champagne at Zoë's book launch party and made a pretty impressive sum of money out of the deal. She used some of it to take her daughter away on holiday, and has been promising to buy her a pony ever since, but hopes that she'll soon get bored with asking about it.

Ben and I both changed our relationship status on Facebook when we got back from London, which is the modern day equivalent of 'going steady'. We went on our first ever weekend away soon after, and guess where he took me? Dublin!

And last I heard, Mark and Rachel were divorced and he was living on his own with just a PlayStation to keep him company of an evening. Never mind, eh?

Hip, real and raw, SASSY books share authentic truths, spiritual insights and entrepreneurial witchcraft with women who want to kick ass in life and y'know...start revolutions.

WHAT PEOPLE ARE SAYING ABOUT

VIVA VOLUPTUOUS

Contemporary and real, *Viva Voluptuous* is a raucous and resonant insight in to life, right now.

It felt intelligent and honest whilst still being a page-turner; a behind-the-scenes account of what it's like to be a woman caught in the chaos of work success, a challenging economy, modern relationships and the big one – self-image. You know this girl. Ellie Johnstone and Co are the type of friends you'd love to find yourself with. You'd cheer each other on, you'd sympathise, you'd laugh and you'd drink Pinot Grigio. The message is important still. What would it be like if we accepted ourselves, loved ourselves? Would that be OK? What would it mean for us? What would happen if we stopped all the bitching and criticism? What if we stopped the un-nourishing diets and the un-nourishing lifestyles? What if we focused on being the best versions of us and really started enjoying life?

Viva Voluptuous explores the answers in a decadent and diary-esque way and I loved it.

Lyndsey Whiteside, Inspired PR, www.inspiredpr.co.uk

I really enjoyed this book. So great (and unusual) to find a heroine who is comfortable with her bigger body. Inspiring, funny and real.

Keris Stainton, author of *Emma Hearts LA*

As one of Sarah's regular blog followers I was looking forward to reading her novel and I wasn't disappointed.

Viva Voluptuous is both fun and deadly serious. I loved the way Sarah combines feminism and no diet messages and concepts with a good old rom-com style story. If you're fed up of dieting

and looking for a good read, this is the ticket.
Audrey Boss, Co-author of *Beyond Chocolate* and *Beyond Temptation*, and co-founder of the Beyond Chocolate programme.
www.beyondchocolate.co.uk

What a voice! The character is so likeable. I'm already rooting for her. I want to know what happens next!
Suzy Greaves, Editor of *Psychologies Magazine*
www.suzygreaves.com

There's a lot of talk around the facts of dieting and not dieting, but very little consideration to the feelings of the individual.

What's really missing though is the stories, and as more women come to realise that they've been sucked in by the pursuit of thin and decide to point their lives in a new direction, I hope that more stories will emerge.

Sarah's leading the way with a heartfelt, honest and humorous tale of living life confidently after saying no to dieting.

Just what does happen after you turn your back on dieting? We're told that dieting can make drastic improvements in our confidence levels, yet these are rare, and certainly not long term. So does dieting bring that longed-for confidence? Just how do you feel great about your looks when you're told by all around you that you need to be thin to be good-looking?

This is a must read for anyone who would like a glimpse into life after the diets. I laughed, I cried, I nodded like a loon in places but most of all I loved every word.

More please! Highly recommended reading.
Jenny Jameson, founder of F*ck The Diets!
http://www.fuckthediets.com/